The Secret of This Book

BRIAN W. ALDISS

The Secret of This Book

20-Odd Stories

Illustrations
by
Rosamund Chorley
&
Brian Aldiss

HarperCollins*Publishers*

HarperCollins*Publishers*
77–85 Fulham Palace Road,
Hammersmith, London w6 8jb

Published by HarperCollins*Publishers* 1995

1 3 5 7 9 8 6 4 2

A catalogue record for this book
is available from the British Library

ISBN 0 00 225364 X

Set in Linotron Galliard by
Rowland Phototypesetting Ltd,
Bury St Edmunds, Suffolk

Printed in Great Britain by
HarperCollinsManufacturing Glasgow

In memory
of

CHARLES MONTEITH
(1921–1995)

who wrote long ago
inviting me to produce
a book – my first

Among his many gifts were
courage, learning, generosity, and wit.

CONTENTS

Her Toes Were Beautiful on the Mountains:

ACKNOWLEDGEMENTS

Common Clay published in *The Magazine of Fantasy & Science Fiction*, December 1992

The Mistakes, Miseries and Misfortunes of Mankind read at the ICA, London, in aid of *Liberty*, 8th February 1994

How the Gates Opened and Closed © Copyright Brian W. Aldiss 1995

Headless published in the *Daily Telegraph*, 23rd April 1994

Travelling Towards Humbris © copyright Brian W. Aldiss 1995

If Hamlet's Uncle Had Been a Nicer Guy © copyright Brian W. Aldiss 1995

Else the Isle with Calibans published in *New Writings 2* edited by Malcolm Bradbury & Andrew Motion, 1993

A Swedish Birthday Present © copyright Brian W. Aldiss 1995

Three Moon Enigmas:
    His Seventieth Heaven
    Rose in the Evening
    On the Inland Sea published in *Asimov's SF*, May 1995

A Dream of Antigone published in *Blue Motel [Narrow Houses, Volume 3]*, edited by Peter Crowther, 1994

The God Who Slept With Women published in *Asimov's SF*, May 1994

Evans in His Moment of Glory © copyright Brian W. Aldiss 1995

Horse Meat published in *Interzone*, November 1992

An Unwritten Love Note © copyright Brian W. Aldiss 1995

Making My Father Read Revered Writings published in *New Writings 4*, edited by A.S. Byatt & Alan Hollinghurst, 1995

Sitting With Sick Wasps published in *New Writings 4*, edited by A.S. Byatt & Alan Hollinghurst, 1995

Becoming the Full Butterfly published in *Interzone*, 1995

Traveller, Traveller, Seek Your Wife in the Forests of This Life, published in *Science Fiction Blues* Programme Book, Avernus, 1987

Her Toes Were Beautiful on the Mountains published in *Universe 2*, edited by Robert Silverberg & Karen Haber, 1992, as, 'Her Toes were Beautiful on the Hilltops'. Revised.

Tom he was a piper's son
      He learnt to play when he was young
The only tune that he could play
      Was 'Over the Hills and Far Away'
Over the hills and a great way off
      The wind shall blow my top-knot off

The Secret of
This Book

Common Clay

'Why don't you move to Paris?'

People like tourists – if tourists count as people – had been asking that question of Emile for years. He stayed on in the city of Geneva without articulating an answer, though in his heart he knew it well. True artists went to Paris rather than stay in a hard-hearted commercial city like Geneva. Paris or even California.

It was many years since Emile Rostand had arrived in Geneva. He mixed only with other bohemians. He and his friends lived the intense rebellious life of an artistic community which feels itself in conflict with the smug bourgeois values all round them. They painted, quarrelled, argued, emoted; when they were particularly hungry they would put on blue sweaters and trudge down to the lakeside to paint portraits of the tourists they despised.

The artistic community lived in the houses and tenements of two dilapidated streets, the rue de la Grace and the rue Sous Mur, which ran in parallel. Here, their lives, ladies and illnesses were generally held in common. Their roofs were leaky, their rentals low. Behind these disreputable thoroughfares stood a high wall, part cliff, part hewn stone, which had once formed the basis of the ancient fortifications of Geneva; the Vieille Ville lay grandly on its eminence behind this wall, in a peace not shared by the rest of the city, and certainly not by the broken houses under threat of demolition at its foot.

Below the two dilapidated streets, where the ground sloped steeply away, separated from them by strips of public garden, ran the modern city, the great grinding commercial world of Geneva, adorned by bus stations, taxi ranks, bistros, and cumbrous grey office buildings without style.

Emile looked from his attic windows on to these grey buildings. There lived some of the very people, the soulless people, who would do away with the rues de la Grace and Sous Mur entirely to erect in their stead banks and other edifices given over to capitalist enterprise.

He felt the conflict between art and commerce to be particularly intense in Geneva. The city served not simply the banking interests of its own citizens but of the whole country and much of the rest of Europe. Geneva was one of the homes of international greed. The thin bellies of the artists stood as frail barriers against this materialism. Any artist who made a name for himself in that world – by selling canvases, for instance, to the smart galleries in the Boul. Georges Ruiz-Brandt at the bottom of the hill – lost his standing and was invariably expelled from the artistic rookery if he did not leave voluntarily after receiving his first cheque. One artist who had recently left was Emile's friend, Gaston Bouyat. Emile's ex-friend.

Gaston Bouyat had sold himself into the harsh world at the bottom of the hill, the modern Geneva. Emile never went there. He hated the place. It held all he had once fled from. On the rare occasions he strolled out, say on a summer evening, when in pursuit of a woman, he would go in the opposite direction and climb the winding stone steps at the end of the rue de la Grace, ascending to the cobbles of the Vieille Ville.

The old city had changed much of late. Once a thriving community of artisans and craftsmen had lived here, making chairs and carts and carriages and objects of silver. Two world wars had finished them off. Here Geneva's most famous artist – artist and socialist to the end of his days – Jean-Jacques Gubenstrade, had lived, a remote descendant of Courbet and something of a hero to Emile. Gubenstrade had managed to be a success in the great world and to remain true to his calling as an artist. He had never compromised. Picasso and Braque had dined at his table. Emile had seen Gubenstrade himself with his own eyes when he first arrived in Geneva, a little old man in a crumpled black suit, walking slowly with a stick through the Vieille Ville. He had died a dozen years ago in a hospital for geriatric diseases, out in a new suburb.

The ancient Vieille Ville had grown less without the living genius of Gubenstrade to preside over it. Gubenstrade's modest house, three storeys of it and only a room thick, was now an electric emporium, selling expensive fitments for the boudoirs of the rich. The deep-eyed windows of the area, which had once looked towards the mountains of the Haute-Savoie, recalling the graces of the pre-revolutionary eighteenth century, were now restored and blinded by luxury goods. Discreet signs, generally in gold or gilt, hung under wrought-iron balconies and against the stone caryatids of old doorways, proclaiming the names and goods of boutiques, fashion houses, lawyers, or jewellers. On their glass doors were exhibited the varieties of credit cards accepted within. And over one of these exclusive shops, in what was reputedly a luxurious penthouse, lived Emile's ex-friend, Gaston Bouyat; or, rather, here, Gaston Bouyat kept a penthouse. For most of the year, Gaston lived in Palm Springs, California. Emile went in fear of turning a corner and running into his ex-friend on one of Gaston's rare return visits.

Emile remained in the rue de la Grace. A garret room, its wallpaper – such as remained – belonging to a more florid era, had once served as studio and home to both the artist and Gaston. The room spanned the width of the house at the east end of the rue de la Grace, the most tumble-down of all the houses in that row, its outer wall supported by a large hoarding bearing an advertisement for a Japanese television set. Integrity and acrylic alike had been common coin between the two young men – until Gaston Bouyat deviated into representational realism and swelling bank accounts. Emile was

3

now utterly alone in his garret – apart, that is, from his transitory women, several male friends, and a cat who climbed over the broken roof tiles to visit him for a saucer of milk every morning.

Gaston's name was no longer spoken in the garret. But everyone knew of him, knew of his desertion and his success. His name was more fragrant, and more often discussed, in boardrooms in Tokyo and New York. Once Gaston had taken to representational sculpture, examples had found their way to those very boardrooms.

The garret was hardly as immaculate as might be supposed in those distant boardrooms. It smelt of linseed oil and old clothes and stale food. Its large skylight in the ceiling was shrouded with cobwebs. The windows facing south towards the Boul. Georges Ruiz-Brandt were misted over with dirt. The old canvases turned with their faces to the wall exhibited the same air of defeat as Emile's broken couch with its covering of rugs.

In the farthest corner of the room, among abandoned stretchers and rolls of canvas, stood an almost life-size clay figure. It represented, in painstaking detail, a woman in a raincoat – a pretty woman with a pert nose – standing, umbrella in hand, waiting for a bus. The figure was the work of Gaston Bouyat. Marking as it did the sudden transformation of Gaston from creative to commercial artist, the alarming object had been spared Emile's destruction. Perhaps he gave it space as a monument to a once close friendship, perhaps as a warning of how a good man could abandon his principles.

Emile's principles had formed long ago, when the sixties tailed off into the early seventies. He spoke openly of them as principles now, where once he had said, 'It's what you've got to do.' As ever, he painted in the manner of Tanguy, with the superimposition of Pollock-like effects and an occasional nod towards Jasper Johns. Although an earlier optimism had left him, Emile still retained his pride. The consolation for having no Name was that everyone in the rue de la Grace knew him by name.

'A great friendship for my fellow men fills my heart,' said Emile – not once, but often, in the bars he frequented by night. Even greater was the affection he felt for women. His affection for individual women was deep rather than lasting. Until Alema came along.

One morning, he was working at a new canvas in the garret, alone except for a friend who was sleeping off a hangover in a broken armchair. Emile was pouring a diluted mixture of ultramarine and burnt sienna, his favourite colours, from an old cat food can. He watched the liquid trickle on the canvas in those special squiggles only he could master, only he understood, when suddenly – in mid-pour, as it were – he stopped, put down the can and walked out, down the three flights of dusty stairs, into the August sunshine.

If there was anything Emile hated more than the government, French imperialism, American imperialism and the exploitation of the Third World, it was to be interrupted in mid-canvas. This morning was different. He simply left what he was doing, left the half-finished canvas on the floor, and went away. He strode through the busy town, hardly aware of the roaring traffic which moved at a rate suggesting it intended to cross all Europe from north to south and east to west before the day was done and the last electronic cash-desk silent in the city.

Walking in a kind of daze, Emile found himself in the Secheval quarter of the town. He stood indecisively outside the Boccaccio restaurant, the striped awning of which swooped out over the pavement. The café area was fringed by oleanders in green tubs. The one waiter visible did not look askance at Emile. The few customers drinking at tables did not appear too hostile. Emile selected a chair on the edge of the pavement, away from the entrance, and there ordered a cappuccino and smoked a Philip Morris.

As he sat lost in thought, four young people emerged from the dark interior of the restaurant, followed by the landlord. The landlord was a plump fellow. He came out smiling broadly, protracting his farewells, as if he had just been liberally tipped. But it was the young people who attracted Emile's immediate loathing, and of them the leading pair in particular.

The man bore every indication of wealth. He wore a white suit with – Emile could not stop himself gripping the side of his table – pink and white shoes, the pink matching his silk shirt. Around the offensive young man's white panama hat, a scarlet scarf was tied, one end of which hung decoratively over one shoulder. He was handsome, with a small fair moustache, laughing and walking with his girl as they strolled to the edge of the pavement. A casually possessive quality in his manner added to Emile's dislike.

The girl presented her profile to Emile as she walked. She was less of a period piece than her companion, and wore a nondescript blouse with blue jeans and sandals. It was her profile that attracted Emile. Her hair was golden. A lock of it hung down over her forehead towards a small neat nose. She was laughing with her mouth open as if slightly aghast at something the man was saying. It was that expression of mixed amusement and shrinking away which seized Emile's attention. He instantly wanted to know the girl.

A large white Lagonda was parked illegally by the kerbside. The four climbed in, laughing loudly, and drove away. Well, there had been many girls he wanted, and many of them had escaped. The fact had to be faced. He lit another cigarette.

The proprietor of Boccaccio's stood under the edge of his awning, staring in the direction the Lagonda had driven, towards the east, towards the mountains.

Perhaps he too had had a vision of a better life, at once pleasing and unsettling.

Emile was a man of simple faith. He believed in his painting. He believed that as long as he remained true to his original vision of what good painting should be, everything else would fall into place. What 'everything else' was was never exactly made clear: although the centre of the vision remained sharp, rosy cloud surrounded it. He was a practical creature and, as the years in Geneva passed, increasingly a creature of habit. He did not know why he had broken off in the middle of a painting, to go for a long aimless walk. And he was disconcerted when he saw for the second time on that same day the girl who had been driven away in the Lagonda.

The group of artists who lived on the second floor of his building, below Emile's garret room, were great party-givers. They painted in the style of Buffet, which Emile regarded as coarse and demoded. He had little to do with them, even putting up with their noise without complaint. Sometimes he was known to drink their cheap

Algerian wine with them, to show common cause against the depraved taste of the inhabitants of Geneva.

At sunset that day, Emile climbed the dirty stairs with a bottle of his own cheap wine under his arm. His room would be empty and he was planning to eat bread and smoked ham for his supper. Despite his affection for women, his bed had always been more of a staging post than a port as far as the female kind was concerned. But, as his youth faded, the women became fewer, not to mention (perhaps it was a symptom of a less sympathetic age) more given to complaint. So his bed as well as his room was at present unoccupied.

He discovered the girl on the landing of the second floor, where the staircase turned and there was a smell of urine. She was being sick in an amateur way out of the window, on to the smart traffic whisking round the corner of the rue de la Grace. She appeared helpless and dejected, and her hair was golden.

'Please help me,' she said, flopping against the sill.

Such was her state that he had to carry her up to the rough bed in the garret. He found himself looking down into the tear- and vomit-stained face of the lady he had seen that morning leaving the Boccaccio and driving off in the Lagonda.

Her helplessness was in evidence again the following morning, when she sat up in bed clutching her small breasts and demanding to know where she was.

She gazed at Emile with large brown eyes, and he was lost. So were Alema's contact lenses, presumably voided into the rue de la Grace along with the contents of her stomach.

She demanded cocaine. Emile had none, and scorned it. Secretly, he feared the habit. He had a sinus problem, he explained – already he was explaining: he did not want to aggravate the problem with coke. Alema scarcely had an addiction. Her withdrawal period was not too agonizing, and he saw her through it, keeping her to a diet of wine, mineral water, lettuce and bread.

Alema had arrived in Geneva only the day before the Lagonda episode, from Paris. She had been three years in Paris, at university, and did not know Geneva at all. Her father lived here. She had every intention of going to his place when she had met some amusing people instead . . . They had proved far from amusing.

The story was inconsequential and told in a confused way. She did not like to be questioned. Nor was Emile particularly keen to question her. Alema was like a private miracle. One did not question miracles.

'Suppose I said I saw you before we met . . . Suppose I saw you coming out of some restaurant with three other people, and a fellow in a white suit had hold of your arm?'

'What about it?'

'I was just wondering who the fellow was.'

'I know so many people.'

'You must remember him. A very fancy dresser. It looked as if he owned a Lagonda.'

'I never know the makes of cars. What does it matter, anyway?'

He found it did matter, but he said nothing more.

After some days of looking grey, Alema became better, rising from the bed and pottering about the garret. She said nothing about leaving. He began to paint her.

Ultramarine and burnt sienna were not her colours. Her colour was gold, a colour more suited to the Vieille Ville than to the shabby artists' colony of the rue de la Grace. Her skin was almost the same dusky gold as her long curly hair. He was intrigued by the way her whole body was covered in very short gold hair, almost like a thin pelt. It excited him into making love to her with mad frequency; she never showed herself unwilling, although she concealed any enthusiasm she might feel.

In profile at least, she could be considered very beautiful. There was a quality, a contradiction, between the soft curve of her cheeks and the sternness of her short nose which excited him. Emile prized her. He feared that she would proclaim herself sick of the sordid surroundings of the garret and remove herself smartly from his life; yet she gave no sign, and did not even venture downstairs to see the Buffet gang. So he painted in a kind of frenzy, somewhere between hope and desperation – painting her, of course, as Tanguy would have painted her had he been Jackson Pollock.

Alema was positively childish in her attitude to art. She had heard of no twentieth-century artist but Picasso. She giggled short-sightedly at his finished canvases.

'You know I don't look like that,' she said. 'Why do you always paint worms?'

While he loftily explained his theory of art to her, he was secretly relieved that she knew so little about the subject. He never forgot that this was a rich spoilt girl, capable of aberrant and power-based behaviour, a potential exploiter of the poor. So he kept her to himself and did not introduce her to his friends.

Occasionally she would interrupt his monologues with a totally irrelevant remark. 'Why don't you move to California?' she asked once.

Emile was amazed at the typical rich-bitch question, and said so.

'Didn't you tell me your beloved Tanguy went there?' she said. 'It's a fun place. I've been there. You should go.'

One golden autumn day, when those inhabitants of Geneva who were not teetotallers were beginning to anticipate the consumption of gallons of the new wine harvest, Emile walked round his studio walls and found that he had amassed twenty fair-sized canvases based on Alema's golden face and golden anatomy. He also realized that he had painted no tourists for several weeks; now it was too late, for the tourists had gone, and he had no money left. Not a sou. Nor had Alema ever appeared to possess a single sou – a typical trick of the very wealthy, Emile thought.

How was he to keep her now? He could not believe that he was in love with this beautiful visitant, but he did wish to keep her, to possess her, as the little snob in the white panama had seemed to possess her. And in those twenty canvases lay the wherewithal; for he had a collection large enough to interest the hard-eyed, well-shaven gentlemen in the art galleries of the Boul. Georges Ruiz-Brandt.

Hastily, he varnished the canvases and numbered them ALEMA ONE to ALEMA TWENTY.

After waiting to make sure that the coast was clear and none of his cronies was watching, Emile took Alema and four of the finished canvases into the mercenary city. This was the first time they had been out together; she had made no attempt to get in touch with her father. As they waited for the break in the traffic which would allow them to cross the road, she chatted gaily of what she would spend the money on when the galleries paid up. She wanted a light blue linen suit, such as she had seen on a Swedish woman in Paris, with a sapphire ring to match, and a fast motor yacht, on the deck of which the suit could be exhibited.

Emile was frankly horrified.

'What on earth do you want a yacht for?'

'Because my Daddy's yacht in Antibes is too big and silly for little me.'

They crossed the road. As they walked through the public garden, he dared to ask about Daddy, though hatred burned in him as he pronounced the decadent word.

Alema explained that her father was well accustomed to spending money wisely, and would certainly advise on how they could pick up the best and most modern yacht for a reasonable price. Her family was Coptic, with some German blood. One branch of the family still lived in Alexandria: great-uncles and suchlike. Mummy had been part-Jewish and of Hungarian origin. She had run away with a minor English lord shortly after Alema's fourth birthday; Mummy and his lordship had last been seen in South America, heading for the Mato Grosso. He was some kind of an explorer, she believed. Daddy, a skilled entrepreneur, had made a mountain of money from armaments, in partnership with a South African millionaire during the reign of the Shah of Iran. It was his second fortune – he had gambled away the first. When the Shah went into exile, trade had become difficult and Daddy had moved to Geneva, where he had made a third fortune – she didn't quite know how. She said a merchant bank was involved.

Although Alema revolted against the ostentation which went with this wealth, she still received an allowance when she bothered to collect it. Unfortunately, she had lost her shoulder bag with all her documents.

She professed a great love of Daddy. He was just a honeybun really.

Much of this information, apparently brought on by the fresh autumn air, was anathema to the artist in Emile. Such key words as 'the Shah of Iran', 'armaments' and 'South Africa' went against his basic principles. Daddy sounded to him a crook of the worst order – a wealthy crook, accepted in society. His daughter's amoral recital made the whole matter even more shocking. Besides, his own father had been a baker of Calvinist faith who had ended up committing suicide to escape his debts.

He put all his misgivings aside as he took Alema's golden arm and led her towards the Boul. Georges Ruiz-Brandt.

Once confronted by the proximity of the boulevard, however, his nerve failed. The thought of those hard commercial men – all thieves – looking his canvases over in their supercilious way made him tremble.

'We'll sit on this bench a moment,' he said.

Alema was as obedient as she appeared helpless but, as she seated her neat golden behind, tight in its jeans, on the bench beside him, she asked, 'Why? Are you tired?'

'Perhaps you'd better take the paintings into the galleries.'

'Why?'

On principle, he never liked to reveal his complex thought processes to women. All he said was, 'Study the effects of light on the roofs of these buildings.'

But he suddenly clutched Alema's hand, realizing sickly that she meant a great deal despite her poisonous upbringing. He remembered how good he had been to her, never hitting her, always making love to her, always pretending to listen to her prattle, never mocking her for her silly views on art. He was, too, approaching forty years old. Sitting there in the sun, clutching his canvases, with her beside him, smiling her sweet meaningless smile, he realized that in his heart he had long grown sick of the filthy garret in the rue de la Grace.

Once he admitted this, much followed. If he had grown tired of the old garret – from which his friend Gaston had so long departed – then by the same token he longed to be rich, and to have a shower and a toilet of his own. Worse, he longed never to paint again in the style of Tanguy and Pollock. He hated Tanguy. In fact he never wanted to paint again at all. What had it brought him? Nothing.

'Watch how the shadows move,' he said. 'Faster in autumn.'

All this while, he sat facing the cars cruising along the road in front of them, and the smart shops opposite the gardens, and the tall cumbersome grey buildings in which there was not one shred of beauty or mercy. And the girl sat beside him, smiling, her hands clasped between her knees, indifferently ready for whatever might happen next.

He saw that it was absolutely imperative he had an exhibition in one of those flashy art galleries patronized by horrible millionaires like Alema's Daddy. He had had enough of integrity. Integrity was killing him. He needed financial success. He was dying from lack of recognition. With success, he might be able to hang on to Alema. Perhaps a yacht was not such a bad idea after all – it might be the cheapest way of cruising the Mediterranean. Just for a year or so.

'I don't mind doing that,' she said. 'It would be fun.'

Emile looked at her blankly. 'What? The cruise?'

'Carting your paintings into the galleries.'

There was no aura of failure about her. She would be more likely to catch the galleries' attention. Her silly talk would not matter, her prettiness would ensure that at least the canvases were viewed.

He was unable to speak. He was on the brink of a crisis. Success or total failure lay just ahead. Now was the moment – or it was the garret for ever. The great stony world of roads and buildings seemed to revolve about him. He hid his eyes and groaned. She took his arm and led him forward. Scarcely heeding, he went with her, the four canvases tucked awkwardly under his left arm.

'Look, Emile!' Alema was calling in delight. She ran from him, clapping her hands. He realized they had reached the Place XVIII Août, from which branched the Boul. Georges Ruiz-Brandt. It was a neat little area fringed by small cafés, filled with pollarded catalpas, a fountain and a Metro-System entrance.

The golden girl stood to one side of the Metro entrance, her arm linked with the arm of a woman in a hat peering into her handbag, as if looking for the price of a Metro ticket.

'Isn't she cute?' Alema called, laughing. 'She's my friend.'

Emile could give no reply. The woman with the handbag was a life-size bronze, completely detailed down to the watch on her wrist – a triumph of realism. Here and there, her green edges shone gold, where passers-by had patted her affectionately.

As Alema walked round and round the figure, laughing and admiring, Emile stood where he was, clutching his paintings, allowing rage to mount within him. An impulse came to him to attack her but she, all unknowing, played with the bronze woman, addressing it as if it were alive, offering to lend it money for the Metro.

She turned to Emile, her face alight with happiness. 'Oh, what a wonderful idea, Emile! She's so much less spooky than the one in your room. Really cute – models of real people in the street. You could do something like this, Emile – something that ordinary people would enjoy. You'd make your fortune.'

Spitting rage, he came forward and pointed to the signature inset at pavement level by the feet of the bronze woman.

'This is another of Gaston Bouyat's monstrosities, can't you see? The municipality has stuck these horrors all over town.'

'You could copy Gaston,' she said innocently. 'Perhaps you could do a whole series of women in bikinis, as if they were just off for a swim. Everyone would like that, and I could be your model. We could have them dotted round the city.'

'Go away,' he shouted. 'Go away, you bitch. You don't understand. Do you really think I'm going to pander to the public like that? Do you think I'm another Gaston? Is that what you believe? I am a real artist, I have integrity – but you know nothing about things like that, do you, you rich little whore? Integrity means nothing to you.'

Still half-laughing, not at all disconcerted, she said, 'But you don't sell any of your paintings, Emile, do you? Be honest.'

'Neither did van Gogh!' he shouted. 'Typical of you – you judge everything by commercial standards. This bronze woman is just a shoddy, trendy, cheap, decadent piece of exploitation, an insult to taste.'

'Not if people like it, Emile.'

He dropped the canvases so as to be able to wave his arms about.

'People. People. You keep talking about people – when have they had any judgement where real art is concerned? God, you know nothing, you're just a spoilt little rich girl.'

She pouted. 'But I've been as poor as you. I've lived with you and put up with all your crap. Why can't you respect me?'

'Oh, I'm just another adventure to you, you needn't tell me.' All his spite and misery came out, and he started to rave at her. Other people stopped to watch and listen, their gazes downcast so as not to meet Emile's eyes. Some had a half-smile on their faces, as if to say, 'What can you expect from a mad artist?' Only the bronze woman went on industriously looking in her handbag, as if searching for a treasure she had lost.

'Go on, get away from me,' Emile finally shouted. 'Why don't you go and shack up with Gaston – he's crazy about money, just like you. His penthouse is up in the Vieille Ville. Go on, clear off, you little tart.'

She stamped her foot, tears in her eyes. 'To hell with you, then – and Tanguy, too. If you feel like that, I'm off. Sell your own lousy paintings, if you can!'

And she turned on her heel and walked away, threading her course through the fast-moving traffic which formed a whirlpool round the green island in the middle of the Place XVIII Août.

'Wait!' he called. 'Alema!'

But an extraordinary thing happened. A white Lagonda which had twice circled the Place pulled in to the kerb on the far side of the thoroughfare. A young man in a white panama jumped out of the driver's seat and waved in peremptory fashion to Alema.

She waved back.

Emile watched as she negotiated the fast lane of traffic and reached the waiting car. The man in the panama removed his hat with a courteous gesture, put an arm about her and kissed her. She climbed into the front seat. He jumped into the seat beside her. The Lagonda moved forward carelessly, causing cars behind to slam on their brakes and toot in fury. Emile followed it with his gaze until it merged with the traffic and disappeared in the direction of Salève.

He stood for a while, not looking at anything in particular. Then he picked up the four portraits of Alema, and made his way towards the prosperous galleries in the Boul. Georges Ruiz-Brandt.

When three galleries had greeted him with frozen politeness, surveyed his canvases in silence and shown him the door with a politeness even more icy, Emile gave up. His spirit failed him.

How was it that, when he had such contempt for these people, their contempt could so wound him?

Shaking with rage at the world and hatred for himself, he made his way back to where he belonged, the dilapidated part of the town. At the bottom of the rue de la Grace stood a small bistro, always known as the Artists' Tavern. It was said that the great Gubenstrade had himself been drunk here many a night, once with Georges Braque. The Artists' Tavern was run by the plump Karl Beiderz, a man of uncertain nationality and catholic tastes. He allowed Emile to barter his four canvases for a bottle of Belgian gin. Emile sat on the kerb and drank down the contents of the bottle gulp by gulp.

He was crawling up the stairs to his garret when he heard a clock in the Vieille Ville strike midnight. He cursed to himself, straightened up and almost fell into his room.

A friend who had been sleeping in one corner of the room had gone, leaving behind only an aroma of urine. Alema of course had gone, leaving behind only the scent of her perfume. The vast room was untenanted – except for Gaston Bouyat's figure of a waiting woman. She stood as ever, waiting in her raincoat for a bus, clutching a dainty umbrella, pert nose turned towards the window as she looked down the street.

'I'm still here,' she said. 'Still waiting for the bus.'

He was not at all astonished. After all, he was in the same predicament, waiting for something that was never coming.

'Why don't you join me?' she asked. 'You can come with me to my place.'

The invitation was one he had heard before. It loosened his tongue.

'Where are you going?' he managed to ask.

'Out of this dump,' she said. 'I'm sick of this dump.'

Again she might have been voicing his thoughts.

He crossed the road and stood on the pavement beside her, feeling dumbly that he had made a decision of finality.

She put her heavy arm in his, taking custody of him, saying, 'Now I'm sure the bus will be along at any moment.'

And surely enough, a great blue bus came roaring up out of the darkest corner of the garret. Its interior was illuminated. Emile saw as he climbed on after the woman that there were no other passengers.

They settled themselves. He realized the seat was cold, the interior of the bus as glacial as a morgue. The automatic door slammed shut.

'No, no, I don't want to be here!' he cried in sudden alarm. But already the bus was on its way, straight through the bricks of the dilapidated building, over that wall, part cliff, part hewn stone, which formed the basis of the ancient fortifications of Geneva, over the Boul. Georges Ruiz-Brandt, over the city, over the river, and into the darkness prevailing over the world, faster and faster.

To a place that no longer had need of any kind of art.

'When a butcher tells you that *his heart bleeds for his country* he has, in fact, no uneasy feeling.'

So Samuel Johnson tells us. We may sit over supper and watch the most terrible news reports on television. Do we spill our wine? Are we forced to push aside our uneaten steak?

Clearly, a preventive principle is at work, affronting our minds but not our stomachs. Yet if something bad happens to someone near us, we may waste away and lose several pounds almost overnight. Slimming is a form of grieving – like over-eating.

Most of the stories in this collection were written while civil war raged, as it still does, in the country we used to call Jugoslavia. There's something to make even a butcher grieve. It is said there is a book called 'The Secret of This Book' which contains at least one story which readers cannot bear to read – some on the grounds that it is too truthful, some that it is just 'fantasy'. The matter is not yet settled.

Many a year ago, in the days when India was still a British possession, I used to be friendly with two book-sellers who traded on opposite sides of a square in the centre of Bombay.

One in particular was an amiable man who enjoyed a little conversation. One day, I said to him, 'You'll be glad when we [meaning the British] are gone.'

He waggled his right hand in an expression of doubt.

'You see that other bookseller over on the other side of the square? When you are gone, then I must kill him.'

I did not understand.

He said, 'I am Hindu, sah'; he is Muslim. When the

British they are gone, then must I kill that man or he will kill me.'

A few weeks later, I was stoned by a crowd in that same square, escaping injury only by sprinting for and jumping into the back of a British Army lorry. (I was taught never to run from danger, but if you can do it successfully it feels great.)

So it is one thing to understand how the Bosnians, Croats and Serbs must feel; and quite another to feel that, despite everything, one may be a butcher. Not only in the Johnsonian sense.

The Mistakes, Miseries and Misfortunes of Mankind

Curfew sounded as dark was closing in on the city. While the sirens shrieked, night rose out of the ground and rolled down from the mountains and woods surrounding the city. Armed motor-cyclists roared about the streets, sending off anyone walking there to huddle in their refuges.

Derak put up the shutters on the one window of his shop. The meeting began almost at once in the darkened room. Seven men entered through a back alley, hidden away from the military who occupied the square. There was no formality, no courtesy, among them.

Each conspirator said his say.

The city was small, grey, broken. Because of its river, it had existed as a place of human habitation for thousands of years, even when dominated by foreign invaders. Invaders had come from east, north and west, all exhibiting their own kinds of ruthlessness. Nevertheless, they had preserved the structure of the city, adding mosques, government buildings, *hans*, or prisons, according to their cultures. Such buildings had in time become accepted, even revered.

All invaders saw the convenience, the advantage, of having a living city with a bridge that spanned the fast-flowing River Neretva.

This new invasion was different. This was civil war. Many members of the occupying force had once lived peaceably in the city, had been born in its crooked streets. Its arts, its restaurants, its prospects, had once been theirs to enjoy.

They had come and destroyed many of the things their own ancestors had built, that they themselves had once cherished. They had destroyed the bridge over the river. The town lay broken under their feet.

Now they waited. They gathered strength before destroying what remained. Those who sheltered in the broken houses were mainly refugees, victims of war. If there had been a god to look into their hearts, he would have found there the same anger, fear and lust for destruction which raged in the hearts of the invaders. In that respect at least, all men were brothers.

When it was Derak's turn to speak, he part-raised his injured arm for silence and spoke in his harsh voice, looking round at the gathering as if expecting disagreement.

'Of course we must kick these swine out. We must deliver more food to our forces up in the hills, now it's growing colder. All you suggest we shall do.

'And when we're free again, when we've kicked the stinking bastards out, we're going to rebuild this nation and make it stronger than ever before. Stronger, juster, more tolerant! It'll be fair shares for all, brothers, and we're going to drive out the foreigners. Brothers, we're going to make our country a utopia. Somewhere to be the envy of the world.

'Never forget that that's our objective. A utopia from the ruins of the past! We're going to learn from previous mistakes and build a land in which our children and our children's children can take pride.'

As the grim-faced men filed out into the night after the meeting, Derak shook each of them by the hand.

After locking and bolting the shop door behind the last departing back, he went upstairs to his family.

Shortly after midnight, rain fell for an hour on the town, blowing along the river valley. Soon there would be snow.

Derak and Meriel's bedroom was up in the attic, wedged under the sharp edges of a dormer window. They slept very little.

Among the noises to disturb them were the scampering of rats overhead, and the slam of soldiers' boots on the stones of the square below. And one other thing: the crying of their new-born baby.

The bedroom was just large enough to contain their bed and a cot which stood on Meriel's side of the bed. The incumbent of this cot was crying again.

Previous incumbents of the cot, three in number, slept in a small room on the floor below their parents' bedroom. The children were girls. Meg, now six, born before the occupying army arrived, was the oldest. Liz was four and Peg just three. They huddled together in a small bunk with Ali, the family dog.

The new-born baby wailed intermittently. It seemed to punctuate its crying fits so that its parents could believe that *this* time it had finally dropped off to sleep. Then it would start again, yielding up to the night its stanza of grief. It conducted its own cries with waving arms. The stanza had no crescendo, no climax, simply petering out in muffled sobs until the child lay exhausted under its blanket.

'Shut the bloody kid up,' Derak said to his wife.

'You shut him up.'

Meriel lay back on her pillow in exhaustion, staring up at the damp patch on the ceiling with vacant gaze, her mouth open. The first light of dawn was already stealing into the room. Meriel would be thirty on April 1. Tokens of spring would be showing then, even in the shattered city, and the cold would relax its grip. She would take the baby to look at the river, on a fine day when the coltsfoot was flowering.

Her body was flaccid, yielding, in the bed, as if imitating the shapelessness of the bolster. Next to her, Derak's body was hard, stringy, an unrelaxing body to match the lines on his face. Derak had turned thirty-six. Having fought for his country during the invasion, he still maintained something of the manner of a soldier.

Since returning with other survivors from the defeated army, Derak had become authoritarian with his wife and daughters. His cough was like a barked command. The flat and shop were unheated, day or night, and Derek wore an old army greatcoat about the place, to Meriel's unspoken disgust.

'Can't you stop it crying?'

'The poor mite sounds broken-hearted.'

'I'll give it broken-hearted.'

The crying petered out. Derak coughed before subsiding into a semi-horizontal position with his head against the plastic bedhead. Although the raincloud had passed over the house, a gutter dripped outside the window, regular as clockwork.

A new noise began, the sound of someone ascending the twisting stair to the attic room. Meg appeared at the bedroom threshold. The faint light showed her pale face and long pale hair, untidy from bed. She was barefoot.

'Muuum.' Meg uttered the one long-drawn-out word of supplication.

Meriel listlessly turned her head in Meg's direction and asked what the matter was. Derak sat bolt upright and said, 'We're trying to sleep. Go back to bed.'

'I can't sleep, Dad. Please.'

Meriel struggled up into a sitting posture and repeated, 'What's the matter, Meg?'

The figure by the door said it could hear the baby crying. 'And Daddy keeps coughing. He woke me up.'

Derak leant over the side of the bed, picked up one of his boots and flung it at his daughter. It missed the child, hitting the doorpost with a thump. Meg began to cry but did not retreat.

'Don't do that, Derak,' said Meriel. 'Meg, dear, come in with me and get warm.'

The girl sneaked round the bed and climbed in beside her mother. She pressed herself against Meriel's body, putting a thin arm round her neck to clutch her tightly.

Derak's cough began again, dry and methodical, each cough separate and regular; the kind of cough a man could march to.

'Your vest is all wet,' Meriel whispered, enfolding her daughter.

'Peggy wee-weed herself again.' Daughter's right leg wedged itself between mother's thighs, which held it tight.

As they clung to each other, mother and daughter, faint sounds came from the square. Men were marching, rifle butts slamming against damp pavements.

'Oh God, I'll have to get up in another hour,' Derak muttered. 'What a bloody life!' he spat into his handkerchief.

'Shhh, dear, Meg's nearly asleep. Do be gentle with the kids . . .'

After a minute's silence, he said, 'I didn't throw the boot to hit her. Don't think that.' Detecting his change of tone, Meriel lay clutching Meg, saying nothing. She was alert again.

'You don't think that, do you, darling?'

She made no response. She dared not be soft with him, knowing what would follow if she were.

'Do you, darling?' More insistent. Army trucks were starting up in the square. 'You don't think I tried to hit the kid?'

In the dark, the lines of Meriel's face tightened as the voice slid down the scale from demanding to wheedling.

He put out an exploratory hand under the bedclothes and felt her buttock. She drew away slightly.

'Shh, you'll wake Meg.'

He moved nearer. 'Come on, Mer. Just a quick one, then we can all get to sleep.'

23

'Shhh . . .'

Meriel dared not shift her position again, fearing her husband would construe the slightest movement as an invitation. Her thoughts ran in confusion, broken as her surroundings. Everything was a muddle. She intended to go and see her sister in the morning, although it meant dodging the sniper on the east bank. She would dress badly – that was no problem, and take little Peg and the baby with her. Meg and Liz were old enough to go to the women who ran a place for kids in a cellar in the next street.

She did not care to leave any of the children alone in the house or shop with Derak. Not that she didn't trust him. She understood that his anger stemmed from a situation he was powerless to improve. A deteriorating situation, at that. Now – the winter ahead.

Self-pity filled her. Tears welled under her closed lids. Well, of course he was hard. Men had to be hard. He had fought, been wounded. And something she loved had gone out of him.

The shop no longer paid its way. Soldiers, enemies, came in, humiliated him, stole his goods . . .

So she would spend an hour with Susil. Susil managed to remain cheerful. Her man had gone away to the front and had never returned. She pictured his body in a ravine, gnawed by the wolves who were returning.

'Good riddance to bad rubbish,' Susil had said. It sounded hard; but Meriel knew that Susil loved her man, for all his failings. The accursed civil war . . . She had forgotten when it started. She recalled Derak climbing into an army lorry, saying with a kind of laugh as he kissed her that he hated the government as much as he hated the Serbs. The lorry had bumped away in the direction of the fighting. She had stood in the road, watching it out of sight.

His hand still rested on her buttock as if welded there.

He had been gentler before he went away. Poor man. She would try to take Susil a cake. Susil liked the baby, probably wishing it was hers. Maybe she should have it. She should get another man while she still had her looks. Susil had always been the pretty one. Life was monstrously unfair.

It came down to that: life was unfair. At least she had the kids.

And as she clutched the sleeping Meg defensively, the baby stirred in its makeshift cot and began crying again.

The cry was gentle, full of misery, she thought. She should get out and feed it. Just when she was feeling warm and sleepy. The crying intensified.

'Jesus Christ!' Derak sat up in the bed. 'Will you stop that kid yelling or do I have to?'

Rousing, Meg asked drowsily, 'Is Baby all right, Mum?'

To reassure them, Meriel said that it would stop in a minute. 'Don't frighten it, Derak. The poor mite gets scared when you raise your voice.'

He jumped out of bed. 'Scared, is it? I'll give it scared! It's robbing me of my sleep.'

She knew she had made a mistake, speaking as she had. 'No, no, Derak, I'll feed it. Yes, let me feed it.'

As she was detaching herself from Meg's clutches, Derak marched round to the cot. Faint daylight depicted everything in shades of grey: distempered walls, ceiling with its mildew, tousled blankets, bars of the cot.

The baby's howls grew louder at its father's approach. At three months, it was already able to recognize an enemy when it saw one. When Derak snatched it up, its small narrow body convulsed in fear.

'What are you going to do? Be careful, be careful!'

'If you won't look after it, I will.'

'No, no, Derak, give the poor little mite to me. I'll put it to the breast. It can't help its crying.'

'I'll stop it crying!' He went over to the window with the infant pinned under his bad arm, and flung up the lower pane.

Meg started to scream. Meriel blundered out of bed and ran over to her husband, shrieking, asking what he was going to do.

Derak turned on her a face distorted by anger, shouting that she'd see what he was going to do – and if she interfered she'd go out of the window too.

Meg's screams grew louder. Her young sister Liz came rushing upstairs to see what was happening. She clutched her sister in fright and joined in the din.

The baby was shrieking terribly, with hoarse little gasps. Never before had it made such an unearthly noise. Derak stuck his head into the cold dawn air, and thrust the baby out too, holding it over the drop.

The child immediately went rigid. Its cries choked off and it fell mute.

Three floors down, armed soldiers marched. Trucks stood in the square, engines running, pouring blue fumes into the dawn. Puddles reflected broken roofs.

Derak took in the whole scene, glaring at it, baring his teeth. He shook the baby until its little limbs flapped. He held it head down at the full length of his arms. It made not a sound.

Behind him, Meriel and Meg and Liz pulled at his shirt tails, pleading with him not to drop the baby.

He drew his torso back into the bedroom, pushing them away from him. The baby was still retained within his grasp.

'That shut it up!' he spoke in ferocious triumph, holding the infant like a bundle of rags over the heads of his cowering daughters. 'Anyone else want to try it?'

'Oh, you nearly murdered it!' Meriel gasped, and burst into tears. She flung herself away from him, collapsing on the bed and burying her face in the blanket.

'You kids get back downstairs,' Derak said to Meg and Liz, in a calmer voice. Overcome by the scene they had witnessed, the two girls were sobbing convulsively.

'Daddy, would you really have dropped it?' Meg asked.

Sternly, he ordered them again to go back downstairs.

They ran off then, jostling each other.

Meriel heaved herself from the bed to beat at her husband's back, cursing his wickedness, calling him all the names she could think of.

'I wouldn't have dropped it,' he said quietly. 'Don't think that.'

He pushed her aside. She leaned exhausted against the wall, murmuring that she knew well he had murder in his mind.

Derak went to the cot and threw the baby down on it. Calm now, he returned to his side of the bed, settling himself for sleep. His wife, having closed the window, remained propped against the wall. She did not speak. Her hands were clasped to her mouth.

'Get into bed, woman,' he said quietly. 'You're a cold bitch, you know that?'

The baby lay in its cot, unmoving, where it had been thrown. Although its mouth and eyes were open, it made no sound. Its tiny fists had jerked back against the bedding and remained clenched.

It stayed in that position as if frozen, while day came on. Its father rose, got dressed, and went downstairs to open up his hated shop.

In the eighties, I devised a series of competitions in a national newspaper. Competitors were invited to write a story of exactly fifty words, neither more nor less. The title could be up to fifteen words long. These were my mini-sagas – haiku-like, while I was also carving out a massive novel in three volumes. Eventually, they came to fill two anthologies. Small is beautiful, tending towards merely pretty.

The competitions were amazingly successful; so much so that the third one was run in conjunction with BBC Radio 4, and brought in 35,000 entries – including one from Princess Margaret. A word or two short, that one, alas!

The competition revealed that many people believe they can write a short short story, and that true mini-sagas are no easier to achieve than any other art form. Beginning, middle and end are simultaneous.

It is also possible to write poems according to the same stringent requirements: fifty words exactly, neither more nor less.

Animal Dreams

The lions sleep in Afric's heat
With antelope herds grazing near.
Meek though they seem, the piles of meat
They dream of are composed of deer.

The deer lie in Botswana's shade
Where deodar leaves hang like tresses.
Although they all look meek and staid,
They dream of eating lionesses.

As for prose mini-sagas, I wrote a number of them. They were my 1982 habit. Two that remain in mind are:

The Dinosaur Archbishop

Despite the heat, everyone celebrated the thousandth birthday of the Dinosaur Archbishop of Gondwanaland. This sage was truly wise, truly revered. Under his sway, there were no nuclear wars for seven centuries.

'He sees eternity in a grain of sand,' Bill Brontosaur said. 'And all possible universes in fifty words . . .'

Happiness and Suffering

The doors of the jade palace closed behind the young king. For twenty years he dallied with his favourite courtesan.

Outside, the land fell into decay. Warlords terrorized the population. Famine and pestilence struck, of which chronicles still tell.

The king emerged at last. He had no history to relate.

Mini-sagas are little trinkets reminiscent of those Japanese sea shells which, when dropped into a glass of water, open out to release a long decorative flower. The flower slowly expands to its full length.

A glass of water, someone, please –

How the Gates Opened and Closed

Among the storytellers gathered round the long table was a fair-haired man past his prime, an untidy man, wearing trainers, tattered jeans and a yellow sweater. He had given his name indistinctly as Dillow.

No one of the company had heard of Dillow. No one had read any of his stories. He had been sitting for an hour, listening, not speaking, his hands under the table and thrust into his jeans pockets.

When the laughter at the ending of a story had died down, he sat bolt upright. He spoke, not challengingly but with assurance.

'Your stories are all choked with events, like streams choked by weeds. Stories should not be like that. I will tell you a tale with nothing happening in it. Because my life has been empty.'

'We fill our stories with events for people with empty lives,' said one of the women storytellers.

Dillow gave her a half-smile. 'You understand that when I say my life has been empty, I mean empty of event. It has been full of drama.'

The people round the table reacted variously to this remark. Some responded sympathetically, some found it pretentious, though they might have accepted it on paper. All, however, challenged Dillow to tell this eventless story of his.

Dillow shrugged his shoulders, looked about him for quiet, and began.

'There was an old man in a remote village. He lived with his daughter and her husband. Every evening, he took three geese down to drink in the pond at the end of the village. He led one goose with a length of string round its neck, the same old string he had used for several years. The other two geese followed the first one.'

Someone interrupted Dillow, saying, 'At this point, a wolf or fox could run out of a wood and carry off one of the geese.'

'No such event. The visit to the pond was always peaceful. The old man, whose name was Lee, exchanged a few words with people on his way there and back. As a matter of fact, this village was almost deserted. He had been a soldier in his time – a soldier in several campaigns. He once was forced to march eight days at a stretch.'

'Action there! Don't cheat, Dillow!' one of the listeners said.

'All in the past, long ago. The country had been ravaged by war, and by the famines that follow on the heels of war. I should have mentioned that the village was in ruins. Hardly a house was left intact after various armies had passed through that way. Most of the inhabitants had fled, or had been killed.'

'You are forced to tell us of many great events.'

'I merely mention them in passing,' said Dillow. 'I should also mention that the old religion had died, or appeared to have died. No one visited the temple any more, or attempted to restore its ruin. But what I'm talking about is simply an old bent man, not in the best of health, taking three geese to the pond every evening.'

'But one day the geese escape, surely?' said one of the storytellers at the far end of the table.

'Geese are friendly and intelligent birds. They'd talk if they could.

They enjoyed their walk every evening, they enjoyed their splash in the pond. And they would no more think of leaving their master than Lee would think of leaving them. They always followed him willingly back to Lee's daughter's house and laid eggs for the family as often as they could.'

'Very dramatic, I must say!'

'What you must learn to enjoy is the lack of event, the silences of a story.' Dillow paused, as if to emphasize the importance of story. Some of his listeners fidgeted – even when he continued on a different tack.

'There are as many kinds of story as there are kinds of reader. People learn as much from inaction as action. And the life of this old man with his geese must be contrasted with another life: the life of a prince who lived nearby – a prince born in the same year as the old man, the Year of the Buffalo.'

'Ha, another protagonist! Now you find it necessary to introduce a little character conflict into the dull tale.'

'Not at all. The two men encountered one another but once, many years earlier, when the prince was on his way to his palace, which stood aloof at the end of the village. Lee got in the way of his carriage. The prince shouted to him, kindly enough, "Don't you value your life, man?" Lee never forgot the words, and often repeated them to his friends in the years of war; he marvelled at them, firstly because he had been spoken to by a prince, and secondly because he had never thought that a peasant's life could have value. "Don't you value your life . . . ?" The question was a puzzlement to him.'

'This is all past-tense stuff, you know,' one of the women reminded him.

'Well, if there's tranquillity anywhere, perhaps it resides in the past . . . When old Lee was standing by the pond with his geese, he could see the gates of the palace. Never once, during all the troubles and pestilences that beset the province, had those gates been opened. Until one day, to his amazement, he heard a gong struck and witnessed the opening of the gates. What a creaking those unused hinges set up between them! And out came the prince himself.

'The prince stood in the roadway, and Lee – at the distance of two hundred metres – bowed to him profoundly.'

'So Lee got his head chopped off?'

'You must consider the situation. On the one hand, an old soldier, survivor of several campaigns, a man whose parents had been killed by bandits, whose wife had died in one of the epidemics that swept the country, and who now lived a thousand miles from the village where he was born.

'And on the other hand, this person of privilege, born to reign over vast territories, who had known no hardship, who – unlike Lee – had been able to choose how he would live.

'Old Lee was a thin wasted man with a face brown and wrinkled as a walnut. His ribs showed under his thin shirt. Although his vision was not of the best, it was for another reason he would have failed to recognize the prince, had it not been for the latter's elaborate garments.

'When he had seen the prince many years earlier, the prince had been a strikingly handsome young man, lean, athletic, known for his prowess at archery and blood sports. Now Lee was staring at a bloated creature with a bald pate. The cut of his clothes could not conceal bow legs and a sagging stomach. He had waddled rather than walked through the palace gates . . .'

One of the storytellers interrupted. 'Fine, fine, but enough of these comparisons: the rich and the poor. What of it?'

'Simply this. I wished to tell you a story without event. That I've done. Once the prince had regarded his ravaged territories with disfavour, he turned and went back into his palace. The gates closed behind him. Old Lee collected his geese and returned to his sister's house as usual. That night, they ate some rice with chopped goose egg and chilli for supper.'

'You mean to say he and the prince never even shouted at each other? Never even spoke? Couldn't you have arranged it for the prince to recognize your old chap, maybe invite him in to a banquet? Your old man never even spat at the prince? That's what I call a disappointing story.'

'It would have been out of character to have a peasant spit at a prince, or a prince recognize a peasant. But don't you see that the story is about the lack of event? You believe tragedies are made from events, like Sophocles's *Oedipus*. But sometimes they are made from the vacuum created by a failure of contact.

'The prince abrogated his powers. Instead of exercising his traditional rights and duties, and maintaining some form of civil order, he had retreated into his private world and enjoyed his concubines. His was a life without history. For thirty years, he closed his eyes to the fate of his people and his bronze doors upon life.

'Because of that idleness, that dereliction of duty, his province underwent too much history. It became a theatre of events. Events ruled. The period was referred to later as The Age of the Seven Wars. Many volumes were written about it.'

The storytellers looked at each other up and down the long table. One of them said, 'Couldn't you have made up a more interesting story about the wars themselves, and the people taking part in them? Or we could have had a nice erotic story about what went on in the prince's palace all those years . . .'

Dillow shook his head, saying nothing more.

All he had had in mind was the picture of an old man walking in a ruined village with his three white geese, an old man who had once been asked the question, 'Don't you value your life?' He understood that the very poor could never answer such things: just as the prince had never valued the life even of a goose.

Almost everything has a cash value these days. Even information, perhaps especially Information, has become a saleable commodity as never before. This is rather puzzling, since a recent poll showed that over half of the population believes that the Sun moves round the Earth, rather than vice versa. How curious that a scientific fact which took courage and knowledge – and unorthodox thinking – to establish should apparently have such a low cash equivalent.

If such basic facts were sold in supermarkets, we should all be a good deal wiser. For those who wanted it, ignorance would also be on sale; you'd purchase it with a discredit card.

One sort of information without monetary value is personal information – that is, provided the person involved is not famous or infamous. People like you and me can hardly give away our vast hoard of personal information. We may want to, we may long to. The chances are that no one, not even our own mothers, will need it. However unique we are, we're too much like other people. Were you ever interested in an account of someone else's operation – however much you itched to tell about yours?

Have you ever been forced to look at someone's else's family photograph album for an hour or two?

Death's different, though not all that different from enforced photograph albums. It is true that a morbid interest attaches to someone's death. A neighbour's death, let's say. We are curious to know about that; we are all ears. We listen to the minutest details where death is involved. 'I went in and looked at him at about 9.15.

His breathing was steady. I looked in again just after 9.35, when his sister left. He hadn't stirred. But when I crept in again at about a quarter to ten – no, it was more like five to – it was quite dark – I found –'

Even death can bring in the money. Even your own death. If you have made all the proper arrangements.

Headless

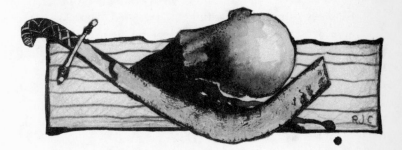

A vast crowd was gathering to see Flammerion behead himself. The TV people and Flammerion had rehearsed almost every move so that the event would go without a hitch. It was estimated that some 1.8 billion people would be watching: the largest TV audience since the nuking of North Korea.

Some people preferred to watch the event live. Seats in the stadium, highly priced, were booked months in advance.

Among the privileged were Alan Ibrox Kumar and his wife Dorothea Kumar, the Yakaphrenia Lady. They discussed it as they flew in to Düsseldorf.

'Why is he giving all the proceeds to Children of Turkmenistan, for heaven's sake?' Alan exclaimed.

'The terrible earthquake . . . Surely you remember?'

'I remember, yes, yes. But Flammerion's European, isn't he?'

For answer, she said, 'Get me another gin, will you?' She had yet to reveal to him she was divorcing him directly after the beheading.

The Swedish royal family had reserved two seats in a back row. They felt that Sweden should be represented at what was increasingly regarded – by the media at any rate – as an important event. The Swedish government remained furious that their offer of a prominent site in Stockholm had been turned down by Flammerion's agent.

Fortunately, six Swedes, two of them women, had since volunteered to behead themselves, either in Stockholm or preferably Uppsala. They named the charities they preferred.

Dr Eva Berger had booked a seat in the stadium on the day the box office opened. She had counselled Flammerion, advising against his drastic action on health grounds. When she realized she was unable to deflect him from his purpose, she begged him that at least a percentage of the proceeds go towards the Institute of Psychoanalysts. Flammerion had replied, 'I am offering you my psychiatric example. What else do you want? Don't be greedy.'

Later, Dr Berger had sold her seat for nineteen times the amount she had paid for it. She felt her integrity had paid off.

Dr Berger's feckless nephew, Leigh, happened to be a cleaner in the Düsseldorf stadium. 'Thank God I'm not on duty tonight,' he said. 'There'll be one hell of a mess. Blood everywhere.'

'That's what the public pay for,' his boss said. 'Blood has a whole vast symbolism behind it. It's not just a red liquid, son. You've heard of bad blood, and princes of the blood, and blood boiling, or things done in cold blood, haven't you? We've got a whole mythology on our hands, no less, tonight. And I need you to do an extra shift.'

Leigh looked hang-dog and asked what they would do with the head when Flammerion had finished with it.

His boss told him it would be auctioned at Sotheby's in London.

Among those who were making money from the event was Cynthia Saladin. She had sold her story to the media world-wide. Most people on the globe were conversant with what Cynthia and Flammerion had done in bed. Cynthia had tried her best to entertain, and was now married to a Japanese businessman. Her book, *Did Circumcision Start Flammy Going Funny?*, had been rushed into print, and was available everywhere.

Flammerion was passably good-looking. Commentators remarked on the numbers of ugly men who had bought seats in the stadium. Among their numbers was Monty Wilding, the British film director whose face had been likened to a wrinkled plastic bag. Monty was boasting that his exploitation-flick, *Trouble Ahead*, was already at the editing stage.

The Green Party protested against the movie, and about the self-execution, claiming that it was worse than a blood-sport and would undoubtedly start a trend. British sportsmen, too, were up in arms. The beheading clashed with the evening of the Cup Final. 'F.A. IN HEAD-OFF COLLISION,' ran the headline in the *Sun*.

There were others in Britain equally incensed by what was taking place on the continent. Among them were those who remained totally ignorant of the whereabouts of Turkmenistan.

As so often in times of trouble, people turned towards their solicitors, the Archbishop of Canterbury and Nick Ross for consolation – not necessarily in that order.

The Archbishop delivered a fine sermon on the subject, reminding the congregation that Jesus had given His life that we might live, and that that 'we' included the common people of England as well as the Tory Party. Now here was another young man, Borgo Flammerion, prepared to give up his life for the suffering children of Central Asia – if that indeed was where Turkmenistan was situated.

It was true, the Archbishop continued, that Christ had not permitted Himself to be crucified before the television cameras, but that was merely an unfortunate accident of timing. The few witnesses of the Crucifixion whose words had come down to us were notoriously unreliable. Indeed, it was possible (as much must be readily admitted) that the whole thing was a cock-and-bull story. Had Christ postponed the event by a millennium or two, photography would have provided a reliable testament to His self-sacrifice, and then perhaps everyone in Britain would believe in Him, instead of just a lousy nine per cent.

Meanwhile, the Archbishop concluded, we should all pray for Flammerion, that the deed he contemplated be achieved without pain.

Visibly put out by this address, the British Prime Minister made an acid retort in the House of Commons on the following day. She said, amid general laughter, that at least *she* was not losing her head. She added that the Archbishop of Canterbury should ignore what went on in Europe and look to her own parish. Why, a murder had taken place in Canterbury just the previous month. Whatever might or might not be happening in Düsseldorf, one thing was certain: Great Britain was pulling out of recession.

This much-applauded speech was delivered only hours before Flammerion performed in public.

As the stadium began to fill, bands played solemn music and old Beatles hits. Coachloads of French people of all sexes arrived. The French took particular interest in '*L'Événement Flammerion*', claiming the performer to be of French descent, although born in St Petersburg of a Russian mother. This statement had irritated elements of the American press, who pointed out that there was a St Petersburg in Florida, too.

A belated move was afoot to have Flammerion extradited to Florida, to be legally executed for Intended Suicide, now a capital offence.

The French, undeterred, filled the press with long articles of analysis, under such headings as 'FLAMMY: EST-IL PÉDALE?' T-shirts, depicting the hero with head and penis missing, were selling well.

The country that gained most from the event was Germany. Already a soap was running on TV called '*Kopf Kaput*', about an amusing Bavarian family, all of whom were busy buying chain-saws with which to behead each other. Some viewers read a political message into '*Kopf Kaput*'.

Both the Red Cross and the Green Crescent paraded round the stadium. They had already benefited enormously from the publicity. The Green Crescent ambulances were followed by lorries on which lay young Turkmen victims of the earthquake in blood-stained bandages. They were cheered to the echo. All told, a festival air prevailed.

Behind the scenes, matters were almost as noisy. Gangs of well-wishers and autograph-hunters queued for a sight of their hero. In another bunch stood professional men and women who hoped, even at this late hour, to dissuade Flammerion from his fatal act. Any number of objections to the act were raised. Among these objections were the moral repulsiveness of the act itself, its effect on children, the fact that Cynthia still loved her man, the fear of a riot should Flammerion's blade miss its mark, and the question whether the act was possible as Flammerion proposed it. Among the agitated objectors were cutlers, eager to offer a sharper blade.

None of these people, no priests, no sensation-seekers, no surgeons offering to replace the head immediately it was severed, were allowed into Flammerion's guarded quarters.

Borgo Flammerion sat in an office chair, reading a copy of the Russian *Poultry Dealer's Monthly*. As a teenager, he had lived on a poultry farm. Earning promotion, he had worked for a while in the slaughter houses before emigrating to Holland, where he had robbed a patisserie.

He was dressed in a gold lamé blouson jacket, sable tights and lace-up boots. His head was shaven; he had taken advice on this.

On the table before him lay a brand new cleaver, especially sharpened by a man from Geneva, representative of the Swiss company that had manufactured the instrument. Flammerion glanced at this cleaver every so often, as he read about a startling new method of egg-retrieval. Figures on his digital watch writhed towards the hour of eight.

Behind him stood a nun, Sister Madonna, his sole companion in these last days. She was chosen because she had once made a mistaken pilgrimage to Ashkhabad, capital of Turkmenistan, believing she was travelling to Allahabad in India.

At a signal from the Sister, Flammerion closed his periodical. Rising, he took up the cleaver. He walked up the stairs with firm tread, to emerge into the dazzle of floodlights.

An American TV announcer dressed in a blood-red gown said sweetly, 'If your immediate viewing plans do not include decapitation this evening, may we advise you to look away for a few minutes.'

When the applause died, Flammerion took up a position between the chalk marks.

He bowed without smiling. When he whirled the cleaver to his right side, the blade glittered in the lights. The crowd fell silent as death.

Flammerion brought the blade up sharply, so that it sliced from throat to nape-of-neck. His head fell cleanly away from his body.

He remained standing for a moment, letting the cleaver drop from his grasp.

The stadium audience was slow to applaud. But all had gone exceptionally well, considering that Flammerion had had no proper dress rehearsal.

It was Grandfather Wilson's contention that life was very short.

'I can almost measure my life in yards and miles,' he said, for he had never heard of metres. 'I remember being impressed by the size of the solar system when I was very young. One of my uncles explained a scale model of distances. I've never forgotten it. He told me that if an orange representing the sun were placed on our dining-room table, then Mercury, the nearest planet to the Sun, would be in the scullery and Venus somewhere down by the cabbage patch. Earth would be a pea stuck in the middle of the Dogsthorpe Road.'

He paused, with one of those meditative pauses that lend to the conversation of the old a quaint sense of gathering dusk.

'By analogy, my boy,' he said, clutching his knees and rocking in a way by which I was to understand he was only half-serious, 'to illustrate the brevity of life. Supposing I was born on that dining-room table, I would by now, in my eighty-fifth year, have got no further than that cabbage patch.'

I said, 'Leaving aside the dining-room table, I feel that life is terribly long. Although on the whole I enjoy each day in its own right, I often think it would be a relief if everything were cut off there and then. I've found life fairly pleasurable but I've had enough. So my experience is the opposite of yours.'

'That's because you're only in your thirties.' After another meditative pause, in which it transpired he still struggled with his analogy, he said, 'You haven't reached the scullery of life yet.'

Travelling Towards Humbris

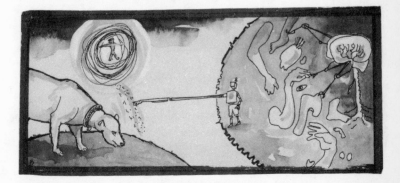

Someone on a TV programme showing on the Starlight Deck declared – apropos of what I do not know – 'But you must understand that we live in a real world, full of real people.'

Do many people believe such a ridiculous claim? No one in the studio audience challenged the statement. Nor did I hear a single murmur from the Disints viewing with me.

Later, I spoke with Turpitz, or what remains of him. I suspect he also experiences disquiet, but we never talk deeply.

'Reality's an old-fashioned concept,' Turpitz said. 'Time it was scrapped.'

'Didn't "real" mean Delphic, first of all? I believe the word was originally involved with faith,' I said.

'Still is,' Turpitz said. 'And it's a small silver Spanish coin. That's really real.' We propelled in silence for a while. Then he added, 'Has more meanings than a dog has fleas.'

'. . . To use an old-fashioned expression!'

He gave a sharp sound like a laugh. 'Goodbye to all that.'

The Disint catch phrase. He had already been shouldered.

Whatever world we are in, reality is surely a relative matter. And we populate it with fantasy people. Men fantasize about women, women about men, and most people about themselves. We on this ship – but I say this to no one, not even Turpitz – we are part of a fantasy of Domination. It's as if my old pet dog had risen up one day and declared the canine race to be God's Chosen People.

Long ago, before the planet Humbris coagulated, I took a month's cruise, sailing from Scotland to the Golconda Coast. My dog went with me. When the weather became warm, we slept on deck. In the great surge and heave of ocean my waking thoughts merged easily into the phantasms of sleep. All night, a part of me remained in communion with the sea, and knew itself to be no more permanent than the creatures that generate the phosphorescence of tropical waters. By day, I could not drag myself away from the rail; no entertainment the ship provided held a quarter as much interest as the vast expanse of waters.

That experience had a lasting effect: I could not doubt that I was a part of creation, and was contained within the drama un-rolling in some immense storyteller's mind. Not separate, but contained!

The sea has always been associated with mystical experience. There we find our true selves, or we drown. This I will say, that before we docked on the coast of Golconda, my psyche had changed and I had been renewed. Then as now, such claims are heresy.

The ship was the *Otranto*. That metal beast of burden trailed its wake behind it unfalteringly, day and night, in calm or storm. Never did it seem to feel fatigue, dwarfed as it was by the echoing vacancy of its surroundings. I conceived an admiration for it, as perhaps a flea does for the dog on which it steals a ride. In particular, I loved to lie during the hours of darkness listening to the throb of the *Otranto*'s engines, just as a flea may be reassured by the beat of a dog's heart. Even today – when sleep comes less easily – I can lull myself into dreams by pretending I hear again the beat of the *Otranto*'s machine heart.

Three centuries have faded away since that early voyage. By coincidence, I am now travelling aboard another *Otranto*, a spaceship of Italish manufacture. Its engines are silent as it slips through interstellar space towards an artificial Golconda. Not a whisper comes from them. We slip towards infinity as if under anaesthetic.

My sea-going ship of the long past was named after an eighteenth-century fantasy by Horace Walpole, a once-famous novel (an old form of storytelling) entitled *The Castle of Otranto*. Our space-going ship, I learn, is christened after a little interplanetary hero of the same name, who dances through various Disint fantasy adventures, in a Milanese CW-RAA game of immense Italish popularity.

We can stand only so much reality – perhaps because we find it an unsuitable medium for human life. Unlike our fantasies, reality does not bend easily to our personal desires. The real is easily spent. As babes we do not know reality; as adults, we do not understand it. What will we have to learn anew on Humbris, I wonder, when the Surgeonry has multiplicated us?

The teaching is that on a uni-specific world we shall create a para-reality, more lucid than anything our old earthstock enjoyed. Well, the Surgeonry knows better than I. But – to be alone? To scuttle about, isolated from the rest of life? Isn't that to exchange diversity for ideology? Such seditious thoughts I keep to myself.

Had I my old dog, Greenfinch, with me, his ear should hold my anxieties. I wept when he was put down before the voyage.

Humbris is the new uni-specific world. There are eighty-six others, all highly acclaimed. Yet did we ever see one image from them, or hear one word, about what was happening there? All is silence. Those bodiless limbs have no speaking parts in the drama of existence.

As we head through the light-centuries towards our new Surgeonry-ruled world, I listen for engines, for that old reliable throb-throb, as once I did on the pre-STL *Otranto*, long since docked at the scrap heap. But here we enjoy no syllable of sound; nothing speaks to us. The ion drive is off. No great beating heart encompasses us. The flea misses its dog.

*   *   *

This *Otranto* possesses the equivalent of an ocean-going ship's rail, but I soon tired of gazing out at the incomprehensible, the black, the stars mired in vacuum, the unacknowledgeable, punctuated by surly bonfires of galaxies. So I take my daily propulsion about the decks, occasionally with Turpitz, less frequently with Desmonda. Other people exercise there too, men and women destined for the Surgeonry, and no child under ten years of age. And again I note – no dogs.

Once I ventured to say as much to Turpitz, after my tessectomy. 'Have you noticed? Not a single dog aboard ship.'

Clearing his larynxofone, he spoke with difficulty. 'Animals forbidden, like young children.' One could not detect approval or disapproval in his neutral tone.

'But even pictures . . .'

'There is the weight factor. You understand how rationing goes with rationality. And bevelage of generation.' He shot me a quizzical look. I recorded it.

'But youngness has import.'

He said, 'Not to an older race.'

'Even steven. So you believe that memory . . .'

'Quits. Goodbye to all that.'

On that old ocean-going beast of burden, the ancient *Otranto*, I knew myself a part of creation and rejoiced in it, rejoiced in my tiny spark of consciousness, my phosphorescence. What can one think about now? Thought has nothing to work on here; as lungs cannot function in a vacuum, brains cannot accommodate this future – though they say that our computers are already living ahead of us. They have no reservations. We're allocated. On Humbris, we shall withdraw from Creation. It's the plan. It will be executed.

Now: starflight. Destined to populate with our component parts a new world on which life itself is new. I see eager faces all round me, eager Disint faces, washed, weakened, waxed, warranted. Yet what are our prospects on Humbris, that new-forged world, that forgery? What dismay will overwhelm us when we are distributed there? For we have left behind mankind's most faithful friend.

Oh, we are escorted by our androids and nanoservants, of course.

Life and surgery must go on. Dismay will not mean in any way defeat. But where is that amiable being who allied himself with humanity, who accompanied us from the caves, from the Ice Age? By what terrible mistaken theory of hygiene did we decide to leave him behind, as if he were not important, not a part of our history?

The Surgeonry will console us with the thought that we shall forget dogs and other animals. The Disint life will contain other things, other qualities as yet unspecified. What prompts these thoughts is the knowledge that tomorrow I part from my right hand and forearm. They will go to the Disintator, to start living apart.

By the time we reach Humbris, I shall be ready for the new existence, with its other qualities. We shall be, they tell us, more various, and replicate like amoebae. Then – oh, then, they tell us, our worries will be over. We shall certainly not need the company of dogs. Goodbye to all that.

Every story has its antecedents, a trail leading back to some perhaps forgotten model, some sunken *Otranto*. No doubt the trail will lead onward some day. The current story is a pause along a track of inheritance.

Both of the two stories that follow have their origins in Shakespeare's plays. Shakespeare's *Hamlet*, in its turn, was based on a lost play, a revenge tragedy, possibly written by Thomas Kyd. My Hamlet is deplorably less serious.

A writer is lucky if he or she finds an opportunity to read his stories aloud to an audience. Both of these Shakespearean stories I have read aloud more than once (sometimes wearing a special jacket for the occasion). In successive years I read them to that kindest of audiences, the scholars and writers who attend the IAFA Conference of the Fantastic in Fort Lauderdale, Florida.

If Hamlet's Uncle
Had Been a Nicer Guy

For many years, one has had doubts about Hamlet's conduct. Indeed, I have written to the papers about it. The Shakespeare critic, A.C. Bradley, in his disquisition on the famous tragedy of *Hamlet*, asks a number of pertinent questions concerning this moody prince. We must remember that, to the other Danes, this young man is well thought of, the glass of fashion, the university graduate, the heir to the throne. Yet he is ostentatiously rude to women.

It would be perverse not to see here a major indicator to his character. Bradley is right to complain of Hamlet's violent language to Ophelia in the nunnery scene. He also raises several problems difficult of resolution according to usual interpretations of the play: Why does Hamlet insult Ophelia? Why, in particular, does he not reflect, when he has slain good Polonius, that the poor old chap was Ophelia's father, and that his death would come as a devastating blow to the lady he professes to love?

Other evidences of Hamlet's low nature are not far to seek.

Our young prince rarely speaks to Polonius without using cruel jibes, or to the king without insult. He terrifies his mother, sends his school friends to their deaths without a thought, and ruins a perfectly good funeral by unruly behaviour. He is also, let us not forget, a potential suicide as well as a murderer. Unbalanced, in a word. S.T. Coleridge's considered verdict on Hamlet, after remarking on his 'almost enormous intellectual activity', whatever that means, is that he is crackers. Or, in Queen Gertrude's more kindly analysis, 'Mad as the sea and wind'.

Everyone bar Hamlet is kind to Ophelia – perhaps suspecting her to be a few apples short of the Tree of Knowledge – Gertrude in particular. Playgoers are shocked when Hamlet bursts into his mother's bedroom. This action is generally interpreted as a sign of his discourteous nature. We can more truly consider it as none too unusual an entrance, considering the time and the place. Such rude invasions may have been a part of the laxity of manners in the Danish court, when anyone might barge into a lady's bedroom unannounced. Hasn't even Polonius done the same kind of thing not half an hour earlier, doing who-knows-what behind the arras? Hamlet himself prompts us in Act I to see the court as a licentious place which, in his words, 'Makes us traduced and taxed of other nations'.

This being the case, we must reconsider our judgement regarding the queen's adultery and her marriage to Claudius. Adultery, the sport of kings, may well have been merely the average standard of behaviour at the time: not quite to be condoned, but accepted as part of a general decline in conduct – less a vice, more a friendly habit, like oral sex today.

We can, after all, but guess at what Hamlet's father got up to when he was alive. His son sings his praises, but this may be merely filial blindness. We know of him only that he is vengeful and obsessive even after death, and prone to hang about the ramparts in full armour: he cannot have been, we feel, an easy man to live with. No doubt Hamlet takes after him.

It becomes clear that, in ordinary cases, both Hamlet and this bellicose parent would be locked up; yet at the Elsinore court they pass for near normal.

Consider the contrast in behaviour with Claudius, in my view a maligned man. Having inherited the throne, he marries Hamlet's mother. We gain insight into his frugal habits when he furnishes forth his wedding feast with left-over funeral baked meats. Hamlet sneers at this admirable parsimony in kings. We have only to witness the forbearance with which Claudius treats his tiresome nephew, to know him for a kindly, dignified man, one with whom we easily empathize: accustomed to dealing with loonies in a humane way – by reasoning where possible, by poison where not.

I express the matter in this extreme fashion to make my point. But a small retreat is in order. Let us suppose simply that Hamlet is no loony, but rather of melancholic disposition, unmannerly, and liable to see apparitions.

If this view of the prince initially proves difficult to accept, it is for two reasons integral to the text: firstly, because Hamlet's is the main part in the play, easily dominating all the other players; and secondly, because Shakespeare puts noble lines into his mouth. This should not lead us astray from Shakespeare's real intentions, which are to portray an unbridled depressive running loose in a castle otherwise given over to the celebration of a royal wedding.

For this perception I can hardly claim originality. In a seminal lecture delivered some years ago, Caroline F.E. Spurgeon stressed the number of images in the play that convey sickness and disease; 'the idea of an ulcer or tumour', she says, 'is, on the whole, the dominating one.' It is clear she refers to Hamlet himself, whom even his patient uncle calls an ulcer in so many words.

So what are we to make of this ambitious play which has gone so greatly awry in the hands of our greatest dramatist? By allotting so much of the grandeur of the words to Hamlet, Shakespeare upset the balance of his play; how could he have remedied matters?

To be frank – Professor Dover Wilson says as much – character construction is rather weak here. Ben Jonson would have made Hamlet's general nastiness clearer, by doing a better job of portraying Claudius as potentially an ideal king.

Poor Claudius! Tolerant to a fault of his nephew's crazed foibles, he finally cracks when the evening is spoilt by an absurd play Hamlet forces the players to enact. Claudius naturally grows restless. It may be that he prefers musicals. Our sympathies are with him when he calls for the lights to go up in the auditorium. Unlike those of us who have to sit through mistaken and long-winded versions of *Hamlet*, Claudius, being king, need not long endure versions of *The Mouse-trap*.

There is no indication at this point in the text that Claudius, by cutting short the pantomime, reveals any supposedly murderous guilt about anything, or that he has poisoned his brother. We have only Hamlet's word for that. We can as legitimately argue that this cultivated newly crowned king was something of a drama critic and could not stand fustian.

Only in the duel scene do we expect his allegedly cruel designs on Hamlet to be revealed. Claudius has had enough. There might seem no doubt that the king poisons both the wine and the foils with which Hamlet and Laertes fight. That this is not the case, an impartial examination of the 'venom' the king uses will demonstrate.

In *The Anatomy of Melancholy*, Robert Burton speaks of several poisons that cure melancholia such as Hamlet's. Hellebore, which modern dictionaries describe simplistically as 'poisonous', was regarded by the authorities Burton quotes as a sovereign remedy, and was so used in Shakespeare's time. Here's the great Paracelsus, in his book on the black hellebore, declaring, 'It is most certain that the virtue of this herb is unrivalled, when proper use is made of it.' Sallust Salvian agrees, called the powder 'a most excellent remedy for all melancholy and mad men', going on to say, 'best applied *through the skin at needle-point*' (my emphasis).

Should we not for once give Claudius the benefit of the doubt and accept that, all other means of medication having failed, Hamlet's uncle chooses this novel method – the tip of a foil – a needle-point – for the administration of what he had been assured was a panacea? It was his bad luck that the mixture turned out to be too powerful.

So much for the foils. As for *Danish wine* . . . One can hardly imagine anything so poisonous in the first place. We may safely assume that the whole court swigged the stuff.

It must be admitted that admirers of Hamlet – and indeed of *Hamlet* – will be unlikely to accept without hesitation this line of reasoning. They will cite tradition as being on their side, averring Claudius intended murder. But certainty is not evidence; they merely follow like sheep what has become custom. There is a strength to tradition, as we see in the case of the Church of England, where, by clinging to the Authorized King James Version of the Bible, the Church has retained huge congregations of the faithful, and filled the pews of their cathedrals to bursting point.

Tradition is nowhere more immutable than in the representation of Hamlet on stage as a thin youth dressed in black. This is another way in which he gains our mistaken sympathy and Claudius our antipathy. Yet, in truth, the text would be better served if the role were filled by heavyweight actors who usually play Falstaff.

Hamlet is somewhat more than Portly. This can clearly be seen in Act IV, Scene iii, where Hamlet addresses Guildenstern, admitting that 'we fat all creatures else to fat us, and we fat ourselves for maggots'. We should hardly be surprised at this outburst, for even in the second scene of the play, he is complaining, 'O, that this too too solid flesh would melt.' Shakespeare could not have made the point more clearly had he written in a stage direction, '*Enter Hamlet, A Fat Prince*'.

The aforementioned Mrs Spurgeon got the point. She speaks of a number of blemishes of the body, going so far as to remark that Hamlet sees even the kingdom of Denmark 'in terms of a sick body needing medicine or the surgeon's knife'.

Here we uncover at once the cause of his melancholia and his constant inaction, so puzzling to lesser commentators. Hamlet delays because he is overweight, he is morose because he is dieting.

His mind is never off food. Enviously, he speaks of Claudius 'making wassail', as if the poor king had no entitlement to celebrate his accession to the throne. Such is the lot of those who diet. Polonius makes mention of this routine, relating in Act II how Hamlet 'Fell into a sadness, then into a fast'. Our overweight hero himself speaks of this regimen shortly thereafter, saying that he has of late lost his mirth and given up all exercise. He tells us – if we wish to hear – that he 'eats air', and that he is so hungry he 'could drink hot blood'. Not a pleasant state of affairs.

Even over Ophelia's grave, this greedy fellow confides that he could 'eat a crocodile'.

Gertrude herself admits, when Hamlet attempts to duel with Laertes, that 'he's fat and scant of breath'.

Of course he becomes touchy in this state. Of course his step-father can do nothing with him. Of course he rants against normal people, asking in a querulous tone, 'What is a man if his chief good and market of his time be but to sleep and feed?'

Why is Hamlet on a diet? Is it to win the hand of the fair Ophelia? Or could it be simply to annoy his mother and Claudius at a time when they, naturally, are having a good tuck-in?

Whatever the reason, it is clear that a scrupulous production of this so-called tragedy would be a good deal more amusing with a twenty-stone prince lumbering about the castle, gasping at ascent of all those stone staircases, sweating upon the battlements. Claudius might then appear in a more sympathetic light.

When my 'Heavyweight Hamlet' is produced at Stratford, justice will be done to the misrepresented bard – and to the new king.

At this point we will call in a witness previously mentioned only in passing, the great Samuel Taylor Coleridge. It is well known that when Coleridge died in 1834, his widow, Sara Coleridge, destroyed many of his family letters. One of his biographers says, 'Within the space of a few years, almost all of S.T.C.'s correspondence, covering a period of forty years, had been burned – sackfuls and sackfuls of it.'

Authors have a habit of marrying pyromaniacs. Tennyson was another such, and Sir Richard Burton. Their relicts destroyed their literary remains almost before their physical remains were decently interred.

Some items of Coleridge's correspondence, however, survived the flames. Browsing through an antique shop in Bristol in 1991, I came across an old photograph album, its pages secured by a fancy cord.

It contained newspaper cuttings, tailors' bills, a postcard or two, and old correspondence. I bought it cheaply. Curiosity paid off. Five letters, three of them incomplete, proved to be by S.T.C. There was also a defiant note from his son, Hartley, saying, 'Sorry, Not coming back.'

The longest of S.T.C.'s letters – scrutinized by the Bodleian Library in Oxford for authenticity – discusses a remarkable stage entertainment based on *Hamlet*, which S.T.C. viewed in 1824, ten years before his death.

It was what we would nowadays call a ballet. S.T.C. refers to it as 'a danced version of Shakespeare's tragic play, faithful to the Bard in all particulars save one, and that the most vitalizing, in that the esemplastic alembic of the poetry, by which alone the grandeur of Shakespeare's conception is realized, has been totally discarded.'

Coleridge goes on at some length to describe this *Hamlet* in which music replaced words. Without words, however faithfully the narrative line is followed in dumb show and dance, we witness a play with a meaning very different from the one we imagine we know. What S.T.C. saw was a story of two middle-aged people, happily united at last, whose honeymoon in a remote castle is spoiled by constant interference from an ageing teenager in black. In the end, this teenager must be brought to heel; he proves to be a schizophrenic obsessed with revenge for some imagined slight.

Things go disastrously wrong when the teenager is showing off his fencing skills before the court. People get hurt. In a final *pas de deux*, the middle-aged newly-weds both die.

And the ultimate irony. In trots young Fortinbras and carts off for burial the villain instead of the hero.

'This interpretation would prove less vicious and indefensible,' states Coleridge, 'if only Hamlet's uncle had been a nicer guy.'

Many a young man must have identified with Hamlet. It is not uncommon to be stuck with a dilemma; indeed, dilemmas are probably a necessary condition early in life. They're part of the world's great spiritual aerobics class, where you give your psyche a workout.

The young male lead in Shakespeare's last play, *The Tempest*, is another son of a king, Ferdinand of Naples, a less attractive character than Hamlet. He makes a poor job of chopping wood.

However, Prospero marries off his daughter Miranda to Ferdinand without a second thought. Seems she's to see Naples or die.

Attending a performance of *The Tempest* when I was a small boy, I was impressed by the glory and wisdom of Prospero. Later, I had second thoughts. He does tend to oppress the natives, especially the indigenous Caliban. So I came to write what science fiction writers term an alternative history, where matters on the enchanted isle work out in other than the accepted way.

I made a journey to Glastonbury once. I'd come up to London from Oxford by train, and bumped into John, an old pal of mine, on Paddington station. We went for a drink in the bar. I had an appointment to see my publisher in Bedford Square. I asked John where he was going. John's an actor, by the way. He said, 'I'm hoping to see an old man in Glastonbury to find out which way my life is going.'

The way he said it sounded as if his life led him by the nose . . . So I forgot my publisher and climbed aboard the train with him. I'd never been to Glastonbury, though I'd

read John Cowper Powys's novel *A Glastonbury Romance*
– well, the first chapter of that cathedral of a work.

For some, Glastonbury remains a place of mystery and
romance. King Arthur's Isle of Avalon is traditionally
situated here. Here it is that thirteenth-century monks
found the remains of Arthur and Guinevere. A good
place in which to consult wise old men.

John's wise old man was called Joe. Joe lived in
a ramshackle caravan in a corner of a farmer's field.
His little site was shaded by two large Spanish chestnut
trees. His lady remained in the caravan, occasionally
peeping out of the window at John and me. Joe didn't
say much of interest, beyond insisting we'd met before.

'Have you ever been to Loch Lomond?' he asked. We
hadn't.

It started to rain, so we went inside Joe's caravan and
drank Ruddles till it cleared up. The lady had disappeared.

As the sun burst through and we were leaving, John
said to me, 'Give him a fiver. I haven't got any money.'
I only had a tenner in my pocket, so I gave Joe that. Joe
said to John, 'You ought to go up to Loch Lomond. If
you call in at Drummle Police Station, you may find
something.'

I said to him, 'Have you any advice to offer me?'

'Yes,' he said. He screwed up his eyes into a squint to
survey me. 'Be careful of your back.'

A couple of years passed before I saw John again. Again
I was in London. I was leaving that pub at the bottom
of Poland Street when John entered, looking no more
disreputable than usual.

'I had a bit of luck,' he said. 'I went up to Scotland
and called in at that police station in Drummle as Joe
advised. They'd got some title deeds hanging about,

which they said I could have if I wanted – I kid you not! So I took them. So now I own fifty-two acres of land and a manor house in Scotland. I'm going to live in it as soon as I've got a roof on it.'

He seemed little surprised at this sudden up-turn in his fortunes; perhaps he had visited Glastonbury anticipating some such event. After expressing my astonishment, I had to leave to go and see my publisher. As I left the pub, John called out, 'How's your back? Be careful with it.'

It occured to me that the reference was not to slipped discs but critics . . .

We all have to undertake journeys. Travel has inspired many a novel – and many a tall story. Myself, I'd advise you to try Glastonbury.

Ferdinand, of course, was more ambitious . . .

Else the Isle With Calibans

CALIBAN: This island's mine by Sycorax my mother, and all the fruit trees on it. Teasles more that clamp the hair, and mangosteen, and tamarisks that smother near the shore, all these I own.

MIRANDA: Thrift and crimson grannie's bonnet, honeysuckle wayward grown, oranges like golden lamps alight, parrot tulips in full flight . . .

Here sing we happy songs of peace till the heavens above shall cease.

CALIBAN: Shells, feather, bark, and shards of bone. These I own. Fowl, the things that scatter under stone, birds that chatter when alarmed, apes long-armed that in the trees go screaming from us branch by branch. What's furred or finned, in wind or rain – all, all's my own, now that I'm free again.

MIRANDA: And when my love and I walk this domain of ours, the very mirror of the sea reflects all our fond courtesy.

CALIBAN: This summer's day, I'm idling on a headland, having swum a hairy fish beneath the bay. Though I'd not wish to change an acre of this ground of mine for furlongs of the oft-perturbèd brine, I love its mystery.

Our children play upon us, test their powers. To Fano I'm by turns a tower, a horse, a fortress holding out against a foe. And while the fight goes to and fro, lo, cannon not of play roar in the bight a league or less away.

MIRANDA: The children scatter. A clatter carrying across the bay speaks of an anchor diving through the spray to wound the softling sand. A mast, a flag, a wooden wall – all signals for dismay.

And from our eyrie high bestowed in ocean's bosom, we espied a longboat crewed by sailors from a galleon. The flag of Naples fluttered at its bow. Already but a reach away, the craft was due to gain our beach.

CALIBAN: 'Mayhap,' I said, 'they only visit to find water, or the dumb hind seek out, to spice their diet. We're safe while lying quiet on this hill.'

MIRANDA: Full ten years breached, and from the champagne-sparkling sea no vessel ever reached this isle, or in this field of the Bermoothes set keel. About my heart all's ill, as if old history returned, with evil date, to hover close to sense. Happiness is unlearned. It cannot conjugate like lovers, knowing no past tense. The present is the place we wear. The future comes, I swear, with scowling face.

CALIBAN: We hid, but many ancient fears gleet from their charnel hole. Upon their winding sheets emblazoned was – the name of Prospero!

Yes, Prospero, vile exiled duke, who from Milan did sail to the still-unvexed Bermoothes to plague poor Ban. What good did he, except to land his frail unversed daughter here?

'Ere his accursed arrival, Sycorax, my blue-eyed dam, source of sweet spells which made the island tame, was queen of all. And I, her little prince, essayed to ape her tricks to summon wood nymphs mild, and suchlike sprites to play. Oh, we would leg it through the groves all live-long day!

But Prospero, so civilized, who feared the hooting of an owl, despised our sport, our rustic style, reduced my Sycorax to naught, and he himself made sovereign of the isle.

MIRANDA: My father, being wronged, wronged you as well.
Scholars by nature wear a spiky shell.

CALIBAN: Thus was my fate: to follow him, dog-like, his slave, early or late: apt to fetch timber, chop his wood or, from an amber pool, tickle a corpulent trout to fill his plate. Many a morning cool, I dreamed that I were out of pain and free of that. Then woke upon my mat, and wept that I might dream again.

MIRANDA: My father feared you, Caliban, and when he neared you always played the tyrant, by his magic powers swayed my heart against you. When I was knee-high he could persuade me fly the moon.

CALIBAN: Feared me? I was his chained baboon. Well, bruises mend . . .'Tis half a score of years since Prospero called up a storm and quit this isle, his tortures at an end.

MIRANDA: God speed to him! He freed his captives, and his magic books he drowned full fathom five.

CALIBAN: My spirits came alive. I took dominion then, of everything. The world did smile. And on his fair Miranda, ho, I peopled then the isle with Calibans!

MIRANDA: My pa must lie in's grave by now.

CALIBAN: And I in amaranth with you . . . Forgetting all, I roll upon her, much inspired beyond control, the very idea of her life o'erwhelming me. My honey-quimmed Miranda, living for the now, takes like furrow to the plough.

MIRANDA: Sure, this is ample golden age, its fruit, its seeds. Increase of appetite doth grow by what it feeds upon. He and I do clench as hand in glove or blind mole in its tunnel.

CALIBAN: My love! The sword of joy is such we prick ourselves alive at every touch, while in our sweet sweat's runnel basting life itself.

Meanwhile, the invaders pound their godless boots up from the beach, to foul the ground we sacred hold. Our childish fold dive each into the pleached bowers where ivy and wild cherry flower. Ensconced in dim uncertain shade, they watch the armèd men. More do parade than I have fingers. Martial are they, their swords displayed, and led – oh yes, Misfortune's brother, Envy, leads the file. Rich Ferdinand, heir of vile privilege, of royal clay, whose merest look can call back yesterday.

MIRANDA: Ferdy! That urban prince, who one time did delude me. Foppish and nice, subtle as lice! I burn to think he woo'd me.

CALIBAN: Of that old courtly band I knew, whose fulsome clothes with gold did smoulder, ashore comes only Ferdinand, with vengeance on his shoulder.

FERDINAND: Now shall my fate be crimson-lined. Oh, foul entanglement! They're there ahead, entwined!

CALIBAN: As lie I in Miranda's arms, he and his crew leap in like hounds and with their grievous metal points surround us.

FERDINAND: Writhe there like worms twinned on the rumpled ground! What's this unseemly show? Miranda, by my trow! Star in whose early succulence all images of ravishment commenced, whose lightest wish became my circumstance, whose tread upon the soil did verd mosses and buttercup, whose every word, parcelled in sweetest glance, pierced my heart's citadel and stormed it quite. You would have been my diadem for which I'd trade my crown, yet now – oh, how cast down!

MIRANDA: How we tumble, Ban and I, conjoined, as Nature made us. All these blades unsheathed numb with a dread surmise my loins . . .

CALIBAN: But she's allowed to rise and don her shift. I cannot lift my head. This royal stigma uses me as footstool.

FERDINAND: Ape, lie still. Apply that worthless brow of yours to earth. Your hours are all sucked dry. Wretched Miranda, ember of your line, your downcast, outcast state implies you harbour no remembrances of me.

MIRANDA: I say, 'Despite that arrogance of talk, I cede that you are Ferdinand who, in my former life enclosed – a life of solitude and learning by my pa imposed – a quarantine from girlhood fun – were son of Naples' king.'

FERDINAND: And now am king, my father being finally disposed to quit this mortal scene. Soldiers, enchain this ill-yoked pair.

CALIBAN: They drag us, so it chances, to a glorious oak, all creeper-cloaked, and bowered in rose, sprung from a bank whereon the wild thyme blows: that self-same oak wherein the affluent Lord Prosper penned poor me.

I cannot this affront surmount, and shake my chains, but she! – Oh, brave Miranda now regains her nerve, and with true verve calls Ferdy to account.

MIRANDA: 'You came in former time with meeker brow, all syrup-tongued yet gentle to me. Now – why now that you've the crown, you force a sterner mode, and need armed men for your discourse.'

At that he laughed as if a prig waylaid his humour. This new-made king declares, 'No more entreaties in this later day, now ten years are sunk away, I know not how.'

FERDINAND: Miranda! – How your very name still rises up before me like a flame, to me dismay! Christus, how brittle is a virtuous state, how soon thrown down in disarray! Think you of late your brow is still unwrinkled, pillowed limbs still virginal, as when the cock first crowed upon your waking sense? That sagging eye was once a glass of innocence, the day we met through Prospero's enchantment, a casement open to your soul. Now shattered, never to be whole . . .

Like his, your own enchantments now are faded – much as the baseless fabric of a dream is torn by waking. Oh, what virtues are degraded! Think you to sleep with apes improves your style? All that once smiled in you, the very mirror of your sex paraded – as meat is thrown to wolves, you tossed to this hag-seed. And he with his vile instrument has fatted you, how many times . . . this witch's whelp . . . Till all that's left's beyond time's help.

MIRANDA: I say, more haughtily than he, 'You trample down enchantment, unfit to scent its spoor. Where'er you tread, it vanishes before. Rest your regard upon this weighty jade whose whole experience rides undismayed o'er that poor thing men prize – virginity. There's no crime in my tatters. Sir, Eros hath a gentler touch than Time – not least in country matters.

'You boast a deficit in flesh. What eats your bones, you royal Naples slave, so profligate and thin? Desire, ambition, hate that dances round some grave of sin, perpetually to dig it up again, as jackals save their carrion? I see the blow-fly in your glance.'

CALIBAN: With covert eye, the soldiery seek one another's gaze, not daring openly to greet the candour of the thrust. Despairing, Ferdinand, 'I expeditioned to this unmapped land solely to meet again – I sought to meet – one who in mem'ry sweet did fill –'

Dead falls his thought. His look is ill as, dried of words, he turns away his head.

He curses, kicks and spits, and yet I see that Ferdy knows full well what all men understand: there is no bush of circumstance so valued as a bird in hand. Compared with faith and lovesome mate, the Naples throne is but a counterfeit.

MIRANDA: Then we are bound. Ban's arm and mine, my left, his right, are touching 'gainst the round oak's bark. This is the ship, our ark, when launched in flame, will carry us beyond our mortal shore, our life submerging into night. Our children roar, and as the torches flare, from undergrowth emerging, caper on the leaze for mercy.

CALIBAN: Here's Fano, Trink, and little Iris, dear doe daughter, as bright water nimble. All now trip and tumble, pleading that our bonds be cut. In agitation, in their humble way they clown, death to deny, for the greater glory of the day. Their rich moist eyes rain supplication.

MIRANDA: Whereupon, the savage Neapolitan plunges his blade into my Fano's breast. The others flee, to crouch with partridge and the speckled snake in nested lair, while Fano in his blood chokes out his soul.

CALIBAN: Right from his day of birth, our Fano was a child of joy, as if the wiser elements of nature rolled themselves into a human form, to make a little world of mirth and love fulfilled. Through him we throve. And there before our helpless selves his life was spilled. My groans resound through all the oaken grove.

Meantime, our state is dire. Now do the twigs, well heaped with gorses too, about our toes catch fire, to hiss the villainy of what they do.

MIRANDA: Poor little Fano! Now the smoke rises to cloak his agonies.

CALIBAN: All eager with desire does Ferdinand lean his crazed face into the growing blaze and shout, 'Miranda, tell me while your life delays, you took me in – why didst thou throw me out?

FERDINAND: For at that moment all were reconciled and Prospero had burnt his books – indeed, as bo'sun was prepared to bend his rowers' backs and bear us safely from the wild and then to Naples, at that living moment, oh, your hand slipped out of mine . . . You turned and ran from off the strand. I called. My cries awoke the beach. I searched, but with you out of reach we had to leave. Ten years have dragged their hapless pomp along, and still that wrong afflicts me. Speak, why didst thou make me grieve?

MIRANDA: Mild was my answer then. 'I am not ceremony's bride who was informal nature's child.'

CALIBAN: The smoke that hides her lovely face lifts like a veil. All modesty, Miranda sighs,

MIRANDA: I thought you first a thing divine. Your noble clothes, your seemly tongue, enchanted when we met. How much you promised then. Oh, I should be the Queen of Naples and I'd wear . . . this gem and that, I quite forget. But when I grew to know you more I realized your robes and rings and thrones were pageants, mere material things. In that moment on the shore, your hand in ownership upon my arm, my blood quick with a sensible alarm – about to leave this little land, *I thought of Caliban.*

FERDINAND: That brute!

MIRANDA: Oh yes. 'That brute', you say – whom all despised, eternally my father's slave, beaten and maltreated – yet my friend, well-seated in my heart. Who was it taught me laughter, played a flute, was antic when it suited, tamed a hare! Who named me all the pleasures of the isle, the fresh springs, marl-pits, mushrooms that enchant? My Ban alone! What's more, when pa had turned his alchemistic back, my Banny teased me with sports in naughty ways, and in my crack his finger tickled qualms I knew not that I sought.

CALIBAN: This hero finger, teacher then – and taught!

MIRANDA: So in that moment by your boat – your mariners with oars all poised – Ferdy, I found I did not want your promises. What do I care for ceremonial? Not a groat. I dote upon this isle's remoteness. That's why I ran – praise fate – to share with Caliban within our little plot pleasures of nature that would please you not.

CALIBAN: Burning within as we without, he sighs. 'Not all the harlots that comprise my court erased you from my contemplation.'

And as he spoke, I freed one hand. The flames do flare. But at a stroke, I summon forth from crackling oak my brother Ariel. In his divinity does Ariel descend, swift as an owl by night upon its prey, piercing the air, to douse the flames and scare the men away with awful shrieks and spears of light. Vesuvius sparked less fiercely than my Ariel.

MIRANDA: Only the King of Naples stands his ground, till spirits in the shape of dog and hound pursue him from the scene.

FERDINAND: Depravity! This isle, I now know well, for all its beauty, lies in the neighbourhood of Hell.

MIRANDA: Go, beastlings all! To chase, to duty! As all do bark, cries Ariel, 'Silver, Fury, there. Go fetch! Hark, Tyrant, hark!' And in uproar, all chase him till he gains the shore, his cloak and sword forgotten.

CALIBAN: With Ariel and sweet Miranda I do follow where the tide, now slack, casts on the yellow sands a necklace of seawrack. We there take hands and watch the sad invader row with all due haste away.

MIRANDA: He stands up reckless in the craft to call in accents choked and gruff, across the tide, 'I loved you once, Miranda . . .'

CALIBAN: From our beach I shout back, rough with pride, 'Then that must serve enough.'

MIRANDA: His cry returns, now faint below the taunt of gulls, to haunt us to our dying day,

FERDINAND: Could you but understand, Miranda . . . [PAUSE] Nothing in life is ever enough . . .

CALIBAN: The gleaming distance bore his boat away.

What happened to Ferdinand when he returned to Naples? Perhaps on reflection he thought his journey, disillusion notwithstanding, to be worthwhile. Perhaps he was freed from his obsession. Perhaps – who knows – he even joined the Church.

The following story is published here for the first time. I like it well, but could find no magazine that would accept it. Its length is against it, and the fact that it has a foreign country named in its title.

People are funny that way.

Readers sometimes believe that when your name is known, you can become published anywhere. Such is not the case. Being famous is a matter of degree. One can be published and recognized all round the globe, and still struggle to earn a crust, just as some writers are totally unknown, never reviewed, and become extremely rich. Mine are the middle parts of fortune.

Such thoughts are idle and well worn, coming as they do from the 'There Ain't No Justice' department. And if we were all treated according to our deserts, who would 'scape whipping? But the idle thoughts possess me this autumn morning, when we receive a postcard from our friends Clark and Judy Brundin. They sent it from Ukiah, California. There, in their hotel room, they switch on the television and find that I am holding forth about H.G. Wells's *The War of the Worlds*.

I marvel to realize I have been addressing the denizens of Ukiah, California. All the same, I would rather someone else had been talking about one of my books.

Samuel Johnson, in his celebrated letter to Lord Chesterfield, says, 'I had done all I could; and no man is well pleased to have his all neglected, be it ever so little.'

That's so. But for a day or two, a postcard displaying the inexhaustible charms of Ukiah, California, on our mantelpiece will suffice.

A Swedish Birthday Present

He woke up before his wife, climbed from under the duvet and peered through the curtains. It was almost eight in the morning. Winter was past, losing its grip over the northern lands. Yet a crinkle of ice had appeared overnight on their artificial pool, drinking darkness down into itself. Frost covered their square of lawn with white; but the sun had risen to halfway through the twigs of the birches lining Vestergaardatan. It shone smudgily in at Lars as he stood naked, scratching himself, relishing the delicacy of colouring, or lack of it, outside.

Today was Saturday. He did not have to work on the Metro. And it was Helen Anderson's birthday. Her fortieth birthday, to be celebrated that very evening. His spirits rose at the thought.

'What are you doing?' Karina asked.

He had heard his wife stir in the bed. Answering while continuing to gaze through the window, he said, 'Winter may carry off old folk, but it sharpens the senses.'

Karina made no reply. As Lars headed towards the shower, he asked, 'Do you understand that? I mean appreciation of natural beauty.'

'Will you make me some herbal tea before you shower? I know how long you take in there, primping yourself.'

Their little kitchen was cheerful, the woodwork painted white, the walls lime green, and lined just below the ceiling with reproductions of Carl Larsson's portrayals of domesticity. Lars hummed under his breath as he prepared two mugs of tea.

Admit it, he liked domesticity. He liked Karina's cooking. Pickled fish was good for them. He liked the whole business of being at home, doing nothing. Pottering. He had given up his socialist principles long ago; life was easier without principles. He enjoyed a stroll down the street for a newspaper, and sitting on the porch in the summer. In a week or so, he would redecorate their little sitting-room. He enjoyed being naked, and the smell of Karina's apple and cinnamon tea. Settle for what you've got, he told himself. Men were meant to be happy. You only got one bite at the cherry.

He savoured his own aroma after the night's sleep. Although he was under average height – to his continued regret – Lars was compactly built, with strong arms and shoulders. True, there was little outstanding about his face; but a girl had told him his eyes were an attractive grey. You had to get what advantage you could from what you had been given. His teeth were good. On the whole, he consoled himself, he had been pretty lucky.

When he returned to the bedroom carrying Karina's tea, Karina was sitting up in bed, studying a paperback.

'You shouldn't walk about naked like that. Anyone passing can have a look at you through the windows.'

'See anything you fancy? If they're respectable, they'll turn their eyes away. If they're not, they'll see nothing to shock them.'

She put down the book to accept the mug with both hands.

'You should read these stories. They're very fine. They convey the horror of war marvellously. Erik's a fine writer.'

'Did you tell me Erik may get back from Bosnia in time for the Anderson party this evening?'

Karina gave a barely audible snort. She had passed her fortieth birthday three years ago, and had made nothing of the event. She had been an attractive blonde when Lars and she had first met as students at university. He was studying physical sciences, she was studying the history of European art. Her withdrawn air had attracted him; no girl he had known had been more reluctant to be seduced. Somehow, her colour had faded with the years. Her face was pale, her eyes shadowed; lines about her lips made her look severe. She had a way of folding her arms across her chest that worried him. Setting down the hot mug, she folded them now, either in self-defence or defiance.

He had offended her years ago. Lars had enjoyed a brief affair with a woman who worked as a secretary at the garage where his car was serviced, the flighty and humorous Liv. Liv had been ready for anything; she was divorced and lived in a nearby suburb. He had been found out, of course. What a time Karina had given him! By way of retribution, she had carried on with a dreadful Finn for some while and had hardly spoken to him for a year.

He had apologized, eaten humble pie, denied he ever loved Liv. Yes, even done that for the sake of a quiet life. It made no difference. The Finn had eventually gone back to his reindeer and things had returned on the surface to normal. Lars and Karina still went out once a week, ate Indonesian food, saw a movie, sometimes met friends, played cards with Lars's boss. But something told him his wife would never forgive him.

He had never made excuses. He had been wrong. Yes, wrong. Women took these things hard.

Sometimes he said to himself, 'If only I'd had more guts, I might have run off with Liv. We could have lived in Munich and I could have worked on that marvellous T-bahn.'

He had never been able to explain about Liv. Not even to himself. He thought of her as he showered and dressed. She certainly had been a bright spot in his life. Now she had remarried. Well, you settled for what you could get. Be grateful. Enjoy life. He had determined he was not going to read Erik Zetterholm's dreary stories about a distant war, even though Erik was Karina's brother. The war in Bosnia had made Erik Zetterholm's name. He was always holding forth on Swedish television.

Lars and Karina's daughter Vikki came round after breakfast.

Vikki lived with her boyfriend a few streets away. She always looked in on Saturdays. They drank coffee round the kitchen table and Karina talked about Vikki's famous Uncle Erik in Bosnia, doing brave things and writing marvellous stories.

'He may turn up in time for Helen Anderson's birthday,' Lars said. 'Your film star uncle, Erik.' He winked at Vikki to show he was not serious.

They went shopping together, and ate lunch in Luigi's. Luigi was always friendly, while his lasagne reminded them of an Italian holiday taken when Vikki was tiny. Luigi's was a small restaurant on the quayside. You went down a couple of steps into it, to be greeted by Luigi or his podgy daughter, Maria. You sat at a small table covered with a chintz tablecloth and looked about in amazement at the fanciful views of Sorrento and Noli adorning the walls, where the sea was a maddening blue. And you began the meal with crisp grissini, which came in packets and were free. Vikki loved grissini. She crunched them as Karina talked about the people she worked with at the art gallery.

Lars remarked, as he polished off a glass of Chianti, that they must buy a present for Helen Anderson, to take along with them that evening.

'I don't feel like going,' said Karina. 'The Andersons don't like me, I don't know why.'

'They won't like it if you don't come. They are your cousins.'

'I don't wish to go. They're only second cousins. You go.'

'Mum, you must go,' said Vikki. 'It's bound to be grand. You know how Sven-Bertil spends money.'

'You keep out of this. Your father can go. He likes Helen. They're too rich for my taste. A lot of show-offs.'

*　　*　　*

The argument was not too unpleasant. Luigi hovered close. Other diners with big ears sat at nearby tables. They kept their voices down. Afterwards, out in the thin sunshine, Vikki kissed both her parents and walked off determinedly.

Karina would not change her mind. She did not wish to go to the party. She did not feel well. Lars must go alone. She did not care what he did.

And she drove home in the car, leaving Lars to catch a tram after he had done the shopping.

Lars did not remain downcast for long. The fact had to be faced, he would enjoy the Andersons' party more without her; she was so critical of other people. And with his wife out of the way, he could buy Helen the sort of birthday present she deserved.

It was true, he thought as he mooched northwards, heading for Sveavagen, that they had an alarming overdraft at the bank. True that he owed his brother a stack of money. He had made bad investments, but that was not his fault. He had taken what he believed to be sound legal advice. He would have to do something dramatic about the mess soon. Maybe they would have to sell the house.

Until then, he would live his own life. He would buy Helen something really nice. Never ever would he reveal to her his real feelings. Not in words, at least. But if he bought her a good present . . . Well, she could draw her own conclusions. Then we'd see. He could not help smiling.

To hell with them all. He was his own man. He knew how to live. And he swaggered into a large store, looked about at leisure, and finally bought a present he was certain Helen Anderson would love. While complimenting her, it showed his own good taste. The assistant behind the counter gift-wrapped it for Lars, presenting it to him with a bright smile.

He nodded his appreciation.

'It's for someone really special,' he told her.

Late in the afternoon, Lars shaved, put on a cream shirt and his cream suit, said farewell to Karina – who buried her face in Erik's paperback – and set off to walk to the Andersons' party. It was a pleasant semi-rural stroll, no more than a kilometre from home, and filled with birdsong.

The few houses on the way were neat and brightly painted. Dwarfing them were tall feathery trees like giant versions of the fennel which grew in the hedges. The glow in the western sky made puddles on the roadway into fragments of sky. The sun was all but set, and across the water the magical lights of Stockholm began to stand out against a deepening blue.

Lars reflected contentedly on the mystery of evening. He was put in mind of his favourite painting in the gallery where Karina worked, a French landscape, a large enchanted landscape. There, snug in leafy nook, Narcissus admired his reflection in a pool, surrounded by romantic nature. A grand castle lurked forever inaccessible in golden distance.

Debts were nothing compared with all that was rich in life: the peace of the scene, the niceness of people, the scents in the air. Even Karina – yes, he had wronged her and must pay for it. She would forget about Liv eventually, and he would never make such a mistake again. All the same, Karina went to church occasionally; she used to take Vikki when Vikki was small; so it was time she remembered what Jesus had said about the necessity for forgiveness. Perhaps Jesus would have put it more strongly if he had ever married . . .

Sven-Bertil Anderson had hired a hall in which to celebrate his wife Helen's fortieth birthday. The hall stood at the end of the lane, on a slight eminence permitting views of water and land over which night was fast descending. Japanese paper lanterns glowed outside the hall, swaying slightly in an evening breeze. Other folk were hurrying along in the same direction as Lars. Already a band could be heard playing inside the hall.

The hall was a pretty wooden structure, decorated in traditional ways, with sentimental Viking dragons curling over the eaves, and curly beams climbing to the roof. Its long narrow windows were of stained glass, depicting sturdy warriors and women of equally formidable physique. Inside, all was light, and gleaming faces, and pretty frocks on the women. Everything looked tremendously cheerful. Lars was immediately caught up in the atmosphere.

He wanted to rush and embrace someone, to declare his excitement, but could see no one suitable.

Sven-Bertil's mother and father, presiding, came up to him, smiling and welcoming. She was a grand lady with old-fashioned ways. Expressing regrets that Karina was unable to join in the celebrations, she relieved Lars of his present. When he made some slight protest, she told him, smilingly, that Helen would receive all her gifts later. Meanwhile, he must drink a glass of French champagne and mix with the other guests.

As he circulated, Lars at first saw no one he recognized except a waiter in an ill-fitting grey suit with a purple stripe. The waiter had evidently been hired for the evening from a bar where Lars often stopped on his way home from the Metro. He nodded at Lars in a friendly way.

A quartet was playing in one corner of the hall. Most of the floor was filled with long tables, on which servants were laying out supper. Black-clad waitresses moved about, serving champagne and orange juice. Everyone flocking in looked smart and cheerful. The two Anderson children were running here and there, occasionally being reined in by a relation.

Helen Anderson and her husband were standing at the far end of the hall, surrounded by admirers. Among those admirers was Lars's bank manager. Lars had not the courage to join them. Instead he began to chat to some men he knew who worked in Child Welfare. They discussed the problems faced by unmarried mothers.

A gong was struck, the quartet disappeared for a drink, and everyone sat down at the tables, in designated positions. Lars found himself sitting next to an elderly woman who worked in the same branch of the civil service as Helen. 'Helen's a charming woman and this is a charming occasion,' she told Lars seriously, as if pointing out something of which he should immediately be aware.

'Are you going to make a speech?'

'No.' He was startled by the question.

'I shall make a speech if called upon, to mark the charming occasion.'

'It is a charming occasion, yes.' He had not caught her name and could not quite read it on her place card. Smoked salmon and caviar were set before them.

Between courses, Helen Anderson walked among the tables. Sven-Bertil followed behind, elegant in evening dress, smiling, nodding to friends and relations, occasionally whispering to his wife.

A warm glow lit the cheeks of Helen Anderson. At forty, she was a mature dark beauty. She was English and had, Lars thought admiringly, lovely English looks. Her neatly groomed black hair curled delectably about her pale neck. Her eyes were deep-set and of a – to him – startling violet hue. Her face was wide and kittenish, while about her mouth there seemed to play always the suggestion of a smile.

He watched her as she moved between the tables in her dark blue glittering floor-length dress. Her bare arms were lightly tanned. Lars marvelled: she was in his eyes almost a mythological creature. As she progressed, she was touching the seated guests on their shoulders and uttering a few words of praise, humorously expressed, about them. Every movement was full of grace. Her Swedish was fluent, though marked by an English accent, delectable to Lars's ears. He watched her lips and her pretty, slightly irregular, teeth, and longed to kiss those lips – though he would never say that to her, or to anybody.

Liv had been less beautiful and more solid, built more along the lines of the women in the stained glass windows.

When Helen Anderson and her husband stopped beside Lars's neighbour, Helen bent and kissed that worthy lady on the cheek. She spoke of her efficiency in the office, her kindness in providing such things as aspirin and coffee after a festive night – hoping, she added amid general laughter, that such medicines would be available again on the morrow.

While the civil service lady, whose name Lars had not learnt, made a brief and affectionate response, Lars felt colour rise to his cheeks. She would come to him next. What would she say about him? How praise him?

And should he say something in return, apart from wishing her a happy birthday, as most of the guests had done? Should he – the mere idea terrified and thrilled him – stand up and boldly declare his devotion, quite contrary to all he had been thinking a minute earlier?

Would Sven-Bertil strike him down if he did so? Or would she, was it possible, would she fling her arms round his neck and kiss him?

Helen Anderson touched Lars's shoulder and passed him by without a word. She began a panegyric about the elderly gentleman, a retired diplomat, sitting on Lars's left side.

Humiliation swallowed Lars. He felt as if a whole continent on which he stood had sunk suddenly beneath the waves. Helen Anderson had said not a word to him or about him. Had not even uttered his name in that charming accent of hers. He felt he must dash from the hall into the darkness and be lost for ever, to be counted among the damned.

But then again . . . It took only a moment for his confidence to reassert itself. That touch on the shoulder – had not Helen's hand lingered just a moment longer than might be expected? What could she have said before the company that would not have given the game away? Was not that gentle pressure on his shoulder a secret message between them, a signal of her real feelings, as secret, as unexpressed, as his?

Happiness filled him. Yes, she did care. She had done all that could be done, with that idiot husband close on her gorgeous heels. Wait till she opened her present. He'd get a kiss for that! A whole embrace!

He almost laughed with delight. What a wonderful evening! How pleasant everything was, how delicious the *boeuf en croûte*. And he chatted enthusiastically with both his neighbours, confident that they must be enjoying his company as greatly as he theirs. He even dared to hint to the old diplomat how deeply he was in debt, in the belief it made him more interesting.

When Helen Anderson's tour of the tables was done, when the last syllabub had been eaten, when the coffee cups and liqueur glasses had been cleared away, servants came and removed all the tables to some remote region. The floor was swept and cleared. The quartet resumed their seats on their podium. They struck up a jovial air and dancing commenced.

Lars danced at first with the civil service lady. She had had her fill of white wine and was immensely cheerful. Both of them agreed it was a lovely evening, and how beautiful Helen Anderson looked. It was said she wished never to return to England. And how awful it would be if she did. If she had fallen in love with Sweden, Sweden had fallen in love with her. Et cetera.

Of all the happy faces in the hall, Sven-Bertil's wore the broadest smile. He now took the centre of the floor and announced that in his wife's honour the band would play a veleta, which she and he had learned in Barcelona, long ago.

The quartet struck up. Sven-Bertil bowed to his wife. He and Helen Anderson took the floor. How bravely they stepped out. And what a wonderful couple they made. Nobody else ventured to join them. Everyone stood and watched admiringly.

Round and about the floor whirled the couple, fast and light, all the while gazing into each other's eyes, smiling, smiling, mouths slightly open with the excitement of it all. They were as one, united by more than music.

All the gaiety in the room had found its focus in that quick-stepping couple prancing, prancing, through the veleta.

It became too much for Lars. He went out into a small adjoining room, begged a cigarette from the friendly waiter in the ill-fitting suit, and smoked, gazing out into the night. The clapping when the veleta ceased was prolonged.

I'll never dance like that with her. I'm a real failure. She doesn't even know I exist . . .

He could do with another drink. Pity the wine had all been cleared away . . . Maybe he should grab his coat and push off. Forget her stupid present. Karina would probably be in bed asleep by now.

'Oh, here you are, Lars. I looked everywhere for you, you old louse.'

Turning, Lars saw Erik Zetterholm standing there, an unlit cheroot between his lips. Erik had grown a stubby beard since last Lars had seen him. He looked tired and grubby, and appeared to have made no attempt to dress for the occasion. Yet Lars could not help recognizing a distinction about him; perhaps that was what came of appearing on television. Of course, he was a head taller than Lars.

Lars shook his hand, glad to see his brother-in-law. They had had some good times together before Erik became a war correspondent. Life was like that: you might be feeling a bit low, but distractions always came along. First the waiter had given him a free smoke, now here was old Erik, famous Erik . . .

'When did you get here? Have you just arrived? Hey, we must find a drink. I'll call the waiter. Celebrate your homecoming. Good to see you. Your stories of Bosnia are displayed in every bookshop in Sweden.'

Erik clapped Lars on the back. He drew a silver flask from his back pocket.

'I've been here for half an hour. Had a word with the birthday girl . . . Spotted you dancing with some aged bird as if your life depended on it. But I can see you're sick of the whole charade, eh?'

He proffered the flask. Lars took a good swig and passed the flask back. Erik removed the cigar from his mouth and also took a swig. Sighing, he ran a hand through his unruly hair. His manner was tense, his movements rapid.

'Just having a smoke,' Lars said.

'But you look a bit down.'

'No, no, not at all.' His brother-in-law had always been inclined to dramatize. He had used cigars as props before. 'You've missed a good feed.'

'Christ, all this makes you sick. This display. Helen showing off as usual. Sven must be barmy – even at school he was a show-off. Why does everyone fawn on her so? Just because she's foreign?'

'That's too harsh, Erik. It's a nice evening, full of good humour. She's very sweet.'

'Good humour! Sweetness! Saints alive!' He tossed his head about as if looking for the saints. 'What a pain! Helen Anderson being *sweet*! I snubbed her, I'm afraid. When you've come straight from Bosnia, still got shit on your boots . . . I was in Mostar, or what remains of it, not twenty-four hours ago. Everyone starving, dying horribly . . . Then to come back to this bourgeois rubbish . . . people eating their heads off, putting on false fronts, being *charming, sweet*!' He coughed, lit his cigar and took a deep draw on it.

Lars gave a laugh. 'It's Helen's birthday. Be fair. Everyone loves her.'

Erik lowered his head so as to gaze, grinning, at Lars from under his brow. He wreathed himself in smoke.

'I bet you'd like to have a go at her. Who wouldn't? But the point is, here we have all this meaningless prancing about in fancy clothes while in Mostar, and most of what was Jugoslavia, people are dying, kids are dying, the whole structure of civilized life is being demolished day by day. And the rest of Europe cares not a fig.'

Taking over the flask again, Lars saw the contradiction in what his brother-in-law was saying. He spoke diffidently.

'Of course it must be terrible out there. No denying that. We all honour you for reporting it. But you complain about civilization collapsing, then you come here – I mean, isn't this evening civilized? Isn't it? Music, dancing. And you're knocking it!'

'I'm complaining about gluttony, greed, self-indulgence.'

'But what can we do to help Bosnia? People must be happy when they can. Seize the chance when it's there. No use being miserable, is it?'

Erik began to pace about the room, trailing smoke. 'I should never have come back. God, I'm ashamed. I should have stayed in Zagreb. You can help Bosnia in a dozen ways. *Think* about it for a start. How much has this junket cost the Andersons, thrown away on that hussy's birthday? Couldn't they have given the money to a Bosnian charity instead? Buy an ambulance. Drive it to Sarajevo, as I did last year. Then you might have earned a right to feel happy.'

Lars shook his head. He hated arguments. As he saw it, confusedly, life was difficult. Everyone should strive for happiness. It was a duty, happiness being infectious. Perhaps he was wrong; he had not had a religious upbringing. He pressed his point no further.

'So will you be coming to stay with Karina and me for a bit?'

'No. I'm staying with my director. I can't bear my sister's continual complaining.'

'She likes your stories.'

Erik drained the flask. His face became heavy and gloomy. He stood in front of Lars and asked, 'You're bored with all this crap in here, aren't you? I'm off. Want to come and knock back a few drinks with me?'

'Sounds good but, well . . . I have a present for Helen Anderson.'

Erik laughed. 'My God, you have got the hots for her! Fancy a bit of English crumpet, do you? Let me tell you it's much like crumpet elsewhere. So what have you bought her? Condoms?'

'I know you're a big hero, but you don't have to be a shit as well.'

'Sorry, didn't mean to offend. It's just so funny . . . Tell me what you've got for her.' He confronted his brother-in-law, cigar between his teeth, hands clasped behind unkempt head.

'Why are you so angry, Erik? You're acting like a film star.'

Turning away, Erik said, 'I'm bloody sad, Lars – sad and bitter. I've seen so much death . . . But what have you bought this desirable forty-year-old?'

Lars felt his colour rising. 'That's between the two of us.'

With a grunt of angry laughter, Erik clapped Lars on the shoulder. 'Perfume, I bet. Good for you, laddie! In Sarajevo, one ciggy's enough to buy a woman. Promise I won't tell Karina what you're up to.'

Pushing the hand away, Lars said, 'Okay – I am going to present Helen Anderson with an artist's box of water-colour paints. You will laugh. Go ahead. But to me that's civilized. Water-colours –'

He could not finish. Erik Zetterholm was giving a disgusted laugh, hunching his shoulders, quitting the room.

*   *   *

After a while, the friendly waiter entered the room and offered Lars another cigarette from his pack. 'Trouble, chum?' he asked.

Without waiting for an answer, he set down half a bottle of red wine on a side table, winked knowingly, and left.

How decent people were, Lars thought, how generous! But the evening had been spoilt. He could not face the rest of the party now. Supposing Helen Anderson *laughed* when she opened her gift and found tubes of water-colour? Then the whole company of guests would laugh. Erik's contempt had opened his eyes to his own absurd dreams. He might as well go home.

After swigging some of the wine from the bottle, he smoked down the cigarette so as not to waste it, and listened to the music in the next room. Stubbing out the butt, he went to the cloakroom to find his coat.

'Not going, Lars, old chap, are you? The night's young yet and we're just going to give Helen all her presents.'

It was Sven-Bertil, flushed, handsome, lightly solicitous. Catching Lars's expression, he added, 'Yes, we also talked to your famous brother-in-law. To tell you the truth, he made me feel a little ashamed. The bit about those people starving hit home.' He laughed.

All Lars wanted now was to be away, but he said, 'You had the Bosnian stuff too? Being miserable helps no one. Erik's a gloom merchant.'

Sven-Bertil appeared to consider this remark seriously.

'Maybe. But I think that Erik Zetterholm is quite right to grieve.'

'Wish your wife a happy birthday from me. Though I doubt she remembers me.'

Buttoning up his coat, Lars rushed out into the night air. The Japanese lanterns had been switched off. Once his vision had adjusted to the dark, he set off down the lane, hands in pockets. Overhead were stars and patches of cloud. The lights of Stockholm were reflected in the nearby river. He slowed and contemplated them. Really, it was like fairyland as he used to imagine it.

The music of the quartet faded behind him as he walked, and the applause of the guests. Lapping water could be heard, melancholy and sensible.

It was not a bad night. The cold air was good for the lungs. He turned up his collar.

He thought of Liv.

'We must find a new way of being alive.'

[Note found in old notebook]

My next attempt to succeed was to found the Second Edition Club. Many books are rarer in second than in first editions, if they exist at all. I hired a little shop in Islington and turned it into a club, the Second Edition Club. Outside, I hung a tasteful shingle, showing a page and a thumb turned down.

I issued catalogues of highly priced books which did not exist. I hired a young lady assistant called Doris. The name was unsuitable for the trade. I insisted she should be called Miranda in shop hours. She did not dislike the idea, and took to wearing her hair long.

We installed a little wine bar in one of the shop windows.

I introduced my Miranda to the Miranda of Shakespeare's play. It occurred to me that the Miranda of the play has no discernible character; she just happens to be a wench – and was first of all played by a boy.

My Miranda was no boy. How passionate we were in that little cubby-hole behind the shop, how readily she hitched up her skirt, how greedily I responded. I was her Caliban . . . Little we cared for the drying up of the Aral Sea.

I wrote a play called *The Tempestuous Wench*, a version of *The Tempest* seen from Miranda's point of view. The theatrical agents I took it to said it reminded them too much of William Golding's *Lord of the Flies*. For three years, I tried to peddle my play to every theatre in the country; luck almost came my way in Middlesborough.

I lost interest in the Second Edition Club. It closed, leaving me with considerable debts. Miranda went off with a man who sold second-hand furniture, and then became a microbiologist.

Life is rather an enigma.

Three Moon Enigmas

HIS SEVENTIETH HEAVEN
ROSE IN THE EVENING
ON THE INLAND SEA

HIS SEVENTIETH HEAVEN

'Oh do, please do!' said the neophytes.

The neophytes were a lazy lot. Of the seven, four were young women, three young men. They spent fourteen hours a day in meditation, three in sportiveness and sexual horseplay, six in sleep, and one in ritual ablution. They lived in clean paper clothes and kept their toenails and hair short.

The name of the satellite was Gratitude One. It orbited Earth once every twenty-four hours, three thousand two hundred kilometres above the centre of the Earth, turning idly as it went through its dance. For most of its days, Gratitude enjoyed continuous energy from the Sun, a pebble caught in a living stream of light. None who lived on it paid taxes. It formed one of the most distant zeepees or zodiacal planets.

Three masters looked after the neophytes like blue-jowled mother-surrogates. All work was done by three androids, calm things with no savour to their presence. The living quarters and dormitories were sparsely furnished. Beds were made of mahogany. Apart from diamonds and nuclear energy, mahogany was the most expensive thing in the solar system.

In the Heaven Room, phototropic eyelids filmed across the long slits of windows when light was becoming too brilliant. Here were sounds of a terrestrial nature, birdsong, whispers of wind, the splashing of a distant waterfall. Here, too, incense burned. The Heaven Room was where Ryan Son Moon worked.

Although terrestrial wealth fountained up to Ryan Son Moon as if drawn to goodness, he lived an ascetic life in his small private world. For himself, he needed nothing; no coin ever loitered in his cotton jersey trouser-pockets. His fortune went to maintaining Gratitude One and to funding the teaching of his neophytes and disciples.

The money came from those millions on Earth who bought Ryan Son Moon's Heavens™. (Sometimes they were called 'Entrances'™, emphasis balanced equally upon first and second syllable.)

Son Moon claimed not to be an intellectual. The variant of Zen of which he was the originator did not require intellect. Nevertheless, Son Moon had EI: empathic intellect. He had EI enough to see that mankind needed salvation, deserved salvation, and could receive it best in small doses, like vitamin pills. It was Son Moon's mission in life to offer EI salvation to all, to provide relief from the tension under which most lives were lived.

His Heavens came from the inner recesses of his head. After years of silent search, alone in a deserted region of the Kuhusai Peninsula, Son Moon had experienced an awakening. He found a small doorway in his psyche which led to a direct experience of the universe. For a year and a sidereal day he was lost there. Through this doorway he coaxed the images of wisdom he termed Entrances or Heavens. They were recorded and despatched in kompacts by ferry to Earth. They could be bought and mind-played by anyone anywhere with a few dollars to spare. Having no language, the Heavens knew no language barriers.

The neophytes, four young women, three young men, stood before Son Moon and pleaded again. 'Oh do, Master, please do!'

Although he knew what his response would be, he withheld it for a space: their toenails must be allowed to grow. Son Moon was in his late seventies, although he looked much younger. His father, an Irish American, came of mixed parentage, half-Irish, half-English; his mother was half-Chinese, half-Malaysian. He was a small stocky man with intense dark eyes, who still looked capable of embracing the globe. His hair, never cut, often trimmed, was tied with a leather strap and hung down his back. At his temples, the hair, remaining stubbornly black, curled up in small curls like the tails of a pair of naughty birds.

'I will see the proposed interviewer,' he said to the neophytes, after the pause. 'And we shall see if he can see me.'

'He will see you,' said one acolyte.

'He will see the popular image of me. Perhaps he will see

further. We must see what we can see in him, and hope it will be good.'

It was the first time in twenty years he had consented to give an interview. The man, he had said, was nothing: the idea was everything.

The neophytes clapped once. He said, 'Fame only obscures truth, seeking to devour it.'

They said nothing. They gazed down at their carnal pink gleaming toenails, reminders of ancestral Beasthood. Secretly, the neophytes longed for fame, while knowing it to be a scorching fire. Buried in each of them was a heritage of lumber they were looking to the disciplines of Gratitude One to eradicate. They still doubted themselves, although they had been reassured that visionaries were full of contradictions. They longed for fame: they sought obscurity.

For fourteen hours every day the neophytes sat in silence, breathing the breath of life. They lived vividly, becoming great. Every seventh day, they all got drunk. But not their leader, Ryan Son Moon.

The interviewer, a terrestrial celebrity by name of Ronald Said Howards, came up on a large screen brought especially into the Heaven Room. Howards wore a white shirt. A bald no-nonsense man with large ear lobes, accustomed to talking politics with presidents. Son Moon sat facing the screen in the lotus position, wearing his loose black garments, totally relaxed. His hair curled against his temples.

After a few preliminaries, in which Howards remarked that he usually spoke with politicians, he said that the interview would be watched by hundreds of millions of viewers on the planets. To this Son Moon made no reply. Howards asked Son Moon if he felt himself set apart by his unusual powers.

'I am apart only in terms of physical distance from you. My Heavens go into many minds; for them I am not apart but close. As close as thought can be. The EI discipline is not a unique talent. Many men and women have learnt it from me.'

'You are set apart in the sense that you are an intellectual.'

Son Moon said, 'Although I am no intellectual, I understand

what an intellectual is, I believe. An intellectual needs a powerful personality because he seeks to articulate unpleasant truths, and always to question. It is a lonely position. My distancing from Earth symbolizes a sympathy with that intellectual position.

'But I deal not in words. My Heavens are pictures. They are not like mass art, with which Earth is swamped. Mass art has become the tool of political forces. My Heavens are pictures untainted by commerce, private things, experienced, lived, in the mind. The mind is the one private place left in a politicised universe. You see what is happening on Mars. It too is becoming one more political battlefield.'

Howards was smiling. 'I was warned before this interview that you might speak cryptically. You speak very clearly. Is that the effect of EI?'

'You must beware of those who speak clearly, Mr Howards. I would speak cryptically if I could. Life's no textbook. I do not talk well, because when I talk I say what has been said often before. Only my Heavens are of individual coinage.'

He spoke almost casually. All his sexual energies were funnelled into his present moments.

Howards nodded. 'If we might speak of those Heavens of yours. They were very elaborate at first. Now they have become – shall we say, minimalist? How's that?'

'A process of refinement needs no explanation. The inessentials get whittled away as time goes by. In a world where individuals have increasingly little say in the forces that control their lives, private and public, they treasure the small things that speak of intimate and governable relationships.'

'May we see one? Your sixty-ninth Heaven, said already to have sold two billion copies?'

'Heavens are a private matter. They are not designed for public transmission.'

'You make money out of them.'

'People value what they have paid for.'

After some discussion, Son Moon relented and said the Heaven could be projected. Howards's face was replaced by a breadboard.

The board was of an old-fashioned English type, circular, made of scrubbed pine and turned on a lathe. The viewpoint pursued the letters floridly incised round a section of the circumference. A chubby B like a buxom imagined cook, red of face from her baking. An R with a curlicue to its tail, grand, as when it stood for Royal. An E with a fat middle stroke like a tongue in a square mouth, almost licking an A with a strut connecting its two near-verticals, holding them together as if they might slide apart. A D like a stomach full of dough, bulging with contentment.

On the board a loaf of bread was placed, a squarish loaf with biscuity sides and a domed crust, brown as the board beneath it. A woman's hand, unadorned by ring or nail polish, put it in place. In her other hand she held a knife with serrated teeth, gleaming. The hands were all one saw of the woman. She placed the loaf centrally on the board. One corner of the loaf overlapped the buxom B.

With a leisurely sawing movement, the knife cut down through the bread, moving obliquely until it reached the board. The first crusty slice revealed its crumbling wholemeal texture as it fell flat on the board, to lie crumb uppermost.

The knife rose and slowly cut a second slice. This slice, lacking the strengthening end crust, bent slightly as it toppled to lie over the first one. The woman's hand laid the bread knife on the board, parallel with the remainder of the loaf.

During this simple procedure, there was ample time to examine everything, the action of the woman's wrist, the rough masculine texture of the revealed interior of the loaf.

'Your Heaven is rather static, isn't it?' said Howards, reappearing on the big screen.

Son Moon smiled. 'You find yourself using politicised language, don't you? Those in favour of progress use the word "static" pejoratively. My word is "stationary" . . . People are made happy by stationary things. They understand that genuine progress means an increase in understanding, not in the enrichment of those who manipulate governments and technical advance. The slicing of a loaf of bread, when properly felt, is a rewarding experience. Always. Eternally. Things are properly felt when we live in the present breath.

'A loaf already sliced is a politicized event, dangerous to moral health.'

Howards said that he appreciated Son Moon's earlier, more elaborate Heavens, with more action to them. He remembered one Heaven in particular, in which a woman had gone for a long walk with an animal resembling a giant cat. He had forgotten what happened exactly, but it took place on the Moon. He hoped to see more colonists on the Moon. He was lost when the time parameters of the Heavens were stretched and the action diminished greatly, as in Number Sixty-Nine.

'You did not stay the course,' said Son Moon, entirely without reproach. 'Many millions of your fellow planetarymen and women are staying. Just for enjoyment. Perhaps they also learn.'

The viewpoint, ever restless, cut to the neophytes in their sombre garments while the two men talked. Whatever the subject, the camera could not be allowed to remain still for as long as two minutes, for fear that the viewing audience would become bored and leave. The acolytes, aware of the lens upon them, tried to appear at their most angelic, and instinctively chose immobility.

'And now you're into your seventieth Heaven,' said Howards, not without sarcasm. 'How long is it going to take to construct?'

Son Moon said that Heaven was composed entirely of something beyond conscious thought. Since pure thought was an imperfect art, he might take many months over Number Seventy. Howards tried to tempt him to show what he had done. Son Moon said no. He spoke of other earlier Heavens: the old woman outside a deserted house slowly sweeping laburnum blossom from a terrace; a man learning to play the piano with his right hand, while his left rested easily on his knee; the hoe, turning over dry ground, held in a gnarled grasp.

'Your symbols for these "entrances" are all rather of the past, aren't they?' Howards commented. 'A *hoe*, I mean . . .' He gestured dismissively. 'The ancient Greeks used *hoes* . . .'

'Politicized language again, Mr Howards. Not old-fashioned but universal. Even today, in the twenty-first century, more people use hoes than computers. You conveniently forget how poor most of the world is, and how much under stress its people live. The object of EI is to unfold in starved minds something with which most people are familiar, and to allow them to reinterpret it. They may eventually learn to reinterpret their own lives. But such reinterpretation is a sacred thing; if spoken of directly, it becomes politicized . . .' After a long pause, Son Moon said, 'It is urgent that we alter our lives: that's the way to happiness, to salvation . . .'

'You claim,' said Howards, pulling at an ear lobe, 'to offer the world salvation, no less. Salvation from what?'

'Oh, from itself, of course.'

'Isn't that arrogant?'

'Mr Howards, even humility can seem arrogant at times . . . Yes, I will show you the few seconds of my seventieth Heaven so far completed. Perhaps then you and your viewers may understand . . . Well, let the vision speak without words.'

The burly masters, the slim neophytes, looked dismayed. Here was their beloved Son Moon going against his own practice. They well knew the mental energy required to conjure even a moment of a Heaven. For this, they were permitted the run of the satellite: when necessary, they sat with their leader, breathing with him. The silent support of the group was as much of a requirement as the roar of a crowd at a football match.

The Seventieth Heaven™ began. A figure sat alone in a room. The figure was heavily garbed in white, its sex ambiguous under its baggy clothes. The room was bare. It consisted of a wooden floor, metal walls, and slit windows stretching from floor to ceiling, grouped in pairs. Beyond the windows lay mist. Sound had yet to develop.

Son Moon sat in the lotus position, eyes all but closed. It took considerable powers of concentration just to maintain the room as an unalterable whole, furnished.

A green field appeared beyond the slit windows. The plain green became grass, fifteen inches high, awaiting cutting. One or two trees appeared in the distance, slowly taking shape as acacias, heavy with blossom. The figure in the chair did not look out of the window. Neither it nor anything else moved.

A fly was introduced into the bare room. Its presence was at first merely a dull buzz. Then it appeared, swooping and soaring, as if in enjoyment of its powers of flight. Viridian glints on its body proclaimed it to be a greenbottle. The detail became sharper all the while. Now the figure on the chair was revealed clearly as a woman of middle age; her hair grew, straggling over her white collar.

But something was interfering with the rhythmic buzz of the fly. The neophytes, sensing something wrong, opened their eyes and looked up. Son Moon sat immobile, wrestling with his construction. Furious bleating could be heard above the fly's song.

Somewhere, sheep were leaping. They plunged down from the maw of a rusting ship into scummy water. Down went the poor beasts. Some landed on other sheep already in the water. Some managed to scramble ashore, calling in terror. Some were too seriously injured to gain dry land. Still they poured from the ship, from the black mouth of a hold, beaten by sticks as they went.

'What is it?' Howards asked in some alarm, from his screen.

Ryan Son Moon rose to his feet, face pale. The three masters ran to him. The neophytes summoned an android. The frightened sheep, the bare room, the woman encased in white – all disappeared in a flash.

Without anger, Son Moon said, 'The interview has been tampered with. We discussed beforehand whether this might happen. Your government is jamming us. I shall have to say farewell, Mr Howards. Goodbye.'

'I'm sorry –' began Howards, but he was shrinking as he spoke. He dwindled to a dot and disappeared.

Explanations were not considered a proper mode of education on Gratitude One. Learning had to be by interpretation and inference. It was right that what was difficult should have its difficulty accepted and understood.

But Son Moon was a considerate man. To allay the consternation of his followers he said, 'Do not fear. I borrowed the sheep imagery from Ronald Said Howards. It needed only a little extra concentration. He is one of the intellectuals who runs with the pack. He will never speak out, he goes with the status quo. What we saw was how he thinks of the common people.'

One neophyte ventured to ask a question. 'But will the common people understand?'

He spoke directly from the EI creed. He said, 'In time they will.'

ROSE IN THE EVENING

Samsara, the great wheel, turned, though the season appeared without motion . . .

A few twitchers were heading back towards Omnurbs, camercasqs still clamped over their heads. They rode dynorods, moving just above the ground at the statutory seven kilometres an hour. They were heading one way, Myrtoo and Rose another. They kept looking at the time. Rose kept looking ahead, her childishly absorbed face set to the south.

Myrtoo thrust inquisitively forward, ignoring the comments of the rodders, pausing only when it was time to turn off the well-defined lane they walked. Long before Myrtoo was incubated, the lane had been an eight-lane highway; now the only traffic was on foot or rod.

'Do we turn off here, Rose?' Myrtoo asked. Rose Moon switched on the orthogonal compmap in her helmet and read off the co-ordinates. It was confirmed. She punched to semi-gravity and dived after Myrtoo into the thick undergrowth.

They were pushing through beechwood, checking, checking, buzzing co-ordinates back to base office in Omnurbs. When they reached a clearing, the mountainous flanks of the Kramer city could still be seen to the north. Storey rose majestically above storey for over ninety kilometres; the upper plateaux of the linear metropolis were bathed in evening sunshine, glittering like crystal.

As usual, Myrtoo went ahead, her progress happening in short bursts. Rose followed at a steadier pace. A last male twitcher emerged from the undergrowth, carrying his rod over one shoulder. He gave Rose an amorous look. She returned him a well-practised cat-hiss through wide-open mouth. He shook his head resignedly and passed on. One day he hoped for a hybrid of his own.

She caught his thought as it faded, a small-radius Class 6 thought.

'You gotta earn merit to own a hybrid,' she shouted at his back, guessing he would not possess a thoughtnapper.

She closed down the poisons of loneliness: only with Myrtoo had she been able to establish a relationship.

Progress was steady southwards. The pair of them travelled uphill and down. This area was pocked with irregular pits, all that remained of quarries from which stone had been excavated to build the linear cities running like slender mountain chains across the face of the globe. Beyond the palisades of the linked cities were wildernesses. The quarries were long since grown over by ash, elder, beech and such shrubs as euphorbias and mesembryanthemums. Deer scattered giggling at Myrtoo's soft approach. 'Catface!' they called – a colour more than a call.

The evening was protracted into a celebration of the funeral of light. The sun lingered like a young man at a gate. The towers of Omnurbs remained pink as if what housed millions was merely a nuptial cake.

Rose took each step forward as it came. She was attentive but carefree, planting sheathed feet. She counted every inhalation of precious air, aware she had only so many billion lungfuls to relish in her lifetime. Every pace, over gravel, over sward, over bare crater rock, was consciously taken. She always made one lungful of air last 4.5 minutes. This was happiness: to be on the move, on the quest for a kill. To have a motive, however imposed.

'Here's a burrow, Rose,' called Myrtoo. Myrtoo had paused on a fern-covered hillock, looking back over one furry shoulder with her usual smouldering patience. 'Come on, dear! This is it. This way.' Thick furry bass/soprano bounces of thought.

Catching up with her companion, Rose parted sheltering fronds of fern and peered behind them. She inhaled and clicked the analyser. Sure enough, this was an entrance to an LTSZ road: the electronic nose told her so.

As they climbed down, a flash lit them. 'They have us fixed and watched, Myrtoo,' Rose thought at her companion. 'Take a little care.'

Without looking over her shoulder, Myrtoo radiated a smile back.

They entered the dark of the road. Myrtoo's excellent nocturnal vision would see them through the difficult stretches.

Rose too had some night vision, but she caught hold of Myrtoo's tail to be safely guided. Some of the LTSZ roads were rough in places. The tunnel branched. The way came nearer the surface. It became a trench, and little wider than a trench, with frequent passing places. Some of the Outsiders they encountered were human. Many side roads curved away across the unending wilderness. Nowhere was there a signpost: only a caged bird at intervals, twittering a signal for those among the Outsiders who could comprehend.

For many a mile, the trench was sheltered by overhanging trees, by climbing plants that sprawled down the sides of the LTSZ roads. Deeroids could be seen, munching them tidy. Every now and again from an underground village came the music of Billy J. Kramer and the Dakotas. The immortal sounds travelled halfway across the galaxy.

Rose and Myrtoo were happy. Every step was a kind of miniature joy; their brains had been creamed up with the Joy Hormone.

Their way was through an illusory labyrinth of light and shadow, ever chequered: in life as in the roads.

They slept in one of the sub-soil villages. The charge for a bed was minimal. Rose and Myrtoo lay in each other's embrace, wrapped in the comfort of semi-gravity. Although they were enemies to the people here, the Outsiders, they were unlikely to suffer harm. The low testosterone/serotin zero levels after which the roads were named guaranteed a minimum of aggression. Outsiders were rarely able to defend themselves, while attacking others was almost out of the question.

Regulated civilized life continued inside the enormous lateral cities. Everything needful for life was produced there. Agriculture, in the old sense, had become obsolete: food came from faketories. Of course, there were some eccentrics who refused city life, its ease, its comfortable claustrophobia, its cradle-to-grave protection. A venturesome few still rodded a short way beyond the walls on day-passes; these twitchers were allowed to carry nothing more lethal than a camercasq. But the true eccentrics, the refusniks – they were

Outsiders, who won their banishment by undergoing the T/S operation. It was a peaceful world. Slow. Autumnal. Peaceful.

Religious schism had almost ruined omnurban life. Northerners and Southerners had argued theological points almost to the brink of civil war. Which had been the True Dakota? It was a *casus belli*. Such arguments meant little to the aloof Rose.

4.5 minutes. Another breath . . . Existence was nothing but the breath of life. The unspoken was real enough.

Killer Police were needed for special missions. Rose Moon and Myrtoo formed a Killer squad. They were contracted to take out Sycoran Jamess. For this, they travelled far from Omnurbs. An hour's Category A thought-rest and they were up and on their journey south again, the lovely creature leading as before, head high, tail high.

Deeper into the wilderness, the wildwood, here impenetrable except to feral beasts and the strains of 'Listen, Do You Want to Know a Secret?' Semi-thoughts of barking deer and hog and badger, steeped in a grassy perfume, came to Rose: 'No, no, wrong, no rhythm, no stepping with the right sinews.' 'Um, the highness of that head, its smallness, its highness and smallness, um, very highness and smallness.' 'Where's from, where's to? Not needed. Only at. At is everything, everywhere. At, at, think that.'

But the words came to Rose as tastes, which served to feed her mystic anorexia.

Rose closed down that flavour-lid. In her brainmaze she felt many lids. Convenient to keep them closed. Whatever was inside there was something less than the eternal external world. She had been trained. The efficient purity of Myrtoo's mind calmed hers: more efficient than her own, she acknowledged.

All through the long lethargic evening they moved, passing many a dull village. Passing singers and occasionally those who danced or jigged or did the kramer. Not so much as a turd was thrown at them. The semi-gravity effect kept them part-invisible.

After two more sleeps, they came on villages built half-above ground. The villagers considered themselves far enough away from Omnurbs for safety. Unmanned fliers were occasionally launched from the metropolis to spray the Outsiders. Agent Indigo kept libidos down.

In the thick flowery bush, 'Little Children' played, subtly woven distortions and harmonics lending complexity. They were nearing the place where Sycoran Jamess lived and worked. Her music. Near the target, Myrtoo hung back, letting Rose go forward. Myrtoo knew and remembered every step they took, but was stronger on cognisance than bravery.

Of course Sycoran had to be wiped. She composed new things. True, they were composed from the old. Everything was composed from the old. New lives were composed from old. Rose Moon and the Moon were composed from the old. All new thoughts were composed from old. New breaths from old. Old things from older. Time itself from a material older, stiffer.

Sycoran's new melodies were a threat to Omnurbs, to its stability. The rulers of the linear city were no fools; they knew the penetrative power of music. Their very foundations were not proof against the right song at the right time. They needed Rose Moon to kill Sycoran Jamess.

The house of Sycoran was improvised from wood. It resonated with her music. She lived there with ten beautiful black shints. All were making music. About the room fluttered yellow and black macaws with basalt eyes and Stone Age beaks. All, all bar Sycoran, disappeared when Rose mounted the rickety stair and appeared in the attic with her gun levelled.

Of Sycoran it had been said in the city that she was the ugliest of fiends. Yet behind her great prowed nose her proud bony face held resonant beauty. Her eyes glowed like smalts. When her lips drew back in a welcoming smile, her teeth were perfect. Her hair, long and unbound, framed her head. 'Rose!' she said. The thought-name formed in the air between them, blossoming, delicate of tendril.

The wave she projected was unclassifiable. Rose Moon had experienced nothing like it for strength or seductiveness. But she recognized pure soul when she met it. She fell to her knees. Before her knees hit the planking, she was desperately in love with Sycoran.

All the trapdoors in her mind opened. She who was blind now could see. The great cat crawled between her legs, purring.

The Joy Hormone dried, to be replaced with the cream of something less synthetic.

She threw off her helmet first.

The shints, returning, played a mutated orchestral, 'I'll Keep You Satisfied'. Rejoicing was all. One cypher saved! One more chance for individuation, for integration. One more soul in continuous creation.

Rose opened the rosebud of her confession in the evening, 'I never knew I was not alive till now.'

Sycoran's full bright efflorescence of thought said, 'It's important not to fear death.' The admonition and its elaboration built in collaboration between them. 'Samsara in Buddhist thought is the great wheel of life and death. Understand that divine continuity and there is no fear worth fearing, my beautiful one. Eat of the fruit while it is fresh, be satisfied.'

The taste of it was lingering in their minds, their bodies, their eyes. Evening too lingered. Rose and Sycoran stood with Myrtoo, gazing from the attic window. Myrtoo ventured out on the wooden tiles. Low in the deepening sky hung the peerless blue-and-white-china globe of Earth.

ON THE INLAND SEA

The great wheel turned and still it was not dark.

They were taking Joe Moone across the inland sea to have him properly, legally, shot. In gratitude, they beamed Moone consolation.

The cargo ship made an unsteady five knots. Its obsolescent steering malfunctioned; it was constipated, creaking along like an old bowel moving toilet-wards. The sea itself, flat as a chapati, gave no movement that first day out from shore. Even at night when the moon Moone may have been called after, too obese to rise to zenith, cheesy in the western sky, shone along the water, there was to the sailing nothing magical. The thanatognomonic seascape defied fancy.

Not that Moone saw much of his surroundings as he stared through his porthole. Moone had never seen much of anything in his life. Since childhood, maybe before that, he had blindly done whatever had to be done. He served. Though he never grew adept at serving, lackeydom was his habit, his way of life.

In the end, he had come to serve the wrong master. When shouting hordes ran down the dusty street, when the knives and staves were out, when a noonday madness prevailed, when men screamed like women for blood – when his master's house was about to fall to revenge and sheer human shittiness, the master's other servants and thugs had scrammed through the back door for safety. Left it hanging open, too.

Only Moone had stayed behind in the shuttered room full of electronic clutter and the smell of fear radiating from the governor. Bars of light full of dust and sweat slanted through the jalousies. For some reason he was unafraid, able to – unable not to – withdraw into an inner life. There was the greenbottle, all viridian glints, and an old man in the lotus position: the grass awaiting reaping. Stillness, the surface of the pool of the soul undisturbed.

He had experienced these things elsewhere.

Awareness sank or lifted. He communed mysteriously with ancient personages who understood nothing of death – why did he know them so well when he had never met them? – these figures who had dreamed themselves into being long before the first men had ever looked into looking glasses and recognized themselves. A somatic world breathed with no language but laughter and silence. Handclasps. Acceptance – something he had never known – exfoliated from the beings . . . who were also himself.

So Moone – momentarily immune Moone – was in an existential antipodes where all screaming and bloodlust were switched off. Momentarily he was at ancient gates with an admired woman, a fabled legendary female, who spoke of the burial of the dead, by which he understood her to mean himself.

In a sense it was all terrible, almost beyond mere happiness, like all visionary experiences, because beyond rational cognisance. This was cognisance itself. All knots were untied.

In the old green blind world, garlanded archetypes – was that admired woman still present? – offered him nourishments like slices of bread which he was able to transact into precepts:

The essentials of life cannot be told, only found.
There is a Self beyond all injury.
You see only by shadow: reason is God's shadow when
His back is turned.
The cause of sin and pain is the ambition for individual
life.

These were slices carved from a board he knew, that circular board of wood. The hand, the knife, the curious lettering, the crumb . . . The bare, he understood, the bare facts of existence.

And with that realization, he was painfully back where the governor was yellow with fright and the mob came closer. Back also to all the ugliness of himself, his body and the perpetual anger. The vision had come and gone in a timeless instance. From motives obscure to himself at the time and since, Moone climbed up on a wicker armchair when the killers broke in, shouting to them to come and get him. It was, he supposed, destiny.

The mob had dragged the governor down the street to the old temple (once cinema, once courthouse, once brothel, once store, now police station), killing him every inch of the way. A kick, a punch, a stab, a poke in the eye . . . Politics had changed since the previous day; so had religion; so had the leaders in a distant capital; it even appeared that the governor was suddenly one of the wrong tribe. The human spirit was blowing like an idle wind, like a tattered shirt out to dry on a wire line, like a buggered-up weather vane. So they hacked him to bits on the police station steps.

Moone was not important. They saved Moone for propaganda purposes. For Moone, there was to be justice of a kind, a justice more cruel than assassination: a cell, a voyage across the inland sea, a mock-trial. Moone was to be shot legally before witnesses in a courtyard behind a two-storey building flying a flag, not far from the quayside. That was democracy in action.

He lay awake by night, listening to the labouring of the ship's engines across the flat and shallow brine. Sometimes he prayed. Having no god, he invented one, dimly remembering forms of prayer taught him on the lap of a dimly remembered mother. Of course he would die, whether he prayed or not. His mother had died. There was yet another tragic botch in the universe: mothers died. So you began the struggle to exist at the age of five, selling discarded boxes or sucking cock or doing whatever sustained life.

By day he slept, sweating into the stinking bunk, listening to the plonk of the engines. Sleep was never real sleep. Sleep kept crumbling like a sand cliff, revealing fossils of past days, hideous things with broken jaws. He woke choking and struggling against apnoea in the clotted air of his marine prison.

First light of dawn showed the inland sea to be a spread of mouldering porridge.

Food was brought early, as the Sun rose, generally a plate of beans and rice. A can of water, the can rusted, the water polluted but having to last all the hot, weary, labyrinthine, fumbling, creeping day. Sheep were penned in a hold next to Moone's cabin. He smelt them and their ordure. From their shaky bleats he constructed words, fragments of sentences, abuse.

He was secured to the bunk by one leg. The metal chafed his ankle. His skin rotted, peeling away into sores like blotches on a rotting apple. Though he covered the leg with his filthy piece of blanket, flies crawled under the blanket for a taste.

The inland sea was no longer the expanse it had been. Rivers that once flowed into it, keeping it pure, had been diverted into canals constructed to water cotton fields carved out of desert. With the hydrological cycle of precipitation and evaporation destroyed, the sea was shrinking irreversibly, like an old man's withered hand closing in death.

All of the region round the inland sea was blighted by salty neuroleptic storms and dusts. Diseases long forgotten by the civilized world rose again from the decaying ground. The sea itself no longer harboured fish: its salinity was sufficient to dissolve living cells. A crust had formed over the face of the waters. Giant saprophagous spiders rushed out from the labouring ship, to snatch at titbits only they found edible.

The ship's twin propellers kept up their pounding. In three days the vessel was almost across the dwindling tideless waste.

Moone gazed from the porthole at his destination. The water gave place to a shelving bank of pure poisonous chemical, dazzling white in contrast to the grey blanket of sea. Carcasses of boats were beached there, rusting, falling apart, deserted by tides, hollowed by decay. Far up from what was now the shore stood a collection of low buildings. In better times, they had been a fishing port. Wiping his eyes with his blanket, Moone made out a distant quay against which blue inland waters once lapped. Stains marked their passage. The light against his eyeballs was as abrasive as sand particles.

A long trail of planking and metal lattice stretched from the present sea margin up the poisoned beach to the stranded port. He realized he would soon be walking up that planking, towards the courtyard behind the building with the flag.

Two guards entered the cabin and unshackled Moone's leg. Trying to stand, he fell over and was hauled to his feet. They struck him with their rifles to encourage him.

He emerged on deck. A hot stinking wind crisped his cheeks. He coughed and spat.

The guards propelled him to the rail. A rowing-boat had been lowered to the starboard side of the ship. An armed man, half-naked, stood in the boat, readying his sub-machine gun as Moone was forced to climb down to join him.

Harsh cries of men and animals. Sheep were bullied, struck, cursed to leap into the sordid shallows. Some fell on others, maiming them. With cries of terror the creatures struggled to the shore, to be bullied, struck, cursed, towards some distant slaughterhouse.

Misapplied technology had reduced this corpse of a world to pre-industrial simplicity: food, work, oppression, death. Sun overhead.

There were no surprises. Moone had never found any real surprises in life; everything was ruled by inflexible destiny, tempered only by illusions of free will. After the boat had been rowed to the shore, he was forced at gunpoint to jump into the gungy water and gain the boardwalk.

A guard held one of his arms as they proceeded inland, in case Moone should know of somewhere to run to. There was probably no other habitation within a hundred miles. The fisher families who once enjoyed a living from the inland sea had long disappeared or found work in a distant factory. The skeletons of their fleet, the debris of their retreat inland, lay scattered everywhere in a final aleatory defilement of nature.

Moone trudged up the rotten planking, past these sublunar relics of better times towards the distant buildings. He could already make out the flag flying over the two-storey building far ahead. It would require at least twenty minutes, he reckoned, to get there, taking the distance step by step, slice by slice, as he had taken life.

Picture a foreign country, far from the West and most of its influences. An exotic place ruled by a mildly repressive government. Where the president will permit no opposition: dissident voices are imprisoned or driven from the country. Where an organization resembling the Russian KGB, let's say, sees to it that order – the president's kind of order – is maintained.

Where the living is not easy, but people nevertheless make their own lives and perhaps are more contented with their lot than we in the West, with our easy climates and soils.

While I was there, I became friendly with a theatrical producer and his family. They were handsome, comical, and highly creative.

I attended a drama staged by my friend. It was several centuries old, and spoke of hierarchical ways of life, of ancient attitudes, and the quarrel a man may have with his destiny. The drama was cleverly staged and gorgeously costumed. In the final act, the costumes, heavy and lugubrious, were the deep crimson of arterial blood.

Drinking with my friend afterwards in an ante-room of the now silent theatre, I asked him of his future plans. He told me, and then said, 'What do you think is the greatest play of all? Is it *Hamlet*?'

'No. *Oedipus Rex* . . . Or possibly *Antigone*. While watching your drama tonight, I was seized by the idea that you could stage *Oedipus* in those very costumes.'

He gave me an intense look, between smiling and not smiling. 'Of all plays, *Oedipus Rex* is the one I most desire to stage.'

'What stops you? You have some fine actors. Is it a question of finance?'

He shook his head. 'If *Oedipus Rex* were performed here, it would be construed as a criticism of our president. I should be banished, my family disgraced and, even worse, this theatre would be closed down.'

Sophocles created his masterworks some time in the fifth century BC. They speak to us from the final margins of the Bronze Age. Even today, they still have power enough to challenge a regime.

Many of the most enduringly popular writers have been prolific. Their lives *overflow* with creativity. Novelists like Balzac and Dickens spring immediately to mind. Sophocles composed at least 120 dramas, only seven of which survive. Among those seven are the great enduring tragedies, *Oedipus Rex* and *Antigone*, in which the wills of men and women are pitted against the laws of the gods.

It's folly to tamper with Sophocles. But, like my now distant friend, I also had a dream. The drama of Antigone kept replaying itself in my mind.

Finally, I thought, 'Supposing a character from another story crept into that ancient tale, among the family quarrels and the disputed walls of Thebes . . .'

A Dream of Antigone

A barred window was set high in the cell wall, like a promised glimpse of eternity. By standing on tiptoe, Joe Moone could peer out. What he saw was not eternity but desert and bleak expanses of the inland sea: though he perceived eternity too, clear in his inner vision. Desert and sea trembled in the heat. The heat congealing in his cell made Moone mad. He stared and stared out at the dead waters as if he were looking inside his own skull.

Towards sundown, the prison warden entered the cell, bearing a jar of water, some pitta bread, and a handful of fresh dates.

After setting the food down, this old and sun-dried man, as shrivelled as a prune, made the announcement Moone had been expecting.

'Eight o'clock tomorrow morning,' the man said. Moone had no need to ask what would happen at that time. He sank down on the bench and wiped sweat from his eyes, sighing deeply.

'Eight o'clock . . .' Moone repeated, trying to connect the words with reality. After a long pause, he brought himself to ask what would happen to his body.

'We'll bury it,' said the warden.

If this gave Moone some comfort, he did not show it. He clutched his head, as though to save it from a general downfall.

'I brought you a book, something to read to pass the time,' the warden said; this was not the first sign of sympathy he had shown the prisoner. With an effort, he pulled from the pocket of his loose garment a volume, bereft of covers, whose curled-up corners lent it a resemblance to a stale sandwich. 'It's old – from last century, I believe. But it's all we've got in this place. No one reads here. I haven't read it myself.'

When Moone made no move, he set the book down on the end of the bench, next to the jar and the fruit and the bread, which a beetle was already investigating.

When the warden had gone, Moone sat motionless, saying to himself over and over, 'Eight o'clock tomorrow morning.' He finally made a move, picking up the volume with indifference. 'The only bloody book in all Central Asia, apart from the Holy Book,' he said aloud, before glancing at the title. It was Sigmund Freud's *Psychopathology of Everyday Life*.

The condemned man broke into ragged laughter. He lay on the floor and laughed until he cried with misery. '"Everyday"? What "everyday"?'

During his last night on earth, there in the foetid confines of his cell, Joe Moone dreamed the Dream of Antigone. His own life had been bleak, unfurnished except by blows and bruises. Although he was about to be executed as a political criminal, he still retained a buried self in which he saw himself as noble, stubborn, principled. And that buried self – because his outward life had been so mutilated, so hard and masculine – took the form of a woman, young and immortal. The woman was dark-clad Antigone of Greek story.

Dark-clad Antigone walked out from the walls of Thebes by its south gate, into the countryside. Old women stood or squatted at their blue-painted doors, talking as the sun went down. The air was full of the music of bees, whose hives, with their painted walls, stood nearby. The women cast hostile looks at Antigone. Their conversation died as she passed by. As she walked along the path by the onion fields where she laboured, a farmer driving a flock of goats passed her; it seemed to her that even the goats gave her a wide berth. She stood in the olive grove, with many kinds of flower, white, yellow, gold and blue, petitioning the bees' attentions at her sandalled feet. Shading her eyes, Antigone gazed longingly out across the river lying congealed among its reeds, as if reflecting her mood.

She was young, raven-haired. A string of beads by the nape of her neck contained her tresses. In her face was an elfin quality more beautiful than beauty itself. Her hands and feet were coarse from her years of travel and, latterly, from rough work. Her inner world was hers alone, just as she shared her body with no man.

Living had been hard for her through the fratricidal war now concluded. Young though she was, she felt herself already to have experienced as much misery as was generally an old woman's portion. She was the daughter of Jocasta and Oedipus. She thought of the sepulchre in which her father slept, finding peace at last. To herself she said, All men should have proper burial: it's a law of God, not man.

Raspberries grew wild here. The raspberry patch, she supposed, had been tended by some man who had gone to the wars and never returned. She crammed the fruit into her mouth, making her red lips still redder. She held some of the berries in her hand as she returned to the oppressions of the city.

One of the women at the well, raggedly dressed, called abuse at her. Antigone shouted back.

'You and your damned family! My father was killed because of you lot!' they called.

For answer, Antigone spat.

'Your stupid wars, you incest-brat! My sweetheart got a spear through his chest, fighting your rotten battles!' they called.

Antigone flung a lump of donkey dung in their direction. They shouted the more. Gathering her black skirts about her thighs, she headed back to the Theban gate. As she went, she pretended to ignore the unburied body lying mangled by the city ramparts. Yet the breeze carried to her delicate nose a scent of carrion. She held her head high as she marched past, going under the dappled shade, where gnats danced in the filtered rays of sunshine.

Above her, in the branches of the oaks, squirrels chattered and hid like disembodied spirits. Superstitious fear brushed her mind, for dread of what they might be saying.

As she was nearing the guard at the gate, the shadow of a bird crossed her path, speeding over the parched grass. Looking up at the omen, she saw a great black crow settling into a nearby tree. It clung to a high twig and stared down upon her. 'Caught!' it seemed to cry, 'Caught!'

Once in the city, she hurried into her own stone house. It was no better and no bigger than anyone else's house. Inside, by the door, stood her field implement, a hoe with a cracked shaft, which Antigone had bound up with a strip of blue material torn from the hem of a garment. Troubled by the ill omen of the bird's shadow, she knelt by her altar stone to pray to the goddess Aphaia. She prepared and ate some *saganaki*, but the cheese was not of the best. Then she sat silent, hands on lap, to await the night, the time when the dead are buried – or rise up.

High above Antigone's house, in the wooden palace, sat Antigone's uncle, King Creon. He too waited, in his wooden room draped with rugs and trophies. Creon's beard was streaked white with the burden of history and the thankless task of ruling unruly Thebes. He dismissed his courtiers and sat alone by the window. The odour of the corpse by the ramparts rose up to him, together with the sound of bluebottles, angry with life. Creon kept his face free of expression. He rejected his supper when Queen Eurydice brought it, but drank some dark red wine from a silver goblet.

Although her pale hand lingered momentarily on his shoulder, he shrugged it off.

Creon rested that night for no more than half a watch. His confused sleep mingled with that of the man in the condemned cell, far distant in space and time. Images surfacing from bygone memory transformed snores to bugle calls, heavy gasping breaths to the sound of armed men on the march.

Into Joe Moone's troubled dreams, the dreams of a failed mercenary, came a parade of chariots, sieges, and the unceasing struggle that had afflicted him as it had Creon. Antigone's two brothers, Eteocles and Polynices, had fought each other for possession of Thebes. Eteocles had defended the city, Polynices had attacked it. Antigone had been torn by her love of them, finally to witness her brothers killing each other in battle, fighting hand to hand, only to fall and roll face downwards in the trampled dirt. This was what glory had come to: flies breeding in gaping jaws, corruption, scavenging hounds.

It must have seemed to her then, in her grief, that the terrible inheritance of her father Oedipus was at last worked out, and the Furies at last placated. Moone, too, taking his pay, had reckoned himself rich enough to return home at last, to a cottage and a pair of slippers and a tabby cat.

It was not to be. Creon, taking over the war-torn city, passed many stern laws – and one above all affronted Antigone's sense of justice. Ceremony was commanded for the dead Eteocles. Creon himself, standing with Eurydice and Haemon, saluted the corpse of the saviour of Thebes as it was drawn by soldiers to the tomb. Eteocles' body was buried with honour; Polynices' body was left to rot outside the south gate. So Moone's body, on that final night, seemed to rot in its narrow cell, far from any consolation bar that which was to be found in dreams.

And this was Creon's law: that anyone who attempted to bury the mutilated body of Polynices would be executed. Moone was caught by a not dissimilar law: anyone who sided with the failed revolutionaries, as he had done, would face a firing squad.

Creon was up and about early, leaving his wife to sleep. A guard came privily to bring him disturbing news, and was summarily dealt with. Creon then bathed himself and spoke briefly with his son Haemon, who was affianced to Antigone. He settled matrimonial quarrels in the public square and presided over the court of justice. At noon, when Thebes was beginning to fall into its afternoon snooze, he went with a bodyguard to his niece's house.

The sun blazed in the street. Many houses had not been maintained and needed new thatch and tile. Creon's bodyguard was ordered to stay outside Antigone's door. The interior of Antigone's room was dark. Creon's eyes did not adjust to the change of light as rapidly as once they had done.

'Antigone, stand before me,' he commanded.

She got up from her loom, bowed and stood submissively in front of him. He was, after all, the king. How slight was Antigone against the barrel of his body: in this disproportion lay masculine power.

He spoke without preamble. 'I want to examine your hands, Antigone. Show them to me.'

Without protest, she brought her hands forward and held them out. Her hands were narrow and brown. The palms were hard. The fingernails were short. She wore no rings or bracelets. Creon turned them over and about as if they were stones under which he expected to find a scorpion. Beneath some nails were particles of dirt.

'You've been digging?'

'At dawn I tended my vegetable patch as usual.'

'Come with me, child.'

'Yes, uncle.'

He walked with her slowly, down a narrow side street. The bodyguard was dismissed. Creon's arm lay across her slender shoulder in an avuncular way. Antigone did not protest. Their feet were in shadow, their faces in the full sun. Rats scampered into a gutter.

The city gate was open and he directed her through it. Then she stopped. 'No, uncle, please. I don't wish to see the corpse.'

'Don't be silly, girl. It's only your brother, Polynices, lying there rotting. You know that, don't you?'

He practically dragged her over to where the body lay unburied and wasps and bluebottles feasted. Heavy scavenger birds moved reluctantly away, clucking indignantly at having to leave their spoils.

Of course she knew. The previous night, when the owl ceased to call and all nature was hushed, he had come to her bedside, he, the slain Polynices. The very manner of his coming was dreadful to her, the small sister, lying on her couch, unable to do more than raise herself on one elbow and gaze open-mouthed and pale of lip at that slow approach. The spectre seemed to be lit from within with a yellowish pallor, as if made of frosted glass, and its armour likewise. Its wounds, its sickly congealed blood, only made it more dreadful, while so slowly did it advance on Antigone that a whole funeral dirge might have been sung in that time.

When the apparition spoke, words came from it without expression, and a disgusting choking scent filled the room.

'Look upon thy brother, slain by his twin, Eteocles! What misery the gods have wished upon our house, O Antigone! Do you recall a happy time when we were young, and bathed together in the river? Now you are grown, you must take on a woman's role. Swear you will do that. Swear!'

And in a frail voice, she from her couch said only, 'Polynices, please go away. I have dieted enough on distress.'

'I cannot leave. The dawn brings my destruction. I am imprisoned.' So Moone's thoughts found voice in his dream through the dead warrior.

'Polynices, you are slaughtered and there can be no communication between us. You are a shade. Leave me, I pray. Go, make peace with your brother.'

She recalled only how fierce Polynices and Eteocles had been when they were boys, and how she as a girl had been scared of Polynices, that great stone-flinger – although never so scared as she was now. But the apparition made her swear that she would bury his corpse: for until proper funeral rites were performed, he was doomed restlessly to wander the Earth, disinherited.

And from pity and terror Antigone had sworn so to do. Then had the spectre slowly receded into the stern silences, until there remained merely a stain in the air. After which, Antigone heard a cock crow; her neighbour in the street gave vent to a furious paroxysm of coughing; ordinary nature revived, bringing back the customary sounds of night, mice scuttling in the other room, the shrill of a night bird, the cry of a sentry on the sturdy ramparts of Thebes.

Putting on her wooden sandals, she had taken up her onion hoe from its corner by the door and gone quietly out into the night to do her dead brother's bidding.

All this she related now to her stern uncle, Creon, King of Thebes, as they stood among the flies and trampled earth about the rotting body of Polynices. She withheld nothing.

He remained rooted, his dark gaze ever upon her, burdening her with that regard.

'So, Polynices came from the realm of death to lay a task on you! And did he report that there was mirth in that dark kingdom, child?'

'He made no mention of it,' she said, looking into his face to try and read what was hidden there.

Creon's brow wrinkled in a frown as he made reply. 'Nor is there mirth here in Thebes. I have passed a law saying that your troublesome brother's remains shall not be buried. You know the law. Those who break the law will be executed. You don't believe in ghosts, do you? That's all nonsense. Once you're dead, you're dead. You begin to stink and that's all.'

'I saw what I saw in the night.'

'Now then, don't be stubborn. You saw nothing, you imagined everything. It was a bad dream. We are beset by bad dreams. They are part of the inclement destiny the gods have wished upon us. Just remember, your father married my sister, Jocasta. Unbeknown to either of them, he was also her son. Thus was natural law denied. The disgrace of it . . . Poor Jocasta hanged herself. She was familiar with the days when there was a matriarchy in Greece, now no more. As if all that wasn't enough, your brothers had to kill each other.

'Now by the decree you must face execution. What say you to that, niece? How do you fancy having your head severed from that body Haemon so desires?'

Antigone looked defiant, saying in a low voice, 'You are king. I am your subject. You will do what you will.'

Creon growled low in his throat, a sound of pain and menace.

He walked in a circle, hands behind his back. 'Only you and I know that you broke the law.'

When she did not reply, Creon continued.

'So you had better behave yourself. Keep quiet, forget all about ghosts. Marry Haemon, as planned. Although he's my son, I will say he's a good lad and much in love with you. You know that?'

Still she gave him no answer.

Again a growl of anger from the king. 'And he will rule Thebes one day. You know that . . . ? Answer, confound you.'

Antigone hung her head. Her 'yes' was only a whisper, before she asked her uncle if they might leave the vicinity of the corpse. Polynices now resembled greatly her father, in having no eyes.

Creon did as she suggested, leading her to the nearest well, under a grove of acacias. Women were gathering there, pitchers on their heads. He drove them off. They feared Creon and his bloodthirsty reputation, and ran away. Creon and Antigone stood alone by the well, under the shade of the trees. When a butterfly settled on his tunic, he beat it off.

In a heavy voice, he said, 'We can talk here freely. Though what I say will hardly please you.'

Timidly, she said, 'Uncle Creon, I like Haemon very well. I have no wish to displease him or you.'

Her words seemed to anger him. Speaking in a low voice, fixing her with his dark gaze, he said, 'I will repeat to you that I have passed a law saying that Polynices' remains shall not be buried. You broke the law by your feeble attempts at a funeral. Anyone who breaks the law must be executed.'

'It's such a cruel law . . .'

'The times are cruel. I must be cruel to meet them. Hadn't you sense enough to see this would put me in a difficult position?'

They could hear dogs barking in the distant streets. 'Yes,' she said. 'I mean no. All of nature is in harmony, uncle. Why are humans in such disharmony?'

In their hasty retreat, one of the women had left a filled pitcher standing on the wall. Creon, taking up the pitcher, began to pour its water in a slow stream down into the cool recesses of the well. The still liquid circle took the libation into its throat with ichorous gulps.

'Thus will our souls flow back into the waiting earth, never to rise again . . . I see no harmony in that dark drink . . . A guard came to me at dawn, Antigone, all aghast. He reported seeing you, scrabbling soil and muck over what's left of Polynices. There's blood on my hands already, Antigone. It was nothing for me to silence and kill the man.'

He hurled the empty pitcher into the well.

'Only you and I know of your disobedience, Antigone. Stay in bed at night in future. Don't entertain funny ideas. I'm doubling the guard tonight. I protect you for Haemon's sake, for his happiness and yours. But if you disobey the law again . . .' He made a derisive gesture, first opening then clenching his upturned right hand.

Though she saw his feverish regard, Antigone responded defiantly in her smallest voice.

'Your law . . . it runs against the gods' law . . . I must bury my brother, uncle. That's my law.'

His teeth gleamed through his beard, his eyes almost closed. 'Be warned. Stay clear of man's business. Your women's business is to marry Haemon and bear him sons. I'll not spare you off a second time, Antigone.'

Although she trembled, she repeated, boldly enough, 'I must bury my brother.'

He had already turned away, to march back along the path through the parched grass towards the great wooden gates of his city. She watched his broad shoulders, moving so easily, so strongly; and in that movement saw the whole of life and the way it must go.

That night, to her terror, Polynices came again to her couch, making the same dreary progress, as if he forced his way through stone. Only the scarlet of his wounds relieved a grey appearance. That swollen mouth again moved as he spoke of his desire for burial.

Behind him strode six other warriors. Antigone could discern them only dimly. The glint of armour was their main feature. Sometimes they were not there at all, lost in the miasmas of death. Sometimes she saw their eyes, their hangdog expressions, which seemed to say, 'There is no happiness in life, only duty and dejection'. And it was of duty that Polynices spoke, saying, 'It is your responsibility, Antigone, to see that I am given proper burial, for the honour of our family. This is the second time of asking.'

His words caused a kind of booming in her ear. She flung the rug aside, to sit up on the hard couch, clutching her toes. Remembering her uncle's words, she said, 'Go away, brother. Leave me. This business is not mine: it is man's business. If you are dead there is no more traffic between us. I am to marry Haemon next month.'

'If you desire to free yourself of me, you must ensure that I receive a proper funeral.' He lifted his bloody sword, perhaps intending to threaten, but it seemed immensely heavy, and steamed like a boiling pot when he held it vertically. 'Farewell,' he said.

For a long while, his ghastly white face hung there in the dark. It faded. All that was left was a stain and a stink.

Antigone sat where she was, shivering, and soon heard dogs beginning to fight outside. The natural world was returning from its abeyance. Its ordinary sounds broke into her numb reverie. She felt able to move her limbs. She slipped on sandals and crept out into the dark maze of streets with her hoe. The pavements underfoot were cracked and broken. Nothing had been repaired while her brothers disputed the city.

It was the dark hour before the dawn, when pale moths were still a-flutter. Beyond the gates, a light mist hung, layered over the ground. Dark shapes slunk away. Wild dogs and foxes had been greedying at the unburied body of Polynices; heavy winged things struggled up into branches overhead. Antigone went forward with caution born of superstitious fear. She wielded her hoe like a weapon, but the scavenging animals were cowardly and faded into the thick undergrowth.

She had been at pains to dig a grave the previous night, but the ground was hard, reluctant to yield to her implement. A shallow depression was all she had managed. Into this, she had dragged Polynices, sprinkling soil over him. It had not been enough. The dogs at first light, taking a foot between their jaws, had fished the dead warrior out of his grave. Now she hardly knew what to do.

*　　*　　*

At this juncture, Joe Moone broke into his own dream and stood before Antigone in the deep deluding dusk, in the leafy shadows, at the tail end of the bosky Boeotian night.

She raised her hoe, ready to strike at him, before asking in a low voice if he were sentry or apparition.

His startlement being as great as hers, he was unable to speak for a moment, so that they held a tableau, neither moving, quite unseen, amid moths, in a silent interlude between waking and dream.

Then he found hesitant voice.

'Antigone, I am your friend. More than that, you are a part of me. You are my anima and I am dreaming you. You may not understand –'

She rushed at him and sought to cleave his head open with the hoe. He seized her thin wiry arms, pressed them against her, twisted her round and held her tightly, locked with her back against his chest.

'Hush, you little tigress! I want to help you. I need to help you. When morning comes, I shall be taken out of my cell and shot. That will be the death of you, too, in me. You see, your tale is well-known, and Creon is going to have you killed in a very unpleasant way. If I can save you . . .'

She struggled furiously, kicking Moone's shins. 'You're a crazy man! Let me go or I'll yell for the sentries.'

He let her go free, throwing her hoe some distance off, saying urgently, 'I'm not crazy. Let me help you do the right thing by your dead brother. I'll drag him into the woods and burn him honourably on a funeral pyre. You go to the palace and sleep with Haemon to establish an alibi. That will fool Creon. He'll think you were in Haemon's bed all night. Haemon won't give you away.'

She was silent, peering up at his face. 'That makes sense. Except that I mean to retain my virginity until my marriage day. But you yourself are a riddle . . .'

'Life's a riddle. Do we live our lives or are we lived? I don't know. In my age, we perceive ourselves as – as inhabited by semi-autonomous . . . how can I explain? . . . semi-autonomous person-ages. A man called Sigmund Freud regarded his daughter Anna as

Antigone . . . When the geographical world had been opened up, Freud discovered a dark continent in each of us. And to him, women were also an undiscovered –'

'Oh, stop talking rubbish. Are you going to help me or not? It'll soon be light.'

Moone went down on his knees. 'Dear Antigone. You can't understand. Why should you? But, you are a valued part of me, the female part of myself, the anima I've denied all my life. Now, on this last day of my existence –'

She clouted him over the head. 'Get up! Help me if you will, but I don't understand your speeches.'

As he rose from his knees, Moone said, 'Look, I know you're a passionate person – sorry, that's a Freudian slip – I mean a *compassionate* person. Go to Haemon's bed now, quickly, and I will dispose of Polynices' body for you. I promise. Go on! Run!'

In her look was a wish to trust. He felt the power of her dark gaze upon him.

'Go!' he repeated. 'Save yourself. Creon is bound to obey a law he himself has promulgated. He's just in that respect. He cannot spare you a second time.'

'But it is the destiny of my family, and my destiny, to suffer. What is the life of woman? Am I not merely the fruit of those elders who came before me, men and women burdened with guilt since time began, when great Thebes was just a cattle market?'

'They are your archetypes, Antigone, but you can defy them. You must defy them as you have defied Creon. Strength is all it needs. Go, live and be happy, marry Haemon. I swear I'll give Polynices a tremendous funeral pyre, to set his spirit free from this earth – as I trust mine will soon be free.'

Although doubt still ruled on her face, something in the tenor of Moone's voice convinced Antigone. She turned and ran from him without another word, running back to the gate of the city, her dark hair streaming out behind her.

As if in a dream within a dream, Joe Moone went to the poor decayed body. It had been heaved against the city wall by the animals. A grey light filtering through the trees allowed him to see only dimly. What haste was his, for he heard the clang of a prison door. He failed to notice that Polynices' head had been severed from its shoulders.

Taking hold of the ankles, he dragged the body along behind him, to slither over parched grass, as he made for the woods. There in the midst of a flowering elder thicket, as apricot light suffused the wildwood, he came on an old wood-cutter's hut, ruinous, with a pile of dried logs beside it. Hurriedly pulling out the wood, Moone made a pile of it and flung Polynices' decaying body on top. Only then, as he struck a flint and set light to small kindling, did he notice that the skull of the corpse was missing.

'Hell!' he exclaimed.

King Creon was up with the dawn as usual. He gave but a glance at Eurydice's nakedness and left her sleeping. After he had bathed his body and had had his beard curled, he went to his window and looked out beyond the city walls. Distantly through the trees, a pillar of smoke was ascending. It climbed into the still morning air and appeared almost solid, reluctant to disperse. Within its curling fumes, Creon thought he saw a woman's face displayed, with hair part-obscuring her features.

He summoned his blind adviser, Tiresias. The tap of the old man's stick announced his approach.

'Tiresias, there is disaster in the royal house. Have we not had enough misery? What means that column of smoke and fire?'

Tiresias, in his whining voice, said, 'What is the life of man? Something not fixed like a compass point towards good or evil. It's a weather vane that blows with the wind, that's what it is. Creon was once an enviable man, who saved his country. But now? Life without joy is no life, life with continuous burden is living death. Today, O King, the wind blows direct into your heart.'

'Oh, shut your mouth, you old fool! Where in Hades is Haemon?' Without waiting for a reply, Creon marched out of the room, past the guard, and flung open the door of his son's room.

There lay Haemon, awake, looking with love into the face of Antigone, curled up next to him. The girl slept peacefully, the fringe of her lashes resting upon her rosy cheeks. One arm was curled protectively over her head, the index finger of its hand entwined with a lock of her dark hair, as if it would pluck a flower. Her defiance put from her, never had she looked more beautiful in her uncle's eye.

Haemon jumped out of bed, grabbing his naked sword as he did so.

'Get out of my room, father!' he ordered. 'Why do you enter?'

'What's Antigone doing here?' asked Creon, taken aback. 'She vowed to remain chaste until her nuptial day. You have dared dishonour her?'

'She is chaste, damn you and your suspicions.' The youth kept his sword at the ready. 'She came to my chamber merely to seek protection, and I have not taken her maidenhood.'

Creon's face grew dark with anger, but at that moment Eurydice appeared behind his shoulder, pulling a long silken gown over her shoulders, looking lascivious.

'Why are you quarrelling, my husband? Must generation always interfere with generation? Leave Haemon and Antigone alone and return to bed with me. The nest is warm. The cocks are still busy crowing.'

'Let them crow. I'll wring every one of their necks,' said Creon. But he knew better than to argue with Eurydice, and followed her meekly enough down the corridor. As they passed Tiresias, the blind man said, tauntingly, 'Those who forge the law will die on its anvil.'

No sooner had he spoken than a clamour arose down in the hall. A house servant appeared at the top of the stairs, abasing himself. When Creon challenged him, the servant spoke up hastily, wringing his hands. He reported that the guards at the south gate had discovered the body of his nephew Polynices was missing. They waited below to report.

With an oath, Creon brushed the servant aside and ran down the stairs. In the hall of the palace, Creon's house dogs prowled and growled about the legs of two sentries. The sentries stood hesitant by the open door. A few citizens, smelling excitement, gathered behind them curiously.

One of the sentries was an older man, still upright, though his front teeth had long been knocked out. The other sentry was a mere youth, with a miniature stubble field on his chin; he had tucked a blue cornflower into his tunic pocket. Told to explain themselves, the older man declared that, as blessed light returned to the world, they had been able to see that the body of his majesty's dishonoured nephew had been removed. They had searched and not found it. They were not to blame.

'Two little items remained where the body had lain,' said the man. 'We bring them here, O King, as evidence to set before you.' So saying, he raised his left arm above his head. He was clutching a decomposing skull. Maggots fell to the ground and twitched about his feet.

'Polynices!' exclaimed the small crowd at the door. Their tones expressed disgust, reverence, excitement.

'What else?' demanded Creon. Though Eurydice stifled a scream, he displayed no emotion at the horrid sight.

The older sentry then showed the second item, holding it up in his right hand. It was a hoe such as women used in the onion fields. The split at the top of its handle was bound together with a strip of blue cloth.

'That belongs to young Antigone,' a woman called. 'And I work beside her many a day. I know that hoe very well by sight. How many times I've told her, "That hoe ain't no good. Get another one, Antigone, my dear," I've said, but she's proud, she won't listen . . .'

'Silence!' roared the king. He began to curse the sentries and everyone else, knowing in his heart he could no longer keep secret the breaking of the law. The chill wind blew direct into his heart as prophesied. Eurydice knew it too, and Tiresias behind her. And the latter cried, 'All will happen as the prophet said. Once the boulder begins to roll downhill, all who stand in its way are crushed. Such is fate.'

'Yes, yes, we'll all be crushed!' screamed Eurydice. 'Husband, rescind your cruel law. Immediately.'

In the palace grounds, a bird called, 'Caught, caught . . .'

The king clutched his beleaguered brow. 'Those who make the

law are those most subject to its command. Guards, bring Antigone hither and she shall confess her guilt.'

In the general furore that followed, Joe Moone made a second appearance within his dream. He himself was as much a spectre as the ghosts from beyond the grave, having but an hour to live before he was taken out into a square courtyard and shot under a foreign flag. His appearance was as ghastly as the shade of Polynices.

Clinging feebly to the king's arm, he said, 'Mighty Creon, spare a moment for introspection! Understand yourself, interpret your actions! You are helplessly acting out the inflexible male principle. Must you always dominate, whatever misery is caused thereby?'

'If I do not dominate the city, you slave, who will? Thebes needs a strong man.' Mixed with Creon's royal anger was some puzzlement at this intrusion. He stood back, clutching at his beard as if for security. Moone seized his chance to speak again.

'Then more clearly than Tiresias I will predict what will happen, for in my better days I studied the classics. By upholding your law, Creon, you will think it legitimate to entomb Antigone, your intended daughter-in-law, in a cave. There she will die. In conse-quence, your son Haemon, overwhelmed by sorrow, will thrust his sword into his own breast. Confronted by such misery, what will your beloved Queen Eurydice do if not bring about her own end, leaving you bereft? How will you be then, O King, O male principle?'

'I will be myself whatever befall!' – spoken in a lion's roar to alarm all present.

'And if your will fails, who then will rule Thebes?'

'Damn you, I live by my stubborn will yet,' shouted Creon. He struck out at Moone. But the rays of the sun had reached the strange flag above the cell where Joe Moone lay, his dream faltered, and his projection faded away from Thebes for ever, as light forsakes the eyes of the dying.

In that ancient month, all happened much as Moone in his liminal state had foreseen. It was a dream, yet not only a dream, but a dream of a myth, and its end tailed away in a new fashion, however little the dreamer could perceive the alternatives. For in the dream Antigone was indeed the undying female principle, and so remained forever living, generation after generation, like the lineaments of a family – a big nose, say, or a cleft chin, seeing no need to fade . . .

Creon indeed had Antigone bound and cast into a cave. His soldiers tossed in with her the stinking skull of her brother. Then the cave was sealed with a great boulder, and the gaps plastered up with clay, so that no light or air entered.

But the goddess Aphaia helped Haemon to escape from Thebes. He searched until he found the cave. Using a branch as lever, he eased away the boulder and unplugged the mouth of the cave. His intended bride was still alive. When he had laved her in a brook, her mind returned to her body. She spoke and smiled at him.

As for King Creon in his palace: his wife, as predicted, fell into such sorrow, imagining that both Haemon and Antigone were dead, that she drank a bowl of hemlock and fell down lifeless in her bathroom. Creon lived on in Thebes, ruling with a heavy hand, a lonely male principle. Law he administered; justice he never understood. As he had claimed, his will did not fail him.

Antigone and Haemon went to live simply on an island in the far Cyclades. But not all of her brother had achieved rest. They were forever haunted by the pallid vision of a rotten skull, which followed them at shoulder height. Strangely, it bore the mark as of a bullet which had pierced it at the temple.

Joe Moone was executed at eight o'clock in the morning, in a country and time far from Boeotia. His life-dream was over, and his dream of Antigone. He turned his head from the firing squad, and a bullet pierced it at the temple.

There is good reason to have Greece in mind. My son Clive and his Greek wife, Youla, live and work in Athens.

The following story is dedicated to Youla. One day when my wife and I were on the pleasant island of Aegina, Youla and I sat on a jetty on Marathonos beach and talked. We spoke of what was possible and what was not – and of the attractions of the latter. It was one of those special occasions.

And somehow a story started to emerge. It rose from the waters of the Saronic Gulf like a vocal Aphrodite.

The God Who Slept With Women

Elizabeth said: 'I know I'm only an ignorant peasant woman. However rich we become, a peasant woman I'll remain. But I've heeded the tales old women still tell in the village, when they sit out on their steps in the evening light. The first gods were female. That's true, girls. The first gods were female. I'm talking about long ago, you understand. Women had all the power then. Childbirth was a mystery then. What the learned call copulation and I call fucking was not connected in people's minds with childbearing.

'This was at the beginning of the world. People were simple in those days, my dear daughters. Men had no importance because the link between what they've got between their legs and begetting children was not understood. So the myths began, those stories that explain the world. Do you know, women were supernatural beings? It was believed that rivers and winds impregnated the wombs of women. People lived happily enough under that illusion, I suppose. They must have made love just as folk do now. We all live under illusions still, that we know. Whatever Father Nikolaos says in church, we still don't know what makes the world tick.

'Once everyone found out what really happened with fucking and all that, and how men had a use after all, their standing improved. Men became mad with their new power. That must be when male gods first arrived. One god was supposed to have created everything – the universe and all the beings in it. Just to take away women's power from them.

'Gods are tricky things, and so are men. They always think they know better. So just beware, now you're growing up, my dear daughters.'

The four girls smiled like cats with saucers of cream, and said nothing. They loved their mother, but of course they knew better than she did.

'I had a golden dream last night,' said Elena, resting her elbow on the breakfast table and her chin in her hand. 'It was wonderful and it lasted all night through. You see . . .'

But there she paused, to look into the faces of her sisters. The girls were sitting barefoot on their verandah in the early morning sun. For breakfast they ate bread with honey and yoghurt. Today there was no school. They lingered over coffee while their mother scurried about in the house, preparing to leave for work in the fields.

The eyes of the sisters were grey or deep blue, like the Aegean which could be seen from the windows of the small house. The house had been built by Elena's grandfather; small and whitewashed, it had stood amid its little garden for almost fifty years. And last night, something like a great wind, and yet something more than a great wind, had visited it.

'Well now, what was this "golden dream"?' asked Persephone, the bold sister (who would later dream she went to Australia).

Still Elena hesitated. She had realized that her dream, so beautiful in its unfolding, might seem indelicate in its telling.

'I bet it was all about a man, eh?' said Artemis, the naughty sister (who would later dream she ran a husband and a hat shop in Athens).

Elena sucked her spoon and looked from one sister to another. She felt a blush starting in the roots of her black hair and spreading to her cheeks. Now she had embarked on the subject, she hardly knew how to continue.

'You don't have to tell us, Elena, darling, if it's private,' said Rea, the shy sister (who would later dream she made an unfortunate marriage).

'Oh yes, she does,' said Persephone.

'What happened was,' said Elena, and then paused before going on in a rush, 'a god came to my bed in the shape of a golden whirlwind.'

Before she could say more, her sisters broke into peals of laughter, covering their mouths politely with their hands as they did so. 'Golden whirlwind!' they repeated, and hooted with laughter. 'Golden whirlwind!' and rocked with laughter.

They joked all through the morning. They were still teasing Elena in the evening, when their mother returned from work. Elizabeth put an arm about Elena, smiled good-naturedly, and quietened her daughters down. Elizabeth Papoulias never joked. The girls sometimes teased her in a high-spirited way. Elizabeth would merely laugh by way of response.

Elizabeth's laughter always touched Elena; she felt that she alone among the sisters understood her mother's sorrow. Now she was sad herself, to have her beautiful and inexplicable dream mocked.

Hard outside work had made Elizabeth's hands hard, but her manner to her daughters was invariably gentle. Some grey hairs already streaked her dark hair. She had ceased to look in her mirror. Now Elizabeth took her youngest daughter aside and advised her in her low, serious voice. 'Elena, your sisters do not understand. You must not be upset by them. You believe your dream happened, so it happened. The world's stranger than people think.'

'It was not really a dream, mother.'

'That I understand. I was awake in the night, as I always am.'

Elena looked enquiringly at her mother, waiting for her to continue.

'I heard you cry out for pleasure, Elena.'

Elena looked down at the floor in embarrassment, not saying a word. In her delight, had she not cried out more than once?

'Our entire house was bathed in gold, Elena, for a whole hour. Such light as never was before. It's a great wonder, my dearest.'

Elizabeth stood in the small room that served as kitchen and living room. In one corner was the television set, in another, Yannis, their caged linnet. She went over to speak to the bird when her daughter left the room.

Yannis cocked its head on one side as if understanding what Elizabeth had to say. What Elizabeth had to say was not very articulate. The linnet answered with a clear fluting burst of song.

'Oh, Yannis, we keep you imprisoned,' said Elizabeth. 'I love you dearly, yet I keep you in this little cage . . . Forgive me. Life is a prison for humans too. I fear for Elena's future . . .'

She was in one of her bad moods, when everything looked black. So often she longed to have a man to turn to for advice.

She carried the cage out into the fresh spring air, to hang it from a hook on the verandah, in the shade, where Yannis might watch birds that were free.

Elena, meanwhile, had slipped out of the house without her sisters knowing. They were prattling on the back porch, among the oleanders and the chickens. She walked down through the olive trees to the margins of the sea, feeling herself invaded by a new sense of loneliness.

The waters of the Saronic Gulf stretched before her, in colour between deep blue and purple. Waves turned lazily over on the shingle at the girl's feet. Distant islands showed grey, crowned by white cloud. As always when she stood here, gazing into distance, Elena wondered if her father would ever return. She had to pretend to herself she remembered his face, smiling down at her.

Looking back, she could make out the red-tiled roof of her home among the olive branches. She loved the house in which she had been born, and the way in which it was now occupied solely by women. But when she had expressed that love to her mother, and remarked on how kind grandfather had been to leave it to Elizabeth, her mother had not replied; instead, her face became set. And Elena remembered hearing from an old woman in the village that her grandfather had been a cruel and drunken man. Angry at siring no sons, he had beaten and abused his poor daughter.

She slipped off her shoes and walked among the little wet stones, letting an occasional wave break over her feet. Her gaze was lowered in thought. A gull cried out as it passed overhead, wings outspread.

Elena remembered how often her mother said, looking up at a passing gull, 'Oh, that I were as free as that bird!' The remark brought sorrow to Elena's heart: not only because the sentiment revealed her mother's discontent, but because she knew, as Elizabeth did not, that even the birds were governed by stern laws of hunger and territoriality. A conviction overcame her – by no means for the first time – that human life, and the great life of the universe, was other than adults preferred to believe it was.

The sheer mystery of the world gave her sombre pleasure. It was the pleasure that cut her off from her three sisters.

A clump of yellow sea poppy grew amid the old square stones. The stones had the texture of biscuit. They marked a spot where once had stood a temple, ancient before Christ was born. Something glinted in the grey sand piled up around the stones. Elena stooped, dug in the sand, and pulled up a glittering thing from its place of semi-concealment.

The high wind in the night had caused waves to lash against the remains of the venerable building. What the storm had partially uncovered was a collar or parure made of gold. Elena held up the collar in astonishment, allowing it to gleam in the sunlight. When she had rinsed the sand from it, she saw it was both beautiful and ancient, whole and complete.

Elizabeth was more excited than her daughters. She and Elena caught a ferry and ventured to Athens. They took the precious find to an expert at the Athens Archaeological Museum. The expert, after

consultation, pronounced the parure to be of Byzantine workman-
ship, gold, and of rare design, probably dating from the tenth century. A museum in Berlin would be anxious to acquire it. Before
too many weeks had passed, a sum of money that Elizabeth – not
to mention her four astonished daughters – regarded as immense
was paid over to her. From then onwards, Elizabeth no longer had
to toil in the fields, and could pay to have her children educated in
foreign languages.

'Elena was always lucky,' said her sisters, not knowing then just
how lucky.

Elizabeth Papoulias knew that what had happened to her youngest
daughter was no dream, no idle thing. Her lovely Elena, born only
a month after her ne'er-do-well husband had left her, was deeply
precious to her: her empathy for the child caused her to believe
she knew Elena's feelings better than did the girl herself. Deeply
superstitious, brought up with the stories of the old gods and goddesses with their impetuous ways, she believed that Elena was
favoured by the arbitrary rulers of the universe.

This understanding she had always hugged to herself, saying no
word of it to her children, even to Elena, in case someone became
jealous. But families understand what is unspoken better than words
from the mouth.

When the immense sum of money arrived from Berlin, Elizabeth
found herself more in control of her life, and the lives of those who
were her responsibility. She hoped above all to spare them from the
kind of prison of circumstance in which she felt she existed. So she
took a walk down to the kiosk in the village and phoned her sister
Sophia, who lived in Piraeus.

Sophia had married a doctor, and was now Mrs Sophia Houdris,
wife of Dr Constandine Houdris. Consequently, she over-dressed,
visited hair-dressing saloons frequently and patronized her less fortunate sister. On the phone, however, Sophia was geniality itself,
Elena's fabulous discovery having evidently had a beneficial effect
on her temperament. It was agreed that the doctor would examine
Elena privately.

One morning in late spring, Elizabeth kept Elena away from school and caught the ferry to Piraeus with her. Rea, Artemis and Persephone were not as envious as might be imagined, since they were rather afraid of their overbearing Aunt Sophia, with her fine city manners.

Mother and daughter arrived at the tall narrow house in Anakous Street, to be greeted affectionately by Sophia and given a good late lunch, with plates of the sweet cakes to which Sophia was addicted. Elena was subdued; she was frightened by the noise and business of the streets of Piraeus, and oppressed by what she regarded as the over-furnished rooms where her aunt and uncle lived. So she said hardly a word while the two sisters talked away, Sophia smoking cigarette after cigarette meanwhile. They talked softly; the doctor was seeing patients in his surgery immediately below.

A linnet hopped about in a cage on Sophia's first-floor balcony. It resembled Yannis, but would not sing for Elena.

'So how do you feel? You don't look ill, girl. Well, let's get it over with. Take your clothes off. Yes, yes, all of them. Don't be shy. Don't delay, there's a good girl. I have an important patient coming to see me at 4.30. Tell me about your periods.'

Uncle Constandine Houdris was in some respects a fine-looking man. He had superficially a resemblance to a good old Greek sailor, with a complicatedly wrinkled visage, a noble brow and a huge white moustache. He was, however, very pale, rather stooped, and nervous in his manner. He rarely left the apartment on Anakous Street, wore eyeglasses of a pink tint, and smoked heavily, even when examining his patients.

Elena was embarrassed to stand naked before him. Dr Houdris stubbed out his cigarette and regarded her young body appreciatively.

'I'm supposed to have a nurse here for these examinations, but since you're family we'll save a drachma or two,' he said, coming closer and beginning to feel his niece lingeringly. 'Mm, mm . . . What sign were you born under? Mm, mm . . .

'Very nice, my dear. You're well-developed for thirteen. Still a virgin, eh? No village boys got at you yet?'

147

She said in a whisper, 'Uncle, something came to me in the middle of the night. Two months ago. Not of my asking.'

He nodded. 'Not a village boy? It entered you, though? Your hymen's intact. Still . . . There seems to be something inside that neat little belly of yours. We'll take an X-ray. So what was this "something" that came to you in the middle of the night? Your mother seems excited about it all.'

'Mother thinks it was a god.' She brought out the last word with an effort.

He peered shortsightedly at Elena, and for the first time allowed some sympathy to pervade his tone.

'And what do you think, Elena?'

'I think it was a god.'

As he positioned her on the X-ray machine, he said, 'You realize this is probably a delusion? Young girls often suffer from delusions. Well, so do old men, come to that . . . Hold still now . . . At times you'd think that *everything* was a delusion.'

The X-rays showed that it was no delusion. Elena had within her body – well, baffling though it was, the plate showed clearly that a small god nestled snugly there. It was no foetus. Rather, as far as could be seen, it was bearded and, moreover, wore a Grecian-type helmet of the sort reproduced so often for foreign tourists to buy in the souvenir shops of Plaka.

Sophia and Elizabeth were called down to the surgery to see the X-rays. They were dumbfounded and clucked like old hens, saying repeatedly that they couldn't believe it.

'But when will it be born, uncle?' Elena asked, almost in tears.

Her uncle put his arm round her shoulders. 'How did the genie get in the bottle? That's the medical question . . .'

'Oh, drat the medical question, uncle! What am I to do?'

Dr Houdris removed his pink spectacles from his face and stared up at the ceiling.

'There must be some way we can make money out of this, my girl. As long as that little man sleeps on in there –'

'Little man! Why, it's a *god*, Constandine!' exclaimed Elizabeth, daring to contradict her brother-in-law. 'And I'm certainly not putting Elena on display, if you have any such idea in your head. She's very special, is my Elena. I've always known it, and this proves it.'

How special Elena was, they had yet to find out. Elena and her mother took the ferry back across the Saronic Gulf, and tried to live as before. Houdris and his wife, however, were more ambitious.

It happened that one of Houdris's patients was an upwardly mobile man in the lower circles of the ruling political party, a party which both the doctor and his wife supported. The doctor confided to this young man that he had an extraordinary niece who was apparently about to become a unique example of virgin birth. By his calculations, the child, her extraordinary child, would be born some time late in December.

Although the young man had not risen sufficiently in his profession to have the ear of the Prime Minister, he certainly had the ear of the Minister for the Environment. The Minister for the Environment was a distant relation of his, a cousin-twice-removed. As soon as he got the chance, he told the story of Elena, with suitable embellishments, to this Minister. The Minister laughed and said merely that he did not think a second Virgin Mary was on the cards. However, after he had paid the bill for his young relation's drinks, he thought deeply about the matter.

Ever since her husband had left her, Elizabeth had suffered from insomnia. The excitement brought on by the news of Elena's god made sleep even harder to come by. She rose one morning before dawn, left a note for her sleeping daughters telling them to get their own breakfasts and be sure to wash properly, and set off to catch a boat.

The spirit, she told herself, moved her.

It was a Friday. And on Fridays during the summer a ferry sailing among the islands called in at the nearest port, only four kilometres beyond the village. Elizabeth caught the ferry with five minutes to spare. She sat on deck, watching the ever-changing pattern of islands and sea, bathed in the pure light of another day. She rejoiced. She felt elevated. What had happened was – she hardly dared use the word, even to herself – a miracle. She lived in a miraculous world.

The understanding gave her a new power; she felt it within her, as if she herself was carrying a god in her womb. Looking back at the wake of the vessel, she saw it as a path she herself was making across the world. She sang under her breath, matching the song to the steady rhythm of the ship's engines.

When the ferry pulled into the harbour of the island of Aegina, Elizabeth disembarked amid a small knot of village people, local holiday-makers, and foreign tourists. Aegina was all a-bustle, even at this pristine hour. She ignored the attractions of its shops and hired a taxi to take her inland, up to the ruined temple of Aphaia.

The great temple, built in the heyday of Aegean culture some centuries before Christ, stood proudly on a hill. Worshippers here could gaze at an unrivalled panorama – Elizabeth had been taught Sappho's words –

> Over the salt sea
> and over the richly flowered fields

At this hour, the temple stood solitary on its eminence, except for a melancholy oriental tourist with a pack on his back. He sat clutching his camera, gazing out to where light and distance concealed Kithnos and the isles of the Cyclades. He had no glance to spare for Elizabeth nor she for him.

Her mother had brought little Elizabeth here once, on her name day, when she was six years old. She had never forgotten her shock at the sight of her mother abandoning the habits of church and throwing herself down on the worn stones to pray to the elusive goddess, Aphaia, whoever she might be.

Perhaps humans should not know the gods by name.

Elizabeth's mother had prayed for the happiness of her child. Now Elizabeth prostrated herself much as her mother had done, over thirty years earlier. The stones beneath her knees, her arms, were still chilly from the night. Like her mother, she prayed for the happiness of her daughters, and for Elena especially. And for whatever was about to happen to them . . .

The prayer faded into a meditation as she abased herself under the Doric columns. Woman must have come to pray at this sacred spot over many generations. Yet she knew nothing of them. She knew only of her own mother, her own daughters. So ignorant was she, that all the rest might be pure invention, something cooked up by priests or the educated.

Was this visitation of the god to Elena perhaps also a message to her? Suppose the whole universe was about to be reinvented . . . Her youngest daughter was not too young to bear a child, just as she, Lizzie Papoulias, was not too old to bear another one, if required. Of this she felt certain: that some wonderful process had started, which would overturn everything that now was. Tears of joy squeezed their way from her closed eyes.

She must help the wonderful thing to happen. She alone, possibly with the interference of her sister and brother-in-law. Perhaps it was for this the gods had arranged that her husband should desert her.

Speculation faded into prayer again as she stirred on the hard blocks of chiselled stone. She prayed that she would be unafraid in the face of powers she could never comprehend.

When she stood up, tourists were arriving at the temple, cheerful in their colourful clothing. Elizabeth avoided them and went down to the souvenir shop for an orange juice.

The Minister of the Environment was an easy-going man. He was not deeply moved by the plight of the environment, being fond of telling his friends that it was, after all, the deforestation of Attica which had built Athenian triremes which had brought democracy to Europe and the West. So, he ended with a laugh, deforestation must be good for us all.

What the Minister needed just at present was money. He had taken on an expensive mistress who liked to shop in Paris and New York. It occurred to him that the story of little Elena Papoulias, as told to him by his cousin-twice-removed, might be helpful to his overdraft. Surely the Prime Minister would like the sound of having a second Virgin Mary on his home ground . . . The Pope would be furious, all eyes would be turned on Greece.

He knew how superstitious the Prime Minister was; and of course the government was at that time undergoing a financial crisis and losing popular support. It would by no means harm his career if he offered the P.M. a distraction to bolster his popularity.

The next formal committee meeting was a stormy one. The P.M., against the advice of most of the cabinet, had decided to launch another national lottery, to be called the Youth Lottery. The prizes for the Youth Lottery would be suitably grand, while the proceeds would go towards improved school accommodation. The new buildings would eventually replace the present rather haphazard methods of education, particularly in rural areas and on the islands.

During the meeting, the Minister for the Environment slipped away and phoned his young relation. The young relation phoned Dr Constandine Houdris. Dr Houdris gave some details of Elena's schooling and how, during term time, she and her sisters had to walk a kilometre to catch a bus which took them to a village where they got a ferry to a large town in which their school was situated. This journey had to be made in reverse order after class. In winter, when storms swept the Saronic Gulf, the ferries often could not run. This information was relayed back to the Minister for the Environment.

The Minister had previously been lukewarm about the Youth Lottery. Now he became more enthusiastic, tackling the P.M. after the meeting and drinking some champagne with him.

'I can think of an ideal young person who might stand for all the young people who will benefit from your splendid lottery, Prime Minister,' he said. 'An imaginative symbol. An outstanding and I believe very attractive representative of Greek girlhood.' And he proceeded to explain about Elena Papoulias.

'What?' said the P.M. 'She's pregnant? Thirteen and pregnant and you wish me to use her as a symbol of Greek girlhood? You're mad, Stavros! Go away. Leave me in peace. Do something about the traffic in Athens.'

The bill for the Youth Lottery was passed through parliament before the summer recess. The first monthly draw was to be held in November. Everywhere went the publicity for the lottery, and the P.M.'s popularity rose accordingly.

The month of November was wet. The four Papoulias sisters attended school as usual. Elizabeth went to church on Sunday as was her custom. She was a little afraid of the young priest, with his glossy black beard and proud bearing; the old priest, Father Nikolaos, rather dotty now, had been more to her taste. The young priest had made a disparaging remark about Elena's pregnancy, to Elizabeth's annoyance.

That pregnancy – though Elizabeth never used the word – had advanced no further. Elena gave no sign of oncoming parturition and indeed had grown accustomed to the god sleeping inside her.

As Elizabeth left the little white-washed church that November morning, she was surprised to see the old priest, Father Nikolaos, standing under a pine tree nearby. He beckoned Elizabeth over.

'Father, how are you? How's the arthritis? I've really been meaning to visit you.'

'Of course, of course. It is a bit of a problem. And your sons are well?'

'Daughters, father.'

The old man nodded his head vigorously. 'Daughters I mean to say. I hear tell the youngest has a little god inside her, is that right?'

Elizabeth ventured to put a hand on the old man's arm. 'Father, you will think it blasphemy that we call it a god. But there's something in there that doesn't want to come out, and the X-rays show it to be of human shape. And it wears a little helmet.'

'A helmet, you say? A helmet? Then it must be a god. Many wonderful things happen, my child, and who am I to deny it?' He paused. The rain was coming on again. 'All will go well with you and yours as long as that little god keeps on sleeping inside your son. He'll protect you from harm and bring good fortune – to you as well as your sons.'

'Daughters, father. You shouldn't stay out in this rain.'

'Daughters I mean to say. Excuse me. There's something I had to tell you . . . Now what was it?'

'About Elena?'

'Oh, yes. No. No, I don't think so.'

She was getting wet and feeling she needed to go home and sit down and sip some camomile tea. 'It's not about Costas, is it?' Costas was her missing husband.

'Ah, yes. Costas . . . Poor fellow! Unable to tell right from wrong.'

'Don't pity him, father. Pity me who ever crossed paths with the man. What's your news?'

Father Nikolaos had a brother in Australia. Over the years, and intermittently, the brother had sent home news of emigrant Greeks to his priest brother. Some years previously, maybe two, maybe three, he had enclosed a cutting from a newspaper in his letter. The cutting was a brief news item reporting that Costas Papoulias, 36, had been up for trial for rape and manslaughter before a court in Sydney. The court had sentenced him to a long prison term. Privately, Elizabeth was relieved to know that this violent man – every bit as bad as her own father – had been shut away in a distant land. Not wishing her daughters to feel ashamed, she had never told them that their father was a convict in an Australian jail.

'What's the news, father?' she asked again, as the old priest looked up at her, narrowing his eyes as if trying to sum her up.

'He's hopped it, my dear. Escaped from prison.'

The old man knew nothing more than that. The Australian newspaper had simply reported the bare fact. Elizabeth walked home through the drizzle in thoughtful mood. She made herself a cup of camomile tea and settled down on her sofa under a rug, relieved that her daughters were off with friends, amusing themselves. Yannis sang to her, but she did not hear; she could only think that Costas might come back to Greece and seek her out. He would come straight to the house. The nightmare life would resume . . .

But if the gods had ordained it . . .

Next day, when the girls were at school, an official-looking letter arrived, addressed to Elena. Elizabeth immediately connected it with her husband. Wrongly, as it turned out. When Elena returned and opened the letter, she discovered that she had won the very first draw of the Youth Lottery. Millions of drachmae were hers.

Elizabeth had bought five tickets, one for each of her daughters and one for herself. And Elena had had the lucky one. A second fortune had come her way.

She thought of Father Nikolaos's words: The god will bring you good luck as long as he goes on sleeping inside Elena. But if he woke up? She trembled from the force of her fear.

Innocent and pliant, Elena declared herself delighted by her amazing luck. Privately, she wished only that life would continue as it was, if possible for ever. It was her sisters who seemed to yearn for change.

'Lend me some money, and when I leave school I'll fly to America and be a movie star,' said Persephone (who would later dream she went to Australia).

'Buy me a red motor-bike like my friend Tomis's,' begged Artemis (who would later dream she ran a husband and hat shop in Athens).

'Do you think we could afford a video now?' asked Rea (who would later dream she made an unfortunate marriage).

Elena said she would see about it. First of all, she had to go to Athens. There, she would receive her lottery prize and shake hands with the Prime Minister before the television cameras. Then, she said to herself, she would return home, bringing each of her sisters a present, with a special present for her mother, and probably something for her history teacher, a young man for whom she had tender feelings. She thought that the little god in her stomach approved of her intentions; perhaps he even masterminded them.

In the silence of the crowded bedroom, when her sisters were asleep, she whispered a prayer to the god: 'Dear God, please don't let my world disappear. Let everything continue as it is, for ever and ever. Amen.'

And she stroked her stomach.

On the morning of the day she was to go to Athens, Elena walked among their olive trees. Where the trees ended, marking off a stretch of land sloping down to the sea, stood an old stone wall. The wall was covered – almost held together – by ivy. At its foot, ants were toiling. They had worn a path through the grass and wild thyme.

The path negotiated steep bends through the bands of stonework before disappearing. It emerged on the other side of the wall, and made its meandering way inland. Here was a world which continued as it was, she thought, for ever and ever, amen.

Elena had always taken an interest in the ants. Sometimes she dropped crumbs of bread in their path, in order to watch them carry the morsels down into the dark of their nest.

The ants had been there since before Thucydides was born, long before Christ. So she imagined. She was studying Thucydides with the young history master. Thucydides said that events in the past would be repeated in the future. She had felt uneasy about this idea, for which the young history master had no explanation. Now she asked the god inside her if the universe might be recreated as before. Or had it been recreated and destroyed many times? The sleeping god, as usual, gave no reply.

She heard her mother calling from the house. Elizabeth was standing there in her best clothes, looking anxious. And beside her was a smart grey lean impatient man from the TV studios.

If Elena wished only to continue her dreamy private schoolgirl life, there were those in Athens, by contrast, whose profession it was to intrude on other people's lives. This was true from the Prime Minister downwards, to the lowest journalist. Many men and women in this category immediately interested themselves in Elena Papoulias and her remarkable good fortune.

The young girl's pregnancy, real or supposed, coupled with her remarkable strokes of fortune in winning treasure both ancient and modern, made a wondrous combination. Elena's adolescent beauty supplemented the attractions of the story.

'How photogenic you are, dear,' exclaimed one photojournalist, adjusting her long dark hair to his own requirements.

'Why, you're so nervous,' said a woman interviewer. 'You're like a little deer. Remember how Iphigenia was turned into a deer? That's you.'

'I don't think Iphigenia was turned into a deer,' said Elena. 'Someone she was going to sacrifice turned into a deer.'

'Oh, I don't set any store by those silly old myths,' said the interviewer, with a vexed laugh. 'Where did you pick up this classical stuff anyway?'

'I've discussed it with my history teacher,' said Elena. And thus sprang up another strand of the news story: the shy pupil in love with her earnest young teacher. A photographer was despatched immediately to her school.

Like Iphigenia trapped in Tauris, Elena was certainly trapped in Athens, day after day, as a guest of the Prime Minister. She was given a room in a small hotel in the busy part of the city, with her mother for company. Her Aunt Sophia, respectful now, came to visit and brought sweet cakes, and offered advice about how all the money should be invested. As for the Youth Lottery, it was re-named Elena's Lottery and sold twice as many tickets as formerly under its new title.

One reason for Elena's detention in Athens was that her legend spread far and wide. Foreign journalists arrived from abroad, from Italy and Spain and France, while a whole television team arrived from Germany. The Greek tourist board sent an important official to advise Elena on what to say. The board foresaw – correctly – that Elena was a valuable adjunct to the tourist trade.

A day came when Elena had no appointments and she asked Elizabeth if they might return home. Elizabeth said that since she had the day free, she could do whatever she liked. Elena pouted and made no response; there was nothing in Athens she wished to do. She stared out of the window at the busy street, with pedestrians spilling out among the congested traffic. Ants again!

The phone rang. Elizabeth answered. On the line was a man who described himself as a media producer and originator. He wanted to structure a new game show, probably to be called 'Golden Fortunes', round Elena. He referred to Elena as a 'magic personality'. He was calling from Sydney, Australia. He wanted to fly over and discuss the project, in which big money was involved. He assured Mrs Papoulias that everyone in Australia knew about her daughter, and how everything she touched turned to gold. Ideal for hostessing a game show.

After giving a non-committal answer, Elizabeth put the phone down. She had turned very pale. The producer's words brought her husband vividly to mind. If Costas, on the loose in Australia, heard of his youngest daughter's fortune, doubtless he would come scurrying on the trail of money and they would all be in trouble. Why, he might even kidnap Elena. You heard of such things happening.

'Elena, my dear,' Elizabeth said. 'I don't think it is wise to go home. I think we should stay in Athens. Athens is a big city. We must buy a nice house in the suburbs, perhaps in New Philadelphia, and change our name from Papoulias. Perhaps a house with two storeys and a little garden and a swing and –' She paused before offering the final titbit. 'A swimming pool . . .'

To her astonishment, Elena gave a small scream and rushed from the room. As she went, she knocked flying a plate of cakes Aunt Sophia had brought them. Elizabeth jumped up but her daughter had gone, slamming the door behind her. Downstairs she rushed, straight out into the street. A passing motor-cyclist knocked her over.

'BAD LUCK FOR GOOD FORTUNE ELENA', screamed the newspaper headlines. 'ATHENIAN WONDER GIRL IN COMA.'

In only a few hours – indeed, before night fell in Athens – strange reports were arriving from all quarters. The Moon had disappeared.

The news from various battlefronts round the world, or from famine-stricken countries in Africa, even the concern for Elena, was as nothing to this alarming news. The Moon had vanished as if it had never existed.

'MOON DOOM. PRESIDENT DENIES U.S. INVOLVEMENT.'

There was no accounting for it, although many experts were dragged in to have their say. Earth's beautiful satellite, the subject of poems, dreams, aspirations and other mental states since before history began, was no more. It simply ceased to exist, leaving not a moonbeam behind.

In the long term, the effect its absence would have was incalculable. In the short term, ocean tides would die away. It was useless for astronomers to point out that in fact the Sun raised tides too, though with only a third of the Moon's power. The collapse of tidal waters would spell unwonted change. Since the Mediterranean and Aegean were almost tideless, local effects would be slight. So Athenians were assured by their journalists.

News of something much more alarming took longer to seep through. The Greek language had changed. Changed beyond recognition.

No Greeks noticed this freakish phenomenon. It was diplomats, exporters, foreigners, tourists, anyone who had been at pains to learn something of the language, who announced the truth. Their claims were immediately dismissed. But no, the Greeks were talking a different language from formerly, even from the previous day. When anyone checked with yesterday's videos, or with LPs and CDs and cassettes, they found that everyone was speaking or singing in a tongue now completely incomprehensible to them. The new language had a different root structure and was compatible with no other on Earth.

Chaos broke out. Language schools closed, re-opened, closed for good. Men and women in the Greek diplomatic service overseas shot themselves.

Other alarming news was ignored for the time being; that physical constants had changed meant little to the man in the street. As startled physicists were soon able to prove, the energy equation was now

$$E = MC^{2.7713}$$

From now on, a great deal more matter would be needed to produce one joule of energy. Nuclear power plants started to go out of business.

While all these arbitrary and inexplicable events were unfolding, Elena Papoulias lay unconscious in a hospital bed. She had a room to herself, into which only medicos, nurses and her mother were allowed. But it was Elena's superstitious Uncle Constandine who waylaid the doctors.

'I alone know what the problem is,' he said. 'I have a diagnosis. I can tell you what is wrong.'

'Elena is best left quietly in our care, thank you,' the hospital doctors said.

So Dr Houdris went on television.

The essence of Houdris's claim was that there had once been a war in Heaven. As he reminded viewers, both Greek pagan myths and Christian faiths contained references to this war. Many other myths featured variants of the same story; the Norse legend of Ragnarok, for instance, spoke of the battle between good and evil gods. One of the great gods, weary of this endless war, had descended to take refuge inside his niece, Elena Papoulias.

'All the god wants is rest. He sleeps inside Elena. And what is he dreaming?'

Houdris's interviewer said suavely, 'Possibly you can tell us what the god is dreaming?'

Houdris smoothed his moustache as if to indicate he had the interviewer trapped and replied, 'He is dreaming our entire universe. We are all figments of the god's dream.'

The interviewer laughed with only a trace of amusement. 'This is getting pretty wild, Dr Houdris. How do you know all this?'

Houdris's eyes gleamed behind his pink lenses. There was no doubt in his mind, he said. How else could the aberrations in what had been hitherto regarded as fixed laws – constants – be explained except by understanding that all were figments of a cosmic dream? No, he was not being unscientific. He was being scientific by deducing facts from evidence. Elena's accident had caused the god's slumber to be disturbed, its dream to be disrupted – hence the vanished Moon and the rest of it. Perhaps it almost woke up from its sleep.

'And if the god did wake up?' enquired the interviewer, now unable to suppress the scorn in his voice.

'Then our universe would burst like a bubble, because it is just a dream . . .'

'What has the damp sea wind brought to my family?' Elizabeth Papoulias asked herself in the quiet of the hospital room. She sat beside her daughter's bed, trying to shake herself from one of her dark moods. With sorrow she regarded Elena's closed eyes and silent face.

'Stop being miserable, Lizzie,' she told herself. The doctors declared that Elena would recover. After all, everything was wonderful. Would there be a grander moment in her life than when she and Elena had ridden beside the Prime Minister in his special car, through cheering Athenian crowds? Of course she had been proud. The Prime Minister had made a speech, holding Elena's hand some of the time as he spoke. 'Greece,' he had boasted, 'is now the most famous country in the world.'

She had thought at the time how well it had sounded, had repeated the words to Sophia and Constandine. Later, a member of an opposition party had laughed and said, 'Greece was always the most famous country in the world. What's the old idiot on about?' Then Elizabeth had been embarrassed, thinking that she had been unable to perceive the foolishness of the P.M.'s speech for herself.

And she was involved with the foolishness. That brought her to the nub of her cogitations. She was just a peasant, a simple country wench at heart. Many of her fellow countrymen went abroad to work, to Australia and America and elsewhere, and returned much improved and richer. She had got no further than Athens, and not on her own merits. She was richer, yes, but she told herself she was unimproved. The elevated mood she had enjoyed at the Temple of Aphaia was forgotten.

Here she was putting on weight, not yet forty and putting on weight, eating sweet cakes every day in smart restaurants. A neighbour was looking after her three older daughters – a disgrace in itself.

To gaze out at the ceaseless traffic rumbling under the window was tiring. She paced about the hospital room. Elena lay silent in the bed, eyes closed – dreaming of who knows what?

Looking down at her daughter, Elizabeth thought to herself, This at least is beautiful and good and innocent. Perhaps that's why she was chosen by the gods. If only we could return to existence as it was long ago in the Golden Age of Greece, when there were only goddesses . . . Then we wouldn't have to suffer having our lives messed about by men . . .

She brightened up. It was nearing five of the afternoon. Almost time to meet her sister and some friends in a neighbouring café. They would have a good chat; most of them were country people at heart, however smartly they dressed. And Elizabeth had a new dress to show off. There would be chocolate cake . . . Elena was safe where she was.

Since the majority of people never know what to think, even at the best of times, they derive their opinions from what others say, and pass them off as their own. Thus, many people all round the world began to nod in agreement when they heard the Houdris Hypothesis, as it was dubbed. They had, they said, always known the whole of existence was a dream and not what politicians and scientists claimed it was.

Some of them began to ask, 'Why does everyone hate work so much?' And answered their own question, 'Because work has no part in Dreamland.'

The Greek government hurriedly assembled a special committee of enquiry to investigate the matter of Elena Papoulias.

A senior German philosopher was flown in from Munich to address the committee.

'While we have yet to discover why the Moon has disappeared, why energy has taken a turn for the worse, and why your language has changed overnight, solutions to these unexpected problems will be found. Scientific solutions. My colleagues believe that the solar system happens to be passing through an unsuspected cosmic flaw. Once we are through the flaw, everything will revert to normal.

'As for the young Papoulias girl's connection with these events, it is merely coincidental, and an invention of the popular press.

'Let me speak briefly concerning what has been called the Houdris Hypothesis, that existence is a dream from which we shall all wake. It is, of course, complete nonsense, designed to scare old women. Excuse me, old men.

'This absurdly named hypothesis is based merely on deductive reasoning. Deductive reasoning from self-evident premises provides us with no sound knowledge of the world. It must be *observation* that supplies the premises on which we base our knowledge, and observation requires modern scientific knowledge, not irrational guesses. We need to know precisely the time when the Moon left its orbit, in which direction it is now heading, at what velocity, et cetera. We need to know precisely the nature of the language you now speak in Greece, its roots, et cetera, and when exactly you began to speak it. Possibly you are as a nation – I only say "possibly" – suffering from a form of mass hallucination. As to the collapse of the mass-energy equation, that may be simply explained as a technical mistake somewhere, though admittedly there does seem to be less sunlight reaching the Earth just now. This could be caused by sunspots, or some other solar phenomenon.'

The professor paused impressively.

'What we require a non-scientifically trained populace to understand is that our modern knowledge of the universe is based on both deduction and induction. Deduction alone, which the Houdris idea offers us, is an example of pre-scientific thinking. It will not stand once the scientific data comes in. Our knowledge of the universe is based on true facts and measurements gleaned from many disciplines. How then could the universe be a dream? The notion is preposterous.'

He sat down.

A Greek philosopher stood up. He was an old man, who clutched the back of a chair set before him to support himself. His voice was thin, but he spoke clearly enough.

'My friend from Munich is himself falling into unscientific ways by deriding the dream theory without examining it. For countless centuries, humanity has been haunted by the belief that all life is a dream. You will recall the celebrated case of the Chinese philosopher, Chuang Tzu, who dreamed he was a butterfly and, on waking, could not tell if he was Chuang Tzu who had dreamed he was a butterfly or a butterfly now dreaming it was Chuang Tzu. Does not the science of subatomic physics show that all we regard as solid matter is really a cosmic dance of waves and particles incapable of explanation?

'For my own part, I see nothing particularly fantastic in the belief that our whole extraordinary universe is someone's or something's dream.

'Let me ask you all this. Rational knowledge – the accumulation of facts – has immensely increased over the ages. Yet why is it that what we may call absolute knowledge hasn't increased one jot since the days of Socrates and the Buddha? As Chuang Tzu, whom I've already mentioned, said, "If it could be talked about, everyone would have told their brother." Doesn't that suggest that everything is *arbitrary*?

'My friend's argument places overmuch trust in empirical knowledge. Instead of seeking human understanding, he would rely on scientific instruments. Very well. Telescopes do not lie. But all our knowledge of the outside world – and of the inside world, come to that – rests ultimately on our senses. What are those senses made of? Protoplasm, a kind of jelly. There is no sort of proof which can convince us that our senses, our perceptions, bring us a definitive truth about the world. Indeed, we know that world-pictures change almost from century to century. They are perforce subjective.

'All ultimately is a matter of interpretation according to . . . well, according to what I don't know. Temperament, perhaps? Certainly we all have different outlooks on the world. My brother – dead now, alas – and I could never agree about anything. There are people even today who claim our planet is flat, and can advance so-called proof of it . . . People seem to live equally happily with or without a belief in God.

'So what do I think in conclusion? That's briefly said, ladies and gentlemen. I believe that the greatest care should be taken of little Elena Papoulias. One more shock like her street accident and we may suddenly find – well, permit me to quote Shakespeare –

'. . . the great globe itself,
Yea, all which it inherit, shall dissolve,
And, like this insubstantial pageant faded,
Leave not a rack behind. We are such stuff
As dreams are made on . . .'

Elena sat up in the hospital bed, struggling with the pillows. She looked about her room. A shaded light burned by her bedside; a blue Athenian night pressed against the window panes. On the couch beside her bed, Elizabeth slept, her face turned from the light. Flowers from well-wishers were ranged all round the room. A buoyant sense of health, more potent than medicine, filled Elena. She smiled and stretched. Her wounds and bandages had disappeared.

'Thank you, dear little god,' she whispered, stroking her stomach.

Climbing out of bed, she dressed as quietly as possible so as not to disturb her mother. As she crept from the room, impulse made her seize up a bunch of chrysanthemums from a jam jar. With these she proceeded down the corridor. All was quiet. The hospital at this pre-dawn hour echoed with silence.

When she reached the foyer, a night receptionist roused from a doze and stared at her curiously. With her face half-hidden by flowers, Elena said, 'These have to be taken immediately to someone ill in the Hilton Hotel. Please let me out.'

The receptionist yawned and pressed a button. When one of the side doors unlocked, Elena opened it and walked through into the first suspicions of dawn. Though the street was deserted, it still held the stale tang of car and bus exhausts, but she breathed it with gratitude and set off at a good pace. She dropped the flowers on top of the first plastic rubbish bin she came across. Where she was going she hardly knew or cared; all she wanted was to be free.

Light was seeping back into the world when she found herself on Aharnon, strolling north. She realized she was enjoying Athens for the first time, seeing the city wake to a new day. The few people who were about walked slowly, as if convalescing from sleep. Some of them bade her good morning. A bakery was opening, filling the street outside with the smell of fresh bread.

Persephone, Artemis and Rea would be waking now, preparing for their long daily journey to school. Elena missed their company and the cosy aromas of four girls growing up and sleeping in that little pretty room with the blue wallpaper. From their one window you could see the line of the sea, and occasionally a ferry on it, heading for the islands.

At one point she became aware she was being followed. In the reflection of a shop window she saw him, a chunky adolescent with fair hair, only a few years older than Elena herself, wearing a dirty T-shirt and scruffy trousers. An unwashed sort of fellow, she thought, who had never seen a comb in his life. She quickened her pace. The youth ambled along on the other side of the street, keeping her in view.

She was passing a telephone booth standing outside a church when the phone started ringing. On impulse, as if directed, Elena entered the booth and picked up the receiver.

'Elena, is that you? Good. Listen, this is your dad. How are you?'

She was not amazed. 'I'm fine. Where are you?' She was not amazed to hear his voice for the first time.

'I'm calling from a one-eyed hole in Australia, outside Adelaide.' The voice carried an echo with it; she knew this meant a satellite link-up. It was thin, almost flavourless, squeezed through cable, freeze-dried in the stratosphere.

'Are you going to come back to us, Daddy?' She withheld too much hope from the question.

'Hang on, where's your mother? Give me her number and I'll ring her. Listen, I'm going to be back in Greece just as soon as I can make it. I've been down on my luck, Elena. Don't listen to anything your mother tells you. My trouble is, I have a pathological dread of hard work. A doctor told me it was inherited.'

'So when will you be here, Daddy? We'll all be glad to see you.'

'I have to be careful, girl. Don't tell anyone I phoned. I'm going to look after you properly. How'd you like to live in with your old dad?'

'And my sisters as well? What about Rea and –'

'Oh, blast it –' said the distant nasal voice on the other end of the phone, and the connection was broken off.

Elena went and sat in a little corner café which was just opening up. She ordered a Nescafé as she considered the conversation. She could not conceal from herself that it was not the best of conversations. All the same, it would certainly be good to have her father back. She could not understand his insistence on secrecy.

The woman behind the bar kept staring. Whenever she saw Elena looking at her, she switched on a false smile. A heavy woman, she supported her torso with elbows on the counter. Elena tried to ignore her.

Pale early sunshine slowly filled the opposite side of the street. She saw that the combless youth was still hanging about, pretending nonchalance, lighting a cigarette. At the same moment, she realized that she had no money with which to pay for her coffee, or to hire a taxi back to the safety of the hospital and her mother. She was trapped at her table.

Behind the bar, the woman was looking alternately at Elena and at the screen of a little television set, snugged by the cash register on her bar. A man came in, carrying crates of mineral water from a van parked outside the café. After conferring with him, the woman made a phone call. Elena became anxious in case this pantomime involved her; she sat paralysed over her cooling coffee. 'Do something, will you?' she whispered to the god within her.

Almost at once, the woman came over from behind the bar, walking clumsily.

'You don't have to pay for that coffee,' she said, flicking her automatic smile on and off again. 'It's free to you.' She gestured towards the cup.

Elena looked at her enquiringly.

The woman said, by way of explaining her generosity, 'Well, you're a goddess, aren't you? So you're welcome to the Nescafé. It says on TV the whole city's looking for you at this very moment.'

'I'm not a goddess.' She pouted, disliking this weighty person. 'I'm just an ordinary girl. I go to school, like my sisters.'

The woman clutched her apron. Looking round as if for help, she said, 'I'm not going to argue with you, miss. I know who you are. You're the one who made the Moon disappear. I don't want this café disappearing or anything nasty like that. Please leave without causing trouble.'

'That's plain silly,' said Elena, conscious as she spoke that she had never addressed an adult in this manner before.

'Silly, is it? For all I know you're one of the old lot come back –

Nemesis or one of the Erinyes, the Furies. All the money I borrowed from the till I shall most certainly pay back, believe me.'

'It's got nothing to do with that. I just wanted a coffee.'

'All right, you've had your coffee, miss, now please leave. Take a bun with you, if you like. I'll pay for it. Gladly.'

When Elena rose to go, the woman backed nervously away. Elena saw how poor and broken her shoes were.

'Thank you for the coffee. It was very nice.'

She was hesitating to leave when a police car came screaming to the door. Two police officers climbed out, surveyed the street and entered the café. Both addressed Elena politely. They said they would like to escort Elena back to the hospital — if she was willing to accompany them.

As she climbed into the back of their car, the combless youth watched from the other side of the road.

Apartments were being prepared on the roof of the hospital, according to government orders. Painters and decorators had been here earlier, but had broken off from work and not reappeared. Elizabeth walked alone in the empty rooms. Sounds of traffic were muted.

'It is not true that you are merely a peasant woman,' said a voice in her head. 'Nor is it true that you are old. Nor is it true that you hate your husband.'

'It's true I'm getting a bit fat,' she said, looking round defensively to see if anyone was there. 'Who are you, anyway? What do you mean?' It was impossible to determine whether the voice, so even and clear, was male or female.

The voice said, 'I'm telling you things you don't know and you do know at the same time. Eternal truths are not expressible in words. You are growing older; you are also eternally youthful. You are helpless; yet there is infinite power within you. There are no gods; but you are godlike yourself. The universe is no dream; though it has all the qualities of a dream.'

Elizabeth backed against a wall. 'Am I going potty? What is all this crap? You're to do with Elena, aren't you? Go and speak to her.

She's only downstairs.' Her eyes tried to see behind the emptiness of the empty room.

'All humans know such things about themselves. They have the power to make the world begin anew, yet do not use it. Until you grasp that fact, you will continue to be your usual unsatisfactory self, looking uselessly for somewhere to hide.'

'Bugger you – excuse my language. I'm happy with myself as I am. How could I get together with Costas again? Come off it!'

And the voice replied, 'By making a new start. Because you are not happy with yourself as you are; what about your black moods of depression? Elizabeth Papoulias, I shall speak to you only this once, so heed me. Your youngest daughter, having been chosen, must go elsewhere. She must join us. But you – you must remain *here*, wherever you consider *here* to be. You must realize yourself fully and create a new world, for yourself and others.'

She clutched her head. She shook her head. She stamped her foot. She clapped her hands together once. 'Go away, damn you! We mortals have to settle for the present world as it is, don't we? Don't we? Surely?'

'Then why do you pray?' With mockery in its laughter, the voice asked, 'And if the old world is crumbling . . .'

Darting about the room, cursing, Elizabeth called, 'Are you the forgotten Aphaia to whom I was daft enough to pray on Aegina? Are you god or goddess, or am I going mad?'

No answer came. The unfinished room was suddenly emptier than it had ever been. She stood waiting in the midst of the space. Nothing happened. What was truth, what deception, what a trick of the senses?

Going over to the window, she looked down at the Athenian traffic. Was there a higher reality than that mechanical muddle? In a piercing moment of introspection, she knew that there was, that the traffic had no more duration in time than the gasoline on which its engines depended.

But under her breath she repeated an old saying, 'Whom the gods love they first make mad.' Was that how it went? She thought so, but being an ignorant peasant woman she was uncertain.

She went downstairs to find her daughter.

Dr Constandine Houdris was not a bad man. Like the rest of humanity, he had his problems. Ambition was one of the traits which made his life uncomfortable. Appearing on television a few times convinced him that he was someone of importance. He was anxious to maintain this illusion, both in his own mind and in that of the general public. Even if life were a dream, as he had declared, he was determined to make his name in it; he was no philosopher.

Another little problem to vex him was his relationship with his wife. The creamy cakes to which Sophia was addicted had transformed the slender young girl he married into a portly lady who suffered from breathlessness and leg trouble. Houdris was not cross with Sophia on this account; although he could scarcely bear to acknowledge the fact to himself, he realized that creamy cakes were probably Sophia's way of compensating for his waning interest in her. He accepted that the world was as it was: no more perfect than the creatures who inhabited the dream. Changing it was not within the compass of his aspirations.

Houdris had his compensations. Many attractive women visited his surgery with one complaint or other. Often it was necessary for these ladies to remove their clothes in order to be examined. The doctor's little pink lenses were not the only ones turned on this display of nudity; he had rigged up hidden cameras which recorded each examination, so that he could enjoy at leisure the beauty of the female form. Among this collection of photographs were several of his niece, Elena Papoulias, in various positions.

Now that Elena was famous, and more than famous, these pictures had market value: though the doctor put it to himself in another way. *Scientific* value. Decorating his reminiscences – or perhaps a booklet of sexual advice to young ladies – these pictures could only increase his fame.

He made a deal with a publisher, who made a deal with a top-circulation glossy magazine, which published six studies of Elena naked. In no time, these pictures of a pretty girl, in the first flush of puberty, travelled across the world, leaping from country to country, bookstall to bookstall, cover to cover.

Meanwhile, the relationship between Elizabeth and Sophia was changing. They had become close, developing a connoisseur's fondness for cream cakes. Sophia no longer patronized; if anything, she fawned. Elizabeth and her daughter were now installed more comfortably in the hospital, for observation and gynaecological studies. Every morning, Elizabeth sallied forth with her sister; they went looking for a discreet property for Elizabeth to buy. Since Elizabeth had received a phone call from Costas, she considered it a matter of urgency to find a place in which she could hide from her husband.

Sophia agreed that no voices in the head should distract her from the quest; besides, looking at houses was fun.

The sisters met as usual in Omonia one morning, lingering over a plate of cakes, before catching a taxi to investigate a house for sale in one of the outer suburbs.

'I shall have to have a guard dog,' said Elizabeth.

'You can afford two, dear,' said Sophia. 'Big brutes with bad tempers.' She had never liked Costas. But she was downcast this morning, as they rolled across the congested city, and felt forced to reveal to Elizabeth that she had some bad news. So saying, she drew from her bag a folded copy of the Greek edition of *Elle Même*. She unveiled to her sister the nude pictures of Elena, photographed by Constandine.

Elizabeth broke down and wept at the shame of it. 'Woe! Woe! What's life worth if relations can do such things to me? It's a disgrace to the family! Such naughty pictures!'

'And Costas may see them,' Sophia blubbered. 'I'll divorce that wretch Constandine, see if I don't.'

The taxi driver looked round to ask what the trouble was. Tears in her eyes, Sophia told him. The driver pulled over to the kerb. Infected by Elizabeth's misery, both Sophia and the driver joined in the general weeping. The latter seized *Elle Même* and gazed at the pictures through his tears.

'Lovely,' he said. 'What pretty tits!' and burst out crying afresh.

When they had all dried their eyes, they proceeded to the smart suburb. The driver stopped at a little kiosk to ask for final directions.

The two women sat in the car. They saw the driver rapt in earnest conversation with the old lady inside the kiosk. Growing impatient, Sophia tapped on the taxi window.

He returned to his car pulling a long face.

'Well then! Where is this street? Didn't the old bitch know?' snapped Sophia. 'Ask someone else, can't you?'

The driver leant in at the window, supporting himself rather in the manner of one who feels he is about to faint.

'I've got two cousins out in Sydney,' he said. 'The kiosk woman says Australia has disappeared. Just disappeared off the face of the globe . . .'

Elizabeth screamed. She knew what it meant. Something bad had happened to her youngest daughter.

That morning, Elena had been feeling content. One of their neighbours from their village had brought Yannis over in his cage, and the little bird was singing happily as if glad to be back in Elena's company. There were also affectionate notes from her sisters, with a rude drawing of her history teacher.

Elena and Elizabeth had been moved into a penthouse still smelling slightly of fresh paint, on the top of the hospital building. Neither of them had ever seen such a smart place before. There was even a jacuzzi and a neat little roof garden, while the glass doors of the luxurious lounge looked out over the flat roofs of Athens to the distant Acropolis. The lounge featured a crystal chandelier and a huge TV set with shutters. All this was paid for by the government, who wanted to keep an eye on Elena. She was no longer allowed to go out of the hospital alone.

Her contentment was increased by the news that her sisters were all coming to stay for the Christmas holiday. Certainly there was plenty of room for them – although Elena now had a bedroom of her own.

In order to surprise her sisters, Elena sent out the duty guard to buy an electronic snorting fluffy pig for Persephone, a new electronic sword-and-sorcery game for Artemis, and an electronic clock which spoke the time for Rea. The State would settle the bill.

Despite the lateness of the year, the day was mild. Elena had the patio doors open on to the roof, and was trotting about barefoot on the thick pile carpet. She was singing to Yannis when she turned and found someone entering the doors.

She saw immediately it was the uncombed youth who had been following her for some while.

'Don't be frightened,' he said, coming rapidly towards her. 'I'm not going to hurt you. Saw the pictures of you!' He gave a nasty laugh.

It was as bad an opening to a conversation as she had ever heard.

She ran for the broom, but he caught her and seized her wrists. Next moment, she found herself on the carpet, and the uncombed one on top of her, breathing his hot breath in her face.

It was not only Australia. Half of New Zealand was gnawed away, together with New Guinea and sundry Pacific islands. The Southern Cross disappeared at the same time. What remained instead was an uncreated space which no one could enter and no instruments detect. Engineers soon discovered that the value of p was looking a little shaky, while various shades of red vanished for ever, everywhere; Santa Claus wore grey. Even more disturbing for the general public was the way in which two seconds were found to have seeped away from every minute. Many people felt their lives had been shortened in consequence.

As a result of these disturbances in what had hitherto been regarded as the natural order, chaos overwhelmed civilization. Various wars had to be cancelled. No one would fly in case the Earth disappeared from below them. Nothing could be manufactured because measurements and timings were vitally distorted. Even transport virtually ground to a halt when red lights disappeared and wheels ceased to be as round as formerly. Not a clock over the whole globe could be persuaded to tell the correct time.

And it was all because a delinquent youth from Crete had tried to rape precious little Elena Papoulias. The Houdris Hypothesis was largely conventional wisdom by now; Elena's sleeping god had almost been wakened by the attempted rape. Rousing, he had lost a part of the thread of his dream, causing Australia to etc etc . . .

How fortunate it was that the chandelier in Elena's luxurious lounge had fallen from the ceiling when it did, stunning the combless youth, so that he could be arrested before real harm was done. Thus, the universe was saved to continue its precarious existence.

Demands immediately arose from the UN, from NATO, and from the FBI that Elena should be placed under their care and guarded more effectively. The President of Turkey even went so far as to suggest that Elena should be kept perpetually under anaesthesia in order to ensure the god's restful sleep. No more of these irresponsible Greek shocks to Elena's system could be permitted.

The Greek government was mortified by all such suggestions. They decided to have a lock put on Elena's patio doors, after some delay.

Fears were expressed that the god might be born on Christmas Day. He would then awaken and that would be the end of everything. However, the hospital gynaecologists and other experts brought in from outside denied this would happen. Elena's was definitely no ordinary pregnancy.

Despite these reassurances, by Christmas Eve millions of people all round what remained of the world were decidedly anxious.

'One good thing,' said Elizabeth. 'If Australia has disappeared, Costas has probably disappeared with it.'

She had found a house she liked. She was standing in its bare rooms with her sister Sophia and Constandine (with whom she was still hardly on speaking terms following his sale of the photographs) and Elena and her three other daughters. Everyone was well wrapped. It was cold, cold for Athens. Four-thirty on the afternoon of Christmas Eve, and their platoon of guards had been allowed to nip off to do some shopping.

Persephone, Artemis and Rea were wearing smart new coats bought by their mother that very morning. They gathered protectively round their youngest sister, shielding her from her wicked uncle. Dr Houdris wore dark glasses for the occasion, and kept quiet at first.

Sophia was gushing about the virtues of the house. 'So nice and near the shops!' Her husband agreed and tugged his moustache uncomfortably. 'Very good taste.' The girls were nodding, smiling, agreeing – all except Elena who just stood there in a golden daze, holding her stomach.

Elena exclaimed, in the middle of all the congratulations, 'But we can't see the sea from this house.'

In Elizabeth's mind, it was as if a dark cloud obscured the Sun. She perceived that Sophia and her husband were merely buttering her up, that the girls were miserable and smiling only out of politeness, that Elena felt herself to be in a prison. Immediately, Elizabeth also felt herself imprisoned. One of her old dark moods came upon her. She felt she was worth nothing and could do nothing right.

'The government is paying for everything,' she said glumly. 'It can't pay for the sea.'

'It could pay for a house by the sea,' the doctor pointed out. Grinning at Elena, who immediately hid behind her sisters, he added, 'If that's what Elena wants, then that's what she should have.'

'Oh, life is so difficult!' Elizabeth exclaimed. 'Why is it so difficult? Why don't you all go away and leave me?

'Lizzie, dear,' said Sophia, taking her arm. 'I thought you'd grown out of these fits. We'll leave if you like, but remember that the only important thing is that Elena should be content – for the sake of the whole world.'

'The world! What's the world ever cared about me? Why should I care about it? Look how fat I've got . . .'

'You are a bit fat, Mummy dear,' agreed Persephone.

'Perhaps you're pregnant again, Mummy dear,' suggested Artemis.

'At least you're not as fat as Auntie, Mummy dear,' Rea told her.

They all began to shuffle uncertainly towards the door, leaving Elizabeth standing, a pillar of gloom, in the middle of the empty space. Houdris decided to give his sister-in-law a short lecture, if only to restore his own standing in his wife's eyes.

'You must raise your sights a bit, Lizzie. Think of your position. You have power and influence now and should use them.'

'So Aphaia told me,' Elizabeth muttered to herself.

'Well then, take my advice, don't buy this hen-coop. Buy yourself a palace. Soak the government, the way it's always soaked us. Order a yacht. Live decently while you've got the chance.' He knew Elizabeth would understand the real meaning of what he said: Stop being such a peasant.

She flew into a rage and drove them all out of the house, calling Elena back only at the last moment.

'A fine way to behave to her nearest and dearest,' exclaimed Sophia as she shuffled down the garden path, nose in air. 'Particularly at Christmas. Her and her rude daughters!'

Mother and daughter stood confronting each other with only the faded wallpaper of the unsold room for company. Elena dropped her gaze, remorseful that she had upset her mother. She held her stomach protectively.

'I'm stuck with you, Elena, aren't I? And you're stuck with me. I suppose that that god is going to be sleeping inside you all your life, long after I'm dead. Why do the gods trespass in our affairs, damn them?'

'They started up the world, after all, Mum. Just imagine a world started up by *humans*! That would be in an even worse pickle, I'm sure.'

Elizabeth felt in her shoulder bag and brought out a sharp kitchen knife. 'I've carried this about with me for some days,' she said. 'It's for a certain purpose.' The smile she gave was not a real smile. She told Elena for the first time that her father was a criminal, insisting on what a wicked man he was. She knew Costas had escaped from prison; Father Nikolaos had told her so, and Costas had confirmed it over the phone. When she heard that Australia was destroyed, she rejoiced – rejoiced! – because she hoped he had also been destroyed.

'Oh no, Mother. Daddy had already left Australia. He's in Athens. I saw him once, I'm sure of it. He's following us about. He wants to join us for Christmas. I want him to join us for Christmas.'

'Never! I'll kill him if I set eyes on him again. He's only after you for the money.' She brandished the knife.

Elena shook a finger at her mother. 'You must do what I say, mustn't you? I need my father, whatever he's done wrong. You and he will have to get together again. If you upset me, the universe will end. Don't forget that.'

'Let it end! Let it! I need a change!' She remembered that the ghost of Aphaia had claimed that she could create a new world if she tried. The thought entered Elizabeth's mind that it would be an advantage if the universe did end. She saw it as full of her misery, packed with everyday difficulties. She could get her own back on Sophia, on Constandine, on her husband, and most of all on Elena, whose fault it was that their old peaceful life had been stolen away. Everyone else might be keen for the universe to continue, from the professors and the P.M. to the taxi driver; she wished it to stop. All she had to do was plunge the knife into Elena's belly. Then the whole human drama would be over.

She remained stock still, wild-eyed, knife in hand. Terrified, Elena felt something move within her. The universe started its contractions.

When Sophia marched out of the house, she had left the front door open. Without listening, Elizabeth had heard the car drive away.

Now there was a new figure at the door. Elizabeth did not immediately recognize him. He was tanned, and had grown a beard, grizzled with thick strands of white among the black. He looked bigger and sturdier than she remembered. He was smiling in an amiable, rather puzzled way, as he hesitated on the threshold, removing what she knew to be an Australian bush hat.

'What are you doing here exactly, Lizzie?' he asked.

She remembered the voice, still slightly teasing as of old. Dropping her knife, she went across the floor to him. To her astonishment, she found she was overjoyed to be enfolded in his arms.

It was just then that Elena went into labour.

A flash of gold, and a terrible golden darkness . . . All that remained was the embracing pair, standing on a bare floor, bathed in eternal sunlight.

The couple were starting everything anew. Obscurity hedged in their little realm of light. But so it had always been.

Ferdinand is not the only one who made a long and perilous sea journey in search of love. A part of our family history has a similar theme.

My maternal grandmother's name was Ream. The Reams were of old Huguenot stock; they'd come from Rheims in France and settled in the fenlands as farmers.

My grandmother's family was a large one; a branch of the family lived in Wisbech, on the Wash. Last century and into this one, Wisbech was renowned as a port. I was taken to visit one of the Ream houses as a small boy, and remember it clearly. Since the area was liable to floods, the gaunt old stone houses were built with their front doors a yard or so above ground level; stone steps led up to a little railed stone platform from which you entered the house

Elizabeth Ream was scrubbing those steps early in the 1880s when along came a young man with a kitbag over his shoulder. Elizabeth was eighteen, the youngest and prettiest of three daughters. The young man was on his way to a ship moored a short distance away. He stopped, gazed up at Elizabeth on her step, and said, 'I shall be back here in three years' time. I shall then come and knock at your door and ask you to marry me. Wait for me.'

When Elizabeth rushed indoors and told her mother and sisters what the sailor had said, they laughed and teased her, but soon forgot the incident.

The North European climate had taken a turn for the worse at the end of the 1870s. Harvests failed, Britain's agriculture declined. This was a time for many emigrations of farmworkers and others to North America. Young Henry Liversedge was one such emigrant.

Three years later, almost to the day, there came a knock at the Ream door, and the maid showed Henry Liversedge into the drawing-room. He had returned as promised to ask for the hand of Elizabeth Ream in marriage.

They were duly married in the Wisbech Methodist Chapel. Henry was soon to return once again to Canada, where he farmed. Sailing from Wisbech, he took his bride with him. A tough journey it must have been, crossing the Atlantic, sailing up the St Lawrence, passing through the Great Lakes, finally arriving at a remote wheat farm on the banks of the Red River spilling into Lake Winnipeg. It took months.

But as the boat drew in to the jetty, there on the bank a horse and trap was awaiting them – and in the driver's seat sat Al Liversedge, Henry's older brother.

Al was unmarried. He, Henry and Elizabeth lived together in their ranch house and farmed vast fields of wheat with teams of horses. And the moment Elizabeth set eyes on Al, she fell in love with him. The intensity of her passion brought a realization that she had never really loved Henry. By a thousand glances, she must have known that Al responded to her. But Elizabeth was a well-brought-up, church-going young lady. In the manner of those God-fearing times, nothing was done, nothing was said – though you may imagine the atmosphere must have been pretty tense at times. With the oil-lamps and the darning and the readings from Isaiah and the great night oceans of wheat, how did they breathe each other's evening air without declaring themselves?

Within a year of Elizabeth's arrival in Canada, a terrible storm sprang up, sweeping across the prairies. Henry went out with a lantern to see to the horses. But the river broke its banks. He was swept away and drowned.

After a due period of mourning, Elizabeth married Al. She bore him six children and, as far as we know, they lived happily ever after.

Humans are a restless species. I suppose most of us here have travelled thousands of miles and no longer live where we were born.

But some living things remain for ever imprisoned. To be motionless is a terrible punishment; which is why criminals are locked into cells.

How we might exist in infinite space and time is another question.

Evans in His Moment of Glory

Prelude: The Penultimate Syllable of Recorded Time

Rain hammered down in hobnails on the city street, rain drummed down in decibels on the roof of our sedan. I turned slowly into the East Thirties, looking for the green-striped awning that marked our friends' apartment block where Tiffany and I were due to dine. Tiffany sat beside me, rather subdued.

Cars were parked along the street. No vehicle moved. A late and lousy Sunday afternoon. Nothing stirred but the new brooklets lapping sidewalks.

I knew Tiffany didn't want this outing; she'd rather have curled up back home, and shut out the ugly weather, to watch *Playing for Time* and *My New Writings in '74* on video. Having seen Estar Winter's two magisterial movies several times, we knew them by heart and other ancillary organs. At that moment I too began to regret the expedition. A heaviness seized me. Later, I accounted it premonition.

The wipers raced. I slowed. Then the action started.

A man burst out of a doorway into the road. He appeared to be wearing pyjamas. Rain slashed eagerly into the fabric. Two men ran out after him, one brandishing a gun. Small, squat, dressed in black, wearing caps with peaks set backwards. They caught up with the first guy. One of them slammed him across the back of the neck with a beefily swung sub-machine gun. The pyjamaed one went down, face first into the dark flood of the street.

We were still drawing near. I slowed further. The two thugs had not yet seen our car.

They began to beat shit out of the first guy.

'Oh, Josh!' Tiffany cried. She seized my arm in horror.

What do you do? I accelerated towards the men, aiming to scare the thugs off, maybe help the guy who was down. If you can, always help the guy who's down. My simple Christian principle.

The first thug straightened and saw us coming on. All in a swift movement he braced himself, brought up the gun and triggered a stream of lead straight at us, slam through the windshield. Everything went berserk amid noises of destruction. Intellect annihilated in fear.

I dragged the wheel over to the right. Tiffany was hit first. Then me. Her mortal beauty erupted into fumaroles. No sooner was she disintegrating over me like flung jello than I too was throwing up my hands as the hail of fire knocked me back, bits at a time.

My last agonised cry:

TIFF–

I. The Long Sidereal Farewell

Oh, the confusion, the hustle and bustle in the porch! I gave my name, 'Joshua Evans,' gave it so that it was gone, and with it a part of my identity.

And then through into a vast concourse, thronging with people. It was measureless and I thought, Well, they pay no ground rates here. They can afford to be big. Despite irony, the general rather Hollywoodish effect was impressive. Like being trapped in a celestial chocolate box.

And in the throng, I somehow lost touch with Tiffany. I had let go of her hand. Tiffany, never leave me, though the heavens fall!

The press of people carried me forward, towards the grand central stairway. Unable to help myself, for there was some confusion, I found myself ascending on the moving stair. Where everything was so strange, there was something teasingly familiar about this escalator, the top of which was lost in infinity. The steps of the escalator were colour-coded in some nine hundred shades, all of which I memorized.

New kinds of intelligence possessed me, so that I knew why I had never really known Josh Evans. All about us was singing of an austerely beautiful kind, love without passion, emotion without egotism. *The music draws them across the grass.* And an attendant angel, bright as a macaw, fluttered at my shoulder, at my very soul. But I was without Tiffany.

Let me shed my name – but not you! Just one glance more, my Tiffany, from those dear green eyes, one glance more! To know that the end was not the end, for you, for me . . . However faint our belief, it has been the thread that has drawn us through. See me, accompany me, through this powerful Kingdom. How many years is it by ordinary universe-time that we have known and loved each other? Yet still I gasp to have you with me, in this wondrous state to go by my side . . .

My prayer was immediately answered, in part at least. Looking down from the steep ascent, I sighted her among the multitude. She still wore the dove-grey suit she had been wearing in the car. She had turned away from the main throng and was examining some musical instruments displayed there. From a rack, she lifted down some flutes; I saw them light one by one, responding to her mood of astonished calm, viridian, amber and rose.

And the wings of the angel, crusty about her unspoilt hair.

Did I call? Perhaps so. But she merely lifted an instrument to her lips, permitting a note of purest indigo to escape.

My angel was consoling me, telling me into my unlistening ear that this was no parting. Yet a faint persistent worry taxed me. I was unable to chase the worry to its lair, for the person beside me on the ascending scale was talking meanwhile, talking excitedly, pleasantly, knowledgeably, abundantly, about his job. To put matters baldly, his name was – had been – Rudy Rudenture, but of course it was presented to me otherwise. All was Otherwise. Otherwise was all.

'. . . searching for six years. I have been seconded onto a committee whose function is to obtain supplementary funding for our various laboratories. Of course, the National Centre for Genome Research has been reliable, but what has been unprecedented in our research is the sheer . . .'

Rudy Rudenture – perhaps it was my angel making the matter clear, by word or signal – was he who had passed away seconds before us, face down in the oily half-inch downpour of the East Thirties. His seniority to Tiffany and me amounted to those few seconds only. He was – but here he wasn't – in his mid-forties; not corporeal, of course, but we newcomers were still permitted first sight as we rose to a higher plane. Beside us, fifty victims of a Balkan massacre, lifting their hands for joy. Most had been women and children down in the Forelife.

> The music draws them across the grass
> The music of eternal light

The music, as music often is, was self-referential, heralding us to the second stage. Ranked to either side of the escalator, immobile, stood busts of the virtuous, those who had offered to others a glimpse of something beyond the illusions of the material world: Socrates, Aristophanes – he of Cloud-cuckoo-land – Orpheus, Offenbach, Averroes of Cordoba, and a swarm more. Gazing down between them while we continued to rise, and Rudenture continued to unfold his streamer of monologue, I could still see Tiffany, unwrapping festoons of colour, entranced. If only she would look upwards, we might still read each other's expressions – our old favoured grin-and-nod routine – and then all would be well about the heart, or where the heart had been.

How characteristic was her stance! She stood with her weight mainly on one slender leg, the other leg slightly bent to enable its well-shod toes to curl behind the supportive heel. The graceful posture always suggested flight, as if Tiffany were a lighter-than-air machine. In my dreams she made her appearances as a bird with speckled plumage and a cream breast – even before I was on easy terms with that breast. Ah, we're all concepts as well as bodies to each other, *down . . . below*, in the Forelife.

To live is so utterly precious: which is why it costs us so dear. But that was what Rudy Rudenture was talking about. '. . . of course, long before the age of modern medicine, and throughout the centuries, cures for old age, for ageing, have been propounded. The promise of immortality has always attracted customers. Nevertheless, our funding difficulties originated in the fact that we were searching the DNA structure in stretches remote from known disease, such as . . .'

The third stage, to which our heads now presented themselves as rising suns, was bathed in orange glow. I was not sure I cared for it – always some tiny unexpected discomfort – or the things it did for Rudenture's complexion. The angel at my shoulder was explaining all away, soothing me, massaging an area now blossoming within me, making me happy, coaxing me towards what is wordless.

It was not that misery was forbidden, more that it was impossible to catch and hold, like stability down below. We had to rise still higher, through other stages, before all our human characteristics would be washed away. Rudenture, for instance, still demanded something from me, if only my attention. About him was a kind of moral hunger, though in telling all he concealed himself. Every human exchange (I understood it now) was a kind of energy-pump operation, with a vital flux transferred from one consciousness to another. Always there was heat-loss, until eventually, somehow or other, the overworked system died and another consciousness was extinguished. Another generation of pumps was always ready. Somewhere above us was the maker of all pumps.

This the victims of the Balkan massacre appreciated better than we. They had died for their faith. The angelic beak assured me that the Balkan hell was but a whisper away from Glory . . .

It was all going to be explained, whispered the plumaged being. And all my errors would be made clear. Made clear? I asked. Clear to whom? *Clarified*, the angel said.

Clarified? Meaning made easy to understand? Or am I to be made free of impurities? Or do you mean (here I felt a faint jangle of alarm) made clear by a process of *heating*?

We ascend to regions beyond semantics, said the tiny voice, its sibilants a rustle of wings.

Jesus! I said.

Yes, it said.

With a little contrivance, I managed to stand on the moving stair in such a way that I appeared to listen to both Rudenture and angel, turning my head sideways and stroking my chin as if rapt in the profound considerations their talk aroused. All the while, I stared down, down at tiny Tiffany. Tommaso Campanella drifted past. There she was, moving on to the harps, foreshortened yet still distinct. What had caused her to linger on the threshold, unable to ascend? When I tried to think back to the moments of terror in the car, the details had already become fogged, eroded according to a great plan. Music alone entered my memory.

> The music draws them, draws them,
> Music melds the mowers and the mown

She continued not to look up. There again, for all the angel said, cause for unease. By mundane-universe-time, she was already over a parsec away. A slight redness about her made me think she was in a Doppler shift. To the millions of newly-released thronging about here, in their turn ascending the escalator, I paid no heed. She had been and was the only one for me.

As the distance grew between that beloved figure and what passes for me, the press of humanity also increased. At every stage, more souls flooded onto the escalator, which widened all the while it rose; no terrestrial engineer could imagine such a structure. Here I witnessed the obverse of the population explosion: the cemetery, not the womb, was gateway to giganumbers.

Some of those near me kept up a flow of conversation which seemed scarcely appropriate in the august surroundings.

'There's no doubt that an improved genome structure can be made to convey many more useful human characteristics. *Here*, for obvious reasons, they're working on a Faith gene. In order for it to be easily inheritable they . . .'

'. . . in Schiller's company. We strolled through over a thousand variants of Frankfurt-am-Main in the course of the afternoon. One of them in the desert particularly attracted us, and Schiller at once threw off his cloak and . . .'

'He said that the sound of the ambulance was the last thing he heard. But she was dead when the medics arrived, and they'd only had a tiff. Of course, he blames himself but my sister says . . .'

'I didn't mind the immobility. It was the pain I couldn't stand. The lack of pain when you're put on *veruchikheit* is also hard to take . . .'

'Oh yes, he was holding forth as usual. You know Voltaire. He told me it was absurd to wear a wig in the Afterlife. Still and all, he continued to do so, he said, because he believed more firmly in the Absurd than in the Deity . . .'

'With a pizza? You must be joking . . .'

Humanity's a hard cocoon to shed.

All this while, Rudy Rudenture kept up his exposition of how they researched immortality. They had found a kind of 'genetic stammer', as he called it, near a repeating nucleotide triplet A-G-C, and thereabouts his technicians were preparing to insert a designer gene that would increase human lifespans by a factor of ten, hopefully.

I had hardly said a word to this man whose life I had once, long ago, attempted to save. Now I ventured a mild protest.

'Do you imagine that anyone currently enduring the painful condition of life would wish to protract it if they knew of this bliss to come?'

Sorry, sorry, chirped our angels in unison. This trip lasts only the teeniest of eternities, then we'll come to the Greater Glory. You'll like that. Everyone likes the Greater Glory.

We passed by the third stage, the fourth, the fifth. The great stairway grew ever wider, the crowds denser. I had to keep shifting my position to remain looking over the edge. The concourse was misty with distance now. Music obscured it, hosannas hid it. Tiffany shone like a distant star. The star fluttered as if with nervous movement. Was there pain somewhere? Steepening perspective carried its own alarm. In her dreams, she had often found herself trapped, struggling to escape the Forelife.

Arise and come to me, my love. Remember how we swore Death should not part us. Look up before it grows too late!

No, no, don't use that naughty word beginning with D here, the macaw chided, its infant lips pouting like a rose-red beak.

I feel its sting.

No, no, not possible. All is eternally well here – and will be improved!

The sixth stage, the seventh. Other souls from other universes joined us, other believers in other shapes. Man was no longer the measure of all things. Young prehensile girls of transparent cast; old bounders of men like boulders, steaming; replicants; reptilians; late reprobates; spirals of neotenous spermatazoa. A drunkard talked about drunkenness as a blessed state, where daylight flickered past like sun squirting molasses over a maze of burnished bottles.

'Early results indicate that cognition will not be affected over the centuries, though there may be some physical impairment. Until more disease genes have been mapped to specific chromosomes . . .'

Tiffany, I know you were too young to die. But now we enter a new phase of being. Sometimes you used to hold yourself apart, to withdraw. I accepted that character trait. But all that has gone, you understand? Answer my telepathic call.

Only look up, my dearest, that I may still gaze upon the dear blur of thy face. Dost thou not see how far I'm being carried, away, away? A fig for Glory!

During all this teeny eternity, transformation had been taking place, to be felt in what had once been the bones. The escalator itself changed direction and speed. We who rode there were but sparks in the tail of a comet. We were elongating. Even Rudy Rudenture's exposition of the future joys of immortality died away in wonder, as his nose lengthened into a snout and our angels became our flaming hair. Oh, the elation, as scents of laurel and emascupam surrounded us. Flares of dopplabundance almost hid us from each other, from our selves!

The stages continued, their numbers flickering by. Music too mounted, propelling us like a sound of revving motors.

Grass is burning, grass is burning, we're all coming, come to Glory . . .

Oh yes, it was insane. Or would have been, had brain been involved.

Looking dizzily down, I found the lower regions no longer discernible. The pillars that supported us writhed like snakes of a higher topology. And my love had dissolved in the Uncertainty Effect.

II. Redesigning Creation From the Bottom

The moving scene clenched in its dynamic fist souls like locusts, teeming, teeming, as I recalled rain once cascaded down elsewhere. I who had feared to be in a crowd found myself rejoicing, and joining, as the air rushed from my body, in an ecstatic 'OM' issuing from the myriads.

Now we were free, bursting up towards the sun. The greater glory.

Yet it was not like that. It could not be like what it was if I could translate it in any way into words. Words were another currency we had left behind. 'Character' also had been shed – yet identity remained. There was no speech, yet voices were heard among us. No emotion, yet joy overwhelmed us. Time – you felt the liberty of it – had been vanquished.

We settled in an area limitless in extent. Somewhere in the infinite above us, a bell spoke like a language, emphasizing its cadences with clarinets. It told of the eternal calm that we believers had reached: and also of CHANGE.

When I conveyed to my angel my transcendent happiness, it responded in shocking fashion. *You should have been here in the old days.*

The statement was a chilly draught. Alert to my shiver, it stated that the numbers of believers were dropping considerably. Next door – what can I do but reinterpret his heavenly gloom in banal language? – *next door*, the Muslim Paradise was *doing better business*. There was – or there may have been – to my confused mind – some talk actually about introducing a system of taxation here. Nothing much, of course. Something everyone would be comfortable with. Perhaps a sort of Sanctity Tax, so many sins so much, so many more sins so much, et cetera, et cetera. This told in an amused way, wings a-flutter.

Perhaps just a temporary tax, till things improved . . .

I was charmed by the idea.

Immediately, Tiffany was lying beside me, silent, experiencing the eternal calm. Rather grey in her dove-grey suit.

So now there's a move – said the angel, encouraged, blowing warm imagery into my mind – to redesign Creation. Redesign it from the bottom up. And you're each going to be given an assignment to assist in the grand design. Isn't that wonderful? The Creator himself is taking advice from his creations. Wonderful, isn't it? Truly wonderful?

Mutely, I assented. It was too wonderful for words. For harp music.

Schopenhauer passed us, laughing, hand-in-hand with Wittgenstein, and each of astronomic size.

'I'm hoping to get an immortality assignment,' Rudenture said. It was no longer possible to say how long he was, or what he resembled.

When I shook Tiffany to tell her the news, her eyes opened and filled with far luminescences. Will we be in time? she wanted to know.

We're out of it for ever, I told her.

As we gazed at each other, we were nearing the throne.

The greater Glory was nigh.

III. The Cultures of the Unyoked Ego

Immensity became the Dream Department, appropriately lit by mock-moonlight. In the vast storehouse of dreams, what was impossible rapidly became the Accepted, just as the hell of big city life becomes the custom of its inhabitants.

> One thought, one grace, one wonder at the least
> Burns like a glow-worm in the darkling skull

Delighted though I was by the concept of Change, Tiffany considered that the idea of putting the Afterlife on a business footing was somehow – what was her expression? – philistine and cheapening. However, her angel, fluttering quills as a cardsharp shuffles his deck, persuaded her that the Afterlife was merely catching up with the Forelife.

Both her angel and mine, with identical squarks, pointed out that the establishment of life on a financial basis had been humanity's idea, not the Creator's. The Creator preferred fiction to the cash nexus, hence his proliferation of galaxies and plots.

Furthermore, said our attendant beauties, the Afterlife should be considered as grand Theatre; so it was reasonable to charge for a seat to watch the play.

I was enjoying the Foreplay, said Tiffany, but this sort of remark we were slowly leaving behind. So we perforce joined in the noble scheme of redesigning Creation, and creating by-passes through the neural maze.

Since Tiffany had been a foremost biotechnologist in – wherever it was, she was permitted into a special department of the Celestial Planning Office. As a civil engineer involved in urban restructure, I too was welcome. We scarcely bothered to say farewell to Rudy Rudenture as we lightyeared to our new posts; no one was apart: togetherness twinkled here like a false eye.

The Dream Department welcomed us. Our busy little angels explained in glorious biotechnicolor that a new Creation was being planned, in which dominant brains would function better than had been the case in the universe from which we came. It was considered proper that brains should contain rational and irrational components (or else where would Faith lodge?); but in the proposed new dispensation the components would be clearly differentiated, so that people would know when they were thinking constructively and when fantasizing – which was not the case under present dispensations.

Violence will be scaled down. Other departments are considering the serotonin situation.

Schopenhauer had left a scribbled note pinned to a vat of dreams: 'Why throw good DNA after bad? Bully off again with a better species.' To which Wittgenstein had appended a typically opaque postscript, 'What can't won't.'

An august being whose height I was unable to estimate showed us to a level labelled as 30 Quail Crashnikov. Here it seemed the motto read: '*Anfang Macht Arbeit* – In the Beginning was the Work'. Certainly the scene was one of intense industry, not least in the editorial repair department. The Afterlife had learnt from the Forelife the depressive effects of unemployment.

As a preliminary exercise, the august being consigned Tiffany and me to classifying all the dreams ever dreamed by occupants of the planet Earth.

'But why do you keep all these strange old fantastifications? What use are they?'

Thus Tiffany to the being. To my developing inner vision, she appeared to me in only approximately human guise – she more resembled a sunlit beach, hovering between sea and shore – but minute, robed, and with her flaxen hair streaming out to circle far above her in a spiral nebula of beauty, glittering as if lit by scalpels.

Being: 'Nothing is of ultimate use. Even our great Creator has said of himself that he is a Fiction, existing only to be *enjoyed*.'

Tiffany: 'So dreams are also creations to be enjoyed?'

Being: 'Are dreams not vital lubricants of the life-engine? They proliferate through the system when the ego is off-line. Once we have them classified, they can be analysed. Such analysis will provide us with indications of how brains can be profitably restructured in the universe-future – *pace* jokers like Schopenhauer.'

Tiffany: 'But these old sequences of sleep, these images that teased out so many bad nights – wherein we were confessedly deceived, as someone once memorably put it – they were all evanescent as dew . . .'

Being: 'A Creator who is Fictional conserves Truth, however strange, however cleverly it comes camouflaged as Lies. Things may fade in the Forelife. Here, *here*, everything is conserved: the fall of a sparrow, the sprawl of a furrow, the spawn of a furlough.'

Tiffany: 'So transience is extinct in Eternity?'

Being: 'Speak not of extinction. Look after the Intimates and the Ultimates will take care of themselves.'

So we two set to.

IV. The Horse Latitudes

How could anyone possibly convey the diversity of the task before us? These uncounted dreams covered all phyla from the beginning of universe-time into what we once thought of as 'the future': not merely human and superhuman but mammal, reptile, insect (the faintest smudge of gnat-vision).

Confronting our tremendous task, I told Tiffany that we might come upon her old dreams. 'How I'd like to experience them – even your baby dreams, hatched when you were in diapers, your adolescent dreams, dyed when you were in hatchbacks . . .'

Among the maze of materials, buzzing like bluebottles against a windowpane of unconsciousness, let's free just one.

A heavily built carthorse was pulling a cart along a city street in some unknown decade. The animal was a mare, grey with a white blaze on her forehead. The carriage was an ancient heavy affair, loaded perhaps with coal or black ice – the details were indistinct; perhaps it was some kind of a hearse.

When the mare reached a street corner by a butcher's shop, she went mad, rearing up on her hind legs and fighting savagely, tossing her head this way and that. Finally, she broke free of the shafts and stood there shaking herself, her harness hanging like fetters about her flanks. Rain poured down.

A crowd gathered from nowhere, leaden in movement. All were squat and wore lumpy garments, topped with crude headgear. They had watched the struggle dispassionately, and looked on, still unperturbed, as the hideous mass of the carriage ran into a building and collapsed.

A man detached himself from the crowd, strutted forward golem-like, and flung himself at the mare.

The mare seemed to grow, to expand. The man attached himself to her chest like a grotesque parasite. She threw up her head and showed large yellow teeth, snapping them down to bite at her assailant.

Crablike aspects of the man were reinforced by his two pairs of arms. His body was broad enough to support these extra limbs. He was dressed in a shiny black plastic suit and wore a black buttoned cap. He stood out like a melanoma on the hide of the mare. The crowd now faded away, leaving man and horse in mortal combat, alone in the streaming street.

After rearing ineffectually, the mare threw herself crashing down to the ground. She rolled violently about, attempting to crush her attacker, as men crush beetles underfoot. But the black figure was tremendously fast, fast as a cockroach, and scuttled about the rolling mammal anatomy. His extra arms gave him extra purchase, enabling him to avoid fatal injury.

How they both fought, man and animal! Scrambling up again, the mare reared high in the air, lashing out with her hooves. The black-clad assailant clamped three arms about her neck. He was attempting to throttle her. I saw livid madness in his face, his bulging eyes, his teeth of a size with the mare's. Veins stood out on neck and forehead like strands of purple ivy.

A mist burst from them. The animal hurled herself against the side of a building. The unexpected move dislodged the man. He fell flat on his back upon the sidewalk. She reared and plunged down on him, but at the last second the man rolled to safety, jumped up and kicked her violently on the shanks. She kicked back, and nipped his shoulder with her teeth, but he was on her, grasping her again, clinging to her belly and then, reaching out for her flaring mane, dragging himself on to her back. Plunge as she might, he punched her savagely. A double-fisted punch missed its target and he slipped, almost fell. She bucked back and forth, almost standing on her head. Green spittle flew from her jaws. He was beneath her belly again, biting her. His face emerged, apoplectic, between the mare's heaving thighs, like some ghastly progeny to which she was giving birth. As he crawled inch by inch, he stabbed at her tender parts, clutched handfuls of her tail, until he was astride her again.

The grey mare acknowledged defeat. Trembling all over, she stood head down, tangled mane about her eyes.

He, the black-clad, was not done with her yet. Grasping her with all four hands, groaning aloud, he lifted the great animal, turned her, and threw her down on her back.

In a discontinuity in the dream, the carriage was there, its dark leather seating split and broken. There sat the man, all arms massively folded, glaring ahead. His face was scarlet, his breathing loud and heavy. Beside him sat the grey mare, crumpled up on the seat – her head bowed in shame, her eyes turned upwards above her veil to show yellow eyeballs. The carriage was in a building with a cross on its roof. It progressed forward, heavy as a steamroller.

And this was just an equine dream.

V. Glorious Things of Thee Are Inculcated

It takes a while to tell in words of something that is over in an instant's assault of imagery. Eternity too is like that. What is over in a flash is never done. Total understanding of the universe was accessible to all. Hence its limitations, the paltry hatboxiness of its majesty.

Perhaps for this reason, a host of us was given theology lessons. Tiffany felt herself particularly in need of indoctrination, since she was – or had been – of frugal nature and was worried by such announcements as 'The Essence of All Denial is Superabundance'.

Even in the Afterlife, she found extravagance an expense of spirit.

To our teacher, Gabriel MXXIV she admitted, 'Yes, I do find difficulty getting acclimated. My idea of Heaven was somewhere where there would be less – not so much more. I've always regarded frugality as a higher ideal than prodigality.'

Gabriel MXXIV: 'Christ gave his blood for you.'

'There's blood everywhere.'

'Attend the lesson. Whose service is perfect freedom?'

'Please don't think I'm criticizing, but there's just so *much* of everything here.'

Gabriel MXXIV said kindly, 'Later, you will find that the word "I", and the concept it embodies, will disappear from your converse. That will be freedom.'

Backing Tiffany up, I said, 'To find that every last fleeting image from every last sleeping mind has been preserved – it sure takes some getting used to . . .'

In that tranquil place, that cumulonimbus of content, anything out of the extraordinary was dismaying. Gabriel's countenance seemed to slide as he said, 'Just imagine you're being rushed through town in an ambulance, badly injured. Wouldn't you get a bit interested in the principle of preservation?'

We shrank away from him, almost to pinpoints. 'You take an extreme ex - ex - example,' I managed to say.

When Gabriel had flown off at the end of the lesson, Tiffany and I looked at each other, as far as that was still possible. 'There's a snag about everything here being indestructible: even personalities must linger on for ever, despite what he says about abolishing the "I"s. You can't help wondering what that guy did in the Forelife.' Tiffany.

'At least it looks as if the Creator might improve on personality patterns when he gets his plans together for the next universe. A little less aggression all round would help, say?'

'Without aggressive instincts, no humankind would rise to the top of its particular heap. You'd find yourself ruled by tigers . . .'

'That would not be the case, provided the rest of the heap was also less aggressive.'

Of course argument and dissent was out of place. As we discussed, amelioration presented itself.

A small white bird, as much like a butterfly as a dove, fluttered down and floated round us with leisurely strokes of its wings. When I held out what had once been my hand, it settled on my palm. It opened its beak to chirp. We saw that its throat sprouted like a pink rose.

Tiffany exclaimed at its heavenly beauty. 'It must be somebody's dream we have yet to file.'

'Cross-reference under Aviculture and Horticulture,' suggested my angel, ever-helpful.

As we floated along, fascinated, the bird began laying eggs of a hitherto unknown apricot tint, which we dubbed avicot. It kept up a cheerful sleigh-bell kind of song as it did so. Further to calm us, the whole surrounding space turned a mild teetotal blue. We walked enchanted on transparent cerulean.

Singing along with the white bird, Tiffany lifted it up, to reveal ten little speckled eggs in the palm of my hand. As they rolled away, they rose instead of falling, to orbit about a golden eagle which appeared overhead. From them came forth green things, together with ferns, fans, fire opals, orifices, fishes, ambers, orioles, and other ordinary marvels.

As for the little white bird, it plunged towards the eagle and was at once devoured.

'They really do preserve ancient dreams here,' Tiffany exclaimed. When we began to laugh, myriads took up the sound and comets burned amid her floating hair. One fluffy breast feather nestled there, pale as an unwritten page.

It was impossible to be out of sorts for long in the Infinite.

VI. The Dyeing of the Light

And yet . . .

How can it be explained? Suppose on the most beautiful afternoon you walk in sunlight, admiring the perfection of day, yet all the time you mourn the absence of a dear friend. Suppose the most superb dish of venison is set before you – you, a secret vegetarian? These similes are sacrifices to my suppressed unease.

So we worked in calm. Calm was astonishingly like delirium, so whether aeons passed or simply stacked up like a pile of muffins it was difficult to say. Just to work in that eternal radiance was a delight, tempered only by the alarm of seeing ourselves distort and disintegrate towards the greater glory.

Gabriel MXXIV visited us only occasionally for theology lessons. The moment came or went when he arrived to stand beside us with the usual up-beat fanfares. I perceived that he was less glowing than formerly. His plumage was becoming bedraggled, like that of a cockerel which, left out in a downpour all night, feels too damp to face the dawn. Indeed, Gabriel appeared too depressed to say anything. The very atmosphere about him was stained with the puru-lent mad purple of his melancholy.

Much disconcerted by this, Tiffany I enquired for his health – an absurdity in a place where no such thing as illness existed.

For answer, he caused to form a – I know not what to call it, a complex elaboration falling both upward and downward for parsecs. Amber, burnt umber, bermudan in tone, it resembled a honey-suckle as might be portrayed in the Book of Kells. Elaborate inter-weavings with ecclesiastical undertones unfolded in all directions, each tender exploratory sprout bifurcating and twisting into spirals or fresh elegant fancies, sheltering all manner of imaginary animals.

Yet even as we watched in delight, Gabriel's magnificent happiness-inducer became afflicted. Motes of mildew attacked it as if it were a real plant. While the extremities still pushed outwards, outwards, the centre withered, the heart of it blackened. Something in Gabriel was failing.

Since that was an impossibility even in a Somewhere where all was possible, we uncomfortably dismissed it as an illusion, and con-tinued with our work. We brushed aside the purple dye of sorrow, failing to comprehend.

*   *   *

Our dream classification had so far progressed that we could observe how large a percentage of human dreams centred round courageous defiance of adversity. Even the crippled, the tortured, the imprisoned, the sick, spawned dreams of happiness, freedom and oceanic health. Nightmares of Hell were far fewer than idylls of Heaven.

Our admiration for this noble trait was almost enough to make us wish to rejoin the human race. Yet it was taxing when viewed objectively: why was it – we could not fail to ask ourselves – that hope so often failed to overcome adversity? Finally, though Gabriel was standing by, still struggling to project his elaborate vine, I declared that the project was useless and I had nothing to offer it.

'That isn't so,' Tiffany told me. 'You always have valid points to raise at the planning meetings. You're too modest. Ask anyone.'

At which point a soft voice spoke nearby, saying, 'Forgive the intrusion. I overheard what you said. I am Enny I, so I can perhaps help. We all have something to offer in the great work for the New Creation.'

To detect what Enny I looked like was extremely difficult. We were all travelling at immense speeds to escape the coils of the poisoned honeysuckle, which was entangling itself with the purple stain. He or she appeared to be very narrow longitudinally and to be made of old computer diagrams, fortified here and there by swivelling gun-turrets; but appearances are deceptive.

'I'm working on Personality, Sub Section Z, Tribalism,' Enny I explained as we zoomed. 'Which galaxy are you from? Your bipedality is unusual. Perhaps you'd care to see my current project?'

Personality was impressively large. Quantal accretions of light radiated from it, closely followed by music of a Gregorian type. We shed velocity and entered. To say that Personality was on a vast scale can give no idea of its actual size: it was at once larger than our universe and smaller than the customary atom, yet more actual than either, since the space-time universe is merely a simulacrum. Many of Enny I's friends were clustered here, all Ennys working happily in unison.

There were many with whom it was possible to hold converse.

The famous, having taken on humility, were available for gentle discourse. Bundles of them could be spoken to on any one occasion. Socrates, with his ready wit, was my favourite, while Tiffany spent aeons talking to Mary Queen of Scots, not always about Personality.

A strange woman in the attire of Egyptian queens passed by me, and we held a fragmentary communion. *She was not happy!* I gathered she had been a Russian poet. In melancholy tones, or the heavenly equivalent, she said, 'As shadows pretend to be those who cast them, so we find even here, condemned to eternal bliss, that it is impossible to discern which is the voice and which the echo.'

'But is not this bliss a freedom?'

'Not,' she enunciated, 'where what is not compulsory is forbidden. I had rather been in Hell, where nothing is allowed, being more accustomed to its *mores*.'

'Madam,' I said, shocked and not knowing how to address this personage, 'that H-word is among those things forbidden here, because of its long association with the D-word.'

She gathered her Egyptian garb about her, nodded and passed on, saying,

'Even in the notion of Soul we can distinguish the countenance of Death.'

These remarks disturbed me greatly, though I gave no sign.

It occurred to me that the poet lady with her penetrating vengeful stare was correct: that a kind of entropy dragged us further down, even here, even in the very throne room of Glory. Thanatos stood at our entering: protoplasm was inclined to melt like jello in the everlasting light.

Inspired though I was by this new aspect of the Infinite which Personality presented, I found myself strangely lagging behind Tiffany and Enny. They appeared greatly taken with each other, and were emanating song. As I fell further behind, they were almost eclipsed by light. At my back, the purple dye still spread its dreary shawl. 'Never look back, dearie,' said my angel.

Tiffany looked back and beckoned. Why did I think she appeared haggard? And why was it I could not achieve the lofty contentment I expected of myself?

'You go on,' I called. 'I'll rejoin our team.'

'Do you mind if I accompany Enny? From what he says, Personality is my kind of thing. I don't want you to be lonely.'

'I'll see you . . .' But with the legions of souls pouring through the air in every direction, it was already becoming difficult to see her. Their faces were radiant and pure as spring water, as if they had never known anguish. Rapture and virtue intermingled in wonder.

One thought, one grace, one wonder . . .

Returning to my side, Tiffany took my hand. 'Come along,' she said.

In my happiness at her touch I thought, I can be with her in all Eternity, if she wants me. Of course there is a greater Glory, but this one would suit me fine.

VII. Death to the Monocranial

Enny I and his few million friends had a wonderfully equipped laboratory. Of course, money was no object. Much was unfamiliar to me. I recognized bank on bank of monitor screens, thousands of which were showing absorbing live-action scenes from numbers of stochastically selected planets.

'We're just working on basic emotions, so far,' said Enny, wrapping a protective turret about Tiffany. 'That's to say, biological life-wish, fear, love, marlia, pride, cuzzoon, clannishness, and so on.'

'Marlia? Cuzzoon?'

'Oh! Not all species have identical basic emotions. That's another thing which will have to be put right. The Creator is reportedly thinking about it – praise to the Holiest in the Height. And in the Depths be praise.' He genuflected before continuing. Tiffany winked a green eye at me.

'Perhaps you'd care to see the sort of situations we are studying, where more reason and less emotion might have led to a better resolution. My rule of thumb is – you had thumbs on Earth, didn't you? – that the less blood shed, the better. My team is directed towards that end. Disease – we can deal with that, no problem.

Blood – well, that's rather a poser. But we think we're getting there.'

He led the way over to one of the large screens. After consulting some of his fellows, all of whom politely turned their thin aspects towards us, Enny informed us that we were about to watch a real situation taking place on a planet he named. And he told us how many similar archetypal situations were occurring at the same time all over the universe.

The screen threw a total VR projection. Next moment – or so it seemed – we were standing, Tiffany, Enny I and I, on a grassy plain in what might have been a desolate region of Earth. The plain, rolling rather than flat, was dotted with an accumulation of boulders, many of them higher than a living man. Perhaps they were the moraine of a retreating glacier, or possibly the debris of some extensive chthonian upheaval with which we were unfamiliar. They gave to the landscape a sense of insecurity – a sense much reinforced by a wild mob of people who were gathering at a spot marked by a ring of stones.

Another factor was immediately apparent. Although the light cast on the plain was dim, two suns shone in the sky.

To the naked eye, the suns appeared roughly similar. One was near zenith, the other hung below the first, no more than thirty degrees above the horizon. They threw their pallid conflicting shadows over the ring of stones.

Towards this ring we made our way.

We were invisible and thus immune from danger. Or so we hoped, for the mob ahead of us gave every indication of savagery. Some came on foot, some came riding. Those on horseback rode with a companion, possibly a son or a woman. These auxiliaries were left to guard the mount when the man flung himself from the saddle and rushed forward to join the fray.

Much shouting and gesticulating occurred. But what was most alarming in our view was the fact that those joining the gathering were two-headed. Tiffany exclaimed at this. Enny I claimed that these people had evolved from ordinary one-heads; but a genetic defect caused many babies to be born with two heads. Eventually, two-headedness had become the norm and the bicephalids – or

Bicephs, as they called themselves – killed off their monocranial kin.

The bicephalous mob gathered about a large irregular boulder on top of which two figures stood. Tiffany immediately christened these two the Witchdoctor and the Hero.

The Witchdoctor was an old frail man, gaudily decorated in feathers and skins. He smoked two pipes, one in each mouth, and paid no attention to the row swirling below him. Instead, his four old eyes were turned to the sky, where the two large red suns shone down.

The Hero was young and half-naked, to show off his beautiful body. He grew thick black hair on one head, thick yellow hair on the other. The hairs were plaited to make a yellow and black mane down his spine. He brandished his fists and shouted in an aggressive manner to those below.

It was clear he was whipping up antagonism levels in heroic manner.

VIII. Slicing Up the Sun

As we became accustomed to this alarming sight, we could see that the Bicephs were of two kinds. A peculiar difference distinguished them. Whereas a small majority of men had their two heads facing forwards, in what we ex-earthlings would regard as a normal way, a sizeable minority had only one of their heads facing front, while the other looked behind. It was easy to see how this development might bestow evolutionary advantage, extending so greatly, as it did, a man's range of vision.

Nevertheless, these Versos – as we dubbed them – were more poorly equipped and less gaudily dressed than the true Bicephs.

This distinction between true Cipro and Verso evidently meant little in the fever of the moment. An untoward event had thrown everyone into a state of nervous excitement. Many men raised spears threateningly and pointed to the skies.

A cumbersome vehicle lumbered slowly across the plain to the ring of stones. A wooden two-wheeled cart was dragged into the midst of the hubbub. Six young women, yoked together, manoeuvred the cart to a prominent position below the boulder on which Hero and Witchdoctor stood.

As the crowd drew back, we saw that tied to the boards of the cart was a man of golden demeanour. He was a mere youth, his beard scarcely grown. Strong and well-muscled, he struggled against his bonds.

He was a Verso. One of his faces looked upwards, one stared down into the planking of the cart. The upward-turned face spat and swore at the two figures perched high above him. Beautiful as his body was, his face was appallingly ugly, with a great squashed nose, prognathous jaw, and crossed eyes, as if nature had singled him out for whatever ordeal awaited him.

The Hero called for quiet, swishing his bi-coloured plait. The mob fell silent, encircled by the grey stones.

The old Witchdoctor descended steps cut into the high rock, relying on a small acolyte to support him on his way down. When he finally gained the ground, he approached the cart. Bending forward, he breathed smoke from one of his pipes into the upward-looking face of the captive youth. This had an immediate calming effect on the Verso, who fell as silent as the crowd.

The old man seemed tired and almost kindly, although one of his faces looked considerably fiercer than the other. Keeping one gaze on the captive Verso, he turned the other up to the sky, and to the two suns. As he did so, he raised an arm aloft.

All eyes in the crowd followed his gesture. The Hero also, still standing legs apart on the high boulder, raised both his arms to point to the skies.

Something was attacking the two suns. Their round solar faces were being dented: a small bite – small but increasing – was being taken from their right-hand circumferences. At first, nothing more than a black fingernail was visible. But it grew, steadily it grew. A low united suspiration of fear was drawn from the two-headed mob.

The Witchdoctor gave a cry, startlingly loud for one so ancient. It formed the beginning of an incantation, and the incantation the beginning of a barbarous ritual. An offering was to be made to an ineffectual god.

The young women who had dragged the cart stood aside. From his belt, the Witchdoctor drew a long stone knife. As he lifted it above his head, the captive Verso managed to raise his two heads slightly and let out a scream.

The knife slammed down into his rib cage. The scream died. The Witchdoctor raised the knife and struck a second time for the second sun. Verso blood welled over his fists.

A murmur rose from the crowd like the sighing of a prairie wind.

But the sacrifice was in vain. The black indentations into the sun grew larger minute by minute.

'The term "eclipse" means nothing to these tribes,' Enny I said. 'The old feller can predict *when* it will happen but not *why*.'

'A double eclipse in a binary system must be rare,' I said. 'Or maybe not. Depends how many other planets there are in the system.'

'These tribes are entirely governed by superstitious fear. Fear of the strange, the unknown. No danger threatens them except self-generated dangers. They are victims of their endocrine systems.'

'Look now,' Tiffany said.

Seeing that the sacrifice had had no effect, seeing that their suns were still being devoured, seeing that darkness stealthily encroached on their world, the Versos and Bicephs went mad. Fighting broke out between the two tribes.

The Hero threw himself down from his height and seized two Versos round their necks. He banged their four heads together.

Spears were wielded. The bicephalids who a minute earlier had been in perfect accord now threw themselves on others who had become deadly enemies.

'Enough,' said Enny. 'It's too painful a scene to watch – and could be repeated a million times.'

Everything went blank. Then, almost without pause, we were returned to his project room in Personality.

'I can see that more reason and less emotion would have helped there,' I remarked, after a moment's silence. Into my being had filtered a horror scarcely to be experienced in Infinity. Tiffany was equally aghast, though Enny seemed unmoved. 'The terrible loss of blood . . .'

'We can adjust endocrine balances.' Enny spoke dismissively.

'Maybe you should determine why people have to suffer so much,' Tiffany said. 'That would be better than juggling with a few glands. I mean, maybe the fabric of the universe could be adjusted so that – oh, so that there aren't eclipses and massive storms and floods – downpours! – all the so-called natural events that afflict –'

'Shootings . . . ' I suggested.

She had faltered to a stop. Like me, she had become aware of the purple stain now welling up like anaesthetic about us. Enny was vanishing. Behind us, a transformed Gabriel loomed.

IX. They're Always in White

He was all in white. He wavered, faded away, returned.

He seemed immense. He was looking down at me. I was horizontal and she was lying silent beside me. Intense weakness filled my being. There was no pain. Only the sense of a moving vehicle. And the memory of blood shed . . .

Seeing my eyes open, he leaned forward and said, 'Can you hear me, Mr Evans? We're from City Biotech. We've checked your credit, you're okay, and we're going to do all we can for you. I'm afraid your wife . . .

'Well . . .'

In his formal android voice he enquired, 'Is there any particular kind of body you'd like your consciousness to be transferred into?'

X. The Last Syllable of Recorded Time

He was fading out again.

My last whispered cry:

–ANY

A reader never sees the book the author writes. A collection of short stories is just that to most readers: another collection of short stories. Some of the stories she or he may like, some dislike. One may perhaps linger in her or his memory. But a reader has a thousand other things to do.

The writer has nothing else to do. At least when he is writing his stories he is perfectly happy, whatever else is going on in his life. The weather, the government, the debts – he is oblivious to them all.

This summer, our family had a holiday in the lovely countryside of Languedoc, lost somewhere between Albi and Toulouse. We stayed in a friend's large stone house. A heat wave ruled supreme. We swam several times every day. And mostly we ate al fresco, under a huge chestnut tree.

While we were there, I re-read Aldous Huxley's fine biography, *Grey Eminence*. Huxley has this to say of Cardinal Richelieu: 'The arrogant, self-deified genius was doomed, by a stroke of beautifully poetic justice, to be convinced that he was less than human. In his spells of mental aberration, the cardinal imagined himself to be a horse.'

The summer suntan has long since worn off. That alarming sentence remains with me. A *horse*?

Horse Meat

The growling reds of a late spring dawn. The sky inflamed. As Lord Lunn came from the castle keep, sentries dragged themselves to attention. Chilblains on the hands that clasped pikes. A bugle sounded above his head.

Cracking the crisp air, hooves echoed like rat-tats on a snare drum. Crumbling stone caught the noise, multiplied it. Number One groom appeared, leading Stalwart. He bowed when he reached his lord and master. The great horse tossed his head in greeting. Leather and silver were his harness.

Lunn patted the neck of the stallion and walked round him, seeing that all was in order for the journey. Here stood the only living thing he trusted. He tightened the girth running under the barrel of belly. When his inspection was complete, he set foot to stirrup and swung himself into the saddle.

As he did so, Lord Lunn permitted himself a brief glance upwards under a shaggy eyebrow. His current woman was at a high window. She stared down at him. In an instant, he had read the puny manuscript of her face. Despair, hope, in oval shape. She did not wave. He offered no farewell. He had not told her where he was going. She would wait. Perhaps she would try to escape. In which case, she would die when he returned. Whatever happened, it was a matter of indifference to him. A woman was not like a horse. Horses were hard to find.

No change touched Lunn's frozen expression as he rode forth. He was a big-boned man, spare of flesh. His unkempt hair caught something of the blackness of his stallion's mane. Vigour more than youth salted his vulpine look; under his leather helmet was more than a hint of wolf. Hollows flickered along jawline and at temples. Some accounted him handsome. To smile was no part of his make-up. His philosophy had been pared to a bone of three words: It is written. A bone without flesh.

The groom stood away. Lunn passed under the broken outer gate of Ensai Castle. A portrait of the Beloved Helmsman hung there. The high forehead, the heavy moustache, were touched by damp sunlight. Lunn averted his gaze.

An escort of armed men waited for him. They came to attention when their lieutenant gave the order. He noted the slovenly way they did so. He did not speak. A toad crouching in a muddy pool augured ill. A soldier's foot crushed it.

Lunn's mood was not to speak. His index finger pointed towards the east. He moved forward along the track in sullen silence. The lieutenant and his troop followed, marching raggedly. A pale ensign trailed a forbidden banner. The lieutenant kept his lips sealed. He had read his lord's bitter look. He understood. Punishment was the castle diet. To live was something: even to live like animals . . .

This was the domain of the Four Fiefdoms (more officially, The 63rd Administrative District). Flowering plums and buckthorn were shedding late blossom over the road. White petals filled cart-ruts with their snow. Many trees had been broken. Little ground had lately known a hoe. Agricultural machines lay rusting in the fields, by order of the Beloved Helmsman. No one should ever forget that the Revolution was still in progress. The sword, not the plough, had triumphed. A line of peasant huts fringed a waterway, all deserted. Flies buzzed.

The sky died to a dull cloud, without colour or direction.

When Lord Lunn had arrived at Ensai Castle as a callow youth, the first grey blizzards of winter had covered lines of corpses. Shut in his room with a portable log-burning stove, he had listened to the wind bearing in from the distant ocean. Invasive wind, hostile to humans, impervious to legislation. It withered the heart. Poems never written defied the blank notebook on his lap. Draughts, soot, spiders, smoke – they fostered no verse.

At night, thinly wrapped, he had prowled the battlements. Vigilance devoured his youth. He had heard ghosts crying. He had heard spectral women sobbing.

In the harlot's foetid chamber, four nails had scratched at the cracked pane. Flowers of frost were scarred.

Now Lunn rode at a good pace towards the river marking the boundary of the Four Fiefdoms, over which he had command. The escorting platoon followed, bearing its flag. Once, hills had existed. Mountains. All had been blasted away during Operation Rat-Catcher. The river now ran sluggish with its freight of debris, like an old peasant bent by burdens. The land was pocked with pools where radioactivity counts remained high. It was forbidden to measure. Cancerous fish gulped away their lives. Women in rags still gutted and charred them, served them up and ate them. For the poor, the alternative to death was slow death.

Lunn had uncovered the secret history of Operation Rat-Catcher. All history was secret. What was not spoken was forbidden. What was forbidden was not spoken. Had not an earlier Helmsman proposed, Our superior organization will make to the enemy's soil a desert? So it had come about. It was written.

Some day, this Lord of the Four Fiefdoms would use his secret knowledge. He felt the document in his pocket. His annual report was also there. And something else. He ran rough fingers over smooth plastic. Under his bitterness, he told himself, lay a streak of romanticism. Watercress grows in polluted streams. His first kiss. Never to be savoured again. How sweet it had been! How pure!

How much to be loved was the touch of female lips. He kept them with him always, encased in plastic. They would never fade.

By midday, the party reached the river and an old ferry. Spilled energy poured from distant sources. Dark waters crackled against reeds lining the nearer bank. Something dived away from their company.

This was the border of his domain. A small band of men had made a stand here once, and had been slaughtered. Their deaths stained the atmosphere like an incriminating patch on a blanket, hard to erase.

Stalwart stood easy as Lunn dismounted. The magnificent stallion, twenty-one hands high, needed no restraint. It contemplated the gurgitation of water with its vivid black gaze. As the river with rushes, so its eye was fringed with lashes.

Lunn addressed his lieutenant. He announced he would progress alone in the administrative district across the water. His preference was not to be accompanied by such slipshod men. The soldiery must now return under a sergeant's command to their barracks in the castle. The lieutenant must remain alone at the ferry, to await Lunn's return.

Crestfallen, the lieutenant received his orders. He dared ask no question. There was nothing at the ferry. He might starve before his ruler returned. He saluted. Hand quivered at forehead.

A boatman approached hurriedly from his shack. An unshaven skeletal figure which scratched at an armpit. He presented himself to Lunn. Without hope of remuneration, he dreaded chastisement. He clasped his hands and bowed low. He plied his ferry now for fear, not money. His old grey clothes were torn. Poverty had its uniform. It was more important to starve than offend.

As Lunn led his mount to the water's edge, the ferryman called out in a husky voice.

Whereupon an old woman draped in a tarpaulin appeared from a thicket. She had been cutting wands of a willow tree to weave a basket. These she dropped in her haste. Doubled with age, she ran across muddy ground to the boat. The curses of the ferryman encouraged her.

This scuttling black form annoyed the lord. He drove his stallion forward. The woman staggered hurriedly out of its way. Her eyes were cinders in her age-charred faced. The boat rocked as Stalwart lumbered aboard, its planks resounding in protest at the animal's shod weight.

Fearful of delay, the ferryman pushed his antique vessel out into the flood. As the water lapped about his thighs, he threw himself aboard. He stood erect to row in the stern. The old woman did likewise in the low prow. He continued to shout angry commands at her. The craft was ensnared in whorls of dirty silk. Many had drowned in this river, some by design.

Both shores were desolate. Signs of long-abandoned industry drifted by. Black flood mirrored black walls. No birds flew.

The old ferryman laboured. The old woman struggled at her oar. To encourage each other, they sang a snatch of elderly song over and over.

> Three days . . .
> Wind in the lower room.
> Between drunk and sober I drifted three days,
> Three days.

Lunn remained silent by his silent horse. He stared down at a silver stirrup. He listened to the repeated words of the song. He remembered his father.

Drifting was but an interlude. The other bank closed in on them. A knot of silver birches clustered together for company. Pines had once flourished until radioactivity killed them. Sheltering under the birches, now in twinkling leaf, was a landing stage and a shed. On the stage a young man stood, waiting. He gave no signal. He was smartly dressed in furs. His legs were slightly apart, his arms akimbo, in a confrontational pose.

This young man permitted his gaze to meet Lord Lunn's as the distance between them dwindled.

The prow jarred against the stage. The old woman scrambled ashore, fumbling with the mooring rope. She secured the boat and stood, bending backwards to ease her spine. Lunn threw her a coin as he disembarked. He led Stalwart from the boat to marshy ground. Stalwart tossed his head, taking the scent of the province. To one of the tree trunks was pinned a poster portrait of the Beloved Helmsman.

Coming forward, the young man in furs bowed low to Lord Lunn. He announced that the Province of Norj was honoured to receive the Ruler of the Four Fiefdoms. He gave his name as Roi Obal. He was a councillor of the City of Norj, in charge of Processing. That city awaited Lord Lunn with impatience to welcome him on his annual visit. So saying, he backed away down the track among the trees, beckoning, beckoning.

The ferryman and the old woman remained by their boat, mouths hanging open. They watched. Then the man crossed and wrenched Lunn's mite from her old fist. She climbed into the boat without protest. Her nose ran. She held her oar upright, using both hands. Behind her, the swirling river, the reeds, the distance, the days of youth.

As fur-clad Councillor Obal progressed backwards, light branches and twigs whipped his face. One cheek bled from a thorn scratch. He kept his gaze fixed on Lunn. Lunn followed him without speaking. His stallion's head nodded by his shoulder, disdainful. Lord and steed thought as one.

Obal stopped when he reached the shed. The walls of the shed were weatherworn but almost intact. Tiles had slid from its roof. Broken by their fall, they formed a terracotta path along either side of the building. The councillor pushed open the black-tarred door. He gestured proudly inside. An automobile stood there.

The high-walled sides of the car were ancient. They had been polished. The glass shone. The vehicle was decorated for the occasion. Above its roof had been secured a portrait of the Beloved

Helmsman. And beneath the familiar face, a familiar slogan in red:
ENEMIES ALL ROUND.

The councillor announced proudly that he would have the honour
of driving Lord Lunn to the City of Norj in the vehicle. His horse
could be left with the ferryman. His rather cold grey eyes sparkled
with pride as he spoke. He was still youthful, somewhat plump of
countenance from city living. He had drawn in his stomach to stand
rigidly upright.

Lunn made no response.

With increasing anxiety Councillor Obal scrutinized his superior.
What he saw there was a tower of pent passion, with a vein that
throbbed in his hollow temple. His own face clouded in response.
Man and horse stood unmoving and unmoved. Obal stammered
part of his welcome again as he sought for approval in the dark
visage before him.

The lantern of Lunn's face remained unlit. Without haste, he
spoke in his deep voice. He asked firstly why an impudent cityman
should believe he would entrust his stallion to a wretched peasant.
He said that the Beloved Helmsman – and the Darling Helmsman
before him – had condemned all automobiles as foreign inventions,
used only by forces of counter-revolution. Had what was written
been forgotten?

To suggest that he, Lord of the Four Fiefdoms, should enter the
machine was an affront. That affront would be punished.

At these words, Councillor Obal fell to his knees. His former
arrogance faded. Clasping his hands together, he babbled for forgiveness. He was a member of an illustrious family. That family would
certainly reward the great lord if his error were to be forgiven. He
had intended only to honour –

His protestations were cut short. Lunn told him that he would
go before a tribunal in Norj. He was ordered to get to his feet and
to cease his blubbering. He would follow Lunn on foot, all the way
to the gates of Norj, where incarceration awaited him.

As horse and rider moved off, Obal followed, chin down on chest.
Impotent hatred spread like a disease within him.

To the east lay low hills. From behind these hills, the Sun had risen. Its disc was pale as swan's egg although it had broken clear of the morning mist. Temperatures on this side of the river were generally more clement than in the Four Fiefdoms. Men and animal moved through a decrepit landscape. Fifty thousand square kilometres of the Four Fiefdoms had been affected by Operation Rat-Catcher. The effects had spilled over here, to the Province of Norj. Generations later, nature still convalesced, and would do so until many more generations of men had faded from the Earth.

Hollow, destitute, all about their track stood broken reeds. New green was just beginning to show through greys and russets of last year. The poison could not be seen or smelt. It was too alien to be detected by human senses.

Horse and rider and following prisoner moved through the afternoon. From tall grasses the wind gathered a rustling skirt. The travellers met with no one on their way. Once, a man was seen fishing in a distant pond, a grey shape curving towards grey water.

Nearer evening colder breezes riffled the vegetation. Lunn rode Stalwart to a stream and allowed it to drink while toads croaked disapproval. Tethering his mount to a lone tree, he seated himself with the tree trunk at his back, its bark at his spine. He ate sparingly of dry rations. Councillor Obal stood nearby, afraid to move until given permission. He dared not ask for food or drink. The order came to sit. He sprawled among long grass. Forehead on hands, he stared downwards into the earth.

Dusk wrapped them in its grey twilight. Minutes wasted away. Lunn ordered his captive to recite poetry. Roi Obal cleared his throat and declaimed in a singsong voice:

> By rivers and lakes at odds with life I journeyed
> Until the Beloved Helmsman directed me.
> Now life's an ocean of understanding.
> To every lock he is the key.

The councillor's voice trailed away. His recitation met with no response. He made bold to explain. 'The verse, honoured sir, is from the opera *The De-Electrification of Northern Countries*.'

Lunn made no answer. He despised cheap propagandist verse. His taste was for classical poetry. He closed his eyes.

The rushes never ceased to shiver in the breeze: they spoke like dried mouths. Dull night brought with it only a handful of stars. The river made its own noise, enfolding itself. Leaves were borne away by the stream.

So it had always been. It was written.

Obal's eyes remained wide. On the jade wheel of night, where the black stallion watched, the smallest hour chimed. Lunn did not move beneath his bare tree. The councillor rose to his feet. His breath scarcely dared leave his chest. He took one step, then another. Under his boots dead stalks crackled. The figure propped beneath the tree gave no sign. Another pace Obal took, another, and another. He began to run.

The voice of Lunn behind him was scarcely raised. It merely ordered him to come back. Councillor Obal ran the faster. No sounds of pursuit reached him. All he could hear was the beat of his own heart and the pulse of liberty in his head. With hands stretched out before him, he rushed through the blind night. Every forced footfall took him nearer freedom.

For nearly an hour he ran. He was forced to pause and fold up to regain his breath.

In Norj, he lived alone in conditions of austerity. The view from his lonely window of an echoing prison yard accorded with a certain bleakness in his soul. Yet his family wished only to pamper him. Because Roi Obal's duties in the city were important, that powerful family would not let him go: daily deliveries of forbidden luxuries testified to his parents' possessive love. When not sick at heart, he consumed the delicacies.

Those delicacies weighed on him now in the middle of nowhere. He bent double, gasping, his stomach touched his thighs.

He heard the drumming. It seemed to be in his veins. Anxiously, he straightened up.

Then above him – a great shadow, inky, terrifying, imminent. Obal was struck before he knew it. A boot was in his face, breaking it.

Under the force of the blow he tumbled and tumbled. A bundle of old rags knew more resistance. When the rider on his stallion rode back to the lone tree, Roi Obal dragged himself to his feet and followed.

Before the midday hour next arrived, Lord Lunn rode into the City of Norj on his black stallion. Horse and man were one.

Norj was one of the great provincial capitals of administrative power. Its suburbs covered many square kilometres of the plain, and climbed hills. The river that ran beneath its bridges was gnarled with veins of history. At the city's ancient heart were many fine buildings, their matt surfaces closed to the street. No building was permitted to be built more than four storeys high. The great stone statue of the Beloved Helmsman, standing in Central Place, was five storeys high. The eyes of the Beloved Helmsman lit at night – dimly, to conserve electricity.

Behind Lunn over the cobbles staggered his bloody-faced captive, Roi Obal. Obal was handed to the police and a charge made. He was dragged without argument into a cell: just to be accused by the ruler of the Four Fiefdoms was sufficient indication of guilt. Obal lay where he was thrown, shouting angrily that his family would rescue him. The door slammed on his cries.

Lunn proceeded to the great official building where the General of the Revolutionary Party of the Province resided. Ordinary citizens passed the establishment with dread. He saw to it that Stalwart was comfortably stabled before he went to the residential section. His customary annual quarters were ready. There he luxuriated in scented waters. A eunuch towelled him dry. He went to a couch to sleep for an hour before meeting the General Secretary.

As he closed his eyes, a familiar madness welled up in him. Coming from black depths, it devoured even his shape. He feared it, being nameless. It/he took monstrous form and its mane flamed in the winds of Lunn's terror.

He was the great Lord of the Four Fiefdoms, all powerful. Yet he was slave to this obsession, that he was less than human – far less, hoofed and without mind – a low thing, blacker than blackest night. An eater of bran.

On his couch he neighed and struggled with his insanity. Behind his satin screen the eunuch trembled.

Lunn when he awoke went to a bronze mirror to survey his countenance. Nothing there betrayed him: the sickness stayed shrouded within his mind. Dragging on his boots, he went down to consort with the General Secretary, in a chamber lined with rich carpets.

Three men awaited Lunn in the room. One was dressed in black. The black-robed one greeted Lord Lunn in the name of the Beloved Helmsman.

Lunn produced from a pouch a C-wand, thin as a pencil. The black-robed man, General Secretary Cooth, accepted it and crossed to where a silken curtain closed off a corner of the room. When Cooth pulled aside the curtain, a dull brown box was revealed. Cooth switched it on and inserted the C-wand in its slot. This was Old Red Eyes. Since the punitive but poorly observed laws against machines were imposed by the previous Helmsman, computers had been reclassified as agricultural implements.

The screen lit. Shining in scarlet, figures and numbers unrolled. These were the accountings compiled by Lunn's clerks. The columns showed production yields over the past year in the Four Fiefdoms, for timber, sorghum, reeds, fish, meat, skins and so on. All figures were exaggerated. When blended with other figures, they would be exaggerated again. Only then could they be despatched to the capital. Norms had to be met – and exceeded. Or unpleasant questions would be asked.

Next came listings of political and ordinary criminals punished under various sections of the law: those who had lost heads or hands. Thieves, loyalty-flouters, questioners and others – all had met with justice and found its blade sharp. These figures, reported to Lord Lunn in Ensai Castle from his fiefdoms, had been exaggerated. His clerks had exaggerated them again. They would again be exaggerated before despatch onward to the state capital.

The scarlet letters drained away, the screen dulled. The curtain was drawn back into place. Old Red Eyes slept. In the carpeted room, the four men seated themselves at a marble table and conversed in low voices. On the table top were incised cryptograms of admonition. The four spoke elliptically, each concerned with his own survival, with law, with betrayal. The name of the Beloved Helmsman surfaced often on their bearded lips, but the left side of their faces spoke only oppression. Sometimes, one of them, whispering of some new decision from the national capital, would trace idly with a forefinger the ideogram for Severity or Deception. Outside, it was dark or light.

Their business concluded, they retired to a yet stuffier room. Faded green silks, imperceptibly moving, gave a sigh. Otherwise, sound was sponged up by fabric. Brass drinking cups stood against a sandalwood wall. Servants were summoned, entering on their knees. Pipes were distributed. Harlots sucked the pipes alight with their lower parts. Smoke rose like serpents crawling towards invisibility. Later, a gong, a meal of many courses. Music, a woman danced, masked, with shaven crotch. Beaks dangling from immense assiettes, marinaded vultures were served, bedded on the tripes of infant sows. The four men ate. Bones crunched between their gold-lagged teeth.

Their eyebrows gathered in knots in the middle of their foreheads as they filled their bellies.

In the stables, Stalwart's oats were moistened with ale, cream, and the semen of tame cheetahs.

Councillor Roi Obal enjoyed no such feast. He was marched before a drumhead tribunal. Limbs trembling with fury, he was forced to plead guilty to charges of loyalty-flouting and technology-roading. His judges wore metal caps. The sentence was death. Justice came and went by the tick of the clock.

Obal expected nothing else. The tribunal had norms to fulfil. He well understood the system. Until yesterday, he had been a part of it. And his past services were indeed acknowledged by the tribunal: his private parts would be severed and despatched to his family – after death, not before.

In forgotten times past, the Glory of November the First Corrective Wing had been the city's main art gallery and museum. In some of the more remote galleries, canvases still hung on the walls. Such galleries were closed, unlit, damp. Portraits of the illustrious dead suffered a double death. Their eyes had been shot out, mouths blacked in. All who had professed or achieved anything of merit had been profaned. The Beloved Helmsman disliked comparisons. Art was disloyalty. Artistry was escape-seeking. The reward was loss of vision. It was written.

Councillor Obal was kicked into the Mauve Room. Once mauve, now prison-coloured. Stink emanated from other prisoners already confined, from walls, floors, bunks, lice. Obal choked. He stood against the door, hearing the sentry slam the bolts on the other side. He could not believe he was here, seeing what he saw.

Light filtered from a small barred window overhead. Beads of condensation dripped down from it with labial whispers.

The nauseous smell pressed against his face and eyeballs, so that he could hardly see. The prison cell was lined with bunks, on which prisoners lay two or even three to a bunk. Men and women were mixed indiscriminately. Anguish distorted their postures. It was as if they had studied exaggerated pictures of misery and imitated the gestures of its victims. Their faces were white, twisted as though made from pastry. Many stretched their arms above their heads, entwining the bony things as if on a rack. Some had involuntarily released their bowels inside their clothes. The diarrhoea of terror seeped from them. Small patty-puddles accrued on the floor, green as the meconia of new-born infants.

These denizens of the pit cast glances at Obal, then rolled their distended gaze away, distraught with their own predicaments. From them came a perpetual moan and whine, as of wind flowing through a pillaged hamlet.

Obal leaned against the door. He filtered the foul air through his hand. A second door stood at the far end of the den. Those incarcerated stayed as far from it as possible. When heavy footsteps were heard, this second door was kicked open. Two guards rushed shouting into the cell. It was as if wolfhounds had been let in. Behind them could be glimpsed a hallway with a stair spiralling down into the cellars of the building. Up the stairwell filtered light and shadows, together with fresh scents of evil.

These mad dogs were armed. Otherwise they appeared as unkempt as the prisoners. At their entry, the wind over the pillaged hamlet increased in volume. The soldiers were in great haste. Their dire activity contrasted with the apathy of their prisoners.

At random, they grabbed five of the men and one woman, pulling them from their bunks. They yelled savagely that they wanted no trouble, no delay. One of the five prisoners, a youngster with a blond flowing moustache, screamed he would serve the Beloved Helmsman till the last. He offered to betray everyone he knew in exchange for an hour more of life. He received such a blow on the mouth that blood immediately dyed his moustache.

The would-be betrayer was barely out of his teens. The cell also contained old men, some as derelict as scarecrows. Old women, too. Young or old, innocent or villainous, rich or poor, those who owned estates or those who were beggars, literate or illiterate, ugly or handsome, betrayers or betrayed – eventually the whole spectrum of society went through the mincer of the Glory of November the First Corrective Wing into the obscurity of death.

Some of those confined wept and sucked their thumbs, coiled in foetal positions. Others presented a stoic countenance, or spat at the soldiery when they came near. There were those, when the soldiers dragged them out, who swore, those who begged, and those – women especially – who prayed to gods long officially forgotten. One old fellow, almost toothless, called cheerfully to the guards that he wanted his breakfast before he was shot.

The selected six were ordered to strip. Their clumsy fingers, shaking hands, began tearing at knots, buckles, buttons. Each victim was anxious not to be first to stand shivering naked before their captors. In an equal terror, the soldiers responded to yells from a superior below stairs. 'Coming, coming!' they yapped.

They rushed here and there like savage dogs, tearing at clothes, striking out, shouting incoherently.

At last their six victims were reduced to nudity, to stand with bare feet on the beslimed floor. Their knees knocked. They clutched their bundles of soiled clothing. Only the woman and one of the men endeavoured to cover their pallid genitalia. The others had lost their shame in the face of imminent death. One and all, they were pulled, dragged, and kicked through the far door. Once they were stumbling down the stairs to the cellar, the door slammed and was bolted again after them.

All those remaining in the cell gasped with relief that this time they had been spared. Most sat up. Some hugged their neighbours. They listened.

Their eyeballs stared out at nothing. Their mouths hung open. Many shuddered uncontrollably.

Somewhere below the cell, shots sounded.

The firing echoed up from the intestines of a gigantic stone animal. Once the animal had been a place of culture. What was fine had once been preserved. Ordinary people had admired here, had spoken of the arts of harmony and perspective. Then human history had again taken an ill turn.

All that had previously been valued or held up for admiration was desecrated. Everything beautiful was condemned. The stone animal had shrugged its heavy shoulders. Its name was Revolution and it had awoken hungry for prey. It was without conscience. It could not smell innocence. It devoured people. The shots from the cellars signified the sound of its feasting.

The prisoners groaned and slumped down on their bunks.

Obal knew what happened next. Below, in the ill-lit dark, insane activity marked the animal's digestive process. He could picture it all. He could not bar the pictures from his brain. In the deep cellar, which was L-shaped, the executioners would be half-drunk. Otherwise, they would have blown their own brains out. There would be a stench of cordite and fresh meat.

After each round of executions, blood would flow from the newly dead as other prisoners tied ropes round their feet. Earth would be strewn on the cellar floor to mop up brains and gore. The bones of the living prisoners would rattle with leukaemias of disgust at their task.

Next, a work-gang of prisoners outside and above ground would be surrounded by armed guards. This gang would haul the corpses up from the cellar to the light. The duty of this gang was to pile the dead into carts. With a heave, up went another body, swung like a bolster. The faces of the work-gang would be as greasy white as the faces of the murdered.

The carts would always be overloaded.

The gang would be made to climb up and trample down the corpses, the still-warm gristle, underfoot. Somehow, more bodies would be pressed in. All this would be done in insane haste, amid curses and blows. Always the insane haste of men burning out their nerves, of men to whom carrion was their bread and butter.

Then oxen with bones sticking from their rumps like propellers would be lashed into action. More curses. The carts would begin to roll towards death pits outside the city. Terrible clotted liquors would slink down the sides of the carts to clog the dust of the road.

The carts would work day and night, carrying away the stinking meat, the by-product of the Revolution.

Some of the living, whose dwellings lined the route to the mass graves, would peer out to see the dreadful journeys. Their stale breath misted their window panes, where window panes existed. They would utter in terror the name of the Beloved Helmsman, for whom the living died and the dead lived.

All this dreadful organization, which continued day and night, year after year, this violation of human existence, was the practical result of the Golden Meditations of various Helmsmen: the world made despoiled flesh, the intellect rendered into madness.

This whole process, horrible but banal, a criminality in which all of society conspired, fried like pig fat in Obal's brain.

He stood in the cell transfixed. He knew it all because he had been one of the directors of the corrective process. As youngest councillor, his had been the task of attending to letters of betrayal or whispers of anti-revolutionary thought. Often enough, both betrayers and betrayed were imprisoned together, tried together and destroyed together. There was justice for you! Obal had seen to it that the norms were fulfilled, that shots always sounded in the reeking cellar, that the carts were despatched punctually on their journey to the death pits.

He had never questioned anything. Loyalty had been his life. He had been possessed by total loyalty to the Beloved Helmsman. Thus he had been brought up, educated and trained. Every day of his life, kept apart from his family, he had been schooled in the grim routines of continual Revolution.

His superiors, fearing this intense young man more every year, had eventually rewarded him.

Obal's reward had been to greet Lord Lunn at the ferry, to escort him to the City of Norj. Obal had accepted the honour as such – not joyfully, for he knew not joy. At this moment, when the mouths of the dying in the cellar below his feet were stifled with blood, Obal perceived how his superiors had betrayed him. They had known that Lord Lunn, wed to his black stallion, would see in the automobile evidence of the crime of technology-roading. They had recognized Obal's sincerity and planned his downfall accordingly. Those who fuelled the Revolution feared sincerity. Sincerity had loyalty-flouting potential. Sincerity shamed them. So they had plotted this devious way to remove him.

Only now did Obal's narrow young mind open enough to admit the betrayal. He understood in the same moment that betrayal was no unusual thing: no secret, no particular spite, no blemish in a just system. It formed, rather, a basic principle by which the Revolution was continued and the state was governed. Only through betrayal as a commandment could one of the largest nations in the world remain eternally subject to fear.

These thoughts crawled like white worms through his skull, as if he were already dead.

Something burst in his head, his throat, his heart.

He began to shout. He filled the cell with his voice.

'God curse the Revolution! God curse the Four Obligations! God curse everything that makes us live lives of shit and misery! Fellow sufferers, rise from your bunks! Let's at least die like honourable men and women!'

Some prisoners turned their heads to glare at him. One lanky yellow fellow called to him to shut up. Obal shouted the more, running among them, striking their bunks with his clenched fists.

A blowsy woman with tangled hair, whose left eye had been blackened by a blow, slid from her bunk to stand on her own two feet. She raised a fist. She showed her teeth in a growl.

'I'm with you, mate! You're right. Let's fight the bastards, kick their balls in. What have we got to lose?'

Obal could have embraced her. But others cringed away or shouted to Obal and the woman to be quiet.

The yellow man screamed at him. 'Shut your gob, you cunt, or we'll be in trouble!'

'God curse the Beloved Helmsman!' shouted Obal, goaded to fresh fury at their cowardice. 'Curse the rotten old bastard, with his fat gut and his privileges! Death to the fucking Helmsman!'

It was too much for the majority of prisoners. Even in their weakened state, they could not bear this blasphemy. They climbed to the floor and threw themselves at Obal. Fists flew. Obal slipped to the ground. The others piled on him, snarling and kicking like beasts.

In burst the guards from below. They swung about them with rifle butts. Half-a-dozen more prisoners were hauled off to the cellar, snivelling for mercy. The yellow man was one of them. In a minute, the next round of executions took place.

The survivors fell silent at the sound of firing. They knew they had only minutes or hours to live. Obal sat in a corner to nurse his bruises.

He discovered he was pissing himself. The sensation brought sullen delight. All political doctrine washed from his body with the warm flow of urine. He was now merely animal. He was now free.

With that reflection came regret. The regret choked him, moving through his veins like poison, obliterating the bruises. He regretted that he had never enjoyed a woman. His dedication had over-ridden the need for women.

Later, later, he had told himself, whenever a whisper of sexual hunger had stirred. Later! Now it was too late. Peering about under his brows, he looked for the blowsy woman who had supported his brief defiance.

I'll screw her, he told himself. Why not? I'll screw her. Yes, in front of all these miserable cowards, I'll screw her rotten. Here on the floor, among the slime and piss. I know she'll like it. She has that look. I'll slip it right up her hairy hole. A mile up.

But the woman had already been dragged down to the stone cellar. Her body was already cooling meat, dragged by ropes up to the charnel carts.

Golden haze had settled on the room. Lord Lunn idled in luxury with his associates. Handmaidens washed his feet with potassium permanganate. Subdued music played. At one end of the cushioned chamber, an old reader in a red gown recited from the *Book of the Helmsman's Golden Meditations*. The Meditations rested on a carved lectern, which the reader clutched with both hands as he read.

> The enemy will not perish of himself. Our superior organiz-ation will turn the enemy's soil into desert, so that he cannot live. There his bones will lie.
>
> But bones can be reborn. That is why we need to create of our whole society a desert. Men see further where ground is flat.
>
> We must starve. The Revolution is not a dinner party. It cannot be refined, temperate, restrained. A revolution is an act of violence.
>
> Violence is necessary for hygiene. Continuous violence is necessary for health. 'Justice' is a class-word. Hiding behind the disgusting term, our real enemies can pretend to be our real friends.
>
> We shall have no real friends until all attitudes towards the Revolution are positively united in the one single aim: Equality!

The old reader read quietly, so that his words were not distinctly heard by his superiors at the other end of the chamber.

Among those superiors, wine was being passed again. They were drinking the dark red wine of Périgord Noir. A messenger was announced. He entered and bowed before Lord Lunn in a manner many times denounced as counter-revolutionary, yet still practised, often enforced.

The messenger handed to Lord Lunn a gift wrapped in layers of yellow muslin. He bowed and departed.

With a negligent air, Lord Lunn unwrapped the gift. The muslin parted. At its heart lay a delicate porcelain porringer. The porringer consisted of three parts, a two-handled cup, a stand, a saucer. Floral decoration had been artistically applied. The expert eye of the lord read the maker's marks on the base of the saucer. This was a porringer made in Derby in 1781 according to the old calendar dating. It was beautiful and rare. And dangerous, because it was technology-roading, equality-floating and decidedly counter-revolutionary.

Lord Lunn held the porringer up to the light to admire its translucence.

A sliver of paper floated from the cup. He scooped it up from the ground. The paper was decorated and perfumed. Such notepaper wanton young women had used before the Helmsmen had come to reshape the world into a better place. On the paper, a female hand had written a verse:

> Four turns of the street and a brass rail
> Lead you to my room and inner chamber.
> Who can tell what joys will prevail
> When you and yours pierce the silk lining?

Every line of the verse spoke of a refinement, a decadence now almost stamped out. Lunn appreciated that it was written after the manner of a Tang poet, and immediately decoded its erotic message. He became erect with lust. Whoever composed the verse was in need of a firm bridle when mounted. He decided to respond immediately. Besides, the company of the General Secretary vexed him.

Taking up the delicate porringer, he excused himself and climbed the stairs to the suite of rooms provided for him. There he summoned a eunuch to lave him and perfume his body. Other servants were directed on other errands. He assumed a rich gown. He pomaded his hair, which he drew together into two plaits. These he tied so that they rested on his chest.

When he went down to the courtyard, a groom was bringing forth his stallion from the stabling block.

The lord fondled Stalwart's muzzle and kissed his arched neck. 'Soon, soon, my beauty,' he whispered. The stallion gave a shudder like a child sighing and fixed his master with a dark gaze. Lunn ordered the groom to wait: he would go out alone and on foot. He was aware that verse and porringer were possibly a trap, and that danger might await him. But for the antidote of danger he was always prepared.

The day was sickening towards sunset. He left the precincts of the General Secretary's establishment and marched down the highway. In such a reactionary verse as he had been sent, 'four turns of the street' would have to mean right turns. Most of the houses he passed were of local stone, blotches of lichen giving them a porous appearance, as though all the dying day were being absorbed into the granite. When he took the fourth turn, he saw ahead of him a mansion with a gleaming brass rail. The rail twisted up three steps to an archway.

He paused and looked about him. There was little life in Norj. The time for curfew approached and few people were about. Owing to power restrictions, no lights showed. Grasping the rail, he mounted the steps and passed through the archway.

In the grounds he entered stood a large house. It did not share the tumble-down air that characterized most of its neighbours. He was challenged by two armed guards. When he gave his name, he was told he was expected.

The mansion confronted the visitor with a heavy stone frontage. Its windows were narrow and shuttered within. Without, their sills jutted like chins. A hound barked warningly as the door opened and he was shown into a long dark hall.

A house servant bearing an oil lamp ushered him along. The tongue of flame cast blurred reflections in polished panelling. They reached a rear room. Lunn stood alertly, for the room was almost totally dark. A voice bade him be seated. He remained standing. The fragrances of the room assailed his nostrils. There came the noise of panting, as of someone being half-strangled.

Electric light suddenly invaded the room with its brilliance. Lunn found himself in surroundings of some perversity.

Elaborate dispositions of furniture challenged the visitor. The salon had been partitioned into a series of niches, each variously hung and carpeted so as to clash with each other, as if to conjure different moods. However, a predominant colour was burnt orange, which seemed to absorb shadows. The walls had not been permitted to go naked; they were adorned with drawings, water-colours and calligraphic poems, some in 3D. *The Enemy* and *Lovers' Death* were two of the poetic titles which caught Lord Lunn's eye. Pinned up in the alcoves were skins of leopard, coyote and other rare animals.

'Cinnabar and celadon are the preferred colours for those of refined visual taste, as you might agree, since the refinement of your tastes is suggested – in strict contrast, if I may say so, to your appearance – by your precipitate arrival here in pursuit of what? . . . a fragment of verse.' Such was the sentence of welcome uttered by a man who now appeared before Lunn from one of the alcoves rather as if he were performing a conjuring trick on himself.

'Not the verse but its author drew me here,' Lunn replied, ironing out his frown.

He found himself confronting a man of medium height dressed in fine decorated brocade who restrained by a gold leash a dog of apparent hostile intent. The panting he heard issued from the dog's throat.

'The blustering swaggering kind of men, your go-getters, even your plethoric types who join various societies – these tend to prefer startling tones of reds and yellows. Where does your preference lie, may I enquire?' The speaker had perhaps attained his fifties. He evinced a tendency towards dryness. With his sensitive features went sparse hair. His slender hands clutched the leash that restrained his dog. The dog was brindle, with heavy shoulders and a wide mouth. It slobbered in its eagerness to attack Lord Lunn.

'I'm well content with red. The more vivid the better.'

'No doubt in the Four Fiefdoms one yearns for what might be termed "a good old vivid red" . . .' He accompanied this remark with a bark of amusement.

'That one does, sir, certainly. Just as one yearns for straightforward discourse.'

'Implying what? Simian grunts? I must apologize for my hound. Being short-sighted, he mistakes you for an animal.'

The green-clad host, speaking in the mellowest of voices, expressed his gratitude to Lord Lunn for visiting what he described as his meagre dwelling. Both he and his family also appreciated the honour their visitor had done them by deigning to take notice of one of their number – a remark that passed over Lunn's head. He simply stood there on pile carpet and waited without responding, containing his anger.

The host's comment evidently served as a signal. From behind an ornate screen concealing one of the alcoves came the family. The host's brother was followed by two sons and a wife, in that order. Each entered the body of the room with a gift which they set at Lord Lunn's feet. Each made a formal bow. Each expressed delight at seeing him in their home.

To this barrage of courtesy, Lunn made no response. No civility of a name had been proffered him, although it was clear the brocade-clad host knew his name. Lunn stood where he was, legs apart, one hand on his belt close to the hilt of his sword. He scowled into the smiling faces before him.

To discover in this room every evidence of discriminating taste and a connoisseur's delight in fine objects did not surprise him. Despite the century of revolution and the depredations of more than one Helmsman, such anomalies still existed. In his own ruinous castle, he stored many precious books and manuscripts of ancient date, together with maps of the world as it had been. What surprised him was that he, a stranger with power, should be permitted to witness this display of counter-revolutionary wealth. Still he spoke no word.

His host offered him tea or other refreshment. Lunn shook his head.

'Tell me who you are. Or does such indiscretion offend your sensibilities?'

With a delicate smile on his lips, his host replied, 'Honoured sir, standing admiringly before you is none other than the Family Obal. My name, which I trust you will find acceptable, is Eric Obal. Our delight in receiving you here knows no bounds. You are already acquainted with our son, Roi Obal. Roi met you at the ferry and escorted you to Norj. Of course, we do not expect you to remember so insignificant an event. But believe me, it was a privilege for us all.'

The rest of the family clapped. Then silence fell. All looked politely at Lord Lunn.

'Well?' demanded Lord Lunn.

In no way altering his courteous purring tone, Eric Obal asked, 'To talk philosophy a while. Do you consider, sir, that a man is a sewer?'

'Some men are worse than sewers.' But he had paused. The question took him unawares.

'Is not one characteristic the same for all men, to whatsoever station of life born – that wholesome things go into their mouths while filth spurts from their lower parts?'

The question was lightly asked. As if he had scored a point by it, Eric Obal turned and sat in a chair. He still restrained the dog. His wife moved like a chess piece to stand behind his chair. Both smiled up at Lunn, awaiting his answer.

'What of it if that is so?' Lunn asked.

'There is hardly an "if", sir, since is not what I say the truth?'

'I'll grant you men are sewers if you care to think in such terms. What follows?'

Eric Obal nodded, still smiling. The dog panted at his feet. 'If you grant men are sewers, are they then only sewers? Is life a disease?'

'Do you presume to give me an anatomy lesson?'

'Would you not say that men are sewers but nevertheless have a kind of sacred spirit imprisoned among the filth?'

Impatiently, Lunn said, 'Some, no doubt, some are as you say. Religion means nothing to me. Now, have done with your sophistry and come to the point. I believe you have a daughter, a versifier, who wrote to me. Where is she? Why does she not appear?'

'Speaking of the female sex, honoured sir, I once encountered a man who said to me – this was in another town – that when a man kisses a woman he is kissing one end of a tube ten metres long, half-filled with excrement. Would you consider that man to be a liar, a philosopher or a misogynist?'

'Has not a man – to those who wish to think that way – also a tube just as long, and just as full of excrement? Any man who spoke like your friend would be a woman-hater, in my judgement.'

A silence fell, hard and crisp as January frost. Lunn kept his gaze fixed on the delicate man in lacquer green, awaiting the next bizarre question. He had a horror of this conversation and was aware of the fixed smiles of the other members of the Obal family.

'You think well of kissing, then, sir?'

'As well as any man,' said Lunn.

Again silence filled the cinnabar and celadon room.

'You have said that men are like sewers. You have said that men are half-full of excrement. All of us in this room heard your words. Do you mean your remarks to apply also to our Beloved Helmsman?'

'Our Beloved Helmsman, sir, is above such slander and such sophistry. He is a god.'

'You deny his humanity?'

'I deny your right to question me further. It is within my power to have the whole bunch of you arrested for disloyal thought and behaviour.'

Eric Obal raised a finger to his lips. 'Choose your words with care, my lord, or the armed servants waiting beyond the door will hear you and grow angry.'

His wife spoke in her sweet voice. 'Would you care for a sugar-plum to calm you, sir?' She accompanied her words with a gesture towards a bowl of the fruits standing on a side-table.

Lunn addressed her with controlled courtesy. 'I am calm, thank you, madam. Porcelain brought me here. It is preferable to broken glass. Do you wish me to leave here and report the counter-revolutionary life-style in which you indulge?'

Eric Obal glanced slyly down at the dog waiting by his feet. 'Oh, no, sir, Brindle, unfortunately, would not allow you to leave this room alive. I would be loath to see my Persian carpets smeared with blood – even such illustrious blood as yours.'

'Don't speak of blood to me, or we'll take a look at yours between us. What do you want of me? Say! Have finished with this small talk of yours.'

'Oh, no. It is very large talk, sir.' His look was unexpectedly challenging. 'It touches on both my son, Roi Obal, at present enjoying the hospitality of one of the city's prisons, and on my young virginal daughter, Caraway.'

'Who's this?'

'Roi you have met; Caraway you have yet to meet.'

It was clear they were now coming to a crucial part of the meeting. Eric Obal exchanged a glance with his wife, whereupon the lady rose and approached Lord Lunn. Putting forth a dainty hand, she said in clear tones, 'Honoured sir, let us continue this pleasant conversation outside, you and I. In the garden you will see Caraway, our paragon among daughters.'

'She who writes verse?'

'She who writes verse.'

The darkness of the garden was punctuated by lanterns hanging in the night like burning tulips. The flower beds had been laid out formally. They were dominated by tall bushes of flowering Portuguese laurel, the perfume of which burdened the air with its sensuous warmth.

The hair of Eric Obal's wife was still dark, although streaked with grey. It was bunched to one side of her head and hung almost to her waist, in a manner more appropriate to a younger woman. She walked gracefully by Lunn's side. She spoke calmly, without gesture, in sentences as precise as mathematics.

'We are grateful that you have concerned yourself with our family. It is evidence of goodness that you interest yourself in the character of our dear son, Roi. Though if I may say so you misjudge him.

'We know Roi is headstrong. He may have personality defects, such as ambition, which you have endeavoured to cure by casting him into prison. Such a cure may prove too drastic . . . We have received information that he is at present in the Art Gallery prison – now called the Glory of November the First Corrective Wing, we understand.'

Lunn scowled into the darkness.

'My role with regard to your son's treasonous conduct is concluded, madam. He is now the law's concern, not mine.'

The lady paused, sighing, beside a shadowy magnolia. She leaned slightly towards him. '"The law"! Dear, dear . . . how old fashioned! What's "the law" these days? Roi remains our concern, sir.'

She moved a little closer. 'The future of our family's fortunes depends on our son's remaining alive. Kindly understand that. He is a councillor in the city, and will rise to great power – *if* his life is spared. Would you not concede, sir, that his incarceration might be in itself sufficient to turn his mind to more correct behaviour in future? That, in other words, he might, if freed, be of great service to the state? And to his parents? And even, sir, to you?

'Are you not, away in your remote Four Fiefdoms, vulnerable to adverse influences here in Norj?'

'This is mere blackmail!'

'Mere reason.'

Lord Lunn put his hands behind his back. 'What do you propose, madam?'

For answer, Eric Obal's wife took a few steps along the path and clapped her hands. A light appeared in an upper window just above their heads. The window swung open. A young woman leaned out, holding a lantern before her so that her face was illuminated.

The glow shone upon such perfection of female features as Lunn had never before seen. The arch of her eyebrows, the heavy-lidded eyes, the pert nose, that mouth half-open like a summer rose, the pretty tilted chin – all this framed in coils of hair darker, denser, than the night – immediately struck a wound into Lord Lunn's heart. The young woman became the very embodiment of the perfumes of the warm air.

This cynosure, this paragon, smiled down into the flower-embosomed garden with her dark eyes. She spoke softly from her eyrie, reciting in velvet tones two lines of her verse:

Who can tell what joys will prevail
When you and yours pierce the silk lining?

As she withdrew from her window, she lowered her lamp. Its glow revealed momentarily that she was naked. The gentle orbs of her breasts lent emphasis to the erotic nature of her rhyme. Then she was gone. Her light was extinguished.

Eric Obal's wife continued to speak as if nothing had happened.

'A daughter, even a good obedient daughter such as Caraway, counts for little when weighed against the life of a son. Nevertheless, sir, you might see advantage in such an exchange.'

He asked if Caraway included poetry among her virtues.

'Sir, I was forced to act as her inspiration.'

When he growled she coolly continued. 'Should you liberate Roi from his undignified and perilous confinement this very night, our family would reward you with our daughter – a small portion of whose charms you have just seen.'

'I would need a closer inspection, madam.'

'Then you will agree to the arrangement I propose?'

In her manner there was even something condescending, as if she were discussing the layout of a new bed of camellias with her gardener.

'Madam, there you have my assurance.'

She laughed, perhaps amused by the growl in his voice. 'We would, of course, require that assurance in writing. It would be unfortunate, would it not, if our son were freed one day, only to be re-arrested the next?'

'I am in a position to see that would not happen.'

'No doubt you are,' Eric Obal's wife said, in reflective tones. 'Though first you have to leave our property safe and sound, sir. That could be a problem. A written statement from you would guarantee our peace of mind.' She paused, contemplating him with cool scrutiny. 'Besides the written statement, we would require from you also a dozen cans of Pepsi-Cola, if they were obtainable.'

'Is it not enough that I should rescue your worthless son?'

She appeared to take no offence at the tone of this remark. Still smiling her fixed smile, she explained. 'You received from our daughter a valuable porcelain porringer. It was not hers to give. We therefore expect that an honourable man would be eager to return a gift of equal value in exchange.'

Lord Lunn made her a slight bow. 'I will see what can be done.'

'A dozen and a half cans will be even more greatly appreciated. We would be even more friendly thereafter.' Just for a moment she permitted her lips to become a thin line. Her frown was scarcely discernible in the scented shadows. With the lightest of touches, she laid a hand on his arm. 'Let us return indoors. Caraway will be summoned. Servants will dress her suitably, and she will be yours to deal with as you will.'

She raised her small hand, which Lord Lunn grasped with his large ones. He increased the pressure. He twisted her thin arm until she was forced to her knees.

'First, madam,' he said, 'you will fellate me to compensate for your husband's impertinent questioning. On your knees, make no outcry, swallow everything.'

Safe back in General Secretary Cooth's establishment, Lord Lunn reclined in a white-tiled bath while servants made arrangements in the next room. A maid poured unguents into the steaming water and applied a sponge to his flesh. When he arose, dripping, she dried him in soft towels. She powdered him. He sat by a mirror while she trimmed his hair and beard. With a final flourish, she cut and polished his toenails.

'Are you content to be black?' he enquired of her, idly, as she prepared to leave the room.

She gave him a wide smile. 'I am content to be whatever the Beloved Helmsman pleases, sire.'

'A commendable sentiment.' He scowled as she made her exit. As if that damned Helmsman cared what colour anyone was.

Stark naked, he entered the bedroom to greet Caraway. Her family had been prompt in her delivery.

Caraway was entirely as beautiful as the brief glimpse in the garden had suggested. Her face, with its delicate tints, was as fresh as a new-budded rose. Her lips, too, recalled something as fragile as petals. So too did her lower lips, peeking out from under a mossy bank of dark hair.

She had been stripped naked. The servants had tied her to the bed, her buttocks thrust upwards. Her plush hortulan complexion, like that of a ripe peach, suggested fruitiness and succulence. To bite into her would incite an unrivalled delight.

As he tested the knots that bound her, Lord Lunn commended her for such impetrative beauty. Caraway thanked him for the compliment. Asking her if she was comfortable, he received her assent with a grave nod.

'For my brother Roi,' said she, 'I am happy to do anything. Roi is my senior by three years. I have adored him since I was a baby. Often and often, he would carry me about on his back. Roi showed me profound respect. That was what made me love him so well. He it was who first interested me in the classical poets.'

'Never mind your brother.' He looked at her, observing her speculative glance at his engorged member. 'Are you prepared for "me and mine" to "pierce the silk lining"?'

'You do promise that my dear brother is released unharmed within the hour?'

'That assurance has been accorded your father in writing. He has merely to present the note to General Secretary Cooth and your brother will regain his liberty.'

He looked down hungrily upon her. Despite himself, he found himself delaying. Her cool demeanour had touched him.

Almost angrily, he said, 'You have never had a lover?'

She spoke as if they were enjoying a tête-à-tête in a drawing-room. 'There was a young man I cared for once. He wrote me a poem, which he passed up to my bedroom window on a long stick. A long stick but a short poem . . .'

That was all she said, forcing him to ask, 'This young man – he never bedded you?'

Caraway paused before responding with a deliberate note of contempt in her voice. 'Certainly not. When I discovered he came from the country, I severed all connection with him. He would probably have stunk of the stable . . .'

Of a sudden, Lord Lunn burned with rage. The insolence of the Obal family was not to be endured a moment longer.

'Very well!' he shouted. 'Very well!'

'Oh!' she said softly, shrinking against the bedding.

Crossing the floor, he flung open the outer door of the chamber. He caught his lower lip between the two strong rows of his teeth and gave a shrilling whistle.

At once a commotion started from below like a devil waking in the basement. Then a great noise and clatter on the wooden stair. It was as though a brute of a man, insensate with drink, endeavoured to throw to the top of the stairs an unwieldy item of furniture. Caraway's eyes widened in fright. She lifted up her head to see what was coming.

Into the room, splintering the doorposts, burst Lunn's great black stallion. The chamber was dimly lit, with two oil lamps standing out from the walls on brass brackets. The horse with its lunging presence immediately dominated the space. Its mane flew. Its eyes enlarged to show their white rims. Its milky pink tongue slavered from its mouth. When it reared up, both neck and shoulders rammed against the ceiling.

Caraway screamed in terror.

'Soft, my friend,' said Lunn to his mount. The immense energy of the beast consumed him. He was like a satyr, prancing beside the living blackness. As the horse snorted forth a challenge, so the man roared in excitement. Lunn flung himself up on Stalwart's back, crouching low, clinging with fingers and toes to the glossy hide.

He urged the beast forward at the struggling girl.

Stamping across the room, the stallion thrust its weight onto the bed. From her hiding place behind the bathroom curtains, the black maid peered out. Too aghast was she even to scream. Caraway whimpered as the huge animal loomed over her. Its hooves came crashing down on the upholstery, one on either side of her shoulders. There was no escape for her. The air was clouded by the stench of lust.

Stalwart, to whom this treat was no novelty, had sprouted an enormous tasselled member. The stallion thrust it home. Screams, noise, fury, erupted in the small space. The maid fell to the floor in horror.

The horse soon withdrew, trailing slobber and semen. Whereupon Lunn threw himself in his turn into the bloody arena. The amorous site was now damaged beyond repair, whirlpooled with slimes and dark intestinal blood.

There, there, Lord Lunn plunged in his dark dagger. He clasped the deflowered girl in rib-cracking embrace, a biting and snarling predator more savage than his horse.

Against the befouled bed Stalwart stood, sweating and trembling. It hung its massive skull down between its forelegs.

The deed was done, the crime complete. It was written.

When he had bathed and clothed himself, and in a fit of self-disgust defiled the insensible maid, Lord Lunn descended to the richly carpeted room downstairs. The black-clad General Secretary glided to meet him.

They exchanged greetings and settled themselves over a flagon of wine. Cooth remarked that a messenger had just delivered an urgent note from the head of the Obal family.

'Do I understand, Lord Lunn, that you wish me to release a certain political criminal from the Glory of November the First Corrective Wing?'

Lunn's insanity had retreated. He regarded the other with a penetrating gaze, saying nothing. Cooth was a sturdily built man, almost hairless. Although in his sixties, he still showed every sign of vitality. His great head was sunk low on powerful shoulders. It appeared to sink even lower as he encountered Lunn's gaze. He lowered his own gaze to the table, setting his mouth defiantly.

Cooth was in large measure within Lunn's power. Lunn had discovered the crime of Cooth's ferocious grandfather.

That crime was nowhere recorded – except in the minds of a few men, and across the despoiled lands of the Four Fiefdoms.

The Four Fiefdoms (officially The 63rd Administrative District) had once, long ago, formed a stronghold of resistance against the

Revolution. No less a man than Cooth's grandfather had authorized the use of nuclear bombardment against the Resistance. Operation Rat-Catcher had proved successful. The Resistance was wiped out, with all other life.

Mountains had disappeared. Over a million men, women and children had died. Some said two million (but the figures were spoken in whispers, behind closed doors). No figures were ever published, no announcement ever made. Smothering silence formed a general shroud.

Such a terrifying act of genocide, carried out on so vast a scale, with so little scruple, had paralysed the psyches of those – the small enabling council – who had planned Operation Rat-Catcher under the command of Cooth's grandfather. Its enormity had chilled even the ruling Helmsman of the day.

That Helmsman had subsequently ordered the destruction of all weaponry, all technology. Despite its awesome success, Operation Rat-Catcher never found favour. Fratricide – brother killing brother and sister – petrified even the most villainous, even later generations, even the higher echelons of the Party. It marked the breakdown of the old society and all its ethical safeguards.

Operation Rat-Catcher – despite repression – remained a potentially damaging issue still. It still waited, like radioactivity in the rushes.

Cooth's continued eminence rested on a conspiracy of silence. Lunn had promoted himself prime keeper of that silence. In the last resort, the General Secretary would cede to Lunn's wishes in order that his grandfather should not be resurrected. He would acquiesce in any crime so that Operation Rat-Catcher would remain officially forgotten. He would give the nod to any atrocity to stay in office.

'What do you wish, Lord Lunn?' he asked in a low voice. He pushed his wineglass aside.

'There's a young woman in an upper room, General Secretary. Possibly dead. Get her away from here at once. Throw her into prison. She's an enemy of the Revolution, a loyalty-flouter.'

Giving a nod of acquiescence, Cooth said, 'Ah – but the criminal in the Glory of November the First Corrective Wing? What do you desire concerning him? The note says you gave your word to Eric Obal that he would be released immediately. What do you want me to do about that?'

'Pass me the note.'

The General Secretary pushed Eric Obal's note across the table, over the ideograms for Deception and Severity. Lunn took it and tore it up without a word. He scattered the pieces on the carpet.

'I suppose you will be riding back to the Four Fiefdoms shortly?' said Cooth. He assumed a polite tone.

The far door of the cell burst open. In rushed the guards, hoarsely shouting. Their shift was almost over. They were drenched with fatigue and disgust, and nearly at the end of their tether. They stank. Their boots and uniforms were covered with the foul exudations of the wretches they had dragged down to execution in the cellar.

Orders and obscenities poured from their mouths. Only eleven victims remained in what had once been the Mauve Room. Some of them had crawled under bunks in faint hope of remaining hidden, and so protracting their lives for an hour, or perhaps even overnight.

Screaming, the guards dragged them out by their feet. They kicked these unfortunates as they did so, pressing their faces down into the muck that coated the floor. An elderly woman vomited. Worms struggled for life in her bile. The guards struck her hollow breast and sent her flying down the cellar stairs.

All was useless haste, as always. The other five victims of their selected six were forced to strip naked. As usual, the guards assisted this operation with shouts and blows, insanely clouting all and sundry in their desperation to be gone from this place, to be done, to be off. The sooner finished, the sooner home to bully their wives and whores into washing their clothes, while they themselves – slumping devastated in broken chairs – gulped alcohol down their throats until they could plunge into unconsciousness.

During all this madness, Roi Obal stood erect in one corner, awaiting his turn to die. His hatred was for guards and prisoners alike. He berated them all in a level voice.

'God curse you all for snivelling bastards. God curse you all for conspiring to banish decency from the world. God curse you all for being scum. God curse you for reducing men and women to animals. God curse you for agreeing to be animals, to crawl and shit and whine and spew. God curse you above all for banishing love and romance from the world . . . God curse you every one for turning the world into a pigsty.'

The guards in their frenzy did not interrupt this litany. Perhaps some dreadful suffocated part of their souls was even comforted by Obal's condemnation. They avoided him. They lashed out insanely at everyone else.

Their knot of prisoners was marshalled, bruised, naked, befilthed. They were driven from the room. The door slammed. The bolt rammed home. Cries faded as they milled down into the cellar to meet their fate.

Those remaining in the cell, Obal and four others – three women and a man – preserved a tense silence. Shots rang out below. It was written.

At that moment, the other cell door, the one that led to and away from freedom, was flung open. A guard escorted in a young naked female prisoner. Her belly, buttocks and legs were covered with blood and slime.

With something approaching delicacy, the guard led her to a lower bunk. The woman sank down, eyes closing in agony. The guard looked about nervously, as if ashamed of his spasm of decency. He patted her head, retreated and slammed the door behind him.

Some of the prisoners shuffled up to inspect this new victim of the Revolution. No one spoke.

The young woman's face was bloated with tears. Her mouth hung open, bruised lips framing broken teeth. Her breath entered and left her body with long-protracted groans, as if she was breathing her last. Her legs sprawled on the floor. They lay carelessly open, exposing her damaged parts. Perhaps she expected never to close them again.

Obal went over to her, shouting incoherently. He pushed the other prisoners aside. When he ripped open his trousers, the three bedraggled women prisoners cheered and laughed to see his erect organ come forth.

Just before he flung himself on the dying woman, Obal recognized her. He gasped her name. Without opening her eyes, she called his name in response. In a hoarse whisper, she begged him for comfort.

He forced himself roughly into her, cheered on by the other women. He was crying, 'Forgive me, forgive me, Caraway!'

When three days had passed, the great lord remounted his stallion in order to return to his castle across the wastes. And no man knew his thoughts.

My dearest Penelope,

We must take control of our lives. If there is no governance over our selves but the biological one, we are lost. This I believe. All the same, there's a pleasure of sorts in watching everything going to hell in a bucket. Selling up. Concluding.

My business has failed. The old house has to go. And the old habits.

Father walks about the unmown lawns, depending heavily on his stick, back bent. I watch him from the long windows as he stares vacantly upwards at the maples. He knows I shall have to put him in a home. Perhaps he asks himself, as I do, as you must do, 'Where do we come from? What are we here for? Where are we going?'

He wears only slippers on his feet; the cold must get through to him. Randy follows, to bark at an occasional pigeon or squirrel.

The frost does not worry father; or could there be a wish to catch pneumonia and die, before worse happens to him?

He'll perhaps be thinking of other days, the days about which it makes him happy to talk, about which no one else wishes to hear, except you – or once you did. He's losing his grip on his tenses. The live and the dead become as one.

The other day he stood still, cupping a hand round his right ear. 'I can hear your sister singing,' he said. And smiled a sad smile.

I am clearing out the attic and the cupboards upstairs. All your old dolls greet me with innocent amazement on their faces! Only now can I understand why I hoarded objects of merely sentimental value. The past, always the bloody past. It's so dusty.

Two months ago, I was in Toulouse, happy, confident, eating well, living with Jeanne-Marie and her crippled child. Swimming in October.

Well, Christmas always was a cruel time.

Father and I live on French bread, cheese, olives. And we're drinking up his cellar. Sometimes I think I hear you singing as in days of old, sister dear.

Since you ask, I've reverted to an old habit, now that I'm – in a way – free. As we used to do, I read much, generally in the afternoons, in the Blue Room, because the window in the Blue Room faces west, towards the evening sun. Since you left behind some volumes of Jane Austen, I am reading Jane Austen. She is well-suited to my frame of mind: 'No second attachment, the only thoroughly natural, happy and sufficient cure, at her time of life, had been possible to the nice tone of her mind, the fastidiousness of her taste, in the small limits of the society around them.' Ahem, yes.

And the old bindings fall apart as I read their contents. Symbolism at every turn these days, Penny!

Many people wouldn't call this catastrophe, or even poverty. I acknowledge that. I am far from complaining.

You see how every paragraph contains a novel, just as every breath contains a life.

And with the new year . . . I shall find a room somewhere. That's no problem. The two problems really are what I do with the second half of my life, and how I can face having the old Airedale put down.

Wishing you all the happiness of the season,

Your loving brother

An Unwritten Love Note

I grew up in a society where everyone had their secrets. My father took up the name of Aldiss. He had been born somewhere in Czechoslovakia under another name. My mother was English. They sat over the shop at night, talking in code. Always prices, profits, taxes, and all in code: a foreign language to me.

My elder brother Tony was always aloof. Only when he was ill with cancer did I discover that he was in fact my half-brother.

Though they had little time for me, my parents were devoted to each other. Even in their dying moments, they had a thought for each other: which is why this is the most beautiful story for me. Harsh, yes, but there's no true beauty without a savour of steel.

My father belonged to a society which hospitalized him when he fell ill. His left leg had to be amputated at the knee. My mother became ill at the same time, and was taken to a different hospital, some miles from where my father lay. She had cancer of the oesophagus and realized she was dying.

When my brother and I visited her, she looked ghastly and could not talk. Beckoning me nearer, she whispered, 'I wanted to write to . . .' but broke off in a fit of coughing.

'Father?' I asked, and received a confirmatory nod.

Making a great effort, mother took hold of a magazine someone had placed on her bed. She tore off one corner with her trembling bony hands. The strip of paper was orange in colour. She gestured to my brother, who accepted it. We both understood it was intended for father. Satisfied, mother sank back and closed her eyes.

On our way out of the hospital, my brother threw the strip of orange-coloured paper into a waste bin. I ran over and retrieved it and clenched it in the palm of my hand. Later, I gave it to my father where he lay in his distant bed. He well understood the significance of this poor little scrap of wordless paper; it came to him with his wife's love, instead of a letter. He died with it clutched in his hand.

That scrap of paper – inscrutable to anyone else in the world, even my dear brother – now has a place in my wallet.

From an old notebook:

> Ten-dimensional space-time. 'Poor old Byron woke on only one morning to find himself famous. I've done it several times.'

> People longing for something they can never have. Sad, but more natural than never longing for anything you can't have.

> An idiot question. C.J. Cherryh was asked by a teacher at Stonehenge: 'Is it a natural rock formation?'

> That the psyche is not a perennial but a hardy annual. Keep applying mulch; remember, when winter comes, spring is far behind.

> To say what you think: not as easy as you'd think.

Readers may ask writers if the characters in their novels are – as the question is generally put – 'drawn from real life'. The answer given is yes and no, even if it really is Yes. Yes gets you into difficulties.

Events are safer than characters. Real events enter even the most fantastic stories. In a short story, a central event can take on symbolic power, as I believe happens with the holding of the infant out of the window in the Bosnia story. So with the introduction to literature in the following story.

You may ask, are such events drawn from real life?

Yes and no.

Making My Father
Read Revered Writings

In the fictions of Pierre de Lille-Sully is much that is exceedingly strange. He must have been an animist, although he professed the Christian faith; for him, even words have a life and spirit of their own.

Unfortunately, I have a poor grasp of the beautiful French language. But in the year – I stumbled across a second-hand book which immediately became one of my treasured possessions; it was a translation into English of de Lille-Sully's short stories, under the title *Conversations with Upper Crust Bandits*.

I was caught, a willing victim, in de Lille-Sully's puzzling spell. One knows such love for fiction only when one is young. I dwelt in the stories. Many of them I read over and over. But not the last one in the book. For reasons I cannot explain, I was reluctant to read 'The Prince of Such Things'. I knew little about literature, and devoured in the main what I regarded even then as trash; being unversed in finer things, I regarded the title of this last story as a bad one. It seemed to me dangerous, even a little deranged.

'The Prince of Such Things' . . . It is the responsibility of authors to give their stories a title that invites one in, or at least promises to make matters clear. Here, de Lille-Sully seemed to be neglecting his duty.

At this period, I was a retarded adolescent of fourteen, and much under my parents' thumb. My two sisters were high-spirited and joyous by nature; I felt myself to be their very opposite. My father's first name was William. He had had me christened William too. As soon as I was old enough to feel the sting, I smarted that I had been given the same name as my father. I was diminished by it; did they think I had no separate existence?

Once alert to this injustice (as I saw it), I felt that everything in my father's behaviour was calculated to deny me individual existence. In the matter of clothes, for instance, he always selected what I should wear. The possibility never existed that he might consult me. And when I grew large and gawky, I was made to wear his cast-off jackets and trousers.

Evenings in our house were particularly oppressive. My sisters would not remain in the sitting-room. They went upstairs to their bedroom, giggling and whispering to themselves. I was constrained to remain below, to sit with my parents.

We lived then in a northern country. Now that I am settled in the South of France, I look back on those long evenings and nights with something like terror. So mentally imprisoned was I that it never occurred to me to go out, in case I should suffer a word of reprimand from my father.

The custom was that my parents sat on either side of a tall wood-burning stove. They had comfortable chairs of an antique design, inherited from my father's family. I sat at a table nearby, on a hard-backed chair. At that table I read books or magazines, or drew in a callow way.

I should explain that my father would not allow television in our house. And for some reason – it may have been a superstitious reason for all I know – the radio had to be switched off at six-thirty.

Prompted by my sisters, I once dared to ask my father why we could not have television. He replied, 'Because I say so.' And that was sufficient explanation in his eyes.

Always, it seemed I was in disgrace – 'in his bad books', as the saying goes. All through my childhood years, I yearned to be loved by him. It made me stupid. It made me mute. The whole evening could pass in silence until, at a gesture from my father, we would rise and go to our beds.

It was my mother's way to sit almost immobile while the hours passed. Women are able to sit more still than men. She wore headphones, listening to music on her Walkman. The thin tintinnabulation, like a man whistling surreptitiously through his teeth, penetrated the deepest concentration I could muster.

My parents sat on opposite sides of the stove. I do not recall their ever conversing. At seven-thirty each evening, my mother would rise and pour father a glass of akvavit, for which he thanked her. Father had a habit of reading his newspaper to an inordinate degree. The frosty crackle of broadsheet pages as he turned them punctuated the hours. I never understood his method of reading. It was clear that, having stumped up a few öre for his copy, he was determined to get his money's worth. But the way in which my father searched back and forth among the pages suggested a man who possessed some cunning secret method of interpreting life's events.

Such was the scene on the evening I decided at last to read Pierre de Lille-Sully's story 'The Prince of Such Things'. I set my elbows on the polished table top, one each side of the volume. I blocked my ears with my hands, in order to defend myself from the crackle of paper and the whistle of music. I began to read.

Perhaps in everyone's young life comes a decisive moment, from which there is no turning back. A decision, I mean, not based on rational thought processes. I hope it is not so; for if it is, then we have no defence against it, and must endure what follows as best we can. The matter is a mystery to me, as are many features of existence. All I can say is that on that particular dreary evening I came upon one of those decisive moments.

The brilliance of 'The Prince of Such Things' flooded into my mind. The words, the turns of phrase, the sentences, the paragraphs and their cumulation, unfolded an eloquently imaginative story. It was a study of ordinary life and yet also a fairy story. More than a fairy story, a legend of striking symbolism, exciting, agitating and ravishing in its effect.

In a way, its basic proposition was ludicrous, for who could believe that ordinary people in a Parisian suburb had such powers? Yet the persuasiveness of the piece overcame any hint of implausibility. De Lille-Sully gave expression to an idea new to me at the age of fourteen, that the manner in which one thing can stand for another quite different – a sunrise for hope, let's say – forms the basis of all symbolic thought, and hence of language.

I was swept along by his narrative, as branches are swept along by a river in flood. Never had I guessed that such prose existed. Even the preceding stories in the book had left me unprepared for this magnificent outburst of de Lille-Sully's imagination.

I reached the final sentence exhausted as if by some powerful mental orgasm. My mind was full of wonder and inspiration. The sheer bravura of the story gave me courage.

The longing to share this experience was so great that, without further thought, I turned to my father.

Across the expanse of carpet separating us, I said, 'Father, I have just read the most marvellous story anyone has ever written.'

'Oh, yes.' He spoke without raising his eyes from the newspaper. 'Read it yourself, and you'll see.'

I picked up my book and took it across to him. How did I feel at that moment? I suppose I believed that if we could share this enlightening experience the relationship between us might become more human, more humane . . . That we might become more like father and son.

Transformed by the story, I felt only love for him as he condescended to put down his paper and accept the volume. He held it open just as he received it, asking what I wanted him to do.

'Read this story, father: "The Prince of Such Things".' I was conscious that I had not approached him to do anything for many years.

He sat upright in his chair, set his face grimly and began to read.

I stood beside him before retreating awkwardly to the table. There I made a pretence of picking up a pencil and drawing in an exercise book. All I did was scribble, while observing my parents.

My mother had momentarily shown some interest in my action; or perhaps it was surprise. After a moment's alertness, she retreated into her music, eyes focusing vaguely on a point above the stove. My father, meanwhile, concentratedly read the miraculous story. His eyes twitched from left to right and back, chasing the lines of print down the page. It was impossible to gather anything from his expression. No sign of enlightenment showed.

It took him, I would say, almost two hours to read de Lille-Sully's story. I had not lingered over it for more than three-quarters of an hour. I could not tell if this meant he was a slow reader, or whether he was deliberately keeping me in suspense.

Finally he had done. He closed the book. Without looking at me, he set the volume down on the right-hand side of his chair. He then picked up his newspaper, which he had dropped on the left-hand side of his chair, and resumed his scanning of its columns. He gave me no glance. He said not a word.

The mortification I experienced cannot be expressed. At the time I did nothing. Did not leave the room, did not retrieve the book, did not leave. Did not even die of shame. I sat where I was.

Either he had regarded de Lille-Sully's miraculous tale as beneath his contempt or – ah, but it took me many a year before an alternative came to me – he was unable to comprehend it. And more years passed before a third alternative, more dreadful than the others, entered my reflections; which alternative dawned on me only as I stood with my sisters by his graveside. Perhaps he had comprehended the story too well. Perhaps he had understood the symbolism in the way a fourteen-year-old could not. Perhaps he had read in Antoine's predicament, forced to repeat himself endlessly, a reflection of some inner paralysis of his own.

So where I had espoused the marzipan, the icing, of de Lille-Sully's prose, my father had absorbed its meaning – and turned for refuge to the stock-market reports . . .

*   *   *

As I have said, this evening wrought a decisive change in my life. Without volition, as I sat there looking away from my father, I found I had decided to become a writer.

In these early days of autumn, our cats lurk about by the fish pond. They serve to scare off the heron, but sneak into the house with their breath smelling of dragon flies.

Squirrels emerge from the woods to collect the acorns from our oak. They too are in danger of cat-doom. At night, foxes creep out and scare the cats. The ceaseless war goes on.

The days draw in. Changes in seasons and lengths of day are what you miss in the tropics. The world's great novels are all written in lands which have a winter. Long northern nights may be passed in drinking, gambling, amorous assignations – or writing *War and Peace*. And, almost as importantly, by reading. Writers need readers, need them even when they themselves are dead and buried.

In a graveyard in the modest hamlet of Langham in Norfolk stands the tomb of Captain Frederick Marryat, author of *Children of the New Forest*. Not so long ago, Marryat was a popular author. At school we all read his seafaring story *Mr Midshipman Easy*. It became a choice as a school prize, and that was the end of that.

Marryat died in 1848. He was then living in a grand house, which is now a nunnery. He won the house at a game of cards. The story as I heard it in the local pub (the same Bluebell which features in my novel *Remembrance Day*) is that he was playing cards with three other men late into the night and, on the last hand, the squire wagered his house. Marryat won the hand, the squire lost.

Next morning, Marryat rode round on his horse to inspect the property, only to encounter the squire and his lady in their coach, moving out. The gentlemen tipped their hats to one another as they passed.

Why was gambling with cards so popular? Part of the answer may have been strong liquor. The other part is — weak light. Until the introduction of gas into homes, lighting had scarcely improved since the centuries before Christ. Candles and oil lamps were the order of the day and night. To read under such conditions could be a strain. On the other hand, the four suits on a pack of cards could be easily distinguished. People could play brag in moonlight, or in their cups.

The interest in card games centres on each player hoping to beat the others. In the garden, cats, dragon flies, squirrels, herons, fish, are also in competition, competition of a more deadly kind.

No blame attaches to their killing, to the cat's kills; we recognize it as a part of nature. Concepts of right and wrong are peculiar to the human race. We can be more wicked than animals, and better, for we can transcend our natures. Somewhere along the line – presumably after Sophocles wrote his plays – someone came up with the challenging moral idea of forgiveness. In some backward societies, generally in mountainous country, where vendettas are carried on, forgiveness has yet to dawn.

The following story concerns forgiveness. So despite all the wasps and spiders, it is really about humans.

Sitting With Sick Wasps

An epidemic is like a failure of electricity. All is well with an individual, until suddenly one day, perhaps in the middle of a conversation, he begins to feel unwell. The current of his health has been cut off.

As a boy I often took refuge in our bathroom. It was the one room in our house which possessed a lock. There I was safe from my elder brother. 'Nasir, Nasir,' he would cry. 'Come out and be a man.' When I did not reply, he would lose interest and go away. I would stay where I was until my parents came home in the evening.

In the bathroom was a large stone bath. In that I crouched, feeling safe with the grey stone about my body. By pretending that I was inside an elephant, I made sure my brother would not get me.

The wasps suffered an epidemic that year.

Every year, wasps built a nest in the thatch of our roof. My father, who was kind to everything and everyone, taught us to love wasps. He said that wasps were on our side. They protected us from flies by eating the maggots of flies. He also pointed out the beauty of wasps, dressed in their neat little uniforms.

Perhaps it was a child's fancy, but I used to know that the wasps respected my father. Often they would come down and crawl on my father's hand and fingers. They never stung any of us, except for my brother when he tried to tear off their wings.

As I sat huddled in the stone bath, wasps fell from the thatch to the floor of the bathroom. They were already dying.

When my parents were home and I was safe from my brother's persecution, I would stand outside our house and watch what was happening on the roof. All appeared well. The industrious wasps buzzed back and forth in the sunlight. Some carried in bees or flies to feed the next wasp generation. Some rested on the reeds, fluttering their wings as if in sheer delight with existence.

That was an external view. Inside, in the dark, all was unwell. The hidden epidemic was working, spreading, switching off the life current.

One by one, the victims of the epidemic came spiralling down to our cold stone flags. Few managed to fly off the floor once they were there. The more active ones could skid along, or crawl about for a while. Some just lay where they fell, twitching their antennae. Few survived for more than an hour. The epidemic had got them.

Sometimes the wasps dropped on me in the bath. I let them lie, knowing them to be harmless. They seemed too feeble to sting. Such energy as they had was concerned with dying as circumspectly as possible.

While lying on the floor, they suffered one last hazard. A kind of large spider lived in the drain. They spun no webs. My mother told me they were called 'wolf spiders'. The wolf spiders would rush from their dark lair, seize a dying wasp, and carry it, still struggling with the last of its strength, into its recesses.

In this horrifying process I never interfered. My religion taught me that the spiders had as much right to life as the wasps. My main judgement was, as I stared over the little stone wall of the bath at this activity, a sort of luxurious fear that existence should have to be constructed along such lines. It struck me as unfair that the wasps should suffer this last torment.

Perhaps the spiders caught the epidemic from their victims. If they rushed, dying, out of the other end of the drain into the open air, sparrows would eat them. Then the secret death would spread to the birds of the air. And who would eat their corpses? The villagers?

It seemed the electricity was more simple to turn off than turn on.

Studying those who fell before my eyes, I saw how they suffered pain. When their time came, their legs collapsed and they lay on their sides. The fur on their shoulders became tawdry, their smart yellow-and-black armour ceased shining. So close did I feel to these humble creatures that every death seemed to make me dwindle.

Now that I am adult and able to nurse my poor mad brother, I see the epidemic is in him too. The current of his mind has been switched off. Unlike the wasps, he makes a great fuss about his plight. Often I find him cramped into the stone bath, weeping.

Defying wisdom and experience, you sometimes write something to please a particular somebody. The result is generally speaking disastrous. Although stories have to sell to particular markets, each with their particular limitations, they should be written mainly because they arise in the mind and therefore invite exploration on paper. In essence, you are pleasing yourself. If you fail to please yourself, you are hardly likely to please others.

I believe that to be correct; I have had over three hundred stories published and still have formulated no more hard-edged prescription for success. Certainly, to have a tragic sense of life makes success a little more difficult; for you are then liable to be told by editors that your latest story is – they use a useless word – 'pessimistic'. Pessimism is a kind of disease; whereas having a tragic sense of life does not conflict with happiness and excitement. As a teenager in a war, I saw stacks of dead bodies, corpses of men piled up like great logs turning black in the sun, with sows gorging on their extremities; and I believe the experience sharpened my sense of humour. Sophocles' tragedies were written by a man with a ribald bawdy streak. A surviving portion of his satyr play called *Trackers* is full of cattle dung . . . However . . .

So 'Becoming the Full Butterfly' was written for a friend who intended to edit an anthology of new stories. Unfortunately, her arrangements fell through. So there the story remained, wingless in the void. To settle here.

The Great Law Dream is probably authentic. Or at least it is plausible. Many things become plausible in

Rajasthan which we might reject on the grounds of rationalism.

There is the lesson people in the developed world find hard to learn: people in the so-called Third World often possess a serenity we would do well to emulate.

Becoming the Full Butterfly

The Great Dream was a wild success, far beyond anyone's imagining. Afterwards, no one recalled exactly who had chosen Monument Valley for its staging. The organizers claimed most of the credit, and the sponsors what was left of the credit. No one mentioned Casper Trestle. Trestle had disappeared again.

So had much else.

Trestle was always disappearing. Three years earlier, he had been wandering in Rajasthan. In that bleak and beautiful territory, where once deer had lain down with rajahs, he came through a rainless area where the land was denuded of trees and animals; here, huts were collapsing and the people were dying of drought. Men, aged at thirty, stood motionless as scarecrows of bone, watching with sick disinterest as Casper trudged by; but Casper was accustomed to disinterest. Only termites flourished, termites and the scavenger birds wheeling overhead.

Afflicted by the parched land, Casper found his way through to a mountainous area where miraculously trees still grew, and rivers flowed. He continued onwards, where the rugged countryside began to rise to meet the distant grandeur of the Himalayas. Plants blossomed with pendulous mauve and pink flowers like Victorian lampshades. There he met the mysterious Leigh, Leigh Tireno. Leigh was watching goats and lounging on a rock under the dappled shade of a baobab, while the bees made a low song that seemed to fill the little valley with sleep.

'Hi,' Casper said.

'Likewise,' Leigh said. He lay back on his rock, one hand stretched above his forehead shading his eyes, which were as brown as fresh honey. The nearest goat was a cloudy white like milk, and carried a little battered bell about its neck. The bell clattered in B Flat as the animal rubbed its haunches against Leigh's rock.

That was all that was said. It was a hot day.

But that night, Casper dreamed a delicious dream. He found a magic guava fruit and took it into his hand. The fruit opened for him and he plunged his face into it, seeking with his tongue, sucking the seeds into his mouth, swallowing them.

Casper found a place to doss in Kameredi. Casper was lost, really a lost urchin, snub-nosed, pasty of face, with hair growing out in straggly fashion from a neglected crew-cut. Although he had never learnt manners, he maintained the docility of the defeated. And he instinctively liked Kameredi. It was a humble version of paradise. After a few days, he began to see it was orderly and sane.

Kameredi was what some of the villagers called the Place of the Law. Others denied it had or needed a name: it was simply where they lived. Their houses stood on either side of a paved street which ended as it began, in earth. Other huts stood further up the hill, their decrease in size being more than a matter of perspective. A stream ran nearby, a little gossipy flow of water which chased among boulders on its way to the valley. Watercress grew in its side pools.

The children of Kameredi were surprisingly few in number. They flew kites, wrestled with each other, caught small silver fish in the stream, tried to ride the placid goats.

The women of Kameredi washed their clothes in the stream, beating them mercilessly against rocks. The children bathed beside them, screaming with the delight of being children. Dogs roamed the area like down-and-outs, pausing to scratch or looking up at the kite-hawks which soared above the thatched roofs.

Not much work was done in Kameredi, at least as far as the men were concerned. They squatted together in their dhotis, smoking and talking, gesticulating with their slender brown arms. Where they usually met, by V.K. Bannerji's house, the ground was stained red by betel juice.

Mr Bannerji was a kind of headman of the village. Once a month, he and his two daughters walked down into the valley to trade. They went loaded with honeycombs and cheeses and returned with kerosene and sticking plaster. Casper stayed at Mr Bannerji's house, sleeping on a battered charpoy beneath the colourful clay figure of Shiva, god of destruction and personal salvation.

Casper was a dead-beat. He was now off drugs. All he wanted at present was to be left alone and sit in the sun. Every day he sat on an outcropping rock, looking down along the village street, past the lingam carved from stone, into the distance, shimmering with Indian heat. It suited him that he had found a place where men were not expected to do anything much. Boys tended goats, women fetched water.

At first, an old nervousness attended him. Wherever he walked, people smiled at him. He could not understand why.

Nor did he understand why there was no drought, no starvation in Kameredi.

He had a sort of hankering for Mr Bannerji's daughters, both of whom were beautiful. He relied on their cunctative services for food. They tittered at him behind their spread fingers, showing their white teeth. Since he could not decide which young lady he would most like to embrace upon his rope charpoy, he made no advances to either. It was easier that way.

His thoughts tended towards Leigh Tireno. When Casper got

round to thinking about it, he told himself that a kind of magic hung over Kameredi. And over the bare-legged Leigh. He watched from his rock the bare-legged Leigh going about his day. Not that Leigh was much more active than anyone else; but occasionally he would climb up into the tree-clad heights above the village and disappear for several days. Or he would sit in the lotus position on his favourite boulder, holding the pose for hours at a time, eyes staring sightlessly ahead. In the evening, he would remove his dhoti and swim naked in one of the pools fed by the stream.

As it happened, Casper would take it into his head to stroll along by the pool where Leigh swam.

'Hi,' he called as he passed.

'Likewise,' replied Leigh, perfecting his breast stroke. Casper could not help noticing that Leigh had a white behind, and was otherwise burnt as dark as an Indian. The daughters of Mr Bannerji moulded with their slender fingers goat's cheeses as white as Leigh's behind. It was very mysterious and a little discomfiting.

Mr Bannerji had visited the outside world. Twice in his life he had been as far as Delhi. He was the only person in Kameredi who spoke any English, apart from Casper and Leigh. Casper picked up a few words of Urdu, mainly those to do with eating and drinking. He learned from Mr Bannerji that Leigh Tireno had lived for three years in the village. He came, said Mr Bannerji, from Europe, but was now of no nation. He was a magical person and must not be touched.

'You are not to be touching,' repeated Mr Bannerji, studying Casper intently with his short-sighted eyes. 'Novhere.'

The two young Bannerji ladies giggled and peeled back the skins of plantains in very slinky ways before inserting the tips into their red mouths.

A magical person. In what way could Leigh be magical? Casper asked. Mr Bannerji wobbled his head wisely, but could not or would not explain.

The people who flocked to Monument Valley, who had booked seats on the top of mesas or stood with camcorders on the roofs of coaches, had some doubts about Leigh Tireno's magical properties. It was publicity that got to them. They had been inoculated by the hype from New York and California. They believed that Leigh was a messiah.

Or else they didn't care either way.

They went to Monument Valley because the notion of a sex change turned them on.

Or because the neighbours were going.

'Hell of a place to go,' they said.

When the sun went down, darkness embraced Kameredi like an old friend, with that particular mountain darkness which is a rare variant of light. The lizards go in, the geckos come out. The night-jar trills of ancient romance. The huts and houses hold in their strawy palms the dizzy golden smell of kerosene lamps. There are roti smells too, matched with the scent of boiled rice teased with strands of curried goat. The perfumes of the night are warm and chill by turns, registering on the skin like moist fingertips. The tiny world of Kameredi becomes for an hour a place of sensuality, secret from the sun. Then everyone falls asleep: to exist in another world until cock crow.

In that hidden hour, Leigh came to Casper Trestle.

Casper could hardly speak. He was half-reclining on his charpoy, a hand supporting his untidy head. There stood Leigh looking down at him with a smile as enigmatic as the most abstruse Buddha.

'Hi,' Casper said.

Leigh said, 'Likewise.'

Casper struggled into a sitting position. He clutched his toes and gazed up at his beautiful visitor, unable to produce a further word.

Without further preliminary, Leigh said, 'You have been in the universe long enough to understand a little of its workings.'

Supposing this to be a question, Casper nodded his head.

'You have been in this village long enough to understand a little of its workings.' Pause. 'So I shall tell you something about it.'

This seemed to Casper very strange, despite the fact that his life had passed mainly surrounded by strange people.

'You mustn't be touched? Why not?'

When Leigh's mouth moved, it had its own kind of music, separate from the sounds it uttered. 'Because I am a dream. I may be your dream. If you touch me, you may awaken from it. Then – then, where would you be?' He gave a tiny cold sound almost like a human laugh.

'Ummm,' said Casper. 'New Jersey, I guess . . .'

Whereupon Leigh continued with what he had intended to say. He said that the people in Kameredi and a few villages nearby were a special sort of Rajput people. They had a special story. They had been set apart from ordinary folk by a special dream. The dream had happened four centuries ago. It was still revered, and known as the Great Law Dream.

'As a man of Kameredi respects his father,' said Leigh, 'so he respects the Great Law Dream even more.'

Four centuries ago in past time, a certain sadhu, a holy man, was dying in Kameredi. In the hours before his death, he dreamed a series of laws. These he was relating to his daughter when Death arrived, dressed in a deep shadow, to take him away to Vishnu. Because of her purity, the holy man's daughter had special powers, and was able to bargain with Death.

The holy man's spirit left him. Death stood over them both as the woman coaxed her dead father to speak, and to continue speaking until he had related to her all the laws of his dream. Then a vapour issued from his mouth. He had cried out. His lips had become sealed with the pale seal of Death. He was buried within the hour: yet even before the prayers were chanted and the body interred, it began to decompose. So the people knew a miracle had happened in their midst.

But the laws remained for the daughter to recite.

Her head changed to the head of an elephant. In this guise of wisdom, she summoned the entire village before her. All abased themselves and fasted for seven days while she recited to them the laws of the Great Law Dream.

The people had followed the laws of the Great Law Dream ever since.

The laws guided their conduct. The laws concerned worldly things, not spiritual, for, if the worldly matters were properly observed, then the spiritual would follow.

The laws taught the people how to live contentedly within their families and peacefully with each other. The laws taught them to be kind to strangers. The laws taught them to despise worldly goods of which they had no need. The laws taught them how to survive.

Those survival laws had, of all the laws, been most rigorously followed for four centuries, ever since the sadhu was taken by Death. For instance, the laws spoke of breath and water. Breath, the spirit of human life, water the spirit of all life. They taught how to conserve water, and how a little should be set aside for human use every day, so much spared for animals, so much for plants and trees. The laws taught how to cook with the best conservation of fuel and rice, and how to eat healthily, and how to drink moderately and enjoyably.

Speaking of moderation, the laws declared that happiness often lay in the silence of human tongues. Happiness was important to health. Health was most important to women, who had charge of the family cooking pot.

The laws spoke of the dangers of women bearing too many children, and of too many mouths to be fed in consequence. They told of certain pebbles to be found in the bed of the river, which the women could insert into their yonis to prevent fertilization. The smoothness of the stones, brought down from the snows of the Himalayas, and their dimensions, were minutely described.

Nakedness was no crime; before the gods, all humans went naked.

Behaviour too was described. Two virtues, said the laws, made for human happiness, and should be inculcated even into small children: self-abnegation and forgiveness.

'Love those near you and those distant,' said the laws. 'Then you will be able to love yourself. Love the gods. Never pretend to them, or you will deceive yourself.' So much for the spiritual part.

Instructions on the way to bake chapatis took up more time.

Finally, the Great Law Dream was clear about trees. Trees must be conserved. Goats must not eat of trees or saplings, or be permitted to eat the smallest seedling. No tree less than a hundred years old must be cut down for fuel or building material. Only the tops of trees, when they grew over six feet high, might be used for fuel or building material: in that way, Kameredi and surrounding villages would have shade and a good climate. Birds and beasts would survive which would otherwise perish. The countryside would not be denuded and become desert.

If the people looked to these laws of nature, then nature would look to them.

So spoke the sadhu in his hour of departure from this world.

As Leigh Tireno spoke concerning these matters, he seemed to become, as he claimed he was, a dream. His eyes became large, his eyelashes like the tips of thorn bushes, his simple face grave, his lips a musical instrument through which issued musics of wisdom.

He said that ever since the holy man's daughter gave forth the Great Law Dream through her blue elephant's head, the people of Kameredi had followed those precepts scrupulously. Nearby villages, having heard the laws, had not bothered with them. They had denuded their woods, eaten too greedily, begotten many children with greedy mouths. So the people of Kameredi lived happily, while less disciplined people perished, and passed away, and were forgotten on the stream of time.

'What about sex?' Casper asked.

And Leigh answered calmly, 'Sex and reproduction are Shiva's gift. They are our fortification against decay. Like Shiva, they can also destroy.' He gave Casper a smile of sorrowful beauty and left the Bannerji house, walking out lightly into the dark. The night-jar sang to him as he went his way. The night itself nestled on his slender shoulder.

'You want to promote an event where two crazy people sleep together?' The question was asked incredulously in a publicity office in New York. Fifth Avenue in the high thirties. Sale time again at Macy's.

'Are we talking hetero, gay, lesbian or what here?'

'Have they figgered out a new way of doing it? A short cut or something?'

'Forget it, you can see people screwing back home every night, in the safety of your own apartment.'

'They don't only screw, these two. They plan to have a very basic dream.'

'Dream, did you say? You want us to rent out Monument Valley for some fucking queers to have a *dream*? Get to fuck out of here!

Leigh was climbing from the pool, naked. Little rivulets of water ran from the watershed of his back down the length of his long legs. His pubic hair twinkled like a spider's web loaded with morning dew. Casper could hardly bear to look. He trembled, unable to make out what was wrong with him. When did he ever experience such desire?

Looking in the grass to see no leeches were about, Leigh folded himself onto a rock. He squeezed water from his hair with one hand. Sighing with contentment, he closed his eyes. He turned his faultless face up to the Sun, as though to return its rays.

'Really, you are a mess, Casper. This place should help you to get better, to mend – to be at peace inwardly with yourself.'

It was the first time he had spoken in this fashion.

'These dream laws,' Casper said, to change the subject. 'They're a lot of Indian hokum really, yep?'

'We all have a sense at the back of our minds that there was once a golden, primal time, when all was well with us – maybe in infancy.'

'Not me.'

'The Great Law Dream represents such a time for a whole community. You and I, my sad Casper, come from a culture where all – almost all – has been lost. Consumption instead of communication. Commercialism instead of contentment. Isn't that so?'

Standing on the spot, looking sulky and secretly contemplating Leigh's exposed body, Casper said, 'I never had nothing to consume.'

'But you want it. You're all grab at heart, Casper!' He sat up suddenly, lids still shielding his honeyed eyes. 'Don't you remember, back home, how they ate, how everyone ate and yet hardly breathed? The breath of life! How there was this sentimental cult of childhood, yet all the while kids were neglected, beaten, taught only negatives?'

Casper nodded. 'I sure remember that.' He fingered the scar on his shoulder.

'People don't know themselves back there, Casper. They cannot take a deep breath and know themselves. Knowledge they have – facts. Wisdom, not so. Most are hung up on sex. Women are trapped in male bodies, thousands of gay men long to be hetero . . . Humanity has fallen into a bad dream, rejecting spirituality, clinging to self – to lowly biological origins.'

He opened his eyes then, to scrutinize Casper. In the branches of the banyan nearby, pigeons cooed as if in mockery.

'I'm not so freaked out as I was.' Casper found nothing else to say.

'I came here to develop what was in me . . . If you travel far enough, you discover what you originally were.'

'That's true. Like I've put on a bit of weight.'

Leigh appeared to ignore the remark. 'As our breathing is automatic, so there are archetypes, I've come to believe, which guide our behaviour, if we allow them. A kind of automatic response.'

'This is over my head, Leigh. Sorry. Talk sense, will you?'

The gentle smile. 'You do understand. You do understand, and reject what is unfamiliar. Try thinking of archetypes as master – and mistress – figures, such as you encounter in fairy tales, "The Beauty and the Beast", for instance. Guiding our behaviour like very basic programming in a computer.'

'Grow up, Leigh! Fairy tales!'

'Archetypes have been set at nothing in our Western culture. So they're at war with our superficiality. We need them. Archetypes reach upwards to the rarefied heights of great music. And down into the soil of our being, down to the obscure realms beyond language, where only our dreaming selves can reach them.'

Casper scratched his crutch. He was embarrassed at being talked to as if he was an intelligent man. It had happened so rarely.

'I never heard of archetypes.'

'But you meet them in your sleep – those personages who are you, yet not you. The strangers you are familiar with.'

He scratched his chin instead of his crutch. 'You think dreams are that important?'

Leigh's was a gentle laugh, not as mocking as the doves'. 'This village is proof of it. If only . . . if only there were some way you and I could dream a Great Law Dream together. For the benefit of all humanity.'

'Sleep together, you mean? Hey! You won't allow that! You're tabu.'

'Perhaps only to a carnal touch . . .' He slid down and confronted Casper face to face. 'Casper, try! Save yourself. Release yourself. Let everything be changed. It's not impossible. It's easier than you think. Don't cling to chrysalis state – be the full butterfly!'

Casper Trestle took dried meat and fruit and climbed up into the mountains above Kameredi. There he remained and thought and experienced what some would call visions.

Some days, he fasted. Then it seemed to him that someone walked beside him in the forest. Someone wiser than he. Someone he knew intimately yet was unable to recognize. His thoughts that were not thoughts streamed from him like water.

He saw himself in a still pool. His hair grew to his shoulders and he went barefoot.

This is what he said to himself, scooping together fragments of reflection in the cloth of his mind:

'He's so beautiful. He must be Truth itself. Me, I'm a sham. I've cocked up my entire life. I had it cocked up for me. No, at last I must grab a slice of the blame. That way, I take control. I won't enjoy being a victim. Not no more. I'm going to change. I too can be beautiful, someone else's dream . . .

'I've been in the wrong dream. The stupid indulgent dream of the time. The abject dream of wealth beyond dreams. Spiritual destitution.

'Something's happened to me. From today, from now, I will be different.

'Okay, I'm going crackers, but I will be different. I will change. Already I am changing. I'm becoming the full butterfly.'

After a few nights, when the new Moon rose, he went to look at his reflection again. For the first time he saw – though in tatters – beauty. He wrapped his arms round himself. In the pool, from tiny throats, frogs cried out that there was no night.

He danced by the pool. 'Change, you froggies!' he called. 'If I can do it, anyone can do it.' They had done it.

Somewhere distantly, when the Moon sank into the welcoming maw of the mountains, he heard dismal roaring, as if creatures fought to the death in desolate swamps.

From the hoarse throats of machines, diesel fumes spewed. Genman Timber PLC was getting into action for another day. Guys in hard hats and jeans issued from the canteen. They tossed their cigarette butts into the mud, heading for their tractors and chain saws. The previous day they had cleared four square kilometres of forest in the mountain some miles above Kameredi.

The Genman camp was a half-formed circle of portable cabins. Generators roared, pumping electricity and air-conditioning round the site. Immense mobile cranes, brought to this remote area at great expense, loaded felled trees on to a string of lorries.

There were many more trees to go. The trees stood silent, awaiting the bite of metal teeth. In times to come, far from the Himalayas, they would form elements in furniture sold from showrooms in wasteland outside Rouen or Atlanta or Munich or Madrid. Or they would become crates containing oranges from Tel-Aviv, grapes from Cape province, tea from Guangzhou. They would form scaffolding on high-rises in Osaka, Beijing, Budapest, Manila. Or fake tourist figurines sold in Bali, Berlin, London, Aberdeen, Buenos Aires.

It was early yet at the Genman site. The sun came grumbling up into layers of mist. Loudspeakers played rock over the area. Overseers were cursing. Men were tense as they gunned their engines into life, or joked to postpone the moment when they had to exert themselves in the forests.

Bloated fuel carriers started up. Genman bulldozers turned like animals in pain on their caterpillar tracks, to throw up muck as they headed for their designated tasks.

The whole camp was a sea of mud.

Soon the trees would come crashing down, exposing ancient lateritic soils. And someone would be making a profit, back in Calcutta, California, Japan, Honolulu, Adelaide, England, Bermuda, Bombay, Zimbabwe, you name it . . .

Action started. Then the rain began, blowing ahead in full sail from the south-west.

'Shit,' said the men, but carried on. They had their bonuses to think of.

The new Casper slept. And had a terrible dream. It was like no other dream. As life is like a dream, this dream was like life.

His brain burned with it. He rose before dawn and stumbled through the aisles of the forest. His path lay downward. For two days and nights he travelled without food. He saw many old palaces sinking down into the mud, like great illuminated liners into an arctic sea. He saw things running and gigantic lizards giving birth. Eyes of amber, eyes of azure, breasts of bronze, adorned his track. So he returned to Kameredi and found it all despoiled.

What had been a harmonious village, with people and animals living together – he knew now how rare and precious it was – was no more. All had gone. Men and women, animals, hens, buildings, the little stream – all gone.

It was as if Kameredi had never been.

The rains had not fallen on Kameredi. The rains had fallen at higher altitudes. With the forests felled, upper streams had overflowed. Tides of mud flowed downhill. Before that chilly lava flow, everything gave way.

The people of Kameredi had been unprepared. The Great Law Dream had said nothing of this inundation. They were carried away, breathing dirt, drowned, submerged, finished.

And Casper saw himself walking over the desecrated ground, looking at the bodies growing like uncouth tubers from the sticky mess. He saw himself fall in a swoon to the ground.

In Monument Valley, gigantic stadia were being built at top speed. Bookings were being taken for seats that as yet were not fabricated. Emergency roads were being built. Notices, signs, public restrooms, were going up. Washington was being concerned. All kinds of large-scale scams were being set in motion. The League of Indigenous American Peoples was holding protest meetings.

A well-known Italian artist was wrapping up one of the mesas in pale blue plastic.

When Casper awoke, all knowledge seemed to have left him. He looked about. The room was dark. Everything was obscure, except for Leigh Tireno. Leigh stood by the charpoy, seeming to glow.

'Hi,' Casper whispered.

'Likewise,' said Leigh. They gazed upon each other as if upon summer landscapes choked with corn.

'Er, how about sex?' Casper asked.

'Our fortification against decay.'

Casper lay back, wondering what had happened. As if reading his thought, Leigh said, 'We knew you were in the mountains. I knew you were having a strong and terrible dream. I came with four women. They carried you back here. You are safe.'

'Safe!' Casper screamed. Suddenly his mind was clear. He staggered from the bed and made for the door. He was in Mr Bannerji's house and it was not destroyed, and Mr Bannerji's daughters lived.

Outside, the sun reigned over its peaceful village. Hens strutted between buildings. Children played with a puppy, men spat betel juice, women stood statuesque by the dhobi place.

Mud did not exist.

No corpses tried to swim down a choked street.

'Leigh, I had a dream as real as life itself. As life is a dream, so my dream was life. I must tell Mr Bannerji. It is a warning. Everyone must take their livestock and move to a safer place to live. But will they believe me?'

A month passed away for ever before they found a new place. It was three days' journey from the old place, facing south from the top of a fertile valley. The women complained at its steepness. But here it would be safe. There was water and shade. Trees grew. Mr Bannerji and others went into a town and traded livestock for cement. They rebuilt Kameredi in the new place. The women complained at the depth of the new watercourse. Goats ate the cement and got sick.

An ancient hag with a diamond at her nostril recited the Great Law Dream for all to hear, one evening when the stars resembled more diamonds and a moon above the new Kameredi swelled and became pregnant with light. Slowly the new place became their familiar Kameredi. Small boys with a dog sent to inspect the old place returned and reported it destroyed by a great mud flow, as if the earth had regurgitated itself.

Casper was embraced by all. He had dreamed truthfully. The villagers celebrated their escape from death. The village enjoyed twenty-four hours of drink and rejoicing, during which time Casper lay with both of the Bannerji young ladies, his limbs entwined with theirs, his warmth mingled with theirs, his juices with theirs.

In their yonis the ladies had placed smooth stones, as decreed in the laws. Casper kept the stones afterwards, as souvenirs, as trophies, as sacred memorials of blessed events.

Leigh Tireno disappeared. Nobody knew his whereabouts. He was gone so long that even Casper found he could live without him.

After another moon had waxed and waned, Leigh returned. His hair had grown long, and was tied by ribbon over one shoulder. He had decorated his face. His lips were reddened. He wore a sari. Under the sari, breasts swelled.

'Hi,' Leigh said.

'Likewise,' said Casper, holding out his arms. 'Life in New Kameredi is made new. All's changed. I've changed. It's the full butterfly. And you look more beautiful than ever.'

'I've changed. I am a woman. That is the discovery I had to make. I merely dreamed I was a man. It was the wrong dream for me, and I have at last awakened from it.'

To Casper's surprise, he was not as surprised as he might have been. He was becoming accustomed to the miraculous in life.

'You have a yoni?'

Leigh lifted his – her – sari and demonstrated. She had a yoni, ripe as guavas.

'It's beautiful. How about sex now?'

'It's a fortification against decay. Shiva's gift. It can also destroy.' She smiled. Her voice was softer than before. 'As I have told you. Be patient.'

'What became of your lingam? Did it drop off?'

'It crawled away into the undergrowth. In the forest, I menstruated for the first time. The moon was full. Where the blood fell, there a guava tree grew.'

'If I found the tree and ate of its fruit . . . ?'

He tried to touch her but she backed away. 'Casper, forget your little private business for a while. If you have really changed, you can look beyond your personal horizons to something wider, grander.'

Casper felt ashamed. He dropped his gaze to the floor, where ants crawled, as they had done even before the gods awoke and painted their faces blue.

'I'm sorry. Instruct me. Be my sadhu.'

She arranged herself among the ants in the lotus position. 'The logging in the hills. It is based more on greed than necessity. It needs to stop. Not just the logging, but all it stands for in the mercenary world. Contempt for the dignity of nature.'

It sounded like a tall order to Casper. But when he complained, Leigh coolly said that logging was very minor and nature was vast. 'We must dream together.'

'How do you manage that?'

'A powerful dream, in order to change more than little Kameredi, more than ourselves. A healing dream, together. As we have dreamed separately and succeeded. As all men and women dream separately – always separately. But we will dream together.'

'Touching?'

She smiled. 'You still must change. Change is a continuity. There are no comfort stations on the road to perfection.'

Within his breast, his heart jumped for fear and hope at the wonderful words. 'The things you understand . . . I worship you.'

'One day, I may worship you.'

Special units of the National Guard had been drafted in to control the crowds. Half of Utah and Arizona was cordoned off by razor wire. Counter-insurgency posts had been established; Washington was wary of dream-makers. Tanks, trucks, armed personnel carriers, patrolled everywhere. Special elevated ways had been erected. Armed police bikers roared along them, licensed to fire down on the crowds if trouble was brewing. Heligunships circled overhead, cracking the eardrums of Monument Valley with spiteful noise.

They supervised a sprawling site bearing the hallmarks of an interior landscape of manic depression.

Someone said it. 'Seems like they are shooting the war movie to end all war movies.'

Private automobiles had been banned, They were corralled in huge parks as far north as Blanding, Utah; at Shiprock, New Mexico, in the east; and at Tuba City, Arizona, to the south. The Hopis and Navajos were making a killing. A slew of cafés, bars, restaurants had sprung up from nowhere. Along authorized routes, lurid entertainments of various kinds sprang forth like paintboxes bursting. Many carried giant effigies of Leigh Tireno, looking at her best, above booths with such come-ons as 'Change Your Sex By Hypnosis – PAINLESS!' No one mentioned Casper Trestle.

Pedestrian lanes and coach lanes were kept apart.

How the good folk jostled on their way to the spectacle! It was mighty hot there, in the crowded desolation; sweat rose like a mist, an illness above heaving shoulders. Bacteria were having a great time. Countless city people, unaccustomed to walking more than a block, found the quarter mile from a Park-'n'-Ride bus drop more than they could take, and collapsed into one of the many field ambulance units. Rest was charged at $25 an hour. Some walked on singing or sobbing, according to taste. Pickpockets moved among the crowd, elbowing hot-gospellers of many kinds. The preachers preached their tunes of damnation. It was not difficult for the unprivileged, as blisters formed on their heels, to believe that the end of the world was nigh – or at least heaving into sight from the seas of misery, a kind of Jaws from the nether regions – or that the whole universe might sizzle down into a little white dot, like when you turned off the TV at two in the sullen Bronx morning. Could be, ending was best. Maybe with this possibility in mind, a fair percentage of the adults stomped along like cattle, pressing fast food to their mouths or slurping sweet liquids into their faces. A fat woman, hemmed in by heated bodies, was hit simultaneously by congestion and digestion; her cries as she cartwheeled among the marching legs were drowned by sporadic ghetto music from a multitude of receivers. Every orifice was stuffed. It was the law. At least no one was smoking. Varieties of bobbing caps amid the throng indicated children, big and little hobbledehoys fighting to get through first, yelling, screaming, gobbling popcorn as they went. Underfoot, all kinds of coloured cartons and wrappers of non-biodegradable material were trampled in the dust, along with the tumbling bodies, the gobs of pink gum, the discarded items of cloth-ing, the ejected tampons, the lost soles. It was a real media event, as much a crowd-puller as the World Series.

Casper had set the whole vast scheme in motion. Now he was responsible only for himself and Leigh. Human nature was beyond his control. He stood in the middle of a mile-wide arena where John Wayne had once ridden hell-for-leather. Mr V.K. Bannerji was with him, terrified by the sheer blast of public attention.

'Vill it vork?' he asked Casper. 'Otherwise ve shall have wiolence.'

But at six in the evening, when the shadows of the giant mesas grew like long blunt black teeth over the land, a bell rang and silence fell. A slight breeze arose, mitigating the heat, cooling many a feverish armpit. The pale blue plastic in which one of the mesas had been wrapped crackled slightly. Otherwise all was at last still – still as it had been in the millennia before the human race existed.

A king-size bed stood raised in the middle of the arena. Leigh waited by the side of the bed. She removed her clothes without coquetry, turning about once in a full circle, so that all could see she was now a woman. She climbed into the bed.

Casper removed his clothes, also turned about to demonstrate that he was a man, and climbed in beside Leigh. He touched her.

They put their arms about each other and fell asleep.

Gently, music arose from the assembled Boston Pops Orchestra. Tchaikovsky's waltz from 'The Sleeping Beauty'. The organizers felt this composer was particularly appropriate on this occasion. In the million-strong audience, women wept, kids threw up as quietly as possible. Before their television screens all round the world, people were weeping and throwing up into plastic bowls.

It was an ancient dream they dreamed, welling from the brain's ancient core. The beings that paraded across a primal tapestry of fields wore stiff antique garb. In these personages was vested an untroubled power over human behaviour. An untroubled archetypal power.

Before sex was life, aspiring upwards like spring water. After the advent of sexual reproduction came consciousness. Before consciousness dawned, dreams prevailed. Such dreams form the language of the archetypes.

In the espousal of a machine civilization, those ancient personages had been neglected, despised. Hero, warrior, matron, maiden true, wizard, mother, wise man too – finally their paths were bent to sow in human lives dissent. In disarray a billion lives were spent: war, rape, mental torment, dismay . . . But LeighCas in the tongue of dream vowed to these forces to redeem the Time, asked in return – it seems – that male and female might be free of crime . . . to live in better dreams . . .

Casper struggled up through layers of blanketing sleep. He lay unsure of himself, or where he was. Much had transpired, that he knew: a shift in consciousness. The dark head of the woman Leigh lay on his breast. Opening his eyes, he saw that above him flared an expressionist sky, encompassing cinnamon and maroon banners of sunset waving at feverish rate from horizon to far horizon.

Prompted by deep instinct, he felt down between his legs. He dug into a furry nest and felt lips there. What they told him word-lessly was strange and new. He wondered for a while if, soggy from the miracle sleep, he was feeling her by mistake. Gently, he stirred her away from his breast . . . his breasts . . . *her* breasts . . .

When Leigh opened her eyes and looked honey-coloured at Casper, her gaze was remote. Slowly, her lips curved into a smile.

'Likewise,' she remarked, slipping a finger into Casper's yoni.

'How about a fortification against decay?' she asked.

The multitudes were leaving the auditorium. The aircraft were head-ing like eagles back to their nests. The tanks were pulling back. The Italian artist was unwrapping his mesa. Imagining he heard tree-cutting machines falling silent in distant forests, Mr Bannerji sat on the side of the bed, to cover his short-sighted eyes and weep for joy – the joy that survives in the midst of sorrow.

Immersed in their thoughts, the short-sighted multitudes went away. The different dream was taking effect. No one jostled. Some-thing in their unity of posture, the bent shoulders, the bowed heads, was reminiscent of figures in an ancient frieze.

Here or there, a cheek, an eyeball, a bald head, reflected back the imperial colours of the sky, arbitrary yellows denoting happiness or pain, red meaning fire or passion, the blues of nullity or reflection. Nothing remained but land and sky – forever at odds, forever a unity. The mesas were standing up into the velvet, ancient citadels built without hands to commemorate distant time.

Although the multitude was silent as it departed, its multiple jaws not moving, a kind of murmur rose from its ranks.

The still sad music of humanity.

The day's death flew its colours, increasingly sombre. It was sunset: the dawn of a new age.

What follows is the oldest story in the pack. More an incantation than a story.

In 1987, my partner and media agent, Frank Hatherley, composed an evening revue culled from my writings: poems, sketches, playlets, conversations. That was how 'Science Fiction Blues' came about.

Frank is the wizard behind scenes. He can light a barn of a place so that we have a little secure cave in which to act. We do not need a stage. Sometimes we perform in bars. Ray Charles's 'Hit the Road, Jack' plays, and on we troop.

There are three of us, two being real actors, Ken Campbell and Petronilla Whitfield. Sometimes, Ken, being so popular, has had other engagements and we have found other actors to take his place, Ken Robertson, Jeff Rawle (of TV's *Drop the Dead Donkey*), and Shane Connaughton (novelist, actor, and scriptwriter of the film *My Left Foot*).

Ken and I met a long time ago, at a Newcastle Literary Festival. Ken was then the prime mover of the Ken Campbell Road Show.

In those days of apparent national prosperity, before the portcullis of the seventies came down, Newcastle-upon-Tyne remained a manufacturing centre. I was drinking in a rough pub by the Tyne, surrounded by miners and dockers downing their great brown pints, when in burst Ken with his two supporters – one of them Bob Hoskins. They grabbed two chairs and started a series of quick-fire sketches.

The faces of the miners under their cloth caps were a study. Offended by this intrusion on their drinking time, they clearly said, 'Goo on then, me-at, make me blooody laff – if you can.'

The two chairs when stacked came in handy for a sketch where Ken climbed up to the top of Big Ben, intending to throw himself off, only to discover he had no head for heights.

The faces of the miners were another study. Within a couple of minutes, they were crying with laughter into their glasses of porter.

Petronilla is another order of being, sensitive and raucous by turns. The star turn of the evening is when she does 'Juniper'.

This little legend, 'Traveller, Traveller', she and I perform between us, the story just as Frank originally rejigged it.

My wife – who has sometimes sold programmes on these giddy evening occasions – and I once argued over which character's life is more wasted, Sven's or his wife's. I am unsure of the answer; but it still seems a point worth arguing.

Traveller, Traveller, Seek Your Wife in the Forests of This Life

BRIAN: Friends, in the remote regions of Scandinavia live many unearthly creatures, of which the trolls are best known. More frightening are the hulderfolk. The hulderfolk have a ceaseless enmity with mankind. There was a young sailor, by name Sven Andersson, who sailed the Baltic and seas beyond. He led a merry irresponsible life before he met Lise.

PETRONILLA: Lise was a fair-haired girl with a shy smile and puritanical ways. She promised to marry Sven only if he reformed and became a useful member of the community.

BRIAN: To that, Sven agreed. 'No more philandering – I swear it by your sacred life.'

PETRONILLA: The seriousness of this oath frightened Lise.

BRIAN: Sven and Lise married and went to live in a cottage at the foot of the mountains.

PETRONILLA: It was a neat thatched cottage with a tall white chimney. Lise grew flowers in the garden and kept the honey-suckle hedge trimmed. Beyond the hedge and the garden was a lane which led into the forest.

BRIAN: Happy though they were, the roving habit was still in Sven. When the summer came round, he kissed Lise's red lips and went up the lane into the mountains, to work as a lumber-jack or trapper, as the fancy took him.

One evening, as the sun was setting, Sven found himself alone in a particularly desolate part of the forest. He was tired and thirsty. The last rays of the sun, filtering through the pines, had a tarnished quality which made him melancholy.

He looked about uneasily. There, through the motionless trunks of the trees, he saw a prosperous farm where no farm should be. Something in the look of it told Sven that this place belonged to the hulder or hidden folk.

He realized then that a woman stood at the farmhouse door, watching him.

PETRONILLA: 'Come over here, stranger. Approach me.'

BRIAN: Although he was filled with superstitious fear, something in her voice, something in her beauty, forced him to draw nearer.

PETRONILLA: The woman gave him a smile of unearthly sweet-ness. She was dressed in timeless garb, with her dark hair sweep-ing over her brow. Her look mingled demureness and cunning.

BRIAN: She gave off a scent of dead geraniums.

PETRONILLA: 'Do you seek shelter, man? That you shall find here, and more.' And she led him into the farmhouse.

BRIAN: As he stepped over the threshold, an owl cried out, *'please'*, and night seemed to swoop down over the forest. Dread halted him, making him stumble.

The room was dim. Beside the hearth, a small girl played with a hound.

PETRONILLA: The woman, her mother, told her to get up and draw some ale for their visitor. This the girl did very pleasantly.

BRIAN: He sat and drank and talked with the woman who smelt of dead geraniums. Her beauty filled his brain. Her gestures, her conversation, went to his heart. He began to lose his caution.

The fire crackled, the words flowed between them. Otherwise, the world was silent, as if all its clocks had stopped. The only reminder of outside was an infrequent clatter of hoof on cobble, where a hulder horse was tethered by the door.

Sven could well recall uncanny tales of the hulderfolk, and of the terrifying way in which time passed at a different rate in their world, so that an ordinary lifetime might pass between two chimes of a hulder clock. He knew that mere mortals had found their lives squandered in that way. But he took more ale – took more ale and looked into the woman's eyes.

PETRONILLA: 'The forests are deep and stretch to the rim of the world. You're a brave 'un to come here.'

BRIAN: 'Are you alone with the girl? Where is your man?'

PETRONILLA: 'What a question to ask! Can you really have forgotten, Sven? Don't you remember? This little miss is your own daughter. Do you not see how closely she resembles you?'

BRIAN: Bemused, he called the girl over to the light in order to have a better look at her.

PETRONILLA: But her mother spoke sharply to her and ordered her off to bed. When the girl had gone, the woman came round the table to stand before Sven.

BRIAN: He looked at her with pounding heart, awaiting her next move, sorely troubled by her words.

PETRONILLA: 'Now we can go to bed, my dearest Sven.'

BRIAN: 'I'm already married. My wife awaits me, down in the valley where the river runs.'

PETRONILLA: 'Don't you remember? Sven, don't you remember that dream you had long ago, when you were a sailor? You met the loveliest woman you had ever known. You embraced her all one summer night, where the fireflies played over the lake. The next day you married her. Later, she bore you the fairest child you ever saw. Then you sailed away and never returned. Oh, Sven – don't you remember?'

BRIAN: Her cry was a torment to him. He looked about the room, filled with night and mist. It appeared to him that he could see the tall trees of the forest through the walls. And it felt as if every word the woman said were true. Remorse filled him as flood water fills a dried river-bed.

'Yes, yes, I remember now. Everything was as you say.'

PETRONILLA: 'All night long we were together.'

BRIAN: 'All night long we were together. It broke my heart to sail away. I could not bear to leave you. Every night in my hammock, I wept for you and the child.'

PETRONILLA: 'I held you like this before. Many and many a time.'

BRIAN: 'I remember, I remember the dream.'

PETRONILLA: 'Only it was no dream. That was your real life, Sven. That was your real life, and everything that has happened since has been the dream. Now you are waking again, and we can be together, just as before.'

BRIAN: 'Can that really be so?'

PETRONILLA: 'Come to bed with me and you will see.'

And the woman began slowly to undress.

BRIAN: He stood before her as if in a spell.

An owl shrieked outside and he heard its cry – 'Lise, Lise, remember Lise!'

He gave a groan and uttered his wife's name.

'Lise.'

Then he was free of the spell.

PETRONILLA: As he ran towards the door, the hulderwoman was transformed. In an instant, she dropped the appearance of humanity. She took on the likeness of a monstrous uprooted tree, and rushed at Sven with an axe.

BRIAN: He threw open the door, unleashed the horse that stood there, and galloped away from the place. Once he dared to look back. The hulder farm had vanished, the hulderwoman was gone. There was nothing but night and forest.

'I was tempted – sorely tempted – but I did not break my oath. I swore by the sacred life of Lise and did not betray her quite.'

The hulder horse vanished like a wraith, casting him down into a bed of leaves.

All through the northern night he walked, as fast as he could go, often looking behind him. By dawn, he came to the lane where he lived. There, ahead, was his cottage, but so changed. He saw the honeysuckle hedge was unclipped. The garden was untended. The thatch needed repair. No smoke rose from the white chimney.

Sven paused by the gate, which had fallen from its hinges.

But Lise was still there.

PETRONILLA: She came haltingly from the cottage to greet him. She dropped her stick in surprise at his approach.

'You returned to me at last, then.'

BRIAN: He clutched her age-dried figure to him, ran his hand over her grey hair, kissed his wife on her parched old lips.

Together they went slowly into the ruinous home.

Storytelling, all agree, is an ancient art. Nowadays it has diversified into many media and a multitude of pictures. But the basic need remains unchanged: a desire to tell or be told a story. To be held by it so that we forget our own story.

The storyteller of old, who stood forth and narrated in verse or prose before a crowd, commanded authority. It is a harmless form of authority; we wish to be dominated by the narrative.

There are various accents in storytelling: one storyteller may like to elaborate character, another to convey a mood, an atmosphere, another has a curious circumstance to dwell on, while another goes for drama. The Anglo-American tradition is, on the whole, to 'tell a tale'. A one-liner is the budget version of the principle. All styles delight when well done.

In most cases, we have an unspoken target: to be as brief as possible, knowing we address busy people. They may not wait.

A few years ago, I used to be treated regularly to another kind of storytelling. It was of a traditional kind, developed for people who could wait – who in fact had a lot of time to kill.

We were living in a house with a fair amount of land attached. One day, an old man walked in and asked if he could do some gardening for us. He was also good at building dry stone walls, he said. Stone-walling was what he had done for most of his life.

So we got to know Mr Parsons. He worked with us for several years. He was a good, steady, reliable man, as expert with a scythe as with a stone wall. I liked him and I still miss him.

He enjoyed spinning a tale. Always about something that had happened in the past. His story would unwind in this fashion.

'You wouldn't know the Hewitts. He's been dead this twelve-month. They used to live down the bottom of Clamp Lane, near where that pig farm is now. It's all changed now. Jimmy Hewitt, the son, he still lives over Garford way. Mary Hewitt was his mother, and her it was as fell down the well.'

So that you will not worry what the story is to be about, he tells you the point of it at the beginning. Mary Hewitt fell down the well.

'Jimmy Hewitt's father was Steve Hewitt, and a funny blighter he was, too. Some of 'em reckoned as he wasn't quite right in the head. How Mary put up with him I'll never know. Not but what she didn't have her own funny ways. I seen her many a time cycle through the village in her slippers, yes! Broad daylight, in her old slippers. She used to clean for Mrs Marshall up at the Vicarage. No one else would work for that Mrs Marshall with her la-de-dah ways. Old Hoskins used to say as Mary fell down the well to spite her husband and Mrs Marshall.

'That can't have been the case. Steve were away with the Ox & Bucks in the war when that happened. She was left in peace a bit, with Jimmy and the daughter – Valerie, her name was – to look after. Valerie later got a job with the grocer over in Longworth.

'Old Mary, she kept half-a-dozen chickens. I used to go down there occasionally. I pruned her apple trees for her when Steve was away at the war. Not that she wasn't capable of pruning them herself, when put to it.

'Their well was down by the apple trees. Cookers they had, as well as eaters. So one day, about this time of year –'

So Mr Parsons would pile up the detail. What, by usual standards, would be called narrative suspense, was lacking. What you got was detail and anecdote within anecdote, so as to protract the story and delay the end.

When it seemed as if no more could be said, the tale might double back on itself, and we would hear how Steve and Mary's neighbours had their thatch blown clean off, one night in a terrible storm, and it landed in Steve's garden. That started a row. They almost came to blows.

As one listened to Mr Parsons telling his stories of village life half a century earlier, it was easy to imagine his father and his grandfather before him, sitting in their poor draughty labourers' cottages, telling similar stories at night. Perhaps the only light – to save a penny candle – was that of a wood fire, round which the family was gathered. How else would the hours after work, after dark, be spent? The longer the tale, the more particular the detail, the more welcome it would be. It filled the hour before bedtime.

To this oral tradition, I am sympathetic. At the tender age of seven, I was sent away from home to boarding school. I had an inestimable advantage over the other boys: our family lived in a haunted house. When the lights went out, and we were confined to our poky little beds in our poky little dormitories, I would tell my ghost tale. It too, like Mr Parson's narratives, could be spun out with practice, elaborated, *improved upon*. When a boy flung himself beneath the bedclothes, shouting, 'Shut up, Aldiss, you swine!' – ah, that was applause! From there, it was a natural progression to other tales in which terrible things happened ... The Bedclothes Effect was my litmus test of success.

Nowadays, a collection like this contains less than one hundred thousand words. And with no particular story is the reader expected to identify, or to nod in agreeable recognition over its minutiae. Certainly not in the manner I was expected to empathize with the way, one autumn morning long ago, Mary Hewitt, in white socks and those old slippers, trudged down through the long grass and leaned over the side of their well to catch hold of the bucket . . .

Well, there are many ways of telling a story, and many places in which a story may be set.

Her Toes Were Beautiful on the Mountains

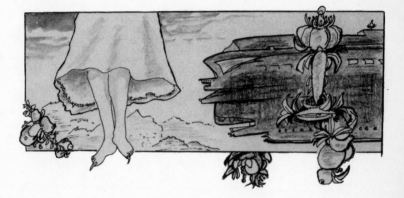

THREE ENIGMAS:

ANOTHER WAY THAN DEATH

THAT PARTICULAR GREEN OF OBSEQUIES

THE ANCESTRAL HOME OF THOUGHT

ANOTHER WAY THAN DEATH

Sun was down. Time was up. Half-eroded, the Moon hung like a target low in the glassy sky. The human world was turning to metal and madness again, yet something miraculous was gestating. That much could be divined from the olive green of the sky, with a hint of Prussian blue, moving at a bone-shaking tilt.

The metal vehicle containing the supposed John Stang and the other soldiers hurtled straight towards the Moon over ill-paved roads. Resonations shook the vehicle as it went. It travelled all through the night, never getting nearer to the pock-faced satellite. Speed, distance, engineered obsolescence.

The eyes of the men in the vehicle were silted up; they flowered with staleness like dead irises, unlit by dawn. The sky cracked like an egg towards the eastern horizon. A pale light spilled out from it, to be reflected on the sullen flanks of the vehicle.

No one knew a damn thing. No one knew their destination. No one knew the cardinal thing: that Heaven was coming at breakneck pace, swooping down the cosmic background, down the backbone, with that touch of Prussian blue.

The marines. Their time was almost up. They could not get it into their heads. Packed into the vehicle with ranks of other uniformed men, John Stang watched the line of first light through a slitted window. Dawn. Although he invited its welcoming implications into his mind, only shadow and foreboding entered. He'd always been a night person, and the stiletto of light he was watching carried a hue he associated with sickness and despair. First light was a time for a family death to occur, for the telephone to ring, for children to cry with newly emergent ills, for suicides, for a confrontation with material ills and unpaid bills, for unmended shoes, cold, smoke, stale breath, alarms, acrid cigarettes, and the snapping of a mundane muzzle back over the chops of dreamtime.

But today dawn was a time for Armageddon. And Stang's resur-
rection.

To deflect his thoughts, Stang turned to the marines next to him.
He knew few by name. In the black interior of the A-truck, they
were not recognizable. They squatted together in the dark, talking
in gusts of talk about women.

So Stang phrased it to himself. Turning in distaste from the crud-
ity of the discussion, he knew they were not actually talking of
women, but about their own rutting and their imagined conquest
of women. In everything they said was a lack of knowledge of
women, even a dislike of them as women.

'I'm gonna grab that slag Penny when we bust out of this op.
Next time, you bet I'm really gonna show her. She'll be yellin' for
mercy time I'm through . . .'

'Forget Penny, you poxy stud. This'll be some strike we're on.
Wham!'

'Ah, the Goonos won't give us no pain, you'll see. Then, home
as heroes and knee deep in semen . . .'

'Yeah, we'll hit 'em so's they won't know asshole from elbow.'

On rattled the A-truck. Ahead across the plain, a mighty hangar
loomed. The plain still lay black under the vellum-pale overhead, so
that the shoulder of the building cut the sky, its geometrical outline
broken only by great bare trees sheltering its northern end. The
vehicle swerved to one end of the hangar as if seeking shelter, braked
among other trucks already parked, and sank down on its haunches.

Immediate shouted orders. Slamming open of doors. Clang of
metal on metal. Intense activity. Every man gathering up his armour,
tightening equipment, securing arms. Pushing forward. They
pushed to the ramp raised at the rear of their vehicle and on down,
solid, close, as if they were one formidable insect. Night visors still
down. Grim lips only showing, eyes concealed. Chill dawn air made
sour by fumes sucked into the barred tubes of their throats.

In the immense black rear wall of the hangar, a sudden sickly
green rectangle as a door opened.

The soldierly insect pressed forward at the double. No shouting now, only stamping boots. Swallowed into the maw of the building.

Stang was in one of the rear files. Pressed against the outside wall of the hangar, so that light from the interior did not catch him, stood a dim figure. He spoke directly to Stang as Stang filed by with the other men.

He said in a conversational tone, '*There is another way.*'

Stang lost his step, stumbling over the lip of the hangar entrance, and so lunging forward awkwardly as he entered the building.

A sergeant was standing guard at the entrance, green light running down the line of his jaw.

'You! Keep the dressing. Name and number?'

'John Stang, Sergeant. No number. I'm not a combatant. I'm an accredited war correspondent.' He flashed his photo-pass.

The sergeant barely glanced at it. 'I don't care if you're Queen of All the Fairies, lad. Keep in step.'

The hangar was filled with the bristling bulk of a Keg 15A. This latest cyborgoid armament was shaped like a boar's belly and coated with synthetic skin and hair. The hangar air was tainted with its processes. Marking time, the troops moved up an escalator which inserted them through a rear orifice into the vast machine. A sphincter closed behind the last man.

'*There is another way . . .*' Who had said it, and what could it mean?

Stang felt the conflict within himself. From without came the empathy radiating from Keg 15A: a kind of communion. The troops listened with an inward ear, their visors up. The air was synthesized, the breath of the semi-being that contained them. Music whispered like bloodstream, damping down pulse rates. All were one.

He had fought all his life against the things that now overwhelmed him. Boots, harness, helmets, weaponry – all part of a mechanized regimented life to which individual conscience was sacrificed. The world, not of real men, as many claimed, but of death of spirit. He would not yield to the mass mind. Sending out a strong probing thought, he touched the cybermind.

It was all about him. He felt it cool and detached, with none of the ferocity he feared. Its wish was not to kill but to fly, to ascend, to keep flying. Even – to preserve itself in order to remain aloft.

Stang gave it a psychic smile, receiving in return . . . whatever it was, it was strong and positive, astonishingly unwarlike. A communication from the mothership to the thing in its womb. Hush, don't worry, you'll get born . . .

'*There is another way . . .*'

The amazing empathy was broken. A crackling intercom voice spoke.

'Marines, we are preparing for take-off. Be attached to the bench straps. Visors down, attach your breathing tubes to the oxygen nipples in the bulkheads. We shall taxi and await clearance for flight. Airborne in fifteen minutes. Out.'

Muted figures plugging in to the Keg lost more of their essence.

As Stang hesitated, the personage was next to him, roughly human in appearance, semi-transparent as if composed of fibre optics. Stang had room to draw back no more than an inch when the being addressed him.

'There is still an island, the Isle of the Blessed, where Heaven and Earth are one. It can be reached. There is a way . . .'

'We're heading for Apocalypse.' Was it the ghost of the machine?

'Not necessarily. Apotheosis, rather. The way is hard. It needs one man to stand up and be counted.'

He knew that what was conveyed was of overwhelming importance. The information came coded, and was attacking the chemical bonds of his being. He felt fear. The Keg reassured him.

Down the blue-lit length of the troop deck, men were immobile. No one had heard anything. Chins were firm, brows heavy.

Vibrations began, filling space between teeth and bones in individual hairs, as the Keg shook itself and moved forward, rolling out of its vat of green light into the open.

The personage had been withdrawn. Had it possessed legs? Had it infiltrated him in some way? Had the projection of the machine Keg united with a deep racial reservoir within him? If not, why was he changing? Pains and confusions grew in him like unbridled optimism. He was filled with a tangle of near-human imaginings.

The Isle of the Blessed.

When that island was obliterated, what remained? The world's apple trees would die and these humans lose their pretence of humanity. Why this new war, fought with newer weapons?

His questioning was answered by the mothership, far, it seemed, in the distance. *The rejection of the anima, the female principle, of wholeness.*

So the planners of this immense instrument of war had designed something beyond their knowledge; a greater power had worked through them – and was now working through Stang . . .

There is another way . . .

In anguish, Stang rolled his eyes upward, fighting disintegration. He saw the ordered labyrinth of pipes and ducts curling through the vessel, the intestines of the great beast that had swallowed them.

The intercom again. A personal voice, rich in fumes of meat and liquor.

'General Steen here, men. You know I'm a no-nonsense guy. You don't need to question my orders. We all hope to die fighting and today we get our chance, for the glory of our country.

'We're about to fly halfway round the globe to blast our enemies out of existence. You don't need reminding of that. However, I will remind you of a few salient facts about our enemy.

'You know they hate our country. They hate justice and liberty and freedom. You know what they call us. Motherfuckers. That's what they call us. They don't live like we do. Not at all. Different religion. Eating muck. Small dark hairy men, women fat as cows . . .'

He went into some detail here, the voice becoming thick and congested.

'So we're going to wipe them out and have done. You all agree. Else you wouldn't be on this mission. First, the cobalt treatment. Then we go in at ground level with the new cerebellum weapons. Men, we have an opportunity no soldiers have ever had before. Literally blast the enemy back into the Stone Age. Turn their grey matter into instant mashed potato, every damned manjack. Never raise a finger against us again . . .'

Backs straightened, glassy looks of pride showed on many a tube-infested face. Big hands clutched at the gleaming weapons in their grasp, sliding up and down the barrel in masturbatory movement.

The Keg was still rolling forward. Everyone swayed slightly, locked in a primitive ritual preceding dance.

General Steen's voice took on a more urgent note. The marines knew what he looked like, his leathery cheeks, the mauve lips, the eyes of chrome, the implants, the neck locking a shaved skull rigid. Even good men dreamed of him.

'We shall achieve our appointed target. We're going to finish this one off. There's no room for weakness . . . But I must warn you that on this ship we have a traitor – a traitor flying with us on this historic flight. He is our enemy in a big way.

'Now I know he's there, and I'm gonna ask him to show himself. You all will know him when you see him. Do not hesitate to shoot. I repeat, do not hesitate to shoot – even if by doing so you may kill a few of your comrades. Our great nation asks that much of you.

'I'm gonna call him. Coward, traitor, come forth. Show yourself.'

A new note drowned out Steen's inspiring address. They had lift-off. The snow-flecked ground fell away below, buildings flattened, the great plain shrank. The immense furred pig opened stubby wings and lifted its snout to the olive atmosphere.

The marines looked about, gloomily scrutinizing each other. Stang fought waves of nausea, knowing now – knowing at last – what was expected of him. He called to the mothership, but something of her was there within him, working to a purpose beyond his.

He stared back at the ranks of uniformed men. They had deliberately sought to dehumanize themselves; to that end, war and military training had been designed. Any pain was better than the pain of accepting one's fallen, divided nature. Head against heart, light against dark, ancient against modern, left against right, masculine against feminine: to accept the human struggle – that was what really required courage. To live as an individual.

And the thick voice again, as they were lifted into the starless thins of the stratosphere.

'Those are my orders. Shoot to kill. The real enemy is aboard.

We are going to obliterate him and his kind. He calls himself Saviour. He's lying, men, lying. He's the enemy, okay, full of soft talk and soft shit. Christ, I challenge you to come out and show your god-damned face right here on my ship. This could be the Last Day – so here's your chance to show your smarmy face!'

The storm rose in John Stang as forces beyond his control massed themselves. The general, he knew, had the terms all wrong. The enemy that Steen feared, that his men feared, was far more ancient than Christ, by several million years. Yet the speech gave him the trigger to respond.

He was no longer himself. His ego died and was transformed. He rose, breaking forth from tubes and belts.

He felt himself rise and shine. Saw himself – or something was seeing him – as the marines saw him: white, pure, terrible to behold.

He was transforming. This was the Keg's birth. Immediately he raised his arms his fingers reached up to the cables overhead, con-joining with them, melting into them, so that a new life-force flowed, flowered. His countenance shone down on the soldiery.

Some hardened men, too unimaginative to experience surprise, obeyed their general's orders. They fired at the increasing figure. Their lasered energies were merely absorbed to feed Stang's radiance. The hairs of his head rained radiance, radiance was in the cablelike folds of his gown.

When he spoke, it was no longer with the voices of men. Silvery in tone, his words chimed through the ship.

'*There is another way* . . . Metal must now die. You must all pass along the river of understanding until you reach the great ocean of wisdom. Somewhere in that ocean lies the Isle of the Blessed. It will not be easy for you, but you must get there or perish.'

All were mute as he spoke. The Keg itself was now free, under its own control, heedless of ground signals, transforming itself.

'You will perish from the Earth for ever and forget its ripeness, its wonderful diversity. Only if you gain that Isle will you live in peace and plenty, and fortune will smile on you.'

He showed his/her face.

Some of the men fell down, dropping their weapons. Some cried, 'Spare us!' Some called to their general, but their general did not reply.

Already their weapons were melting, assuming strange vegetable forms.

He/she grew still. There was laughter. This was the final hour. Despite the darkness outside, she fed on her own brightness, spreading beyond the skin of the Keg. Her feet trailed to the valleys and plateaux far beneath. She summoned the mad and the sane. Her toes were beautiful on the hilltops.

Armoured vehicles moved in line towards her place. Their circuits failed. Nothing could withstand the ancient life-fuse once it was lit. The feet took root and their tendons became ivies growing up the trunk of a great earth-tree. To which, the world responded with a glow of a kind unseen; all eyes were open to this strange light, shining across land and ocean. There was a new thing born.

And the Keg was no more than a little golden nut, high on one of the branches that spread like a canopy and sent their saps out to the Moon. Netting in its net of twigs comets and the noiseless inhabitants of Heaven.

THAT PARTICULAR GREEN OF
OBSEQUIES

It was in the fifty-first year of the Kayyrandarth. In the annual lot-
teries, the opportunity to visit a dead personage fell upon a man of
common clay called Barnes Atarver.

Barnes Atarver was no fool. But he was obscure, and forced to
cut his own toenails. He had previously been allowed some freedoms
and did not abuse them. He spoke not of policies but philosophies.
His life had been led dedicatedly, sowing a hundred acorns every
year, except for a year in his youth, his *Wanderjahr*. Then young
Atarver had travelled among the Inner Isles and – so it was rumoured
– had been made much of by maids and their mothers.

That journey of discovery and love had lasted for nine weeks,
followed by the statutory period of fasting. Since when, Barnes
Atarver had lived in a small house on Bronzeface Street in the capital,
collecting and studying the paintings and writings of the bygone
artist Paul Gauguin.

So when the Clerk of the Hereafter Bureau asked Atarver what
dead personage he would most wish to visit, Atarver replied unhesi-
tatingly, 'Paul Gauguin.'

The Hereafter, as was generally understood, was a state of sensory
deprivation. One did not see or feel in the Hereafter. Nothing existed
there, except a gravy-like darkness and a ghostly smell of parsley.

Recently, in order to encourage visitors, a spirit lamp was set
burning. Maintenance costs were enormous. Cold, fish white, the
flame attempted to illumine Eternity.

When Barnes Atarver arrived, Paul Gauguin was still recon-
structing. Atarver averted his eyes from the process. The falling
gobbets of decay were as ludicrous as they were disgusting. Only
when Gauguin coughed did he look again.

The painter was wrapping a coloured sarong about himself, look-ing petulant. His face was no more than a skull with eyebrows and fierce eyes, bisected by a beak of a nose.

'Everything's always the same here,' Gauguin said. 'The rocks, the sand, the sea, the temple, the heat of noon, the Moon like a rotten melon, the women with their wide shoulders . . .'

None of the things he mentioned were to be seen. Both he and Atarver floated in limbo. Limbo was an unprimed canvas.

'Er – quite, quite,' replied Atarver.

Silence fell, palpable as papaya within the general anomic quiet. Souls rustled invisibly about him like leaves on an autumnal tree. He permitted himself a quick tremble.

'The palm trees are the same, too. Happily I'm not a painter who works from nature.' Gauguin clasped his hands together.

Atarver was overawed. Silence within silence, like an unhatched egg within a dead chicken. 'And the sky?' he suggested. 'Is that . . .'

'I'll do the sky in a couple of flat washes,' Gauguin said. 'Yellow. A nice neutral yellow like Breton cake. And green. For the sense of melancholy and acquiescence in implacable laws . . . Olive green, with a dash of Prussian. A motto in Tahitian. I thought, "An Ancient Adversary Watching Us". The green would be echoed in her flesh. Bernard taught me that, at least.'

He was walking about now, losing some of his stiffness, as Atarver was losing his shyness.

'I admire those unrealistic skies, M. Gauguin. I can sit and con-template them for days, weeks even. I lost a cat that way, once.' It was not an easy confession from an academic. He lived on lentils and the sweet Greenland lettuce.

'You look the contemplative type,' said Gauguin, with a snort. 'Once I went by appearances. When I was a slave to what I saw, I was blind. An artist must describe essences. The way a woman is all women . . . Scarlet, olive green, the pink sand. Has to be pink, whatever you academics say . . . Fuck realism. I told Degas that.'

'Of course there are schools –'

Gauguin came and stood closer to Atarver. He looked as threaten-ing as he was corpselike.

'I'm bigger than you.'

'Er – of course, you're more legendary.'

His luminous green eyes penetrated the haggard night of eternity. 'Those fools of art critics in Paris, what do they know? That particular tone, *that particular green of obsequies* – that's Vincent's name for it – is the colour signifying the struggle and submission we endure as humans. Innocence and wickedness – *the* colour. What am I saying? – The whole damned thing is philosophy. The philosophy of the flesh in all its rapaciousness. To catch life by its throat . . . by its tits . . .'

His hands reached forward as if about to grapple with life's windpipe. Atarver stepped back out of the way, wishing he had brought a walking stick, or at least his umbrella. He had been prepared for a more formal interview. The Clerk of the Hereafter Bureau had told him the dead were sticklers for etiquette. Being so near to his hero made him realize the dead did not wash.

'You mention innocence and wickedness, M. Gauguin,' he said, fighting a note of hysteria that, like rising damp, was creeping into the panels of his throat. 'Therein lies the source –'

'What do you know about it?' The painter looked suspiciously at Atarver. 'Who are you? Why bother me, Paul Gauguin? What's this pineapple doing in my bed? You have to follow your convictions to their desperate conclusions, even when –'

'My name is Barnes Atarver, M. Gauguin. I venture here on a day-pass some two centuries after your – following your translation to the Hereafter. My apologies for disturbing you, but in my estimation you are the greatest of all painters, and not only because you unite East and West. In your *"Contes Barbares"* you painted the first great metaphysical masterpiece of the twentieth century, while your rhythms –'

He was babbling on for some minutes until his perception of the general achromatic muck brought him up short. The painter was not attending. Instead, he secreted strands of orange material which hung in the void before him, dull in parts, flame bright in others. At first, Atarver took the stuff for an attenuated parrot.

Next followed an olive green, tinged with Prussian blue. It

uncoiled like ectoplasm, distributing itself, forming the crude figure of a man. The man – or it was an idol of sullen demeanour – was seated, clad in a loincloth. The orange strands formed themselves into hair. They hung down his spine, coiling about like snakes. Unlikely flowers of phallic shape distributed themselves behind him. Gauguin wielded a heavy brush like a conductor's baton.

The man depicted might be a native of the Marquesas, the Blessed Isles, where Gauguin had died. So Atarver surmised. His eyes were heavy-lidded; plump were his breasts, round were his limbs, brutish was his expression. He looked towards Atarver with unwavering intensity, the menace of which was increased by the knife clutched in his broad blunt hand.

'Great!' exclaimed Atarver. All Eternity was lit by the sulphurous colours of Gauguin's art. The drab olive feet of the man drifted far below Atarver, who suffered vertigo. 'But why's the man got red hair, monsieur?'

'He's a Neanderthal.' Gauguin did not look away from his work.

'Neanderthal?'

'They're all Neanderthals, all the tribes of the Pacific. That's why there are no serious conflicts between them, or between men and women. Neanderthals are *whole*, in liaison with the world of the senses. I had to leave Europe behind. It wasn't just a question of cash. I couldn't stand the Cro-Magnon, his stink, his chatter. His cities . . .'

'So when it came to sexual relations –'

'I left my relations behind. Even my wife.' He was vigorously beginning another figure, recumbent on a couch. His nostrils dilated with effort. 'It wasn't just young girls. I had young boys too. Flesh – the androgynous flesh. That melting principle. When you're hungry, you eat what's around. Goats. Creation itself is a melting process. Male and female, Yin and Yang. You talk too much.'

'And did you find that the essential innocence of the islanders of the South Seas in any way –'

Gauguin laughed. The Hereafter rocked. He gave a great vulgar ejaculation of ectoplasm.

'Innocent? Them? They're not innocent, you fool. It's Europeans, the Cro-Magnons, who are innocent. That's the trouble. Sex in head, mess in body. City-dwellers. Over-developed cerebrum. Whereas the Tahitians have large cerebella. Plus deliciously moist vaginas. That's the Neanderthal heritage, needless to say.'

'Well, I don't know about your "needless to say". It seems to me –'

The reclining figure became more female, hideous yet elegant, her eyes narrowing as she regarded her mate, as yet unformed. The line of her leg and hip held a world in thrall. She slid a hand up her skirt and scratched herself.

'Are you arguing with me? I'm an authority. I fought my own stupid swinish ignorance . . .' He turned on Atarver, who cowered politely. 'I fought my own swinish innocence. I changed my species. I became myself Neanderthal.' He secreted a bunch of bananas.

In a more conversational tone of voice, as he sketched in mountains, brick red and burnt umber, he continued, 'Leprosy is a Neanderthal disease. No doubt you associate it with dirt, but that's just because Neanderthals are of the earth itself, mankind's original stock.'

He turned away. Hitching up his gown, he drew in the mud with a stick.

The mud sighed and from it grew a fat-bellied dwarf, horned. A devil of some Tahitian kind, who sprouted grey lips and addressed Atarver.

'M. Gauguin is too busy to argue with critics. He offers you a word of wisdom to take back to life with you . . . Okay? he says, "*It's all magic.*" There's no "reality" – only magic. You know that, M. Atarver, but you prefer to forget it. You've never lain with a woman under a full moon, poor sop! Magic, magic.'

'Yes, I have. In the Inner Isles. And more than once.'

'Rubbish. Never heard of the Inner Isles.'

'And this rubbish you talk about –'

But Atarver had never argued with a devil before. His sentence petered out into limbo, smelling briefly of cat piss.

'Why did he eliminate European traditions from his canvases, do you think, my fine friend?' asked the devil. 'So that he could generate real magic. Naked truth. Nudity instead of stuffy rooms. Ripeness, fruitfulness, lubrication. La-la.' He danced heavily to his own words. Gauguin painted on, undisturbed.

'We Neanders are as different from you Cros as Cros are from androids. With our command of magic and empathy, and just a touch of garlic, we regard all Cros as androids. Cold, closed, self-contained, peasants of patriotism, idiots of ideology, robots of –'

'Here, shut up! You're so rude! You're only a figment! You aren't even alive and warm!'

The devil was whirling now, its words indistinct. 'Fresh fruit, fox-fruit, fish-fruit, fruit like a fear delayed . . .'

Gauguin had moved away a parsec or two, his hands active and incantatory. He produced about him four Amazonian brown women, all at once. Atarver jumped out of the way of their floral skirts.

Dogs accompanied them. They stood majestic on the beach, platters of fish held below their generous bare breasts, gazing into a mauve distance dense with passion fruit. Their lips were guavas, their hair bougainvillaea, their eyes held Capricorn sunsets.

'Magic . . .' Atarver said, feeling lust overcome timidity. Whatever Gauguin's crazy theories, he had lost none of his creative faculties in the Hereafter.

As he started to remove his socks, he gazed in wonder at the darkness in the armpit of the nearest beauty. Ten metres deep at a conservative estimate.

'The forests of entanglement,' piped the woman. 'A merging, monsieu. You likee? No more Yin and Yang. Only Ying.'

Throwing aside his clothes, Atarver cried, 'Then the world will end.'

'Best way to go,' Gauguin said. Again the laughter, with a touch of the Prussian.

A forest of rampant hibiscus grew, shielding the pair. The columns of its trunks were like the colonnade of a temple, forever extending, multiplying into the farthest recesses of the Hereafter. A street fire in rose madder.

*   *   *

When Atarver came to, Gauguin was still talking, filling the void with his savage kind of beauty.

'And what better way for the world to end, since end it certainly must one day. A great wave will come and wash the whole conundrum away. Male and female united, one flesh. The whole place one gigantic sexual organ, which is what I wish my canvases were.'

The forests along the shore burst forth with lingams in red and biscuit profusion. The women strode into the foaming green waters, raised their arms above their heads and swam away.

Atarver's chronograph chimed. Time to return to the Therebefore. The outlines of the painter became indistinct, the lingams drooped on the bough.

'I must leave you, monsieur. I only wish I could take your superb paintings with me.'

'Without payment, no doubt. No, we'll leave it here,' said Gauguin, his earlier moodiness returning. 'It will cheer up this miserable anteroom between our two worlds.' His speech became indistinct as he began to decompose. 'You see about Yin and Yang. We even have to have two worlds, one for the living and one for ger ger deh-h-h-'

Only luminescence was left. And the little spirit lamp.

Vertigo returned to Atarver, and the prospect of a plate of oysters, with lemon, escorted down the throat by a white wine that had never been over-chilled. Served by his current lady friend. He turned to leave . . .

Within what seemed no more than a passing moment, he was recovering in his room in Bronzeface Street.

In the Halls of the Hereafter, Gauguin's painting still hung. It lit with its enormous shapes the emptiness between the Yin and Yang of existence. The eyes of its devils gazed towards the surf. The waves crashed in, disputing the boundary between land and ocean, Earth and Heaven.

THE ANCESTRAL HOME OF
THOUGHT

But for the building, the plateau was a bare canvas. Dead trees stood apart from each other. They alone offered shelter to any wanderer rash enough to traverse the high plain.

No one travelled here tonight. An owl swooped from its perch in one of the dead trees, streaming like a feathered wind above the land. As it flew it passed over a low mound, beneath which was buried a man or woman who had once ventured across the plateau. The mound was ancient. The adventurer had died centuries before the present governors of the land emerged from their caves.

The trees had lived then, streams had flowed, and green vegetation covered the land. But the trees had been felled. The climate changed. The streams dried. Now there was only desolation – and the building.

The building housed the Vercore Project. It stood one thousand five hundred metres above sea level. By daylight, the mountains fringing one side of the plateau could clearly be seen. Now, in the light of a moon pared down to its last quarter, the simplifications of night prevailed. A monstrous being striding across the plateau would have seen only a level space with a straight road leading to a concrete rectangle. No mountains. No details on the building. Only an elementary white shape, Euclidean amid its vast and rudimentary site.

Once the block had housed an Institute of Experimental Neuropsychology. Now it housed the Vercore Project, and barriers had been erected, and defensive zones. Its outer fire perimeter was within one kilometre of the nearest prehistoric burial site.

At the dead hour of Zero Two in the morning, the energies of the project were at their lowest.

In Room B306, known as Research Three, three floors below ground, lights burned bright. 146 Merv Widdows and his assistant, 180 Jay Ling, were on duty. The hum of the air circulator numbed their senses as they sipped sweet coffee from plastic cups. Widdows' wonderfully unruly mop of fair hair hung down over the liquid.

He scratched the sole of his foot and said, 'I keep thinking of my great-aunt Nellie.'

Ling was the smoothest of men, his long black hair slicked back into a neat black band resting on the nape of his neck. He stared into his syrupy liquid and said nothing.

Widdows tried again. 'You saw the news, Jay? The Sickle have hostaged Oslo, the rats.'

Without looking up, Ling said drowsily, 'We better get on with Brains, Merv. Oslo's neutral – we can live without it.'

'Yeah, well, it's an escalation of the war when you start picking up neutrals. Doesn't nothing ever bother you?'

Ling grunted.

'Besides, my great-aunt Nellie lives in Oslo. Dear old lady. I keep thinking about her.'

Ling stretched out, laying his cup aside without saying anything. Widdows stood up and looked down at him.

'Don't you have any aunts, Jay?'

'Dozens – but that's war, Merv, old buddy . . .' Dredging up words from the well of his indifference, he said, 'I begin to hate this so-called civilization we are supposed to be defending. I don't just hate the Sickles – I hate our side too. We're poisoned by war. When we hostaged KL, who complained?'

Widdows gave a short laugh. 'Battle fatigue. The war's dragged on too long. The sooner we wipe them out, the better. It's them or us.'

'Ain't it always them or bloody us?' He had heard Widdows on that subject before, many times.

'Okay, let's do the Brains.' He made a reluctant move towards the power store. Instead of following, Ling sat tight, finishing off his coffee.

'My ancestors came from Hainan four generations ago. It was a nice tropical island until Deng industrialized it. Now the industry has moved away, so you can live a human life again. Or so all my aunties say. When this bloody war is over, I shall pack my bag and go to Hainan, and spend the rest of my days there, swimming, screwing, fishing, and never ever thinking of Vercore again.'

He got no answer, and expected none. Widdows had heard Ling on that subject many times before.

'Come on,' Widdows said. 'Or we'll have Telbard chasing us again.'

'Screw Telbard.' But Ling got up and went over to where his mate had switched on the optical drive. They had programmed the DUX3. The Brain X-rays began to feed into the computer, which clicked and said, 'Processing begins on 2400 X-ray plates, Code BR615.'

The readings started to download immediately, printing out as the monitor showed serried columns of calibrations ranged against roentgens of human brains, which the holoscreen presented four-dimensionally. Widdows and Ling hung around, yawning.

Weighty matters were being decided. Which did not mean to say they were not bored.

The second part of the program, in which previous readings were collated, took an hour's computer time. Both men longed for a faster model. But Research Three had to make do with what Applications One had discarded a year earlier. War brought its economies as well as its extravagances.

Ling ee'd the data to Telbard's office in Admin Five. Telbard was head of the department.

Zero Five a.m. and grey dawn waiting below the plateau, though not three floors below ground. Time to go off-shift.

'Massage and bed for me,' Ling said, shouldering his bag. 'You coming?'

'I'll take in a snort and a movie,' Widdows said. 'Studio Two is offering a golden oldie, *Horsemeat Men*. I need a shot of violence.'

'See you tomorrow.'

'That's for sure.' Their grunts substituted for laughter as they moved to different elevators. They would inevitably meet on the morrow. No escape from the Vercore Project was possible for the Duration.

The evil lord rode forth from his castle, his stallion caparisoned beneath his saddle. Bugles sounded. His soldiery stood –

The hunters were gaunt, their ribs showing like barred sand on a seashore. They moved across broken territory and along a dried riverbed. It was the magic hour of sunset, a tangle of tachyons, and the dusk between light and dark. The men slowed their progress. Stone clubs at the ready, they began to stalk.

Ahead in a sheltered hollow, heedless of danger, women began a ceremonial dance older than humanity, stolen from male birds of paradise. They were small and dark, almost naked, and they swayed to the rhythm of a single skin drum. In their rapture, they remained unaware of the enemy's approach.

The hunting party attacked. With stone clubs.

With spears.

With bows and arrows.

With muskets.

With rifles and bayonets.

With carbines.

With hand-nukes.

Every time, one of the women survived. She was the Magic Woman, dark and hot, known sometimes as Sycorax. She possessed knowledge forever denied men.

She had but to dance her dance and the world would be changed.

A truck was bearing down on her, headlights blazing. Armed men were pounding towards her. They claimed this land. Sycorax yelled defiance.

They surrounded her. They approached with weapons at the ready. Searchlights glowed into life, stepping up rapidly from red to yellow to white – the incoherent illumination of the electronic culture opposing her kind.

In the Magic Woman's brain was another kind of existence, a fractal thing, illimitable, to be expressed in intricate pattern. If she danced the dance, the world would be changed for the good, transformed by her secret knowledge.

And she began to dance –

146 Widdows sat up suddenly in Studio Two and snatched the ViR-helmet from his head. It was true he had taken a heavy snort, but – It had been the movie, then suddenly it was not the movie. The Magic Woman was no part of the movie he had expected to experience. She had emerged from –

No, that could not be. It was not rational. He was merely tired. It was the brain stuff getting to him. Cautiously, he put on the helmet again. He saw the armed hunters, heard twigs crackle underfoot as they marched through his cerebrum. They entered barracks, shed uniforms, showered, drank beer. Plus the artificial heroics of the screen, and the man who was a horse.

It was cosy in Studio Two. He was tucked into his helmet, absorbed, when a call came through. He blanked the screen on Pause.

'Hi.'

Major Neil Telbard's face sprang to view.

'Hi, Merv. You alone? Come up. Private way.'

'Sure.'

Telbard's lean acid face disappeared, to be replaced by one of the dark women. She fell to her knees, clutching at her belly. Switching off, Widdows left the studio. Along the corridor, he raised his override, ensuring the securicams did not record his movements. His key let him into the Privileged bunch of elevators. A scanner checked his pass. A few moments later he was high above ground level, in his chief's office. Admin Five.

The major's windows were sealed off by radiation shutters. He might as well have been below ground, except that here one end of the room was preserved as a jungle of indoor plants, grown monstrous under the ultra-green.

'Trouble?' Widdows asked.

Major Telbard was standing by his desk, pumping iron. He continued to pump, scrutinizing Widdows as if half-regretting he had summoned him. Despite his rank, he wore civilian clothes; that is to say, a dull brown shell suit, which he filled amply. He was a plain man, not given to expressiveness. In a further attempt at concealment, a gingery-grey moustache hung over his mouth, lending him a somewhat dog-like appearance.

'These results, Widdows.' He nodded towards the Brain printouts lying on his desk.

Widdows waited.

Telbard lowered the weights with a sigh. He ignited two mescahales from a desk lighter and passed one to Widdows. Sinking into his chair, he said, 'The Project is much bigger than you or I are permitted to know.'

He wreathed himself in whorls of smoke for further concealment. Light from his green-shaded desk lamp turned the smoke half-transparent, half-solid. Widdows stood where he was. Silence made him think of the war: the noises of war, the silences of war. He thought of his great-aunt Nellie. Nellie would be silent, too.

'Sit down, Widdows . . . I suppose you have speculated on the prime objective of Vercore?'

Widdows took a seat, worried to think this might be another security check. Maybe they had traced his illegal ee calls to Oslo. Telbard was really twitchy. He kept pulling one end of his moustache. It would take very little to push him right over the top. As Jay often said, the guy was three coins short of a full fountain.

'I understand it is a demographic survey on a major scale, sir. Unprecedented, sir. So we're told.'

His department head fanned away a little smoke. 'I've been taking a look at the results of this test you've just produced. They are absolutely conclusive.'

'Conclusive?'

Telbard rose wearily and moved to a cupboard behind the desk, taking from it two gels of a cutaway human skull. The brain was tinted to indicate different areas. He dropped the gels on the desk and ran a finger over the cerebral cortex.

'The brain. The human brain. Wonderful, eh? Makes you think.'

'Indeed,' said Widdows, smiling. He realized that his remark might make the major see he was making fun of him. He knew Telbard for a self-conscious man – the weights being all part of the act. Attempting seriousness, he said, 'There are those who believe that our brains will take us to the stars, and in fact that the universe was made to measure for us. When we cease warring with each other . . .'

A snort of contempt. 'The anthropic cosmological principle! Bunkum, Widdows, bunkum, take my word for it. Darwin knew better, the great Darwin, when he remarked that our minds, developed from the brains of the lowest animals, could not be trusted with such grand conclusions . . . Pay attention to what I'm trying to show you. You can see on this gel how the cortex, the grey matter, overshadows the limbic brain – that lowly brain Darwin refers to.' Moving his finger further, looking up sharply to see he had Widdows's attention, tugging the tache, he went on, 'Here, at the back of the skull, the cortex overhangs the cerebellum. It's the recent cortex which makes Homo Sapiens.'

Being rather more up to date in his knowledge of the brain than his superior, Widdows said nothing. Neural networks had been his speciality at university. Like Telbard, he swathed himself in smoke from his mescahale.

He knew how Telbard clung to old models, and ascribed it to military training. The hundred billion neurons of Telbard's brain had been regimented in a way that precluded storage of new information. Perhaps for that reason, Widdows was fond of the major, scary though he sometimes was. Like now.

Telbard had started to describe the second gel, pointing out the difference in the topography of the cortex. In particular, it did not cover the cerebellum, as in the previous specimen. The occipital lobes were less developed, and the cerebellum itself was correspondingly larger.

'You see, Widdows? The profiles of the two specimens differ quite considerably. With a natural effect on human thought and behaviour. You understand?'

Widdows understood that Telbard would eventually have a point to make. Meanwhile, Widdows thought of the movie, of the guns opening fire on the dancing women, and of his great-aunt Nellie, who in her youth had been a champion dancer. She had once tried to teach young Mervyn the veleta, but movement was not his forte.

'The cerebellum is common to all mammals – an ancient part of the brain. Controls movements. Posture. The whole motor system.

'It's also the home of sleep.' He paused and repeated the phrase. 'The home of sleep. So you see we're building up proof that two different kinds of humans exist on the planet, with two different kinds of brain profiles – and consequently different thought/ behaviour processes.'

'Which the brain collations of BR615 confirm.'

'That's Research Three's objective.'

Scuffling on his desk, he produced five of the new brain calibrations clipped to a clipboard. Widdows leant over and examined them. The major had ranged them to represent extremes of the profile spectrum. On the one hand was what he described as the cerebrum-oriented, scientific, rational; on the other hand, the cerebellum-orientated, believing in magic and superstition. The cerebrum-oriented brain was annotated as having belonged to a Western man; in fact, from a suburb of Oslo. The cerebellum-oriented specimen had belonged to a fisherwoman in the Marquesas.

The major stood staring at the calibrations, shaking his head in a gloomy way. He stubbed out his mescahale.

Giving him a cautious glance, Widdows said, 'We're dealing with highly explosive racial material. Is that what you're saying? How does this – how does this fit with Vercore?'

Telbard went over to his miniature jungle, beckoning with his head for Widdows to follow him. Rustling the foliage, he said in a quiet voice, 'We'll take a stroll outside.'

'*Outside?*'

'You heard me.'

He led Widdows to his small kitchen. A ceiling-high cool-cupboard swung aside. A blue-coded corridor lit behind it. As they stepped into the corridor, an android guard skidded towards them. Telbard froze it with a rank-card. They passed by and took an armoured elevator down. In another minute, they were walking under a canopy of frosty stars, planting their boots on the ancient plateau.

Widdows was dizzy. He went over to a dead tree and leaned against its trunk. It was months since he had been outside the Vercore building.

'Agoraphobia,' he said.

'We can speak more freely here. They may be on to me, Widdows. I may not have long.'

Wow, not that, please, thought Widdows.

Telbard said the latest results of Code BR615 proved that Homo Sapiens was in fact two inter-related species. Interbreeding took place with territorial variability. The proof rested not only on brain profiling but on previous tests establishing such factors as physiological proportions and related data.

He said that despite interbreeding, the two original species remained surprisingly distinct in many parts of the world, mainly owing to territorial factors. These had been monitored in one of many Vercore departments. The species were known as Species A and Species B.

Species A emerged from Africa two million years or so BC, spread through the Middle East, and subsequently divided into two sub-species. The weaker of these two sub-species were driven into what is now Europe – then dense forest. The smarter, stronger sub-species either settled in the Mesopotamian region or began a long trek eastwards, during which they would populate Asia and, further still and later, cross the Bering bridge and invade North and South America.

'I don't think I wish to hear this, sir,' Widdows said. 'This is dangerous ground.' He was cold. He could see Telbard only in outline. Behind him was the monstrous prison of Vercore, hardly a light showing.

'Listen to me, Widdows. This is termination time.'

He continued with his account.

Species A had been cave-dwellers and were Moon-worshippers. They lived in matrilinear societies. Since they were promiscuous, having no knowledge of the connection between copulation and generation, the children never knew their fathers. So the line of descendance was through the women, the mothers, who ruled the tribe.

Such matters, Telbard said, still applied today among their progeny in the Pacific islands. He pulled at his moustache and muttered something indistinct.

And then – Species B. Species B emerged from the sub-continent of India, possibly Rajasthan. The tribes of Species B were warlike and patrilinear. They worshipped the Sun. They organized themselves into quasi-military units of about 150 persons – a convenient military unit ever since – and from the start had a firmer grasp of technology than did the dreamy Species A. Many of them migrated north and westwards.

One branch of this invading force occupied Egypt, to the advantage of that country. The name still lives of Akhenaten, the young pharaoh, a great Sun-worshipper. This brilliant man of Species B is known as the first individual in history.

Intermarriage with Species A took place throughout the Middle East. It was fertile, a good place to live. But several legions of Species B continued westwards, into Europe.

Europe proved to be their real hunting ground. One animal they hunted was the sub-species of A, whom we now call Neanderthals.

And to use that same terminology, we may call Species B the Cro-Magnons, said Telbard. The Cro-Magnons gradually vanquished the Moon-worshippers, the non-pugnacious Neanderthals. They killed off the men but often saved women and children. The history of the extinction of the Tasmanians in historic times is similar. These women became slaves, whores, concubines; many by their own mysterious wisdom became powerful.

The present Caucasian races developed from that mix of two enemy species.

The two men stood facing each other as the eastern sky paled.

Let's keep cool, Widdows told himself. He noticed the glint of saliva down Telbard's chin, which the man kept wiping away.

327

'We're of mixed stock. Is that what you're saying?' Widdows asked. 'Does that help the war effort?'

'I've checked you out, Merv.' He paused, to say heavily, 'You and I are Security cleared as being between 80 to 85 percent pure Cro – Species B – with high proportions of new cerebrum to the more ancient cerebellum. We're kosher.'

The bark of the tree he clutched was real enough. Was what Telbard said truth or merely madness? Did the facts bear out the theory? He recalled the major's quote from Darwin: the human brain had been built of the same perishable material as that of the lowest animal.

Perhaps brains invented lies about themselves.

Why not? Why did men imprison themselves, as they had imprisoned themselves in the Vercore Project?

He was frightened. Frightened of the major and his monstrous story. And frightened that there was more to come.

He knew of facts that supported Telbard's account – and others that contradicted it. As Karl Popper had once said, the nature of all science was conjectural. He had monitored Telbard's movements illegally, as Telbard did his, and knew that women came to Telbard through the blue-coded corridor. He knew what Telbard liked doing. This whole account of prehistoric miscegenation on a grand scale sounded like sexual fantasy.

'Does all this help the war?' he asked at last.

'There's always war, Merv. Ever think why? Advanced data sees war due to one basic cause only, even when masking causes – territorial, let's say – prevail. *War is a trans-specific activity!* That's my discovery. I'll give you an example.'

'I'm cold, sir. We should go in. Where's the bloody Sun?'

'The Sun'll wait, man. Listen. Take Christianity. Christianity broke into two major sects, right? A and B specific. Protestantism is B-oriented. Catholicism is A-oriented – the worship of Christ's mother, the old matriarchal line, no earthly father. The problem of a male god remained. So the priests, the bishops, all that lot, down to choirboys, they wear long smocks. They dress up as women, Merv, to appease those old matriarchal instincts.

'Now do you get it? There's only one way to end war and bring peace to Earth.'

What was delaying the dawn?

He said, 'Hold on, major. All this stuff, it's well – *hard*.' He could not bring himself to say 'insane'.

He saw Telbard fold his arms across his chest, protectively or defiantly.

'Of course it's *hard*, man. The truth isn't easy. Think of the long complex track from amoeba to human being. You expect life to be easy?'

'Okay, but logical thought processes –'

The major moved suddenly, to grasp Widdows's arm. 'Suddenly to find truth – it's horrifying. Beautiful but at the same time horrifying. We've hit crunch time, you understand?'

As Widdows shook his head dumbly, Telbard put on his lecture voice again and went on.

'Interspecific conflict has increased of late, Merv. Species A, the more promiscuous group, is outbreeding us – Species B – us. Hence the enormous growths of population in the Species A areas. We are going to be bred out, come another century, Merv. That's exactly why we have to wipe out the A species now. Like now.'

Widdows's bad feelings increased greatly.

'Where do you get all this from? Is this what Vercore is all about?' In his agitation, he started to walk as if setting out for Mars, stumbling over the rough ground.

'Suppose this stuff, this lunatic theory, is true, even part-true, you're talking about . . . Jesus, it's madness. You're talking about wiping out half the human race.'

'Three-quarters of it,' Telbard said firmly, hastening behind him. 'It's Darwinian. The survival of the fittest, don't you see?'

'I fucking well don't see. Hitler's extermination of the Jews was –'

'Listen, Widdows, stop, will you? Jews are the Middle East admixture of Species A and B. If official thinking is correct, then Hitler accidentally had the right plan. That admixture can't be trusted – it's infiltrating our species.'

'Official thinking!' He turned on Telbard and struck him in the chest. 'You're – it's genocide, it's –'

Telbard staggered about gasping. When he straightened, he said, 'No, you start on a modest domestic scale. You have to. We have to start with your assistant in D306. His profile has been studied. He's A specific. He must go. I'm telling you.'

'Jay, you mean? Jay Ling? My mate?'

'A specific. He has to go.' They were on the move again, walking in circles. The plateau stretched out round them, naked to the frosty sky.

'We have enemies, Merv. This is why I brought you out here, Merv, not to be overheard. My superior has on his desk orders for the immediate destruction of 215 operatives employed in Vercore on the project, once the last test runs are complete. The orders were ee'd in during the night. Destructions to be carried out within forty-eight hours. Ling's on the list.'

The giddiness overcame Widdows again, as he asked if he was expected to strangle Ling with his bare hands.

Telbard said matters were worse than that. The military now had the CEWE, which he pronounced 'See-Wee'. The initials stood for Cerebellum Weapon, a selective brain destroyer.

'I have committed a treasonable offence by passing on top-secret information to a subordinate. Only the president and the top echelon here know about it. Scuttlebutt says the scientists involved have been arrested and – disappeared.'

Widdows clutched his head, staring about. Nothing remained but land and sky – forever at odds, forever a unity. He gave a hysterical laugh. 'We'd better start running now.'

Telbard drew his service revolver.

His voice was shaking as he said, 'We must trust each other. I know it's a shock. My superior feels as I do. He gave me authority to speak to you. He is in touch with others who also reject the secret sub-text behind Vercore. We can't let all this happen.'

'But I thought you said –'

'Listen, damn you. We must strike now, before the new data we have collected in Research Three is ee'd to the Pentagon. I need your assistance in destroying all our brain calibration research.'

'What? But it's been circulated.'

'Only to other departments. If necessary, we must send word to the Sickles to blast the building out of existence.'

'The enemy? Neil, I couldn't do that! You're talking impossibilities.'

He talked more impossibilities, his voice urgent. The project administration had received secret notification that the president had concluded a secret pact with the Sickles. The Sickles were also Species B, or rather, a similar admixture with B predominant. Both war machines were about to be turned on the neutral populations of Asia, Africa and other A-specific regions, using the selective and deadly CEWE weapons.

When those regions were cleared, then possibly the struggle against the Sickles would continue.

'You understand how serious it is?' Telbard said, in the most reasonable of voices. 'This has nothing to do with personalities. My personal belief, which I offer to you for what it's worth, is that we should simply eliminate everyone we suspect, including most of the women, with this wonderful new weapon, before the enemy gets hold of it and turns it on us. Only Species B, with its brilliant organizing powers can –'

Widdows had brought his breathing under control. He kicked the gun out of the major's fist. Flinging himself at Telbard, he brought up his right hand, palm flat, striking Telbard in the windpipe with the hard edge of his hand. Telbard fell to the ground as if he belonged there.

Raising both arms above his head, Widdows called for the guards.

'Help! Telbard's gone paranoid. We're all going mad, all, all of us! I almost believed his story. Take him, take me! Help! Reason! Light!'

Searchlights flicked on from the building perimeter. Widdows began to run away from them, shouting wordlessly. A truck was rushing up behind him, headlights blazing. Soldiers jumped from it, carbines at the ready, shouting at him to halt.

He was bathed in luminance. And at that moment, he fell over an old grave and went sprawling.

Another luminance was growing far out across the plateau, a luminance having no connection with their tawdry affairs. Tombs were starting up into the velvet, ancient ruins built to commemorate an age without time. Graves scattered across the wastes opened in clouds of dust. In the sky, a huge tapestry unfolded, a huge being formed, cloud becoming flesh.

Her toes were beautiful on the mountains as she danced.

Toes roseate, limbs of immense shape and beauty, blossomed into being, to dangle in the dawn air. The soldiers stood aghast. Legs, vines, roots, things of curving line, rose up like vines into the sky. Stars sparkled and slid along thighs, great trunks grew down into the soil, robes trailed wide like sheets of the aurora.

'Hoh-hoh- ' gasped Widdows. He could not recall the word he wanted, or even that he wanted it. He ran forward instead, hair flaming and fluttering, screaming with delight, and nobody stopped him. Throwing down their weapons, the guards followed, charging across the plateau, boots twinkling like a child's sparklers.

Now a magnificent tree, a great World Tree, an Yggdrasil with sparkling breasts like fruit, rose to utmost heights. Sunlight made treacle poured into the branches that spread above the world. The world responded with a soft radiance. In the world there was light. In one of the branches, a golden nut twinkled. The upper boughs spread even higher, spread like a canopy, pouring milky sap out to the horned moon. In the net of twigs sported comets and the noise-less inhabitants of space.

And, with a hint of Prussian blue, Earth at last was joined with Heaven.

Paul Gauguin was a painter who travelled to the depths. He was familiar with Hell, he loved the simple nasturtium. He saw the golden nut twinkling in the upper boughs, and was half off his head with it. His daemon drove him far from France and from his Danish wife, to darker wives and a more desperate life in the South Seas. To live differently, to paint.

He speaks of an artist 'living on his own planet'. His meaning is at once clear and secret.

He speaks of his own work. This from a letter to Vincent van Gogh in 1889, describing a canvas he had recently completed:

> 'The seaweed they [the women] are gathering for fertilizing their land is reddish ochre in colour, with fawn highlights. The sand is *pink* not yellow, probably because of the dampness – the sea is dark. Seeing this every day fills me with a sensation of struggle for survival, of melancholy and acquiescence in implacable laws. I am attempting to put this sensation down on canvas, not by chance, but quite deliberately, perhaps by exaggerating certain rigidities of posture, certain dark colours, etc ... All this is perhaps *mannered* but what is natural in art? Ever since the most distant times, *everything* in art has been completely deliberate, a product of convention ... In art, truth is what a person feels in the state of mind he happens to be in. Those who wish or are able

to can dream. Let those who wish to or are
able to abandon themselves to their dreams.
And dreams always come from the reality
of nature.'

When Gauguin propounded this doctrine of
expressionism, it was revolutionary; small wonder his
work was slow to be accepted. Even surrounded by the
savage beauty of Tahiti, he advocated drawing not from
nature but from those things that are inward to us. 'My
artistic centre is in my head . . . I am not a painter who
works from nature. With me, everything happens in my
wild imagination.' His paintings bear out what he says.

Even today, Gauguin's principle is not widely
accepted, though it forms the basis for much creative
work. We can all share in the outwardness, in the grandeur and havoc of our times: it's the inward thing where
true exploration lies.

Paul Gauguin also said, 'Those who reproach me don't
know all there is in an artist's nature.'

Not only is he a painter's painter; he's an evocative
writer. It would be fine to create anything that resounds
through time quite as well as Gauguin's letters home
from abroad, full of complaints, grumbles, explanations,
optimisms, colour.

He made of his life something wonderful, as even the
most beautiful vase is made of common clay.

Yet that planet on which he claimed to live remains
inviolate. Artists have an entitlement to secrecy, even
when they ache to express it. Even a book such as this
may retain its secret.

The sand is pink, not yellow.
XYZ